THE
FINISH LINE

Bestselling author and Texas native Kate Stewart lives in North Carolina with her husband, Nick. Kate is a lover of all things 80s and 90s, especially John Hughes films and rap. She dabbles a little in photography, can knit a simple stitch scarf for necessity and, on occasion, does very well at whiskey.

Her series The Ravenhood Trilogy, consisting of *Flock*, *Exodus*, and *The Finish Line*, has become an international bestseller, a TikTok phenomenon and reader favourite.

THE RAVENHOOD

THE FINISH LINE

KATE STEWART

PAN BOOKS

First published 2021 by Kate Stewart

This paperback edition first published 2023 by Pan Books
an imprint of Pan Macmillan
The Smithson, 6 Briset Street, London EC1M 5NR
EU representative: Macmillan Publishers Ireland Ltd, 1st Floor,
The Liffey Trust Centre, 117–126 Sheriff Street Upper,
Dublin 1, D01 YC43
Associated companies throughout the world
www.panmacmillan.com

ISBN 978-1-0350-1352-4

Typeset by Palimpsest Book Production Ltd, Falkirk, Stirlingshire
Printed and bound by CPI Group (UK) Ltd, Croydon, CR0 4YY

Visit **www.panmacmillan.com** to read more about all our books
and to buy them. You will also find features, author interviews and
news of any author events, and you can sign up for e-newsletters
so that you're always first to hear about our new releases.

For Mon Trésor, Maïwenn
And for my readers for taking this
journey with me. Merci.

Prologue

TOBIAS

Age Forty-Four
Saint-Jean-de-Luz, France

"*VIENS ICI, EZEKIEL.*" Come here, Ezekiel. *I walk over to where he stands, his hand lowered, a round, brown seashell with a flat bottom resting in his palm. When I go to take it, he moves it out of reach.*

"*Qu'est-ce que c'est?*" What is it?

"*Un clypéastre, un dollar de sable. Lorsque tu en trouveras un, garde-le. Et lorsque tu seras prêt, alors tu le casseras. Mais tu dois le faire bien au milieu pour pouvoir en récupérer son trésor.*" A dollar of sand. When you find this, you keep it. And only when you're ready, do you break it. But you have to do it right down the middle to claim the treasure.

"*Quand serai-je prêt?*" When will I be ready?

He ruffles my hair. "Tu le sauras." You'll know.

Standing on the shoreline, I skip rocks along the foamed waves flooding in at my feet. I never recalled the whole conversation from that day my father brought me here, only the look of the sea, a glimpse of sand, the flash of early sun peaking behind him, and the strange shell in his palm. It was on my last visit to the institution that he recalled our discussion verbatim during one of his rare and lucid moments. He told me the story of his son, Ezekiel, and repeated our exchange that day with surprising clarity just minutes before he asked me to search for him.

Whether it was a sign, or fate, or something else playing a factor, I'd found a sand dollar on the beach in pristine condition the day I'd broken ground on the house. Though he didn't jog my memory until years after, the why of what had drawn me to keep it when I'd found it was made clear. Somehow, without knowing the details, I'd known the significance of it.

It's ironic and cruel how the mind works, mine especially. Some memories I re-live regularly but would do anything to forget, the details so vivid, so ingrained, it can be torturous. While others, the memories I hold most dear, at times evade me. But it's my fickle memory that planted a seed that day and instinct that had me hiding that shell—that makes it all the more meaningful. And it wasn't until I looked up the significance of the "treasure" that I understood his state of mind that day, a state very much like my own mindset now.

We were never close due to my mother fleeing from him because of his temper and mental illness—a diagnosed schizophrenic—but I feel some connection to him now. However, I've been fearful since the day I found him decades later, covered in his own shit and rambling frantic French at any stranger who passed him on that street in Paris. Seeing him in that state gave way to trepidation that one day I would suffer the same fate—that everyone who claimed to care for me would eventually abandon me—due to mental illness and lack of control. A fear that crippled me for years and kept me from investing, in believing in people fully.

To me, love was always conditional—until her.

My mother never fully understood the extent of my father's illness. It's my belief now that she assumed he'd just gone mad. Although that's partly true, it wasn't by conscious decision. It wasn't as if he'd let some dark side of him take over, which I believe was her stance on him up until the day she died. It was sickness that claimed him and the fear of inherited sickness that's plagued me for so long.

But at this stage in the game, the odds and my age are in my favor that I will never suffer his fate.

Retrieving the sun-bleached stone from where I hid it a lifetime ago, I start toward the winding cliff-side staircase that leads to my finish line. It's more apparent than ever that it was never the house I was waiting for. It was today, this moment of clarity—a day where my head and heart are no longer at odds.

If I had to sum up my life, my journey, in one word, it would be today. I did it all for this moment. The irony is, I never knew through my plotting and scheming a day like this could exist for me. Fate threw me the cards while Karma had its wicked way with me. Luck was never factored in, but it came through for this opportunist enough to know that at times, it was present, and others it had abandoned me completely.

Noted, luck. And fuck you for it.

But if I have to measure my life against the uncontrollable powers of what could be, at any time, for or against me, I'll have to bat them all away. I'll have to choose something else to measure my life by, a different entity all together, a cosmic force to trump all others: *her*.

Without her, my purpose would feel meaningless, as would this day.

Because she wasn't wrong. We, what we have and what we found in each other, is all that matters. The path I traveled to get here would amount to nothing without someone to reflect on it with. And there's no better storyteller, no better reflection of my worth, than in the eyes of the woman who shared in my journey and helped me navigate my way through the worst of it.

She's my mirror, my judge, and has revealed herself as my sole purpose. She brought direction back to my deadening soul when I lost my way, and she continues to guide me back, a star too bright to ignore, no matter how far I stray.

There's no more strength in life than a man's purpose. For so many years, I thought mine was something else entirely—until she showed me the truth. I always considered myself a lone traveler until she blazed her way onto my path as my opponent, lover, teacher, confidante, and best friend.

Any significant sum of every day I've spent on this Earth will always amount to her.

If I had succeeded in throwing my purpose away, if I were successful at self-sabotage, I wouldn't know such a complete feeling existed. I would have never found such peace inside myself. The panic would have seized me long ago and made me sick to the point of no return.

The minute I step through the door of the house, I won't ever look back on the cruelty of the path or how many steps I took alone. Instead, I'll appreciate each bend of the journey, aside from a single blow so fucking merciless, I'll never be able to shake it off. Not ever. A loss so painful, there won't ever be a day it won't hurt.

My brother.

Her savior.

An irreversible scar that will never fully heal, and proof of my weary travels. I'm halfway to the top of the cliff when my phone rattles in my pocket.

Lady Bird is in the nest.

However, I've already sensed her nearby. From above, I hear her shout my name as she races through the house, clear panic and excitement in her voice as I begin taking the stairs two at a time, heart thundering.

"I hear you, Mon Trésor," I reply, hastening my steps, chest pounding, the delicate offering safe in my hand. *I will always hear you.*

Already choked up with emotion, I nod at the two Ravens standing guard at the back of the property as I pass and enter through the back door. Beau greets me with his typical cock check before he allows me to run my fingers over his ears. I've learned to tolerate him over time, despite the fact that he's still ridiculously territorial over our woman.

"Bonjour, you greedy fucker."

Of all the planning I've done in my life, this is the idea I've obsessed most about coming to fruition. But if Beau's here with her, that means not only did she get my text, but she clearly understood the double entendre.

Meet me at the finish line.

Though I've never set foot in this house and have refused to without her, I pay it little attention as I stride past the wrought-iron staircase railing, knowing exactly where I'll find her. I've dreamt this dream a thousand times over the years, and both my heart and head know the way.

A light breeze guides me down the long, Spanish-tiled corridor, past the sand-textured caramel walls. The house is just a few rooms short of a mansion, but fitting enough for a queen.

The details I soak in through passing are few because my sole focus is far more appealing. There's nothing but fire and need in my hammering chest, which is beating as hard as it was the last time I came to her with a request. Back then, I was just as fucking terrified. Terrified she'd refuse to take me back. Terrified she believed my lies. Terrified I believed them for so long, I convinced myself they were true.

Twelve years ago, I forced her out of my life. In doing so, I lost myself, my purpose, my meaning, and my fucking mind.

Over half of those years I spent without her were due to fear, guilt, and self-condemnation.

Today, I come to her a changed man because of the years we lost and because of the years that brought us here. She may not have believed my lies, but I always believed *her truths*, believed in her love, in the surety of her heart.

Because she saved me.

Earning her and her heart has been my greatest accomplishment, making it my most prized possession.

A treasure any worthy thief will try to steal.

A treasure many *have* tried to take and failed. Because I made fucking sure of it. Before, I would never have gloated about such a feat of winning her because of the cost. Before, the guilt made it impossible to make such declarations.

Before . . . was too fucking painful.

I was selfish then, as I am now with her, without much apology, because the need outweighs the guilt—mostly.

After forty-four years of life, I'm positive she's the only thing I can't live without.

And for the next forty-four, I will *never* love another.

She's loved many. That's the nature of who she is. It's what shaped her, but I've been greedy with my heart, and it has one sole owner. Nothing has, or could ever, compare to what she stirs inside of me.

My selfishness, my ambitions, my jealousy, and greed almost cost me my future, cost me her.

Since she accepted me back, I've spent every single minute of our time together paying penance while biding my time for this day.

Sentence served.

My time is up, and I'm officially a free man.

Which is exactly why I have to find her. Right. Fucking. Now.

Napalm desire, along with the ache in my chest, has me hastening toward her as Beau struts next to me, determined to be the first to seek her affection.

"Fuck off, mutt, she's mine for the rest of the night."

Beau continues to prance next to me, ignoring my order. It took over a month to ship him here and another six weeks in quarantine to get him to the house. Now it seems he's already staked his claim as the head of it.

"Go. Now. Or I'll never cook you another steak."

His ears perk up as if aware of the implication of my threat, and he stops when I do, circling at my feet. Snapping my fingers, he returns my gaze, unphased, before he struts off.

Fucker.

When I reach my destination, I find her exactly where I thought she'd be, perched on the balcony, her long, breeze-blown hair tangling around her face. Her hands lay flat on the thick clay ledge as she gazes out at the sparkling sea. She's dressed in white, the silky material dipping low in a V on her back, exposing every inch of her spine. Her skin is golden from the sun, but it's the sight of the delicate wings along her shoulders that gets me hard. My thirsty eyes drink her in with a mix of desire and relief.

Getting her here was the final step of countless many.

I wait for her to recognize I'm near, and within a second of me standing at the door, I see her tense in awareness. Furious, watery, dark-blue eyes find mine as I take her in, emotion clogging my throat.

We've come so far since that day in the parking lot in Virginia, where all I had, literally, was the shirt on my back, an apology that would never be enough, and the fight she stirred within me to win her, to keep her, to reclaim what I stole all those years ago.

And we've come so far.

So. Fucking. Far.

From then to now seems like a lifetime ago.

In a sense, I've been waiting . . . but as of this moment, it's over.

In a matter of seconds, I will have done everything I set out to do. But it's the first day of my sentence that comes to mind when I breach the doorway and charge toward her. In the flash of the seconds it takes to reach her, I re-live it all.

"I was never really insane except upon occasions when my heart was touched."

—Edgar Allan Poe

Chapter One

TOBIAS

Age Thirty-Eight

HELL, DAY ONE.

The sudden weight on my chest jolts me into consciousness a second before hot, putrid breath hits my face. Opening my eyes, I'm met by the unmistakable shadow of a four-legged fucking devil.

The rabid dog stands proudly on my chest as snarl-induced saliva smacks me on the chin and his phlegmy sounding bark rings in my ears.

"Psychopathe." *Psychopath.* I grumble, batting away the crazed French bulldog, whose howl only increases the more I rouse and fight him off. He doesn't weigh much, but his bark indicates he's got an incredible self-image.

The fucker hasn't stopped growling at me since I walked through the front door yesterday, which Cecelia found highly amusing.

I did not.

Lifting to sit in the blackened room, I palm the empty space next to me on the bed. Beau, a namesake I truly wish she hadn't wasted on a dog, snaps his jaws where she slept next to me just hours before, sitting on his haunches, yapping, to make sure I fucking hate him.

And mere hours after our introduction, I decide I do.

Tense due to her disappearance, I glance out the window to see it's still dark, midnight dark.

I run a hand down my face, trepidation sneaking its way in.

I'd shown up after eight months, promised her the world, explanations, breakfast, and vowed to earn her. Instead, I got a brief tour of the house before I took a shower and passed right the fuck out. I don't remember much after the relief of getting through the door, mingled with the hot steam relaxing me to a point I haven't been able to reach in years.

And after all those promises I made, I failed to deliver on every single one a mere hour after I uttered them—due to exhaustion. With the adrenaline gone, I crashed and crashed hard.

What in the fuck, Tobias?

Tossing off the covers, I dress in the clothes I arrived in and slip into my boots.

Searching the room for a clock, I spot a small one that looks antique—solid gold with bells on top—sitting on one of her bookshelves and manage to make out the time.

Four a.m.

The time stamp marks my first day of hell.

Not only that, I'm fairly certain she's freaking out.

Merde. Shit.

I hoped she would sleep through the night, but I knew better. Jet-lagged from a thirty-six-hour trip, I passed out before we had a real conversation, went practically comatose before I could give her a single explanation of what kept me away. Briefly, I recall she changed into head-to-toe flannel pajamas while I was toweling off. This detail I remember because I found it amusing that she would go to such lengths to make sure I knew she wasn't going to reward me for returning—with her body. It didn't stop her at all from eye-fucking me when she thought I wasn't looking.

I'm sure she usually wakes early to open her café, but it's still too early for her to have gotten enough sleep. But I slept like a rock in those hours, better than I have in years, because I was in her bed. I know she hasn't rested for the same reason.

Because of *me* and my grand entrance back into her life.

I may have gotten my foot in the door, but she's still got her hand on the knob, ready to slam it with me on the other side if I fuck up. And I'm off to an amazing start.

I groan in frustration as Beau continues to shriek at me in what seems to be a canine declaration of territorial war until finally, I bark back.

"Putain, tais-toi!" *Shut the fuck up!* Immediately, Beau goes silent, head cocked, beady black eyes questioning the authority in my tone.

"Couché." *Get down.* Beau obeys without issue. He's got the simple commands down pat. Commands he understands clearly, *in French*.

The pointy-eared dog bounces around my heels as my eyes adjust to the dark. Though I'm anxious to get to her—wherever she may be—I can't help but glance around her bedroom out of curiosity. This room is far different than the one we got acquainted in. The room in her father's home where I manipulated her, fucked her, damaged her, before I began to worship her, love her.

She said her place wasn't much, but every part of the space has been touched somehow by color and inspiration, or houses some sort of creature comfort.

It's as if she's carefully designed every room in this house both as sanctuary and proof of her evolution. I can see it, all the subtle pieces of her in this house, in the artwork, in her choices.

Turning on a mosaic-colored Tiffany-style reading lamp on her repurposed desk, I sift through some hardbacks she has yet to shelve and eye a few of her handwritten notes next to a stack of bills, one a to-do list.

Organize a Thanksgiving food drive. (Drop at Meggie's)
Join the Chamber of Commerce.
Take a cooking class?
Hot Yoga?
Girls' Night with Marissa?
Book Club?
Entertain Mr. Handsome?

I tame the surge of fire that threatens and decide not to start our morning conversation with "Who the fuck is Mr. Handsome?"

Everything about my doghouse predicament has me batting away my natural instincts to dominate, so I can make peace with her before I declare any sort of territorial war. And by war, I mean the full-fledged battle to make fucking sure we do everything imaginable to retrieve what we were beneath the ruins of our *last* one.

Perturbed by what I've discovered, I make my way

toward the kitchen in search of her. When I find it empty, my unease kicks up, but I can't help my grin at the sight of the French press sitting on the counter. And that's when my chest begins to ache due to the double-edged sword that is my situation.

I might be here, with her, but not in the way I want to be.

Patience is crucial in winning her back, but it's also my Achilles' heel.

It's been far too long since we were truly together. Merciless years since the day we were last wrapped up in the other while confessing our love in Roman's back yard before being torn apart by the worst of circumstances. Some of which I myself created.

From that point, years ago, to this one, along with all of the hurdles I've dealt with in the past eight months, all the obstacles I've battled in order to get here, to this point, through her door, feel justified.

But even with her near, she's not *with me*. Not yet.

Doubt creeps in when I glance around the kitchen for any obvious place a note might be and find nothing. On instinct alone, I know she's not inside the house. Opening the back door for Beau, a cold gust of wind slaps my face as panic starts to set in.

Did she leave?

Sweat gathers at my forehead as I stare down her Napoléon-complexed mutt as he drops his morning deuce, all the while snarling at me. It's clear we're going to have issues, but the bigger one has blood pounding at my temples.

Could I blame her if she did leave?

Yesterday was a big step, but as the high of my sudden

appearance wore off and reality set in, I could feel her distancing herself for protection.

Monitoring Beau from the porch, I blow into my hands. With Indian summer fleeting, a cold snap seems to have arrived overnight, much like me, without ample warning. Autumn chill seeps into my bones as I step off the porch and further into the yard, relieved when I spot her. She's hunched over her garden, a shop light illuminating where she works in nothing but her flannel pajamas and black Uggs.

The urge to touch her, taste her, fuck her, reclaim her, thrums through me—a low-lying demand I refuse to entertain even though I'm aching everywhere, and I know she feels the same need.

It's who we are.

With us, looking is love, fighting is love, fucking is love, and even now, while we muddle through our collective but distinctly different fears, it's love.

A fact she refused to let me deny. A fact I've come to embrace. The fuel I need for the fight I'm in for. *"No matter how we came to be, we were and still are. You stole my heart, and you let me love you with it, and you made damn sure I knew where its home was."*

I need to believe it. I have to believe it. Her words are my driving force. It may have been eight months, but the journey to get back to her has felt like an eternity.

Everything between us has always come down to love, as she so boldly pointed out until I had no choice but to face it fully and give in to the truth.

The truth being that I love her so fiercely that I can't stand the idea of letting this drag out another day—fuck, another hour. But I will. For her, I'll find the patience.

And my demands will be few.

On the drive home, she glanced over at me in the way of a stranger she was trying to understand, posture guarded. It's the same rigid posture she's displaying now as she stabs into the dirt with a small shovel. She's on the offensive.

When I approach, I know it's just a matter of time before she'll sense me near. She always has, as I have her.

Beau, the greedy fuck, makes it to her first.

"Hey baby," she murmurs to her dog, her voice raw, as she takes off a soiled gardening glove to run her fingers down his back. She doesn't bother to glance my way when she speaks. "Did he wake you?"

"Doesn't matter. It's freezing out here. I'll get you a coat."

"I'm fine." She slides her glove back on and resumes her work, tossing a patch of dirt to the side before grabbing a container of mixed mums.

"Did you have a dream?" I ask, knowing it's some of what's bothering her.

"Don't I always?" she replies in a biting tone.

I kneel next to her as she continues to stab at the dirt.

"Need help?"

"No. I've got it."

"Talk to me," I urge, studying her profile in the yellow light.

She digs and stabs—as does her silence—and I do nothing to stop her. She's nervous or hurting or both, and that's the last thing I want.

Day one, Tobias.

"Talk to me, Cecelia."

"Maybe I don't want to." Her reply is low, so low I'm not sure if she wanted me to hear. But I don't bother armoring up. She's already won. Today's not the day to brawl. It's a day to surrender. I've missed her so fucking much. Over the years, and as the months passed, I sometimes wondered if I imagined some of my need, my affection for her. That theory was blown all to hell the minute I stepped into the boardroom to face off with her after years of separation. It was just another lie I told myself in the days and months after I sent her away. Trying to reason with love is fucking pointless. It doesn't care about your reasons, right or wrong. Love has no regard for circumstance, nor does it give a fuck what state it puts you in. It's a relentless and unforgiving emotion that will never let you lie to yourself.

Fixed on her profile, in desperate need of a hit of her ocean blues, I sit back on the heels of my boots, settling in for the first battle of many.

"Why now?" she asks, palming a mum from the container and placing it in the waiting soil. "You wait until I'm settled into a *new life*. A new life that doesn't include you. That doesn't suit you at all. Why?"

"I had to . . ." I exhale a weary breath when she gives me the side-eye. "No matter what I tell you right now, it will sound like an excuse, but I do have reasons, a lot of them. And I'll give them all to you."

She briefly stills the fingers pressing the soil around the plant. "I'm listening."

"I'm sorry I fell asleep. That's the last thing I wanted to do. I'm jet-lagged."

She doesn't bother asking where I was. She's too used to not being in the know. Or worse, she doesn't care.

"I was in Dubai on Exodus business. We just acquired a company. It was my last task as acting CEO before Shelly took over. I haven't slept in days. When I tied things up, I came straight to you and—"

"Straight to me?" she scoffs. "You know, you're right, Tobias; anything you say right now will sound like an excuse. You should probably go back to sleep."

"Let me explain."

"I don't know if I want your explanations right now."

"Well, you deserve them, and it's fucking cold out here. Let's go inside and talk."

She ignores my request and continues her task as though she didn't hear me.

"I'm not leaving," I whisper softly, knowing I'm getting nowhere. She doesn't want to hear me, not now. I stand and do the opposite of that declaration, entering the house and heading back into her bedroom. I grab a hoodie from her chest of drawers and make my way back outside just as she empties another container. She eyes me when I thrust the thick shirt out to her.

"I'm fine."

"Cecelia, it's freezing."

She stands, pulls off her gloves, and yanks the sweatshirt from my hands before tugging it down over her head, the university logo a glaring reminder that I missed her through four years of college, and the summers she spent in France in between, and the years after. A painful reminder she experienced a lot of living without me. Even with a daily report of her well-being and what I could stomach about her personal life, I don't know most of the intimate details. I couldn't handle knowing them, though I got overly curious more than once and drank myself stupid, setting my progress back. She stands in front of me now, eyes wary, and even so, it's lightning in my veins being so close. Our attraction tangible, a constant pulse thrumming between us since the day we met. Even in the murky yellow light, I can see the faint freckles on her nose. She's symmetrical perfection, from the shape of her face to the tiny divot in her chin. I move to reach for her, and she steps away.

She's swinging hard already, and I feel every blow. Shoving my hands in my jeans, I toe a loose rock that edges her garden back into place with my boot. "What was the dream about?"

She bites her lip, lifting her faraway gaze when she speaks. "I guess if I had to Freud it up, the interpretation would be that I don't *really* know you." She resumes her place on her knees. "I don't know your brand of toothpaste."

"That's an easy fix. What else happened?"

"I don't remember."

"You're lying. I'm willing to bet you're out here because of that dream. Because *I know you*."

She lets out a labored breath. "I need to get this done."

"It's called multi-tasking." I kneel again and nudge her to the side to share workspace. I grab another shovel from the old-fashioned wooden toolbox sitting on the stone sidewalk behind us.

"It's early, you're tired, and I don't need your help."

"We're going to be together. Today, tomorrow, and the day after, Cecelia."

"Just . . . back off, Tobias." The shake in her voice tells me all I need to know as she stands and walks over to a large bag of potting soil before dragging it my way. I don't help because I'm fairly sure she will stab me with her little shovel if I try to come anywhere near her.

She's angry. I expected it, but it hurts just the same. I'd

forced my way into her space yesterday, much like I did when we got together, and I no longer want that to be the case, but the urge is strong.

She hangs her head as if she feels the conflict in me, although I don't flinch. "I don't want to fight, Tobias."

"Since when are you so fucking afraid of confrontation?"

"I'm not afraid." She rips through the thick plastic easily, a very, very angry gardener. "I just don't have anything to say to you right now."

"How many lies are we going to start with?"

Her dark blue eyes ice over. "I made a *life* here. Temporary as it may be, I'm not leaving it *for you*. Not again."

"Well, I can see why. You're on the fast track to one *exciting* life. Hot yoga? The Chamber of Commerce?" I fist my hands at my sides. This is an argument for a different time.

"Of course, you went snooping. Isn't that just like you to come in and invade my privacy after *years* apart."

"You knew who you were falling for."

"Doesn't mean I wanted to."

"Time and separation don't matter when it comes to us. That's clear now."

"But it does. It does *matter*. It matters to me. I know I agreed to try, but what exactly are you thinking will happen? That I'll just fall back into place, no questions asked, legs spread, heart wide open? I'm not that girl anymore, Tobias, and I'm no longer that woman, either."

"This is you we're talking about, so I fucking know better. If you weren't capable of being that woman anymore, the one who forgives and loves the way only you can, I wouldn't have slept in your bed last night. As far as plans go, I don't know because we haven't talked yet the way we need to, or made a single fucking plan, *together*. We're now in negotia-tions. What. Was. The. Fucking. Dream?"

"What else would it be?"

"I'm not leaving you. Not today, not tomorrow, and not the day after. Hell will freeze over. I'll eat a McRib first."

Wrong thing to say.

"You think this is funny?" She glares at me, covered in soil, her eyes gleaming with accusation and residual anger.

"I think a sense of humor may make this a lot less bloody, but it's clear by the look on your face you don't share that opinion."

"You lived with her." The admission is just above a whisper.

"You dreamt about Alicia?"

"She *knew* you. You *let* her know you. *She* knew your brand of toothpaste. *She* probably picked out your fucking ties in the morning. Things you *let* her know."

"Don't—" I shake my head, hating the direction this is going— "don't do that."

"You threw me away, but you *lived* with her. I never even got to see where you lived."

"Yes, you did. You saw the only place I ever considered home. The shithole my aunt owned at the edge of town. That was the only home I knew in Triple Falls. The rest were just places to rest my head between business trips. I haven't had a real home since my parents died, and I didn't *live* with her."

"She made it seem like you did."

"And I let you think that."

"Of course, you did." She lets out an exasperated laugh.

I can't help the bitter edge with my delivery. "Glass houses, Cecelia. Need I remind you that you were wearing a fucking two-carat engagement rock when you drove back to Triple after leaving your *live-in* fiancé? Or is he still an afterthought?"

Chill, Tobias. Right fucking now.

I close my eyes, dreading seeing the evidence of that cutting comment.

"How dare you," she croaks, her voice barely audible. "So, it's my fault? I had to move on. It's not like you gave me a choice."

"I know," I swallow. "I'm sorry. That was jealousy speaking. Ask me anything."

She looks away, and her silence only makes the ache grow.

"We have to talk about this. We've wasted enough fucking time."

"We?"

"Fine, *me*. Merde!" I clench my fists. "If you want to play the blame game, I take it all, all of it, okay? As far as living arrangements, I . . . *we*, have a condo in Charlotte, a townhouse in Paris, an apartment in Spain, and a hideaway in Germany."

"You and Alicia?"

"Are you fucking serious right now? We, as in *you and me*. She was never my future, Cecelia."

She seems to mull it over. "And the finish line?"

I nod. "Still there. Never set foot in it. And you and I practically lived in Roman's house together."

"It's not the same. And that was all an illusion anyway, wasn't it?"

"No, it wasn't. But what you had was just a dream. I know they feel real to you, but it was just a dream."

"Or a warning I should take seriously."

Stab. I feel it everywhere. But I'll let her have this fight and a thousand more.

"We weren't together long," I offer and cringe when I see it does shit to help.

"Neither were we if we're keeping score and if *dating* is what you want to call it."

"What we did was not dating; don't downplay what's brought us back to this point. We fell in love, and it devastated us and everyone around us to the point we destroyed lives, including our own. And I'm to blame. But here we are, and we still love each other, more so now because we're wise enough to know what we've lost. It's not going to take a day to get over the things I've said and done, the lies I've told, or the shit we're going to have to work through. But I'm owning my part, the way you asked me to, the way you need me to, the way *I need to*. And all I'm hoping for is that you ask me what you need to, so I can own up to it, and we don't waste any more time."

She sits back on her heels and drops her gaze. "Fine. Then start with what you promised. The truth. Why did you come back now?"

"A lot of it has to do with carrying out plans I set into motion over twenty years ago, especially Tyler's position in the White House. I didn't expect it to take so fucking long, and the longer it took, the more I was sure I had to get everything off my plate in order to do this right. I had to heavily vet the few I trusted to take over with Sean, so you and I could . . ." I groan in frustration. "The last thing I wanted to do was come after you and turn around and leave while we were sorting ourselves out . . ." Anger surges at the hell I went through after she left. "And you disappeared for seven fucking weeks before I found you."

"I had every reason to."

"For seven weeks, I went off the rails because you didn't leave a trace." I clench my fists on my thighs in an attempt to temper my anger. "You made sure of it."

"Cash," she supplies. "It goes a long way, as you well know. That's why this house and the diner *legally* belong to my mother." She stops her digging. "Maybe I didn't want to be found."

"I was losing my fucking mind with worry."

"I was no longer yours to worry about. You made sure of it."

"You've always been mine. I've had protective eyes on you since you were eleven years old, Cecelia, no matter how I felt about you. Maybe I deserved the hell those weeks were not knowing, but there will never be a time in your life you're not under my protection. I failed you once, and I'll do everything in my fucking power not to fail you again. Believe me, by the time I arrived yesterday, I made every effort to make sure you had *no one* but *me* coming for you."

Chapter Two

Tobias

Her face drains of all color. "What's that supposed to mean?"

"Exactly what you think it means. Another reason it took me so long to get to you. Aside from kicking a hundred things into motion so I could be here, I had bodies to find and *bury*." My sole focus being Roman's old business partner, the motherfucker who sent Miami, turning the confrontation into a bloodbath.

Her mouth parts as her eyes widen, incredulous. "Jerry? You went after him?"

I nod and don't miss her flinch.

"Tobias, what did you do?"

"I made sure he'll never be a threat to you again."

"You said you trusted me."

"I do. I didn't trust him. He's as fucking corrupt as they come. Retaliation was in the works. I saw it for myself. I was tracking both his correspondence and calls closely. He's always been a threat to you. If I had gotten a handle on things when I should have . . ." I clear my throat to stop myself, "I would have taken care of him a lot sooner."

She flicks imploring eyes to mine. "What do you mean?"

Not yet. We're not there yet, Tobias. One thing at a time.

"I got a confession before I buried him. He was the one who sent Miami. Do you want the details?"

She swallows and darts her eyes away. "No."

"You are never to disappear on me again." Her stare is a million miles away before it finally flits back to me, the toll of the first of my confessions heavy in her eyes.

I level out my voice, intent that through her anger she hears me. Adamant she knows what she's in for should the situation ever present itself. "I will *kill* anyone who threatens you. Anyone. I will fucking *end* them, Cecelia. I won't think twice, and I won't lose sleep over it."

She bites her lip, dragging her gaze over my body before turning her attention back to her flower bed. I crouch down next to her as the wind lifts some loose hair from her shoulder and I brush the rest away from her face.

"Does that scare you?"

"No."

"That's because you *do* know who I am. We are not strangers, Cecelia. Far from it."

She doesn't argue that. "Even so, you should know by now. I don't do well with orders."

"On this, I don't give a fuck. Punish me, but never that way. Don't run from my protection. I'll make you promise me that one day and save it for a different fight that will be happening *sooner* rather than later. I can't risk . . ." I resist the urge to rip her from the ground, shake some sense into her and demand she make the promise now, but I know better. It's my selfish need, my own emotions that demand it. Aside from that, she'll never be tamed. It's part of my attraction to her, even if it scares the hell out of me.

A beat of silence passes. "How *did* you find me?"

"Sean. He knew where you were the whole time. After I exhausted every resource, I finally went to him to ask for help. He was expecting me."

I see it the second she puts it together.

"There's a tracking device on the Camaro."

"He installed it before he gifted it to you. He had you followed and put two permanent birds on you the minute you landed here. He knew I was losing my shit, but he wanted to make sure I got my wake-up call. I sniffed out his bullshit when I asked him for help, and the smug bastard finally put me out of my misery when I told him of my plan."

"Which was?"

"You."

She shivers in her hoodie.

"Let's go inside and talk. Your lips are turning blue."

"I'm fine," she harrumphs, wiping the loose dirt from her gloves. "You bastards—even when I did your bidding and kept your secrets, you never once believed I could take care of myself."

"He was sincere about the gift, Cecelia. Dom would have wanted you to have it, but no matter how this works out between us, we're always going to protect you. Always. That's not debatable."

"Yeah? Well, who's going to protect me from *you*?"

Right hook.

I swallow. "You don't need it. I'm at your mercy."

"Until when?"

Still crouched beside her, I place a thumb under her chin and turn her head my way. "I'm in this, Cecelia. I would give anything to go back, to change the things I did. To be the man you needed me to be, but it's never been as simple as giving in to how I feel about you. And it's not any easier now. After what went down, after all you went through, I had to allow you the chance at a normal life, to escape this one." Her frown is deep-set when I lift her chin. "And after years away, you did start a different life. You stayed away. Purposely, even with the excuse of your father's death to come back, you didn't return to Triple Falls. You went to college, graduated, and were engaged to be married to another man. You had a ring on your finger. When you came back, you were selling the company. You were ridding yourself of all ties, from Triple Falls, and *from me*. I had to respect your decision. You were thriving. At least that's what I thought, at first."

"And after?"

"I explained this to you. It was a culmination of reasons, one in particular, and I'll tell you everything, but—" I shake my head—"I need time for that. Not a lot, but I swear I'll tell you."

"You don't think I can handle it?"

"I think you can handle anything," I say honestly. "It's just too much to sort through right now. You haven't slept. I doubt you've eaten."

She stands and wipes her pajamas free of debris, and I take a step forward, but she takes one back, jerking her head. "Don't."

"Why? Because you know exactly how it's going to end up once you let me touch you?"

"Love and sex solve nothing, remember?"

I run my hand through my hair, and she crosses her arms, satisfaction clear in her eyes. She's fully expecting me to give up at some point. It's the opposite of progress, and she puts a voice to it.

"Giving up already?"

"Stop it," I snap. "It was just a dream. Did nothing I confessed to you yesterday make a difference?"

"Yes and no, you just . . ." she rubs a hand over her red nose, "you don't belong here."

"Where do you picture me?"

"You didn't even bring a goddamn suitcase!" She fists her hands on her hips. "Where do you live now? Where are your belongings, Tobias?"

"Packed in a truck with a driver waiting for my say so. Over half my wardrobe are suits that I don't plan on fucking wearing anytime soon. I *live* here. Where you are is home. I made that clear yesterday. I know we can't pick up where we left off—" I step forward, she steps back, and so the tango begins—the look on her face one of a wounded animal.

"You're lonely here, Cecelia. I did that. I've made you lonely *again*. You think I don't know that? You gave up your fucking life for me, so I did the same. I did the only thing I could because I wanted you to take me seriously when I showed up with nothing but the clothes on my back."

She bites her bottom lip, her eyes drifting up and down my frame.

"I gave up the only life I've known for over twenty years and most everything that had anything to do with it, to come here just for a chance to be with you again."

"You gave up *clothes*."

"I gave up *control*," I counter. "Which is the hardest fucking thing for a man like me to do." I step forward, and this time she doesn't step back. I cup her face, her cheeks ice cold. "Because I want *this*, more than anything else. I want this, *you*, *us*."

"Just—" she lifts her hands to my wrists and grips them, intent on pulling them away. "Go back to bed. I need to think."

"No."

"Tobias—"

"Fuck no. I'm not going to give you a chance to think of more reasons to hold a grudge against me." I lean in. "What hurts you hurts me. There's more to say."

"Not today." She drops her eyes and shakes her head before pushing past me toward the house. That's when I snap, rush her, and scoop her into my arms.

"Put me down."

"No," I murmur, nuzzling her neck, inhaling her scent, a scent so soothing it feels like coming home. But it's short-lived because I feel her tensing in my arms.

I bend to kiss her, and she turns her head.

"Look at me, please," I implore.

"I hate you so much," she whispers.

"I know."

Her eyes lift to mine before dropping to my lips. "Plus rien ne nous séparera. Jamais." *Nothing will ever come between us. Never.*

Exhausted, no doubt by me, she drops her head to rest on my shoulder as I carry her inside, Beau hot on my heels until I kick the bedroom door closed in his face.

"Don't take your frustration out on my puppy," she scolds as I walk into the bathroom and gently deposit her to stand in front of the shower.

"Did you sleep at all?" I ask, turning on the faucet.

She stands limp and doesn't respond.

"I'm sorry it took me so long." I slowly lift the hoodie above her head along with her pajama top before gently pulling the tie from her hair. It falls heavy around her shoulders, and at the sight of it, I get hard.

She's sleep-deprived, shell-shocked, and seems defeated, and I hate it. I want her fight, but her game is off. And that's on me.

"I had to come to you ready, Cecelia. I had to. Too many people depend on me. I had too many plates spinning. I had to plan my exit strategy and get my head together. I promise you, somehow I'll make you understand."

"I doubt it."

"Those lies I told you when you were fighting so hard, they were my last," I murmur, pressing a kiss to her temple as I unclasp her bra. Unable to help myself, I bend and pull a nipple into my mouth, and instantly her fingers tangle in my hair, the breath leaving her as she rips at me, full of resistance.

Fighting her, I draw her other nipple into my mouth and suck, flicking my tongue over her silky flesh before lifting my eyes to hers. Her chest pumps with rapid breaths as she watches me, rapt but furious.

"I need you," I whisper before again pulling half her breast into my mouth, drawing a soft cry from her. Her chest glistens when I release her, her body becoming lax as I hold her firmly in place. "I need you, Cecelia. I need to make you come. I need to feel you stretch around my cock. I need to hear my name coming from your lips. But I need *you* more."

Kneeling, I tug down her pajama bottoms before slowly dragging her panties to join them on the floor. Eye level with her pussy, I press my lips to the top of it and inhale her scent, cock throbbing, begging to be set free.

Unable to handle the need for a taste, I run my tongue along her slit as she digs her nails into my scalp, a choppy moan leaving her. I revel in the burn of the pain she's inflicting, because she's fighting, but not nearly hard enough. I pull away and gaze up at her. Her return stare full of blue fire.

Neither of us can fight our draw, and we have never been able to, no matter how at odds we were. But I need more than her body's submission to act.

Standing, I run my thumbs along her jaw before briefly kissing her. She trembles with want. Her eyes imploring, while her lips refuse to move, to ask for what she needs, and it's fucking agony pulling away.

"Shower. I'll make breakfast. We'll talk more."

She nods, her gaze losing focus, to another time—a time where, no doubt, I've hurt her because that's all I've ever done.

"No one hates me more for what I've done to you, than me," I admit before I fully release her and leave her in a room full of steam.

She's been on autopilot since she got out of the shower, mindlessly sipping her coffee while feeding Beau her bacon. It's not the breakfast I pictured we'd have. But I set my hopes high.

"Ask me anything," I urge from where I'm seated at her four-seat kitchenette. She bites into her French toast and downs her coffee before I shove the first bite in my mouth.

Our eyes meet as I cough it down while a faint smile twists her lips.

"Putain." *Fuck*. I grab her plate and mine and walk them over to the sink while continuously trying to clear my throat.

She speaks up behind me with a little mirth in her tone. "It was a good effort."

"I've never cooked with cinnamon." I shove the crisped bread into the garbage disposal and click it on. The slide of her chair alerts me to what I knew was coming. Shutting off the sink, I turn and grip the counter behind me. "You can't take a day?"

She slowly shakes her head, and I accept the lie.

"All right, give me five."

"What?" She frowns, her plump lips twisting in displeasure, and it might as well be a knife in my chest.

"I'm coming with you."

"To my café?"

"I need to borrow the Camaro."

"Where are you going?"

"I need a few things."

She nods to the keys on the counter and collects her purse. "I'll be outside. Lock up."

She leans down to pet Beau and gives him an exaggerated kiss, and I'm instantly jealous.

Chapter Three

TOBIAS

Age Eleven

I GLANCE AT the clock when the front door slams, and a second later, Delphine cuts the music off. The clink of a bottle to glass in the kitchen tells me she's not going to be driving us to school in a few hours, which means it's up to me to make sure we make it. Truancy will have us scrutinized, and we don't need social services at our door, not with the state the house is in. And once again, I'll have to be the one to clean it. It's only been a few months since our parents died, the worst months of my life. Dom's not getting any better. The happy kid he was has all but disappeared because of our aunt's indifference and cruelty. She doesn't have the motherly gene, and she's made it clear, daily, that we're an obligation she never wanted. But if she falls suspect by outsiders as unfit to parent us—which she is—we'll be taken away, and I won't have that. I won't be separated from my brother.

Deciding to get a little sleep, I set my cheap alarm hoping the batteries don't die, and settle back into my mattress when

I hear the unmistakable sound of my brother's stifled sobs across the hall. Tossing my thin, itchy sheet off, I walk into Dominic's room to see him lying on his stomach. His head is pressed into his pillow to muffle his cries, his shoulders shaking. Turning on his plastic lamp, I sit on the edge of his twin bed, and he freezes, fear in his eyes until he sees it's me.

"It's okay, Dom. They're gone. The party is over. Go back to sleep." I cup his shoulder and feel his skin blazing through his thin pajama top. I turn him over, lift his shirt, and realize he's covered in chickenpox.

He stares down at his chest and stomach in fear. "I didn't do anything."

"It's not your fault. You have chickenpox."

"Am I going to die like Mama and Papa?"

I grind my teeth at the ache in my chest. "No. They'll itch for a while, but you only get them once."

"You had them too?"

"Yes, and it made me stronger. I'll get you some medicine to help the itch in the morning."

The door bursts open, and Delphine eyes us both.

"What are you two doing awake?"

I roll my eyes. "How could we sleep with all that noise?"

"That's grown-up business. Go back to bed."

"He's got a fever and chickenpox." She looks at Dominic warily as I lift his shirt for her to see. "He can't go to school. They'll send him home."

"Well, I can't take off work," she huffs. "We can't afford it."

"Then I'll stay home," I argue back. "He's not going to be sick and *alone*."

"You can't miss school."

36

"I'm not leaving him here. *End of.*" That's what Papa used to say when he meant business, and I hope it's just as effective.

She glowers at us before she turns and slams the door.

"I hate her," Dominic whispers, afraid she might hear him.

"We won't live here forever."

"She threw my cars away because she stepped on one."

"I told you to pick them up. I'll get you more."

"You don't have any money."

"Let me worry about that." I'll steal another twenty from her purse. Half the time she has no idea what's in her wallet and is too drunk to notice when it goes missing. I press my palm to his neck again and stand. He's burning up.

"Where are you going?"

"To find some medicine to lower your temperature."

"You're coming back?"

"Right back."

Making my way across the hall toward Delphine's room, I'm stopped at the doorway by a familiar sniffle. I peek in to see her eyes reddening as she studies the pictures laid out on her bed, pictures of her and the husband who left her a few months before Mama and Papa died. She runs her fingers over them before sensing me standing there and lifts hostile eyes to mine. "I don't want to be a mother."

"Then don't. I'll feed him. I'll bathe him. I'll walk him to school. You don't touch him, don't yell at him. I'll do it all."

She snorts. "You're just a kid."

"Plus adulte que toi." *More of a grown-up than you anyway.*

"Surveille ton langage, petit con." *Watch your language, little shithead.*

Opting out of another useless argument, I switch gears. "I need Tylenol for his fever."

She opens her bedside drawer and plucks one of the powdered packets she puts on her tongue every morning for her hangover, and I eye it, uneasy.

"What's in it?"

"Same as Tylenol. Works faster. Put it in some juice."

"We don't have any juice."

She sighs and gathers the pictures from her mattress before lovingly placing them in an old cigar box on her nightstand.

Walking over to her dresser, I snatch her wallet from her purse and take a twenty out.

"What the hell do you think you're doing?"

"I'm going to get the medicine he needs and a new car for him to play with while he's sick." The tone of my voice dares her to object. This is the fight I'm up for.

She opens her mouth to argue and instead sinks back into her mattress. "Fine, whatever."

"We don't want you for a mother, either." I crumple the money in my hand and toss her wallet back into her purse. "Just stay away from him. I'll take care of him."

"Whatever, kid, close the door." She rolls her eyes and turns off her lamp, leaving us both in the pitch dark. She'll pass out in seconds. Fumbling out of her bedroom, I use the dim light from Dominic's lamp to navigate my way down the hall toward the kitchen to grab some water. I pour half the packet she gave me into the cup and stir it up while staring at the full moon outside the window, just as a roach skitters across the glass. Medicine in hand, I bring it back to Dominic, who's stripped down to nothing but his underwear, furiously scratching his arms.

"Put your clothes back on, so you can't scratch."

"I have to."

"You can't. It will get worse and leave marks."

He stills his fingers and groans as he pulls his pajamas back on. Pajamas that are too small for him now. I can still remember the day Mama and I brought them home after running errands together. I'd picked them out. It wasn't that long ago they were here, alive.

Dominic frowns at the glass. "This will make me stronger?"

"Yes. Every time you get sick, your body will figure out how to make you stronger so you're not so sick next time. It'll target the culprit and create antibodies to fight it."

"What's a culprit?"

"The reason why you're sick."

"What are ant bodies?"

"*Antibodies*. They live inside you. They build an army to help fight the sickness."

"How do you know that?" he asks, tilting his head the way Papa used to.

"I read books. Books make you smart."

"Then I'll read books," he says, "lots of books. And I'm going to get stronger. And smart, and then nobody can be mean to me ever again."

"Good. Drink it."

He takes a long drink and makes a face. "I don't want it."

"There's medicine in it. You need it."

"Bleh."

"Drink it, Dom. I'll get you better tasting medicine at the store tomorrow."

Not long after he finishes his drink, he falls asleep, and I drift off next to him once I've checked his skin for a drop in temperature.

When the front door slams a few hours later, I rouse in between the wall and his mattress and gently shake Dom to wake him up.

"I'm going to the store. Don't you leave this bed until I get back."

"I'm sleeping," he whines.

"If you wake up, you pee and get right back into bed. Otherwise, don't leave this room until I get back, and don't answer the door for *anyone*."

"I'm *sleeping*."

"Promise me."

"I promise, gah," he huffs, pulling the sheet over his head.

Gut churning, I lock the door behind me. I start toward the street before I turn back around and head up to the porch, turning the lock with my key. *One, two, three.*

Satisfied with my count, I start at a dead run from the driveway toward the drug store. I'm not far from the house when I notice the sedan that was parked across the street from our house creeping up next to me. I stop mid-stride and turn as the car slows to a stop. Ready to confront whoever it is, I'm surprised to see a woman in the driver's seat. She peers at me before she puts down her window, her eyes swollen and red. "Hi. I'm sorry if I scared you. I was wondering if I could give you a ride?"

"No," is all I say before I turn and resume my run.

She follows for a few wordless seconds before she speaks up. "I'm not going to hurt you."

"I don't need a ride, but thanks." I keep my eyes forward, sweat clouding my vision. I've built up stamina due to my nightly runs since I started going to the place I discovered the night my parents died, but it's hot as hell today, and my shirt is already soaked through.

"I'm going to town if that's where you're headed, and I could use the company."

Annoyed, I stop my run and glare in her direction. She's pretty and doesn't look that much older than me. It's when I finally approach the car that I see her large belly behind the wheel. She's pregnant, *really* pregnant, and something in my gut tells me she's harmless.

"You're a little young to be running around alone, don't you think?"

"I turn twelve in a few months, and what are *you* doing following kids around offering rides?"

She flashes a weak smile. "I'm sure I freaked you out, but it wasn't my intention. I was passing through when I saw you and thought I'd offer a ride. It's hot out here."

"You know the Perkins?"

"The Perkins?"

"The house you were parked at." I cross my arms over my chest.

"Oh? No. I got turned around in the neighborhood. Where are you headed?"

"My brother is sick. He needs medicine."

Her chin wobbles as she speaks. "Is it serious?"

"No. Just the chickenpox."

"Hop in. I'll take you. I promise I'm no threat to you."

Gripping the handle of her car, I hesitate and look down the long road ahead and back toward the house. I locked it three times. He's asleep, but for how long? A few nights ago, halfway on my run to my secret spot, I couldn't remember if I'd locked the door. I ran all the way home, my heart pounding more out of fear than the run because I wasn't sure. Three locks clicking, three twists of the handle. Three checks on him before I leave. It's the only way to be sure. "I have to get back to him."

"We'll make it quick," she promises.

I again glance back at the house, sweat rolling down my temple. I can't picture this woman trying to hurt me at all. Fuck it.

I get in and buckle my seat belt. Her car is older, a little beat up, but the AC works, and I'm thankful for it. She turns the vent my way, and the sweat starts to cool on my skin.

"Can you drop me at the pharmacy, please?"

"Sure."

The more she drives, the more I grow comfortable in the seat. She's *big*, and there's barely an inch of space between her belly and the steering wheel.

"So, is that your house back there?"

"It's my aunt's house. We're staying with her for a while."

"Do you like living there?"

I shrug to make her think, 'it's okay,' but the truth is, I fucking hate it, and I'm almost to the point I hate Delphine.

"Is she, are you . . ." the woman's voice shakes when she speaks, which makes me uneasy. I glance in the passenger side rearview.

Three times. You locked it three times.

"So, your brother . . ."

"Dominic."

"Dominic," she swallows. "Is he in much p-pain?"

I glance her way, and she looks back as if she's afraid of *me*, afraid of what I'll say.

"He'll be okay. I had them when I was his age. Everyone has them, haven't you?"

"No, actually I haven't. I'm sure I'll get them when my baby has them. It's better to get them young, though. I read it in one of my baby books."

"What are you having?" This is the strangest conversation I've ever had. I have no idea who this woman is or why she's giving me a ride, but her AC is making it hard to care.

"A girl. I was thinking of naming her Leann."

I wrinkle my nose, and she doesn't miss it. She lets out a light laugh.

"Don't like that one, huh? Well, it's my mother's name."

"Sorry." I look back in the direction of the house, praying Dominic stays asleep.

"It's fine. I don't have my heart set on it. Maybe I'll use it as a middle name."

When she pulls up to the pharmacy a few minutes later, hand on the door handle, I turn to her. "Thank you for the ride."

"Do you mind if I come with? I can help you find what you need."

I draw my brows.

"I'm kind of in between things to do," she says softly.

"I mean . . . I guess, if you want to."

She nods and exits the car when I do, waddling through the door when I open it for her.

"Thank you," she says absently. Her face is splotched, a lot like Delphine's after she has one of her nightly cries. Together, we walk down through a few aisles until we find what we're looking for. She grabs a bottle of anti-itch lotion that costs eight dollars, and it's then I know I'm screwed.

43

"Thanks," I say as she plucks a bottle of children's Tylenol next, and I see the price on the shelf she pulled it from.

Eleven dollars.

I won't have enough after tax.

"What else do you need?"

"Nothing." I bite my lip, looking at the drug store brand of Tylenol, and snatch it off the shelf. "This one instead."

Face flaming with embarrassment, she grabs another bottle of Tylenol and dumps it into the shopping cart she snatched when we came in. "Let me get this for you."

"What?" We're close to the same height. I might have her beat by an inch. "Why would you?"

"I would just really like to if that's okay."

"I mean . . . I don't—"

"It will be our secret." She gives me a little smile.

I nod because I really have no choice. If she hadn't offered, I might not have enough and would have to steal it. I've been getting away with it a lot lately, and it never gives me a good feeling. But I only started doing it because of reasons like this, days like today when my back is against the wall. Since I have to wait until I'm sixteen to get the money from my parents' death settlement, I'm stuck taking until I can earn it. And until that time comes, I'm going to have to figure out a way, and I have a sinking feeling the five-finger discount will be a lot of the way. But it's a fine line. If I get caught stealing, I'll draw attention to Delphine and Dom. I have to play everything just right, be twice as fast, twice as smart as any simple thief. My life, Dom's life, depends on it. Familiar shame chokes me up, and I vow to make enough money someday, so I never have to feel this way again.

As if reading my mind, she speaks up. "Can you think of anything else he needs?"

"I'm just going to find him a Matchbox car and a book."

"Oh?" She perks up. "I'll help."

"You really don't have—"

"Please let me," she says, her voice urgent and shaking again. "I'm having a b-bad day. You ever have those?"

"All the time."

This seems to set her off, and she turns away from me and wipes her face with her hand.

"I'm sorry. Don't get upset. Yeah, you can help." All I want to do is leave this strange lady and get back to my brother, but it's when she looks over to me the way she is, that my chest aches.

"Don't apologize to me, not ever. I'm sorry. Pregnancy has made me really emotional lately. I'm not trying to make you uncomfortable."

"It's an abundance of hormones," I repeat Mr. Belin's words from during one of our science classes. "You are kind of creating an entire other person at the moment. It's expected."

She smiles at me. "You're a smart one, huh?" She pushes the cart forward, and I follow.

"I have a really good memory."

"That's good. I wish I didn't," she says on a light laugh.

We move to the toy section, and I weigh the price of a few cars with the cash in my pocket when she lifts a set off the shelf.

"This is a set. He can have all of these."

"I can't . . ." Face burning again. I look away. "I don't have the money for a set."

"My treat. Please, it will make me happy."

Dropping my eyes to her bulging belly, it feels wrong to let her. She can't have a lot of money, either. Not with the car she drives and the clothes she's wearing. I pull at the collar of my T-shirt, my skin growing hot. "You don't have to."

"I want to, really. Please let me."

"Okay." I give in because it's all I can do. I have to get back to my brother. The same churning in my gut has me tapping my fingers on my thigh.

You locked it three times. Three.

She runs her fingers over the package as if it's some sort of answer and adds a small blanket covered in cars into the mix of the rapidly filling cart.

"He'll love that. He's *really* into cars."

This seems to perk her up. "What else does he need?"

Everything. New clothes and shoes. *His parents.* Throat burning, I look away. "Just a book. He's getting better with his reading." I don't know why I felt the need to report this to her, but I feel like she wants to know, and I want someone, *anyone*, besides me to want to know. Hardly anyone from the meetings comes around anymore. From what I've gathered, a few months after death is the max for people to inquire about our well-being.

"A book, okay." She smiles, though her eyes are watering again, and I clear my throat, uncomfortable with how emotional she is. This lady is suffering from way too many hormones. I play along with her, unsure of her reasons for helping me, and wonder if she, herself, will be able to afford everything she's tossing in the cart. We go through the book section, and I pick out two. She grabs them from my hands before adding seven more. And then we're in the grocery section as she clears a shelf of soup, tossing it into the cart along with some Gatorade, candies, and chocolates.

"He doesn't eat chocolate," I tell her.

"Do you?"

"Yeah, I love it."

"Then they're for you."

"You really don't have to do this," I tell her, scanning the overflowing cart with apprehension.

"I really do."

"Do you live in Triple Falls?" I need to take my mind off the time. He's awake. I can feel it.

Three times. It's locked, it's locked.

Unable to help it, I glance at the plastic clock hanging just above the pharmacy. Seven-thirty. Sean will be heading over for his walk to school by now. If Dom's asleep, it won't be long before he wakes him. I have minutes to spare.

"No, I used to live here, but I moved away not long ago. I came back today to see someone . . . but I . . ." she shakes her head. "Doesn't matter."

I glance at the clock again, only half listening as my heart starts to race. If he's hungry, he might try something stupid, like cooking an egg.

Except, we don't have any fucking eggs. My palms begin to itch as I turn to her. "I need to get back to my brother. I need to go. *Right now.*"

Her eyes bulge. "Is he alone?"

I nod.

This seems to set her off all over again.

"He was sleeping when I left. I didn't want to bring him with me in this heat. My aunt couldn't miss work. I'm staying home with him. I'm old enough." There's anger in my tone, and I've already said too fucking much.

"I won't tell anyone if that's what you're thinking. This is not your fault," she assures me. "You're a good brother."

She rushes us to check out, and I stare at the sea of bags wondering how I'm going to haul it all home, but excited about the idea of Dom lighting up when he sees what's inside them.

"Come on, let's load the car and get you home."

Relieved, I look her over. "You sure?"

"Of course. You didn't think I'd let you carry this three miles, did you?"

The cashier gives her the total, and I stare at the screen, eyes wide. Two hundred and twelve dollars. She doesn't even blink as she hands him three hundred dollar bills and puts the change in one of my bags. I look over at her, eyes wide.

"In case he needs more medicine," she says, but I know it's pity. And I fucking hate it.

Swallowing hard, I nod because I'm finding it hard to speak. I gather the bags and haul them to the car as she turns the ignition and flips on the AC. The drive home is silent as I glance at the back seat full of bags and then back at the woman gripping the wheel, her fingers turning white. I feel sorry for her, this sad pregnant woman, who's so lonely she needed to shop with me to make herself feel better.

When she pulls into the driveway, I stop her from helping me. As nice as she's been, I won't invite her in. I rarely let any grown-ups near Dominic. I don't trust them. I don't trust anyone here. Once I haul the bags to the porch, I walk back over to the car and shut her back door, and she rolls down her window on the passenger side. "Thank you."

"Really, please don't thank me, it was my pleasure." She shakes her head and again looks like she's about to cry.

"I'm Tobias," I tell her as if it matters.

"Thank you for keeping me company, Tobias."

"I hope you have a better day."

She bites her lower lip as if she might explode before she speaks. "You made it so much better. Thank you for indulging me." She shakes her head. "You must think I'm crazy."

"It's like you said, you're having a bad day. I was too. You made mine a lot better."

"You're a good kid. You deserve—" her eyes drift to the house—"you deserve a lot better than bad days."

I shrug. "We all have them."

"Thank you, Tobias."

Weirded out about the last half hour and the goodbye, I turn to run up the stairs and drag the bags in, closing the door and locking it three times.

Once inside, I peek through the bent-up blinds to see her still parked in the driveway, head bent on the wheel, her body shaking.

She's crying. A part of me wants to go to her. Mama always said never to let a woman dry her tears alone and never be the reason for them, but I wouldn't know what to say to her. All I do is watch her for a few minutes before she wipes her face and pulls away. The aching feeling in my chest stays with me as I unpack the bags. Dom was still asleep when I poked my head in his bedroom. Lining up the cans in the empty narrow pantry, I feel relieved when I stare at the amount of food. No more starving before Delphine decides it's dinner time. She rarely eats, so the stash will feed us for a few weeks. It's when I hear Dominic pipe up behind me that my excitement kicks up.

"All of this is mine?!"

A few minutes later, packages lay scattered on the floor of his bedroom as I try to dot him with pink lotion while he smashes his new cars into my thigh. Bellies full, I think of the woman who helped me and wished I had thanked her better than I had. Once I've fought Dominic enough to get him covered in the lotion, I haul him back in bed and pull the small TV from my room to his. He's halfway back to sleep when his window opens, and a rat's nest of blond hair appears. Sean lifts his head and grins when he sees us camped out on Dom's bed. He climbs through the window dressed in his favorite Batman T-shirt and jeans, already covered in dirt from his trek through the trees in the neighborhood.

"You not going to school?" he asks the two of us.

"No. Dominic's sick."

"He doesn't look sick." Sean stares at us both, running his nails down his arms, and that's when I spot the blistering dots on his arms, face, and neck. I open my mouth to speak when Dom shoots up from his bed and points at him.

"Sean! You're the *culprit*!"

* * *

"Sir?" The unfamiliar voice pulls me back to where I stand. "You have seven bags." The sound of ringing merchandise eases me slowly back into the present as I take my change and receipt from the woman's extended hand. Chest aching from the memory, I gather the bags by the handle and make my way out of the store and toward Dom's Camaro. *"We both know I wasn't going to make it to thirty, brother. Take care of her."*

Chapter Four

CECELIA

STARING BLANKLY OUT of one of the large windows into the parking lot, I refute the idea that I'm searching for any sign of the Camaro—for him. Yet another glance at the clock has me aggravated with the lies I'm telling myself. He dropped me off three hours ago. I know he hasn't changed his mind. I know he's coming back.

He came back, for me.

He left his life, for me.

He killed, *again*, for *me*.

"Where is your head today, woman?" Marissa asks, sidling up next to me at the counter.

"Just . . . distracted." I know I should probably give her a heads-up on what, or rather, *who's* coming, but I have no idea if he has any plans of invading my workspace as he has my home and my new life. I have no idea if he intends to remain incognito here as he has in the past. It's anyone's guess for now, especially mine.

Marissa is the closest thing I have to a girlfriend here, and I've told her enough about Tobias for her to know why I'm not entertaining men for the time being. I hold back in revealing any more for the moment because believing anything at this point is far too premature. He could very well disappear as quickly as he came.

But I don't believe that, despite my need to hold on to my skepticism.

I hate that I mostly believe him and the sincerity he's shown thus far with his words and actions.

But if I do believe him, take his words to heart, will I be forever a fool?

For now, I could be. I can't let him do it. He has to earn my trust again, no matter his place in my heart.

"Distracted? I'll say, you've been shining that napkin dispenser for ten minutes."

"What? Oh." I glance around the café, which is dead after the last of the morning rush. "Did you need me for something?"

"No, just worried. You've been acting out of sorts since the Presidential Address yesterday. Want to talk about it?"

"No, I'm fine, swear." I turn to her and force a smile, and she raises a brow.

"We've been joined at the hip since you hired me. You think I can't tell when you're faking it?"

"Sorry, you're right. Something is going on, and to be honest, I'm still trying to wrap my head around it. I'll explain later."

"Yes, you will, and it'll have to wait because he's back." She gives me a conspiratorial wink.

"What?" Paling, I glance behind me, following her gaze to see Mr. Handsome stroll in. Within the second of seeing he's the man she was referring to, I'm gifted with a little relief, quickly replaced by a spike of anxiety.

"All yours, girl. And in case you're wondering, our omelets aren't that great."

He takes a stool, dressed to impress, his eyes focused on me as I grab the coffee pot, snatch a ready mug beneath the counter, flip it and pour, refusing to meet his inquisitive gaze. "Morning. Western Omelet, no peppers or cheese, right?"

"Most people call me Greg," he quips, "but yes, please."

I give him an answering smile while I write out his ticket and haul ass back toward the kitchen, cutting off any chance to draw out conversation. So far today, I've filled a few salt shakers with sugar, dropped three plates, and in my haste, ran smack into my office door.

Bastard.

The fatigue has finally set in from lack of sleep, and mostly because I stayed up staring at the fucking French Adonis who took up over half of my queen mattress last night wearing nothing but black boxers. He is a dangerous temptation, his profile and build—all hard lines and thickly muscled curves—mesmerizing in half-light. His construct just as incredible as it was when we were together, maybe more so now. His surreal looks are just as distracting as they were before, threatening to replace my resentment with desire. And the minute I woke up from a dream that left me raw and aching, my first instinct was to pull him to me, to wrap myself inside him, and never let go. Oh, how much I wanted to touch. So much so I had to leave my own bed to get away from him. From his smell of citrus and spice. From any familiarity that might bring me comfort.

Because fuck that, I refuse to make it easy for him.

He wants another chance, but he's had years of chances to come back to me. He refused me at every turn in Triple

Falls, forced me to let him go. Purposefully, he let me walk out of his office and his life.

And he's right. No matter his reasons, no matter how justified, they'll all be excuses for me at the moment.

I deserve more.

I *will* hold out for more, no matter how gloriously beautiful he is. No matter how many times over the years I dreamt of him coming back to me and saying the things he said. His words from yesterday cross my mind.

"I couldn't look away."

No matter how much the words mean, I'm no longer a teenage girl or twenty-something woman who'd had her first mind-blowing orgasm gifted by a beautiful, smooth-talking man. Been there, have the tear-soaked pillowcases and blood-stained clothes to prove it.

"Cecelia." Travis, my short-order cook, booms from behind the cutout steel window in the kitchen, making me jump where I stand.

I glare at him, and he winces. "Sorry, you weren't hearing me. Order up."

"Chill." Marissa grabs the plate from the hot bar and walks it over to Greg. She gives me a curious glance once it's delivered, as does Greg. Annoyed by the scrutiny and refusing to look again toward the parking lot, I retreat through the double doors of the kitchen toward my office for a timeout, wishing for the first time in months I had a joint to smoke.

It's minutes later, when I'm safely behind my desk, that Marissa bursts through the office door, a look of utter shock on her face that lets me know I'm not getting off so easily. She darts her eyes around the office in panic, chest heaving before she leaps for her purse.

"Jesus by the river," she says, brushing a week's worth of gloss across her lips, standing at the threshold of my office door. "Please tell me the man that just got out of your Camaro is your adopted brother."

Loathing the relief I feel, I slide my chair back, second-wind determination running through me as she looks at me with wide-eyed hope, while Travis grunts something unintelligible behind her.

"It's complicated."

"That tells me nothing." She's hot on my heels as I toss my shoulders back and push through the double doors.

Chapter Five

TOBIAS

I GATHER THE few bags I need to set up shop before making my way inside. Upon entering, it's nothing like I expected. Though Meggie's sits in a ratty-looking building in an outdated shopping center, the interior, including the paint and the furnishings, are new and somehow distinctly Cecelia. Inside, it's a complete one-eighty in feel from the pothole-filled parking lot and chipped and faded paint of the building. It's cozy. The wall colors are a mix of burnt sienna and azure. Black and white photographs hang throughout with price plaques floating next to them; no doubt, Cecelia's attempt to help support local artists. Large bookshelves line the far walls, and oversized chairs are situated to create a reading nook. There's an internet bar and stools along the floor-to-ceiling rows of windows. Cozy booths and tables sit throughout the middle of the café designating the dining area.

Dominic would have loved it here.

It's the same thought I had when I entered her house yesterday. Guilt blinds me briefly as I try to switch gears when I spot her in the center of the bar pouring coffee, just as her eyes lift to mine.

It's an arrow straight through the burn, and the hole isn't small.

Fuck, I've missed her.

Breaking our stare-off, she paces the counter refilling drinks before stopping just in front of the man I take a chair next to. As I retrieve my new laptop from the box, she sets down a cup of coffee in front of me and a menu while I power it up.

"Thought you were on vacation," she mumbles before setting a check on the counter in front of the suit next to me.

"This is my vacation laptop," I assure her and open the menu, reading the selections.

"Right," she says dryly before walking off. Zeroing in on her, I sense I'm not alone in doing so and stiffen when I glance at the suit before following his line of sight. The plastic on the menu squeaks around my fingers as white fire thrums through me. He's got my attention. Decent looking, close to my age, and he's not here for the fucking coffee.

Mr. Fucking. Handsome.

I've never killed a man in cold blood or out of jealousy. Something tells me today should not be the day I get to check it off my list.

"She's beautiful, isn't she?" I ask, plugging my laptop into one of the ready outlets beneath the counter.

"Am I that obvious? I've been here every day this week."

"That so?"

He nods before lifting his cup in salute. "Greg."

"Tobias."

"That a French accent? You sure are a long way from home."

Cecelia glances our way, eyes our exchange before her attention drifts back to me, lingers, and darts away.

"Actually, I'm right where I need to be. Just moved here." I turn to him in the hoodie and jeans I picked up from the discount superstore. I'm dressed like a fucking teenage boy due to slim options. Casanova is in a suit.

"There's something about her—" his smile deepens—"I feel like a creeper coming back like this, but she's . . ." I can hear the curiosity in his voice. Each word spoken might as well be lighter fluid he's dousing me with. "I'm going for it." Cecelia uses that moment to approach us and genuinely smiles at the motherfucker, before turning to me.

"Are you hungry?"

"Starving," I manage through clenched teeth. "Breakfast was shit."

Day one, Tobias. Day one. No dead bodies on day one.

She's completely clueless to the attention she's getting. Or is she? Her to-do list makes that theory shit, but she won't be fucking to-doing Greg. Not to-fucking-ever.

"Just let me know when you're ready."

"Cecelia," suit dick addresses, an over-confident smile on his face as he stands and pulls out a twenty to cover his check. Cheap fuck. Knowing what's coming, I see the panic in her eyes a millisecond before she schools her features. She's gotten a lot better at bluffing, but I'm the master of bullshit detection. She wants no part of Greg or the offer that's coming, but that doesn't lessen the urge to imprint the Apple logo of my newly purchased Mac into his skull.

"I was wondering if I could take you to dinner?"

Logged into a new email account, I click to compose while keeping my tone even. "The first time I saw her, she was eleven." They both turn to me, but I continue typing, not sparing a glance at either one of them. "She was nothing but a little girl, but she was mine to protect from this fucked-up world. Mine to look out for. Mine to care for."

"Tobias," Cecelia hisses in warning.

"She came in later like a fucking wrecking ball and obliterated the image of the little girl I remembered. I claimed her then as mine to have, mine to touch, mine to possess, fucking *mine*."

Cecelia shuts her eyes, fisting her hands on the counter.

I lift my eyes to Greg, who looks like he's about to shit his silk boxers.

"And so, I would very much appreciate it if you would stop fucking looking at *my* future as if she may be *yours*. The answer is no, Greg, she won't be dining with you."

Greg nods. "I apologize, I really had no idea. She isn't wearing a ring."

I tap the mousepad to open a new email. "Leave your address, and we'll send you a *save the date*."

"Tobias, enough," Cecelia scolds. "Greg, I'm sorry."

"It's fine." He lifts his tweed jacket, *pussy*, from the stool next to him and tosses his voice my way. "You're a lucky man, Tobias. See you around, Cecelia."

"Come back, Greg," she urges, her gaze lingering on him for ten fucking seconds too long as he makes his way out the door, *whistling* like a nutjob.

My laptop is slammed on my working hands before I'm face-to-face with violent dark blue waters.

That's right, baby, fight me.

"If you're going to go all caveman, you can *leave*. That's not going to fly here."

"Two things," I mumble, lifting the screen to type the last of my email. "I would like a club sandwich, fries, and your phone number."

"You are such a bastard."

"*Your bastard*," I remind her, unlocking my phone and pushing it across the counter. "And he can order all the fucking eggs and coffee he wants here, but he doesn't get to look at you like that."

She stalks off through the double doors of the kitchen. Seconds later, a petite blonde with a head full of messy curls saunters toward me. It's then I know Cecelia's back there hiding.

"Has Cecelia got you?" she asks in a sickly-sweet voice.

"By the balls," I mutter, shooting off the email.

"Pardon?"

"I've ordered, thank you. But—" I lean over and engage her—"please make sure she's not back there with a box of rat poison." She laughs like it's hysterical and leans over, giving me an eyeful of cleavage that I opt out of.

"Now, why would she do a thing like that?"

"Ex-boyfriend." I wrinkle my nose. "She's not my biggest fan."

Her jaw slackens. "*You're* the bastard?"

"In the flesh. So, you know about me?"

Good.

She narrows her eyes. She knows enough.

Not good.

"Oh, I'll make sure we take *really good* care of you."

And I'm no longer eating here.

*

"You from out of town?"

Perched on the stool, I peck at the keyboard on my Mac next to my untouched club. The question was raised by an old-timer who's spent the majority of the time since his arrival scrutinizing me. Cecelia's been mostly avoiding me since our earlier exchange. When she realized I wasn't leaving, she had no choice but to resume her shift. She pauses her fifteenth wipe of the counter, her circles in three, no doubt just to fuck with me, in wait of my response.

"Just moved here," I reply over the top of my screen. Though much older than me, he's got near-perfect posture, a thick silver mane, and appears meticulously groomed. Ex-military.

"Moved from where?"

"Not far."

"What for?"

"I guess you could say I just switched careers."

"What were you doing?" the man asks, his tone a little louder than socially appropriate, no doubt due to some hearing loss.

"Lot of this and that. Mostly, I was in service."

Cecelia snorts.

"Military?" he yells across the bar. "Ah, I got you. I served in 'Nam. So, is this your first week back as a civilian?"

Cecelia watches me, and I smirk. "Exactly."

"Hard at first, but you'll get used to it. There are benefits to being a veteran."

Eyes rolling down her frame, she doesn't miss it. "I'm hoping that's the case." My cock springs to life as her lips part slightly, the small taste of her from this morning lingering on my tongue. "It's going to be an adjustment being a real citizen," I toss in for good measure. Getting her to both listen and believe my truths will be a new sport. Fingers itching to touch her, I resist and click out of a few screens.

"What brings you to this part of Virginia?"

"Something I can't live without," I admit easily and feel Cecelia tense just before the cook calls for pick up.

"You don't look the type for a small town."

"Actually, I was raised in a town just like this, about ten hours from here."

"Well, DC isn't far away if you ever need to scratch the itch for some city life."

"Thanks for the heads-up."

"Name's Billy."

"Nice to meet you, Billy. I'm Tobias, Cecelia's boyfriend."

Cecelia coughs, and Billy smiles, his teeth untarnished from age. A good majority of Cecelia's customers are wearing dentures. This isn't the type of hipster town with microbreweries popping up from a population spike. In fact, it's probably one of the last American small towns that the rest of the US has forgotten about. And a damn good place to hide.

"You never mentioned a boyfriend," Billy says to Cecelia.

"I'm a best-kept secret," I interject, giving him a wink.

Billy rolls a toothpick across his lips. "Don't kid yourself, son, every man who frequents the place thinks he's her boyfriend." His grin amps up. "If I was thirty years younger—"

"Try forty, and Billy, don't finish that sentence," I warn, as Cecelia finally smiles and walks over to me. She lifts my sandwich and takes a large bite. It's an act of kindness, a rarity since I showed up, and my shoulders ease back a little.

She chews slowly, and our eyes meet and hold. She's in

there, hiding, both the girl I met and the woman I love, as she was yesterday. Maybe her dream haze anger has passed. "Done with this?" she asks, snatching the plate just as I reach for the other half of the sandwich.

Maybe not.

"It's true, Billy. He's my old flame," Cecelia snarks in an indicative way that means trouble is coming. "He's here to try and win me back. But I'm thinking of passing."

Billy lifts his brows. "Well, what's wrong with him, other than the way he dresses?"

Billy–1, Tobias–0

She crosses her arms, lips lifting. "Quite a bit."

"Does he always dress like that? He could be in one of those rap videos in that getup."

Billy–2, Tobias–0

"It's just a part of his disguise. He's a *professional* liar."

Shit, here we go. And no doubt she's going to make this publicly painful.

Bring it, baby.

"That's never good," Billy says, sizing me up as Cecelia begins to tick off my crimes on her fingers. "He's a thief, a liar, and the first time he kissed me, he didn't ask permission, so definitely *not* a gentleman."

"Shame." Billy analyzes me with a crease between his brows. "You should always ask a woman's permission."

"And he betrayed me," Cecelia adds, and there's nothing humorous in her tone. I feel that blow so much I grunt through it.

You hurt, I hurt. Look at me.

But she doesn't, and it's all I can do to keep from jumping over the counter.

"You did all that?" Billy asks, his frown deep-set.

I nod. "I did."

"You're not even going to defend yourself?"

"No," I reply as she lifts her eyes to mine. "It's all true."

"Well, then, do you have one reason why she should take you back?" Marissa is standing a foot behind me, and I can feel the rest of the sparsely-filled café leaning in on bated breath.

Small fucking towns.

Cecelia collects a tub of dirty dishes when I finally speak up in a shitty defense. "I stopped lying yesterday." I barely get it out before she passes through the double doors.

Chapter Six

TOBIAS

NOT LONG AFTER Billy leaves, she immerses herself back into cleaning and making small talk with her customers. I lay low, hoping the rest of the shift will pass without incident or another public inquisition. The more I try to concentrate on the task of tying up a few loose ends for Exodus, the more I'm distracted by her presence mere feet away.

It's the ache of wanting her. It's the need to erase the distance, not just physically but emotionally. But on the physical side, I'm tamping down a thirst that's been constant since the first time I thrust inside her.

Cecelia has always been beautiful. Her face a mix of innocence and incomparable natural beauty. She measures above the average woman in that respect. Still, it's also in the way she carries herself with confidence, the way she beams when she smiles, the carefully conveyed words that come out of her mouth that express her warmth, empathy, and intelligence. In appearance, I still see some of her lingering youth, her curiosity for the world around her. She's forever a student, and I find that appealing. Where some women seem to be convinced that they're experts on everything after a certain age, she's always searching for ways to understand the world around her, to both learn and grow.

It's clear within just a few hours of being here that she has the respect and admiration of her employees and her frequent customers.

She's impossible not to love.

And the more she matures, the more she's become *that* woman, the unavoidable and irresistible woman who deserves every bit of admiration she gets.

Men have been falling for her since well before I met her.

She's never used her sex appeal as a weapon or fully wielded its power. If she were ever to harness that, she'd be a black widow—sort of fucking lethal.

And I'd be a dead man.

I've barely been able to tear my eyes from her today after denying myself for so long. I've never known another's body as intimately, nor mapped it as intricately as I have hers.

Instinctively, I still know it.

But she doesn't see herself the way men do—the way predators do. Especially because for a majority of her life, she felt like she was undeserving of love. I fed into that ridiculous notion when I was at my weakest to keep us from eating each other alive, but I fucked up royally in doing so.

I refused her heart when she begged me to retrieve it, revive it.

Jealousy isn't something I'm used to dealing with. Women have come and gone with me; my mission always taking precedence. Yet, this one woman has made it impossible to ignore that inside me lurks a heart in need of what only she can give it.

It wasn't until the day I witnessed how they loved her, the way Sean and Dom loved her, that I became acquainted with that type of bone-deep jealousy. And in feeling that, I lost control.

Briefly, I close my eyes and shut my laptop.

I signed up for hard.

I came ready for hard, to face and deal with the impossible, but it's the guilt that makes it the hardest.

It's the tension that's killing me right now. Her hesitation to even look at me.

I recall some of yesterday's conversation in the parking lot. Fuck being okay with whatever ending we get. That's not good enough. I want her happy. I want our ending happy. That's what I decide as I watch her interact with the people in her café. I want her smiling about thoughts of *us* before she ever greets a stranger.

I will do everything, *anything*, to make our ending blissful. Simply being together is not enough. We aren't settling. While she remains weary, I'll be ambitious for the both of us.

In our time at her father's house, we *were* blissful, content, despite our circumstances and the underlying threats to that peaceful state. Despite the fact that I knew we were a time bomb. Despite *me*.

Our pleasures came easy. She could look at me then. Now she avoids it.

Standing abruptly from the counter to stretch my legs, filled with restless energy and entertaining snacking on a napkin, I shoot off a text on my new phone.

It's me.

Sean: Me who?

Funny.

Sean: I'll shoot the number out to the crew.

The bubbles start and stop. I pause when I read his message.

Sean: How's it going?

Do you give a fuck?

Sean: Of course, I give a fuck. Report.

She's fine. She's good. Really good. She bought a café. It's nice. Her house is too. She's doing the daily grind.

Sean: Knew that already. What about you?

I read the text again. A question I didn't expect. When he, correction, when *Tessa* invited me to their wedding, I thought maybe then we might start to repair what was broken between us, but even then, things were off. The day we buried Dom, he looked at me like he hated me. And I know he did. This olive branch he's extending feels just as foreign as my position in my new life. I'm at the mercy of the people I hurt.

And I *want* to be here.

But fuck if it doesn't suck.

When I went to Sean for help in finding her, that's when I felt a little give on his side. Over the years, I've felt his absence significantly. I convinced myself our mutual cause is the only reason we're still part of each other's lives, despite our history. But a hope lights inside. Maybe that's no longer the case.

You really want to know?

Sean: I wouldn't ask, man. That bad?

Cecelia's priorities

Dog

Café

.

.

.

.

.

.

.

ME. And fuck you for laughing because I know you are.

Bubbles. I decide I hate bubbles as much as I hate peas.

Sean: You didn't think it would be easy, did you?

Hell no.

Sean: She's got you by the balls already, doesn't she?

More than that.

Sean: If it didn't hurt, then it wouldn't be worth it. You're too used to getting your way. Let it burn. It will be worth it.

Disgusted I need consoling this early in, and by him, I change the subject.

Things good?

Sean: Can't even last a day, can you, man?

Throw me a fucking bone. I'm useless here.

Sean: You're not even twenty-four hours in. Give it time.

I will. I am. I'm not complaining.

I can feel the hesitation on both ends of the phone. A minute passes before I get another text.

Sean: It's weird, huh?

You have no idea.

Sean: I have some idea. Wait until you go from Maverick to married with three kids.

Two kids.

Sean: Three. Found out this morning.

Congrats, man.

Sean: You going to have any?

I just starved half a day to make sure she didn't poison my sandwich. I think I'll table that conversation for later.

The bubbles start and stop.

Stop laughing. Dick.

Sean: You really have no idea what you're doing, do you?

I want to be here. I know that.

Sean: Go with your gut.

Familiar advice.

Sean: This will work out. Day one.

Day one.

I mull over my word choice and decide just to type the truth.

Thanks, man.

Sean: Anytime.

You mean that?

The bubbles pop up and disappear, and a minute later, he replies.

Sean: I do.

Unexpected emotion clogs my throat as more tension leaves my shoulders. Glancing up, I see Cecelia watching me carefully just before she pushes through the doors with hands full of dirty plates.

I reclaim my seat as she comes back through, and the bell rings for pick up. A second later, a new plate is set in front of me.

"Eat before it gets cold," she says softly. I grip her hand

before she has a chance to walk off and bring the back of it to my mouth. Her eyes drop to where I press my lips to her skin before I release her.

"Thank you."

Chapter Seven

CECELIA

TOBIAS INSISTED ON driving home, and I'm thankful for it—my vision blurry from sleep deprivation, my body aching from a day of roller coaster-worthy emotions. I have so many questions but can't bring myself to ask them yet because any questions I ask right now make me vulnerable and susceptible.

Clearly, I heard him say he'd stopped lying, and that comment landed where intended. It's up to me to believe him. Just months ago, I was ready for any truth, any explanation he was willing to give, and when I left, I made peace with the idea that I would never get some of my answers. So far, everything he's professed makes sense in a way I'm not comfortable with, which only makes it hard to hold on to my animosity. I'm still reeling from his invasion in my life, and I want it made clear that he will not get away with another hostile takeover.

"Stop overthinking this," he says softly, his hand on the wheel as he effortlessly navigates his way back to my house, his profile lit by the fading sun. He's dressed so differently from the way I'm used to seeing him. Hoodie, jeans, cheap

sneakers, hair disheveled, without product and cresting natur-
ally across his forehead. He's the same man . . . yet different
in a way I can't put my finger on. Maybe it's his openness,
his eagerness to reveal secrets and the parts of his life he's
kept hidden. At the same time, I still feel he's guarding something, something I'm missing. I'm still shell-shocked he's in
Virginia, driving Dom's Camaro, with plans of again sleeping
in my bed—more than that—merging our lives.

All things I considered impossible mere days ago. I want
so much just to be happy, accept him here, and throw myself
into the notion that this is permanent, but flashes of the past
haunt me. From my experience, the minute I accept love,
accept happiness, it gets snatched away from me in life-
altering ways. I accused him of being a coward, but I'm the
one now whose fears are overshadowing everything else.

"Ask me anything," he says, glancing my way briefly.

Instead, I rest back against the seat, my eyes dry, my bones
aching. Suspicion gnaws at my conscience. Something wasn't
right today, and I can't quite put my finger on it, but I decide
to compartmentalize that for the moment.

I've never been so tired, but I can't stop staring at him.
His presence here is surreal. Not once have I granted myself
any version of a life here that included him because I was so
intent on letting him go. His revelations this morning changed
some of my perceptions, and maybe that's where my hesitation is. The more it all makes sense, the less angry I'll be.
When he pulls to a stop at the house, it takes effort for me
to open the heavy door of the Camaro as he gathers a few
plastic bags from the back seat, along with a paper bag full
of homemade vegetable soup he requested just before we left
the café.

He meets me at the hood, urging me forward with his free hand on the small of my back as we approach the front door. He sorts through my keys, finding the right one, and sticks it into the lock. Standing to his right, I notice when his shoulders slump forward before he lets out a heavy breath. Confusion sets in as he sets the bags down and turns to me. Placing an open palm on my stomach, a familiar and predatorial look in his eyes, he walks me back toward the brick on the side of the porch, pinning me to the house.

I gaze up at him as he stares down at me intently a split second before thrusting his fingers into my hair, fisting it, and crashing his mouth to mine. Gasping, he takes advantage of my surprise, urging my lips wider before he sweeps my mouth fervently with his tongue, plastering our bodies together and eliminating all the space between us. His erection brushes my stomach as he seduces me thoroughly with his kiss, and in those moments, I forget myself, I forget my grievances against him and kiss him back. Gripping his shoulders, I begin to melt into his mammoth frame, wrapping around him. Somewhere in the back of my mind, there's a voice of protest reminding me that I'm freely participating. But this isn't an exchange of power. This is a lover's kiss, a reminder.

Heart thrumming, panties dampening, I clutch the material of his hoodie to bring him closer. He indulges me, lifting my leg and grinding into me as we both get lost, making a new memory, a searing kiss I won't soon forget. A pained grunt leaves him when he pulls away and gazes down at me. In it, I see—need, want, lust, hope.

"I've wanted to do that all day, and if I did it once we stepped inside this house, I don't know if I could stop myself.

I'm okay with not being a gentleman because that's not who I am and not who you love. Asking permission to kiss you? Never going to fucking happen."

I read into his actions, his intent as he steps away and collects his bags before pushing the door open. He's trying. Trying to be respectful of the clear boundaries I've set, trying to take things at my pace, despite the impatient man he is.

Once inside, he keeps his gaze averted as if it pains him to look at me. "Go take a shower. I'll walk Beau and warm up this soup for you."

"You don't have to do that."

He pauses at the threshold of the living room, his shoulders tense, his back to me. "Just let me take care of you tonight. Tomorrow you can glare at me, yell at me, put me in my place, or whatever else you think you need to do to make yourself feel better about letting me in the door. However, you haven't eaten, and you haven't slept since I got here, and I don't want it to start this way." Without waiting for my response, he makes his way toward the kitchen, and I watch him retreat, shoulders heavy, while I trace my swollen lips with my finger. Every part of me wants to go after him, seek his kiss again, feel his weight on top of me, to give in, but my mind wins, and I make my way toward the shower.

When I'm freshly dressed in my flannel pajamas, I walk into the kitchen to see the steaming bowl of soup and a note next to it.

Went for a run.

His absence brings me no relief. Never would I have thought it would be so hard to communicate with Tobias after all this time. At this point, no matter how well we once meshed, we feel like very intimate strangers. Everything about our dynamic has changed. For the first time ever, he's not sneaking into my bedroom under Roman's radar, and we have the ability to be open with each other, open publicly about our relationship without the repercussions that threatened us before. I take a seat at the table feeling oddly guilty at the space I'm putting between us because I can't fathom how this is going to go, or worse, the feeling that it will end again . . . it's just a matter of when and how.

Will he up and leave the first time the brotherhood faces a serious threat? Will this small town—a simpler life—bore him to the point he'll feel coming here was a mistake? I hate that my fear stems from investing in him again, only to watch him leave. I hate that I'm so fucking afraid to embrace the idea of us permanently. But he'd forced me to let go of it. He forced me to imagine life without that possibility. But mostly, I hate that it's all, once again, on his timeline. Numb, that's what I decide I am for the moment. Numb. And it's for my own protection.

After eating half the bowl of soup, I decide to retire early, irritated by the fact that I'm a little uncomfortable in my own house due to consideration of him and what he might be expecting from me. I only manage to gloss over a chapter of a new book before my errant thoughts start to dissipate, and exhausted sleep claims me.

Chapter Eight

TOBIAS

Age Sixteen

"GET OUT!" VICTORIA screams as I towel off and glance out of the bathroom to see Dominic standing at the threshold of my bedroom, with an eyeful of my naked girl-friend. He plays deaf to her protests, a smirk lifting his lips. "Get out, you little pervert," she shrieks, white-knuckling the sheet she pulled up to her neck.

"Out, Dominic," I bark. As he lingers in the doorway, spiked blond hair appears over his shoulder. Sean is feasting on her as well.

"Get the hell out." Securing the towel around my waist, I cross the room and push them back in one firm shove before slamming the door in their faces. I turn back to Victoria. "Sorry, they're young, curious *idiots*."

"Get a damn lock on your door," she lashes out before dropping the sheet and pulling her bra from the floor.

"No need. I'm leaving in a week."

"What?" She looks over to me, her eyes wide. "Going where?"

Leaning against the door, I ready myself for a conversation I've been dreading. "France. Prep school. I told you I applied."

"You're leaving in a week and just now telling me?"

I brace myself, knowing I'm in for it. I knew better than to secure a girlfriend over the summer.

"I thought France was a long shot." It most definitely was, but my French roots aided greatly in my acceptance, the irony not lost on me that my French roots are precisely why I set my sights on it in the first place.

But that's not why she was betting I had *no* chance.

"Yeah, I guess it was, for a guy like me, living like this," my tone bitter.

"That's not what I meant."

"Yes, it was."

"I'm sorry," she whispers.

I let the anger roll off me, knowing that dig was meant to sting because she feels stung herself. "I didn't set out to hurt you."

"No good guy ever does."

"Don't accuse me of that."

"I won't now. I was warned."

"Let me go handle them." I pull some sweats from my half-collapsed chest of drawers. "I'll be back."

"It's fine." She pulls her sundress on. "I have to be home early since I broke curfew with you last night." The shake in her voice doesn't sit well.

"Victoria." She looks up at me as the first of her tears fall. "I told you this couldn't get deep when we got together because there was a chance I was leaving."

"I know." Her disappointment stems from hopes that she

would be some sort of exception. But our relationship was superficial because I couldn't share anything with her. She was the perfect girl to pass a summer with. Though highly privileged and a little demanding at times, she has a good heart. She harrumphs, fastening her sandals. "I considered myself lucky to be with you. Now I wish I didn't know what it was like."

"I'll call you later."

She doesn't respond.

"I *will* call you."

"And say what? I don't see the point." She shakes her head. "Good luck in France."

She lifts up on her toes to kiss me, and I kiss her back, releasing her as she steps away, hesitating before opening my door. "I love the fact that you're getting out of here. You're so much better than this place."

I watch her retreat down the hall. Shortly after, I hear the front door close. Guilt gnaws at me and I bat it down as I dress. From this point on, anything resembling a relationship will only hinder my progress—another thing I have to give up if I intend to see my plans through. I indulged in Victoria because she was my last for the foreseeable future. After dressing, I take angry strides across the hall and slap open Dom's bedroom door with my palm. Sean sits on his twin bed, pouring some of Delphine's vodka into a flask before replacing the booze with his water bottle. Caught red-handed, he gives me a mischievous grin and lifts a shoulder. "What? I've been doing this for months. It keeps her less drunk and more hydrated."

"I told you to stay out of my room when she's over."

"She's *always* over," Dom says, tapping on his remote

control from where he sits on a beanbag he's outgrown, engrossed in the game. "But I can see the appeal, nice tits."

I slap the remote out of his hand, and he lifts his chin, ready for my wrath.

"What the hell is wrong with you? You know better," I growl.

"I have a dick, too, brother. I notice things," he retorts sarcastically, all for show, and mostly for Sean, who picks up his remote.

"You going to spend the rest of your week with her locked in your room? Do I need to make an appointment to knock on your door?" He's lashing out, and it's no mystery why.

"I *was* planning on taking you both camping tonight, but you can kiss that shit goodbye."

Dom barely flinches, but I know it stung him. Sean spikes to life, tossing the remote and abandoning the game. "I'm down."

"Not acting this way, you're not." I face my brother. "And don't be disrespectful about her."

"You love her or something?" Dom asks, more out of curiosity than anything, but there's no need for us to have *that* discussion. He's way far ahead of the curve on that front, as he is most things. Though I'm positive he's still innocent and hell-bent on changing that status. From the attention he's getting, it won't take him long.

"What did I tell you Papa said?"

"When you love someone, it's never a question you have to ask yourself."

I nod. "But even if you don't, you treat them well. There's no need to act like a dick, even if you're thinking with it."

"Sage advice, thanks, *brother*. I'll be glad to be done with your lectures in a week." He glances back at Sean. "We both will."

"You want a prime example of what the *wrong man* can do to a woman?" I jerk my chin toward Delphine's bedroom. "Take a good fucking look at your aunt."

This sobers them both considerably as I glance between them.

Dominic rolls his eyes. "You want me to feel *sorry* for her?"

"No, I want you to understand why she is the way she is."

"By choice."

"Just like you're choosing to be an ignorant little prick right now."

At eleven, he's twice as smart as I was and three times as hard to handle. I'm partly to blame. I've shared with him most everything I know.

"Don't disrespect women, *period*. They're twice as evolved as most men will ever be. Don't take your shit out on them, either. It's a sign of weakness, and they aren't punching bags. They're a sanctuary, and you need to figure that out quick."

"How many have you been through lately?" Sean pops off.

"Listen to what I'm saying."

"Do we have a choice?" Dom spouts, and I shove him to sit on the mattress he's outgrown. He's been especially aggressive the last few weeks, and it's clear why.

"I'm *leaving*, brother, and I'm sorry that I'm leaving you with her, but it's what's best for us. You have to trust me."

"Thousands of miles away, yeah, that's best for *us*," he retorts dryly.

I cup the back of my neck, the ache growing in my chest. "You'll understand why soon enough."

"I don't have to understand shit." I jerk him up to face me, and instantly Sean's on his feet. I rarely hit my brother, but it's Sean's reaction that lets me know where we stand on that front. And it's relief I feel as Sean bows up, ready to defend him without a second thought. Nothing but pride fills me, but I keep my tone aggressive as I stare down at Dominic.

"You think I wouldn't take you with me if I could?"

"No, you're just leaving for the next six to seven years because it's what's best for *us*."

"And I'm not going *six fucking weeks* without seeing you. I've explained this."

"We'll see," Dom mumbles, clear hurt shining in his eyes. He's just as terrified as I am about our impending separation. Sean's been just as antsy, playing joker and acting out a little more to hide his apprehension about me leaving. My only comfort is that they'll have each other.

"Why Paris? Why so far?" Sean asks as I split my gaze between them. It's clear the ticking of my last days are taking a toll, which cracks me dead center.

"Put her bottles back and pack up right now—it's time you know."

"Know what?" Dom asks.

"That everything I'm doing is for *you*."

"I fail to see the logic, *brother*."

"And when you do, I'll make you eat those fucking words." I turn to Sean. "Grab Tyler and your gear and be back here in half an hour."

Sean opens the window. "On it."

"Sean," I call to him, and he pauses with one leg out the window, "why don't you try using the front door?"

He gives me his signature grin. "Where's the fun in that?"

Shaking my head, I turn my focus on my brother, who studies me curiously. "Where are we going?"

"My spot."

This shuts him up. He's been begging me to take him with me for years, but I never have, until tonight. He'd followed me once, and I caught him halfway and walked his ass straight back to the house. My spot has always been the one place I find a little solace, where my chaotic thoughts and panic morph into something more definable. Where I can make sense of more than I question. And I've never wanted to share it, until now.

Dread fills me when I think of leaving him in this shithole, and at Delphine's mercy, but he's thick-skinned enough to endure it, and his confidence more than makes up for any of his other shortcomings—I made sure of it. I may have over-shot some on that front by the amount of attitude he's been giving.

Across the hall, I shove a few days' worth of clothes into my duffle, just as Delphine comes in from her shift, eyeing us both from the hallway before opting for my bedroom.

"Where are you two going?"

"Camping. We'll be back in a few days. What do you need?"

"Nothing." She crosses her arms from my door, watching me pack. "Thank you for paying the electric bill." With my parents' death settlement, I've arranged to pay a few of her bills for the first year I'm in France, but I refuse to tell her that. To someone like Delphine, that's permission to go on a bender, and she's been attempting to dry up recently, at least on a more functional and less destructive level.

"You good for the rest of the month?" I fold my shirt for the third time.

He'll be okay. He'll be okay.

Frustrated, I unfold it again and restart the process, feeling her eyes on me.

"What?"

"Even if I wasn't okay, I don't want a dime of that piece of shit's money. I'll starve first."

"Yeah, well, it's necessary for me. Don't let my brother suffer because of your prejudice," I warn her. "He's suffered enough."

"Why camping?"

"We have a lot to discuss."

She bites her lip, steps in, and shuts the door. "You're sure this is what you want to do?"

"We've gone over this."

"And you're telling *them* now? You think they'll even understand?"

"They've listened in on some of the meetings. It's a risk I have to take. They need to start paying attention. At some point, they'll either remain at play or step up, but I'm willing to bet it's the latter. He's brilliant, but he's still just a kid."

She laughs. "So are you."

She remains unmoving where she is, and it grates on me as I refold the same shirt, unable to keep proper count with an audience. Sweat beads at my temple, and I fucking resent she's standing there, watching my every move as the familiar pulse and unease sets in.

"What?"

"Your parents would be proud." I look up to see her glassy-eyed. She's gotten softer over the years, more of a sentimental drunk than a mean one. "I've shamed them with the way I've handled this." A rare confession coming from her. Something is up.

I walk over to where she stands. My aunt is one of the most beautiful women I've ever seen but has been tarnished by a life that's stolen most of the good left in her. She'll never walk a straight line emotionally, and I'll never be able to fully trust her with my brother because of the way she treats herself. That's why I'll be home every six weeks and will be spending every single holiday break and summer in Triple Falls. I refuse to let her be the one to shape the rest of him. "You want to make it right?"

"I'm far past the point of redemption, nephew," she admits, not quite meeting my stare.

"Maybe," I agree, "but if you're sincere." I lower my voice. "Traite-le bien." *Treat him well.*

"I've been trying to talk to him." There's hope in her voice, and that aids in lessening some of the panic I feel.

"He doesn't need another friend. He needs authority now, more than ever. But you have to have his respect for him to listen. Tell him your stories. Tell him what you've told me. Tell him your past. That's a good way to earn it. Sois ferme. Mais traite-le bien. Il te résiste maintenant. Les choses ne changeront pas du jour au lendemain, mais si tu restes ferme, il s'y fera. Fais cela et tu auras gagné ma confiance." *Be firm. But treat him well. He's immune to you now. Things won't change overnight, but if you remain the same, he'll fall in line. Do this, and you will have earned my trust.*

"Your French is much better," she comments.

"I know." I was rusty for a while and failed Dominic in keeping his native tongue.

"Smug little bastard," she mutters before looking up at me with concern. I surpassed her height years ago. "You're sure about this? You know who to contact once you get there?"

"I've got it. I've had it for a long time."

"Okay." She pulls the shirt from my hand and rolls it instead of folding it before tucking it snugly into my bag. "It won't wrinkle this way. Not that it matters, but . . ." she shrugs.

I look down at the shirt and then back to her before taking them all out and rolling them up the same way.

She laughs. "Mr. Know It All doesn't know it all just yet. This will honor your papa. He talked a lot about—"

"Talk." I shake my head, irritated. "No more *talk*. I'm *tired* of *talk*, and if they become a part of it—" I nod in the direction of Dominic's room—"they have to know what's happening. He thinks I'm leaving to get away from here, from him." The words pain me.

"I thought you were leaving to get away from me." Her self-deprecating laugh says it all. This is the closest I'll ever get to an apology.

"We've survived this long." It's the nicest thing I can say about it. She leveled out enough after an explosive fight between us and started hosting the meetings. As much as I'm disgusted by some of her behavior, I have some admiration for the way she conducts herself; unshakable in her beliefs, hardcore in her delivery.

"You're not going to let the others in on this?" She's referring to the core members who show up for the meetings.

"Not yet."

"You think that's wise?"

"I think if I fuck up this attempt, it won't help me if they *know* I did."

"Just be careful. These people you're looking for aren't to be messed with, Ezekiel. The sort your father—"

"If you're not careful, Delphine, you're going to sound maternal."

"God forbid," she jests, but it's genuine worry in her voice and her expression.

Not one to linger, especially on feelings, she takes her leave, but pops her head back in just before she shuts my door. "You're really going to do this, Tobias. I know it."

"Yeah, I really fucking am. And they will too." I nod toward Dominic's room. "Mark my words. They were born for this."

* * *

Sitting in the high back chair in front of a roaring fire, fingers hovering above the keyboard of my laptop, I get lost in the memory of that night around the campfire, the night I unearthed my plans. Less than a week later, I was hugging my baby brother tightly to me, fighting tears as he struggled to free himself from my grip. I'd embarrassed him publicly with my emotions. The memory of that has me tightening my grip on the velvet arms of the chair. I come to when Beau pops to life at my feet, ears perking before he lays his jaw back to rest on his paws. It's when he lifts again that I hear a faint, pained mewl coming from the bedroom. Chest lurching, I close my eyes and curse, her agonized whimper growing louder as I close my laptop and jump to my feet. Beau stalks next to me as we rush toward the bedroom. Once inside, I click on her lamp and gaze down to see her face twisted, forehead covered in sweat, and her arm jerking at her side. A dream or a nightmare? Either way, I can't stand the state she's in. When we were together before, she would wake me with her subtle movements or light laughter, and I would watch her, curious as to what she was dreaming about and anticipate hearing about it in the morning. It was a much different situation than now, and these dreams are far different as well.

It's when a sob bursts from her that I clench my fists, determined to take the burden away.

I did this. I will undo this.

Sidling up on the edge of the bed, I lean over and kiss her temple, and she barely rouses before sinking back into her dream state.

"Dis-moi contre qui me battre, et je me battrai jusqu'à ce qu'ils disparaissent." *Tell me who to fight. I will fight until they all go away.* It's when tears start to coat her cheeks that I gently lift her to my chest, her arms limp at her sides.

"Dis-moi comment réparer cela. Dis-moi, mon amour. Je ferai n'importe quoi." *Tell me how to fix this. Tell me, my love. I'll do anything.* Another sob escapes her as she comes to, and I hold her tightly to me to try and keep her grounded.

"Ce n'est qu'un rêve, Trésor. Je suis là. Je suis là." *Just a dream, treasure. I'm here. I'm here.*

My name spills in a guttural cry from her lips as my chest caves in, and sobs begin to pour out of her, her body shaking as tears glide down her cheeks. I kiss them away one by one as she tries to speak but cries instead, clinging to me.

"It's okay, Cecelia. It's okay." Silent cries wrack her body as she claws my back, and I kiss her face, her lips, her nose, her temple before lowering my mouth to her ear.

"I'm here." I can't promise her nothing bad will happen or that no monsters are lurking in the shadows, because there are. I can only try to protect her from them and from the damage the dormant monster inside of me can cause her. Finally coming to, she tenses and sniffles, gathering herself, and I release her, her swollen eyes lifting to mine.

"Tell me."

"Not now," she rasps out, gaze dropping. "I guess I woke you?"

"No, I was in the living room, on my laptop."

"You can't sleep?"

"I'm still a little jet-lagged. You sure you don't want to tell me?"

"It was just a dream." That statement and her posture strips all the intimacy out of the moment. Her guard is back up and firmly in place. I try to crowd her a little to keep her close to me, in hopes of a confession, but release her when she pulls away, shifts around me, and stands. "I'm fine."

I grab her hand before she can fully retreat. "Don't lie to me."

She tenses before glancing over her shoulder down to where I sit on the edge of the bed. Resentment. It's so clear, her voice frigid when she speaks. "That's a bold request."

"I'm aware."

"You want honesty?" She pulls her hand away. "I've been through years of these dreams *without you*."

That statement, along with the firm echo of the bathroom door shutting behind her, lets me know exactly where I stand.

She doesn't need me, but that much I knew. She's become her own woman, independent, fiercely so, and so much fucking stronger. She doesn't need me, and that's a fact I'll have to live with and respect her for.

I just need to make her *want me* again.

Her face is clear when she emerges minutes later, posture stoic when her eyes lift to mine.

Challenge.

My fighter.

She's daring me to press her, but tonight I won't. Fisting my T-shirt, I pull it over my head and toss it to the floor. Her gaze drops when I push off my sweatpants and step out of them. We haven't been intimate in months, in truth, years, because of the way I took her the last time in my gin-infused rage, something I'll never forgive myself for. There's nothing I want more than to erase that as the last time I had her, replace that memory, replace the lingering sound of her anguished cries with moans of pleasure. But even if she were free of those head-to-foot fucking flannel pajamas, I wouldn't take her. Not with the cautious hesitation in her eyes, the fear. It doesn't stop me from needing her or growing hard at the sight of the beautifully structured equal she's grown into. She bristles when I walk over to where she stands, angry, emotionally confused, tormented by a past I can't change and mistakes I can't erase.

"I don't know how this goes either," I breathe. "I don't know how long it's going to take, or what words to say, or what moves to make. I have no plans, Cecelia, none." I grip her hand and lead her back to bed. She lays with her back to me, wordless, and I pull her into my chest, my arms wrapped around her.

Her scent, the comfort of knowing she's safe, eases some of the blow of her cries. I wait, hope for her explanation, hope that I wasn't the cause of her tears, but nothing comes.

Time. My goddamn enemy, an invisible force I've never

been able to defeat. Seconds to save my brother, now years between me and the woman I love, all due to my judgments, my mistakes. And it's time that rears its ugly head at me now, mocking me, the main reason for the barrier between us.

She's lived so much life without me.

The irony? I have to make peace with my nemesis because it's the only thing that can heal us.

"Ce rêve dans lequel nous sommes tous les deux. Emmène-moi avec toi." *This dream we go into together. Take me with you.*

She grips my hand, the one palming her stomach, and not long after, she drifts away and takes me with her.

I wake up alone.

Chapter Nine

TOBIAS

Age Eighteen

THE HEAVY KNOCK on my door followed by, "Come on, King, I know you're in there," has me closing my book with a groan. There's only one person who knows the address of my room in the hostel.

Opening the door an inch, I'm met with a mega-watt smile. As usual, he's impeccably dressed, as if he just stepped out of a men's magazine into the real world. Yet there's nothing real world about him, and I envy him that.

"Yep, just as I thought, it's our last night, and you're intent on fucking wasting it, let me guess, reading? You'd be worthless to me if every girl at school didn't want a piece of you. As it happens, I'm in need of my wingman tonight." It's a lie. He's notorious for his reputation with the coeds and the attention he draws with his personality and antics. Even I took an immediate liking to him, despite my best efforts to steer clear. He's the attention-seeking opposite of me. From beneath his expensive-looking trench, he produces a small bottle of gin and lifts it to my line of sight. "Just once, I'd love to wipe that scowl off your face. Get dressed, and I'll do my best."

"I'm busy."

"Bullshit, you're just as bored as I am. You've got one minute before I start singing fucking Christmas carols in soprano, and if that doesn't work, I'll do much, much worse."

Annoyed, but knowing he'll back up his threat, I step away from the door, ignoring his smug victory smirk as he closes it behind him. Moving toward the rack sitting in the middle of the room, I pick through my clothes and pull off my best button-down. Due to the insanely tight budget I'm on from opting for a single room, I'm practically living on air at this point. New clothes are a luxury I can't afford for the foreseeable future, and the last time I switched a sales tag on the full-price sweater I wanted, I almost got caught. Paris is a city full of expert thieves, and since that day, I've been a keen observer of those I've come across. My higher learning extended beyond my studies to a more skilled sleight of hand.

Preston glances around the room and then back to me, and I'm thankful when I don't see an ounce of pity in his eyes. I would despise him for it.

"It's dreary." Honesty. It's one of the things I appreciate most about him, and I agree with him. There's nothing but a single bed in my room, the provided free-standing clothes rack, and a small desk with a built-in lamp I purchased and hauled ten blocks from a street sale. "A man of little means. I like it."

Buttoning the shirt, I move to grab my worn patent-leather shoes from beneath the bed as Preston sets the gin on my desk before walking over and thumbing through my clothes, looking for something better suited. When he inevitably comes up empty, he turns to me, his eyes looking me over as I tie my shoes. "It's freezing out, man. Grab your jacket. Better yet, I have a spare in the car. Take mine." He slides out of it and walks it over to me. Instead of arguing with him, which is fucking futile most of the time, I push my arms into it as he holds it out for me. The fit is perfect.

"Admit it. You're going to miss me, King."

"What is there to miss? You're a loud, obnoxious, overbearing, ridiculous person."

"Ah, buddy, I feel the same way about you."

Grinning, he retrieves the gin from my desk, uncorks the bottle, and takes a sip before thrusting it toward me. I accept the offered bottle, gulping down a shot of the ice-cold liquor before posing the dreaded question.

"Where are we going?"

"To paint the town."

"I'm not feeling that idea."

"You're not feeling *anything* yet. Take another drink."

Gulping back another sip, I hand it back to him before leading him out of my room.

"Your lock broken or something?" He keeps his gaze on my fast-working fingers. It's then I realize I'm on my third turn, an overpowering need surging up to re-start my count. Instead, I pull my keys out and pocket them in his jacket. I can't help but run my fingers along the expensive lining. "Old habit." I shrug. "It was my lock back home that had issues."

Accepting my excuse, we start down the hall to make our way out of the hostel. Once outside, he leads me past the entrance to an idling blacked-out limousine just as his driver hops out to open the door for us.

"Why gin?" I ask him, sliding into the leather seat.

"Brown liquor brings out the worst in men." He takes the seat opposite me. "That's what my dad says—well, what he used to say."

Like me, Preston is an orphan. His dad was a congressman who died of a heart attack relatively young. His mother followed shortly after a double mastectomy couldn't save her. The difference between us is that he was fed from a platinum spoon and is the benefactor of not only his deceased parents' fortune but the generations before them. Old money in abundance. He'll never have to work a day in his life, which makes him aimless, and from what I've gathered, a little reckless. Newly nineteen, he embodies the realization of the American dream. Yet because he is the way he is, I can't hate him for it. He doesn't treat me like a charity case, but through small gestures and shared stories, I can feel his empathy, and it grates on me at times. Even when you do your best to mask poverty, it can be painfully obvious.

"I was shipped to France on the advice of my tutor and educational planner to broaden my horizons and get some world experience. My semester's over, man. I'm going home tomorrow completely unsatisfied with the size of my horizons." His grin indicates his intent before he puts words to it. "We're going to change that tonight."

"What could possibly go wrong?"

He taps his finger along the leather seat next to him, and I still my own fingers as he graces me with another smug smirk.

"Fuck off," I grumble.

"Let's get you relaxed." He grabs the spare trench on the seat next to him, leaving no doubt he brought the one I'm wearing for me. He pulls a silver case from one of the inside pockets, opens it, and plucks a joint from it before sparking it up.

"We'll start with dinner," he says on an exhale as we pull away from the curb, "a minimum of five courses. We're going to have a gentlemen's night." He pulls a tie from another pocket and tosses it on my lap. "There's a dress code."

Thumbing the silk, I nod and stare down at it as heat creeps up my neck.

"I—"

"Say no more, my friend." In seconds, Preston manipulates the necktie with sure hands into an adjustable noose before tossing it back to me.

Hooking it around my neck, I pull it tight at the base of my throat and glance over at him. He gives me a sharp nod of approval. It's both humbling and humiliating how much I presume to know and how much I'm reminded daily of just how much I have to learn. Spending time with guys like Preston reiterates that for me, which at times can be infuriating. Knowledge is power and key, but so is experience.

Preston has that advantage. He had a mentor in his father until he was sixteen. I wasn't so lucky. The idea that Roman Horner walks around freely, just as privileged, while I agonize over a necktie has my blood boiling. When the time comes, I don't ever want him to have any advantage. For now, while my resentment grows, I'm an observer, but one day, I won't be. That day is what keeps me aware, eager to learn as much as I can. Roman has the advantage of knowledge, age, and experience, and there's only so much I can gain from a book. But more than that, like Roman, Preston seems to already know who he is.

"For once, King, I want you to let me be in charge. I'm not letting you waste another second of our youth."

He's full of shit with that statement, and we both know it. Preston came in on a tidal wave, with his unavoidable personality, grabbed my hand and took me with him for most of his ride this semester at prep. We've been a force to be reckoned with for the last couple of months, mostly due to the attention of our skirted coeds, which only made us more noticeable and got us into a few fights, mostly his, because he loves a challenge.

For some reason, I trust him, and I trust *myself* with him. He doesn't have that edgy look in his eye; he's into this purely for sport, not self-destruction, and that appeals to me. Nothing pleases me more than pushing the limits of what I can get away with.

The few times I've turned down his invitations were to study to maintain my GPA or because I had to fly back home. But we more than made up for lost time with matching hangovers. His is the easiest and most low maintenance relationship I've ever had. With him, I've allowed myself a freedom I'll never have back home. And I know for a fact that once he's gone, I'll go back to my reclusive ways.

"Last night, King," he says, plucking two rocks glasses from the stocked bar and dividing the rest of the gin between them. "Let's make it count."

He extends one glass to me, and I clink with him.

For the last few weeks, I've been . . . off. Though my grades are stellar, my high GPA is no guarantee, and I'm going to have to push myself to be ready for the entrance exam to HEC next fall. It's all up in the air at this point as my efforts to find old contacts of my parents for help and guidance have proven to be fruitless. My birth father seems to have ruined my chances with his past behavior. No one wants to deal with Abijah Baran's son. My list is almost exhausted at this point. With each door that gets slammed in my face, the more I'm beginning to think my presence here is a mistake. An expensive mistake. I'm getting nowhere, and between the stress of worrying about my brother, his safety, and our dwindling finances, while making no progress here, I need all the escape I can get.

"I'm in."

Luniz raps "I Got 5 On It" as heavy bass thunders at my feet. Angelic-blonde hair blocks my vision, tickling my nose before a heart-shaped ass takes up the rest of my line of sight.

"Tu me vexes." *You're hurting my feelings.*

Attention fully drawn back where intended, I'm rewarded with the upturn of her full, bright-pink painted lips. "Te voilà." *There you are.*

"Pardonne-moi." *Forgive me.* Tracking her movements with appreciation, I tuck one of the bills into the string of her thong.

"On ne touche pas." *No touching.*

"Pardon." I lift my hands as the bouncer standing guard next to our booth steps forward with a look of warning. In my defense, her pole and elevated stage sit barely a foot from our table, making it prime real estate, and for me, a good excuse to take a closer look.

"Est-ce ta première fois dans un endroit comme celui-ci?" *Is this your first time in a place like this?*

Neck heating from transparency, I decide there's no point in lying. "Oui."

"Ah, mais un homme comme toi ne devrait pas avoir besoin d'être ici." *Ah, but a man who looks like you shouldn't need to be at a place like this.*

Her voice is pure sex, her body an offering, but I do my best to keep my wits about me, despite the quarter gallon mix of wine and gin coursing through my veins. But she's dead-on in her assessment. I've never been to a place like this, and even I know this club is as upscale and exclusive as they come. And since we strolled in just past midnight, bellies full of the finest French cuisine and expensive wine — that I immediately acquired a taste for — we've gained the attention of a majority of the dancers, especially since Preston has no shortage of money and has been so generous with it. The woman intent on breaking my concentration gently sways her hips in a deliberate taunt as I avert my gaze back to the man sitting in VIP. It's clear he's not a first-time patron. The section where he's taken up residence is just across from our booth, elevated just a few short steps above the main floor to make sure we know our place in the food chain.

What separates us is a velvet rope and an insane amount of influence and money. Though I'm sure if Preston flexed his bank account, he'd be a contender for the highest roller in here.

I'm not obsessed with money, I know the evils of it, but more than once tonight, I've been slapped by the reality of my standing due to lack of it. I think of Dom, still sleeping on the same fucking twin mattress he's had since he was five, the roof leak in the corner of his bedroom, and the black mold growing in his closet because of it. My lackluster room at the hostel is a palace in comparison.

"Je pourrais te permettre de me toucher. Mais pas si tu continues à m'insulter en détournant ton regard." *I might allow you to touch me. But not if you keep insulting me by looking away.*

Light-brown eyes scold me as she arches her back against the pole in another attempt to gain my interest. It's a tempting offer, but I'm too distracted, my reasons for staying in Paris dwindling by the second. I could hang it up now, let some of my aspirations go. I could attend an Ivy League university back home and find a way to pay for it. Four or five years from now, secure a job with a six-figure salary, enough to move Dom out of Delphine's shithole and secure his future.

But it's a gut feeling, combined with the hairs rising on the back of my neck, that has my thoughts shifting again. A tangible tension has been building since the three suited men walked in a half-hour ago. The staff scattered like rats. And from what I've witnessed, it's due to a mix of fear and respect, which leads me to believe they are someone important or work for someone important, and I'm determined to figure out which.

"Dis-moi sur quelle chanson danser. Tu vas voir, ça en vaudra la peine." *Tell me which song to dance to. You'll see, it will be worth it.*

It's the man tucked in the corner booth who I'm most curious about. He hasn't paid a bit of attention to the dancers. Everything about his demeanor screams organizational man. He's a decade at most past his prime and very, very well paid, which I deduce from his dress, the high dollar bottles being delivered to his table every few minutes, and the cigar he's chewing on. It's cliché gangster 101, so obvious and obnoxious. Chances are, they're more drunk on their effect, on the attention they've gathered, than the liquor they're tossing down their throats.

"Arrête de regarder, si tu ne veux pas qu'il te remarque." *Stop staring if you don't want him to notice you.*

"Qui est-il?" *Who is he?*

"Un homme qui n'aime pas qu'on pose des questions à son sujet." *A man who doesn't like people asking questions about him.*

Placing one of the higher bills in my hand at her heels, she glances down and then back to me before subtly shaking her head.

"Je ne sais rien. Personne ne sait rien ici. Et personne ne te dira quoi que ce soit. Mais tout ce que je sais, c'est que si tu poses trop de questions, si tu suscites le moindre soupçon, tu disparaitras, ou tu le souhaiteras fortement." *I don't know anything. No one here does. And no one will tell you anything, either. But what I do know is that if you ask, if you even so much as arouse suspicion, you'll disappear or wish you had.*

I look down at the wad of cash Preston pressed into my hand in the car before we arrived and know if I pocket some of it, it will make life a bit easier for me. Both angered and shamed by the thought, I lay it all at her feet.

"Quelqu'un sait quelque chose. Et si ce quelqu'un c'est toi, je serai très reconnaissant." *Someone knows something. And if that someone is you, I would be appreciative.*

Just as the man's eyes lock onto mine, she blocks his view of me, brushing her nipples along my lips. Both her allure and the gin take over, and I do my best to keep from getting hard. This isn't the place, and though beautiful, she isn't the girl to indulge with.

She grips my shoulders and turns me to face Preston, who's sitting in our booth, two popped bottles open and sweating in buckets. A dark-brunette beauty bounces in his lap. At this point, he looks only half-conscious, the only sign of life a dopey smile on his face as she grinds against him. My dancer runs her palms from my shoulders to my chest, encasing me from behind. Her breath hits my ear a second before she digs her nails through the fabric. It's then my cock can't take no for an answer. Hissing through my teeth, I'm thankful for the cover of the jacket.

"Si tu ne croyais pas aux fantômes avant de venir ici ce soir, il en est la preuve. Il a un intérêt dans ce club. Une danseuse. Elle ne parle à personne ici. Jamais. Elle est escortée partout où elle va. Un des videurs les a suivis une fois et a disparu. Ce ne sont pas les hommes avec qui plaisanter." *If you didn't believe in ghosts before you came here tonight, he is proof. He has one interest in this club. A dancer. She doesn't talk to anyone here. Not ever. She's escorted everywhere she goes. One of the bouncers followed them once and disappeared. These are not the men to be messed with.*

"Merci." *Thank you.*

Just after our exchange, I stop drinking, and after politely declining several appealing suggestions from my dancer, I pry Preston from the brunette. Wrapping his arm around my neck, I begin the task of hauling him out of the club while he struggles against me, whispering declarations to his abandoned dancer standing feet away.

"Je te retrouverai, mon amour." *I will find you again, my love.* Palm on his chest, he grins at her. "Finally, I have found true love in the city made for lovers. And now I have to leave. Au revoir, ma chérie."

"I'm willing to bet she'll move on quickly," I huff as he struggles against me, slurring his sentimental goodbye.

He turns to face me, not at all pleased I've cut this part of our night short. "What do you know about love, man?"

"That it's distracting your feet; do me a favor and try to remember what they're for."

"That blonde was into you. Why didn't you pounce on that?"

"Not my type."

"What is your type? You like a whip cracker and rope, don't you? It's always the quiet ones. Tell me, King, am I right?"

"Use your feet," I grunt as I practically drag him across the room.

"I bet you like 'em mean," he says, stopping the two of us in the middle of the club. "I need to take a piss."

After waiting an eternity outside the bathroom, we make it to the entrance, which is now deserted, thanks to the lateness of the hour and the rapidly dropping temperature.

"Where's the car?"

"I called him while I was taking a leak. He's not far."

He leans back against the side of the building, his eyes closed. "I shouldn't have had that last drink. The air is helping. I'll be all right in a minute. Just need my second wind. The night is still young, King."

"You're done."

"I am, aren't I?" He slowly opens his eyes, not a trace of humor in his tone. "In more ways than one."

"What do you mean?"

"I mean, even with my parents six feet under, I have expectations to meet. A family full of overachievers to impress back home. The minute I step off that plane, they'll be peering over my shoulder for the rest of my life." He exhales, his breath visible and glowing from the neon shed off the club lights. "For you, this was a Friday night, but for me . . . well, it's my last hurrah."

"You've got college."

"No, I don't." He nods over his shoulder toward the club. "No offense to working ladies, but I'm not interested in strippers, man. It was just something to check off my list. Another experience I can say I didn't miss out on. There are no strip clubs in my future. Hell, there's no fucking fun in my future."

"What's in your future?"

"Boredom. A shit ton of it, followed by more boredom. Rich boy problems, I know." He cups the back of his head. His slicked brown locks thoroughly picked through by the fingers of the dancer. "The money is mine, but with it comes the pressure. I have to accomplish more than being a spoiled trust fund baby. Want to know the worst part? The road ahead isn't that unappealing to me. I'm kind of a no-frills guy."

"I'm going to have to call bullshit."

"No, this is different. I'll be honest, man, I've never partaken in half the shit we've done this semester."

I chuckle. "Same."

He cracks a grin. "I suspected as much. And I'll admit I've enjoyed it. I think my issue is that I just want the freedom to decide, you know what I mean?"

My reply is cut off, as is my view of him as he's pinned

to the brick, his eyes going wide at the sudden appearance of the man between us.

"Vide tes poches. Maintenant." *Empty your pockets. Now.*

I didn't see him. Not at all. He was background noise, a pedestrian walking down a typically busy Parisian street. I didn't think a thing about the man approaching us because I was fully immersed in our conversation. Preston seems just as surprised as the man glares between us, producing a knife out of thin air before thrusting it toward me. I barely manage to escape the tip, jumping back to the curb.

Satisfied with the space the move provided him, he grips Preston by the collar, pressing the tip of the blade into the base of his throat. I'm three feet away at most, and I know with just a little more pressure or a fast flick of his wrist, Preston will die.

Something inside me breaks with Preston's expression, and I leap forward, jerking the man's head back by the hair before smashing his face into the brick just next to Preston's shoulder. Adrenaline takes over as I fist the side of his head repeatedly until he goes limp and the knife clatters on the pavement at my feet. Once he's on the ground, I kick him with the hard-edged heel of my shoe until his arms are no longer raised in defense.

With a quick glance around, I see we're still alone and lift him from underneath the arms before glancing up at Preston. He's still plastered against the brick, his eyes wide. I eye the camera at the entrance, thankful we're just out of view.

"Grab his legs," I blurt, panic rising as Dom's face flits through my mind. This can't be it. This can't be the mistake that takes me out. "Preston, I can't go to jail." I don't voice my bigger fear, that I'm unsure if the man is dead or not. I've never hit someone so hard in my life.

Preston leaps into action, and we carry the unconscious man to a nearby alley and drop him behind a dumpster. Bending, I press my fingers to his neck to check for a pulse.

"He alive?"

I nod and stand. "Come on."

Preston stops me, gripping me by the shoulder. "Take his money."

"What?"

He juts his chin to the unconscious thief and flits his hardening gaze back to mine. "It's only fucking fair. Take *his* money."

Turning back, I lean over the man and study the damage I've inflicted. His face is mangled, and there's blood oozing from his ear.

"Do it, King."

Ripping open his jacket, I check his pockets and retrieve a wad of bills, some frayed, some newer looking, and I know it's not his. He didn't earn a cent of it.

"Jackpot. He's been at this all night."

Pocketing the money, I join Preston where he stands before we wordlessly leave the alley, hastening when we see the limo waiting at the club entrance. Once the driver's ushered us inside, he takes his seat behind the wheel. "Where to, Mr. Monroe?"

We stare off before he speaks up. "I'm hungry. You?"

I nod.

"Take us somewhere for breakfast. You choose."

The driver speeds away from the curb. "Yes, sir."

Preston lifts his chin toward me. "You're going to have to lose the jacket."

Inspecting it through the passing street lights, I see a splatter of blood on the coat. It's far too noticeable. While shedding it, I lean in on a whisper. "I've never done anything like that."

"How did it feel?"

I lift a shoulder. "I'm not going to cry about it."

"Me neither." He leans forward, his hands clasped between his legs, his voice low. "And don't ever second-guess what you just did. That man was going to end me no matter what I had in my pockets. I saw it in his eyes. He was fucking high." He sits back in his seat, his expression contemplative. "Along with my father's looks, I was blessed with his judgment. I know when to trust people and when not to. Usually within the first minute of meeting them." Pulling the case from his pocket, he lights the half joint he put out hours earlier, pinching some loose weed off his tongue before he speaks. "The way I see it, there are bad men capable of doing bad things, and then there are good men capable of doing bad things for good fucking reasons." He looks at me pointedly. "You're one of those."

"Which are you?"

"Incapable of being either. Eventually, I'm going to be a man in need of guys like you."

Preston dropped me off just as dawn began to light the streets. After a few hours of sleep, duffle in hand for my flight home, I opened my door to see I was blocked in by six large boxes. At the top of the first lay a note.

Thanks for saving me the burden of packing,
Wingman.

P

* * *

There was a shift between us that night. We were both aware of it. We just didn't know exactly what *it* was. I never knew how instrumental that night would be in my future, but looking back now, I know it was the true beginning.

The memory flitting fresh through my mind, I stand in Cecelia's closet, sweat gliding down my back after another long run with Beau. I pick through her clothes, curious. She's a no-label girl. There's not one designer in her closet. We're so much alike in some ways and polar opposites in others. She's simple with her taste, even as a millionaire. She's never given a fuck about money, which she made crystal clear when she handed me her inherited Fortune 500 company, along with the profit she made from our deal, back to Exodus *in full*.

She never wanted her father's money. She only wanted his love.

That's all she's ever asked of any of the men in her life.

I run my fingers down the fabric of one of her dresses. "I'll make it up to you, Mon Trésor."

I've never lived with a woman, or really anyone as an adult for that matter, and I find it oddly satisfying that my first will be my last. That's only if life and time allow it. Time itself is as fucking merciless as love is—no boundaries or ceasefire. It's an enemy. And since I've been back, we haven't resumed shit.

But time is what she needs—time and boundaries—and that's what I'll have to give her. But is allowing space the right move? Do I treat her with fragility?

That's not what she's used to from me. That's not who we are.

Grabbing some clothes of my own, I toss them on the bed

and walk to her bookshelf, picking through until I see a familiar book. A new library copy of *The Thorn Birds*, similar to the one destroyed at the restaurant months ago.

"I guess I'll always be the girl crying for the moon."

Opening the small book, I thumb a few pages and palm my head when I see the main character's name.

"Why did you name it Meggie's?"

"It's a long story."

"Do I know it?"

"Intimately and from afar."

"King, you fucking idiot," I mutter. I've flipped through the book once or twice out of curiosity, but the character names never stuck. I was too absorbed in Cecelia to see the bigger picture of what the book meant, and all these years later, I'm still as clueless.

She named her café after the lead character of *The Thorn Birds*, the story closest to her heart. Her thieving this book from the Triple Falls Library is one of the reasons we exist. It's obvious she compares herself to Meggie and our own story to the one inside the pages. I'll memorize the fucking thing if it means so much to her. But for now, I'm coming up blank on how to proceed.

This is my first time on the board without a strategy, and right now, she's resuming her life like I'm some obstacle she has to work herself around. She'd left me here this morning, purposefully, so I couldn't be more of a distraction.

Frustrated, I head into her bathroom and open her medicine cabinet, satisfied when I see her birth control.

That's a discussion for a different day. I grab the bottle of lotion sitting next to it, uncap it and inhale.

Immediately I'm hit with the familiarity and one of the

triggers of my addiction to her, her scent. Reading the label, it dawns on me why.

Juniper Berry.

No wonder I'm addicted to her smell. I drink the contents of her scent nightly. *In. My. Fucking. Gin.*

"Well played, queen," I muse, capping her lotion and closing the cabinet.

Rummaging through her drawers, I realize I'm in full-fledged stalker mode with no idea what I'm searching for. Insight? Some sort of aid to help me in winning her back? Frustrated, I slam them shut, knowing I'm not going to find what I need counting her fucking Q-tips. My phone rumbles in my pocket with a text, and I'm thankful for the distraction.

Tyler: Incoming.

The phone rings in my hand a minute later, and I answer on the second, "Tobias."

"Had to make sure I knew my place picking up after two rings, huh?"

"Good afternoon, Mr. President. How's the big White House treating you?"

"The bed is very comfortable, Mr. King," he fires back in the same jovial tone. "I've been meaning to call you to thank you for all your help and for your contributions to the campaign."

"I consider it money well spent. We seem to agree on a lot of policy and change."

"That's another reason for my call. I wanted to assure you that I'll work tirelessly and have the country's best interests at heart."

"No doubt you do, *sir*."

He cuts the shit. "Been a long time since prep, hasn't it, King?"

"Too long. I'm surprised you remember me. You were only there one semester."

It's a lie. Not his time at prep, but the acquaintance-only aspect of our conversation. Someone is always listening, and we're not taking any chances. From the second we stepped into that breakfast café twenty years ago, both slightly hungover and eager for grease in our bellies, we got personal due to a newly formed trust and respect.

For the first time, I trusted an outsider with my plans for Roman, and he shared his aspirations as well. And together we strategized our own agenda, and together, we carried it out to the fucking letter.

Little did I know, we would become the greatest of allies. Upon hearing his aspirations, I knew he was the perfect candidate for an underdog President. Orphaned, but from good breeding, insanely wealthy, good-looking, but someone who could control his dick and treat girls with respect, even behind closed doors. He was one of the first of my major recruits and a damn good decision on my part. My financial backing to his campaign was ironic and brought us full circle.

His ink is there—though it's invisible—and he's one of the founding fathers of the brotherhood, now sitting in the most powerful seat in the world.

"Molly wanted me to extend an invitation to dinner."

"Someday soon, I'll take you up on that." We agreed early on that the association between us needs to stay formal until we have the bulk of our work out of the way—or unless there's an emergency. My contributions to his campaign and our months at the same prep school for one semester our only visible tie. He's one of the only decent men in power, and we have too much to accomplish in the next seven years for our association to taint him—should I ever get prosecuted for my crimes.

Preston Monroe doesn't need micro-managing, and Tyler has been preparing for this since he joined the Marines.

"What are you up to these days, Tobias?"

"Most recently, sir, I've taken an interest in Virginia."

"Ah. Glad to know you're in the neighborhood. Anyone I know?"

"You'll meet her, eventually."

"I'm intrigued. So, I'm assuming you're retiring from politics?"

"It's temporary," I assure him. "I don't golf."

"Well, good luck with that. I'll be in touch."

"I appreciate your call, Mr. President."

"I look forward to seeing you at the House."

"You deserve this," I say honestly.

"Couldn't have done it without you, man."

Ending the call, I glance out the window of Cecelia's bedroom before I shoot off a text.

ETA?

Russell: A little birdie just parked the Audi in the driveway, keys in the visor. I've got two freshly hatched birds coming. Should I send more?

Send four more. I'm not familiar with the neighborhood. And switch the old. They're tired and bored, which makes them useless to me. I want 20/20 fucking vision.

Understood?

Russell: Got it. They'll be there tomorrow. How's Cee?

Good.

Russell: That was an abrupt answer. She can hold a grudge, can't she? Laughing emoji.

When I don't respond, the phone rattles again.

Russell: She's giving you hell, isn't she? God, I love that girl. Take care of her.

Get back to fucking work.

Russell: Aren't you retired?

I'm on vacation. Big difference.

Russell: 10/4 Good buddy. I'm sure you have your hands full. Kissing face emoji.

Chapter Ten

CECELIA

I PULL UP to see my Audi parked in the driveway, and the sight of it jars me. It's part of what I left behind. It seems no matter how much space I put between myself and the life I was living a year ago, I won't ever escape it.

Today I overserved and talked the ear off every customer at the café, intent on resuming my routine. When things got slow, I busied myself scrubbing every inch of my restaurant to avoid Marissa and her questions. This morning, I all but fled, leaving him alone without a car and to his own devices so that I could try and sort my thoughts.

Exiting the Camaro, I inspect my Audi before glancing at the lifeless house, curious as to what he's doing inside.

"You don't look happy about it."

I damn near jump out of my skin and turn to see Tobias feet away from me, his black tee plastered to his monstrous build, sweat trickling down both his temples.

"Or maybe you didn't want to go into that house because you thought I was in there." He tilts his head, his allure drawing me in, his stare skeptical. "Which one is it, Cecelia?" The rawness in his voice threatens to open the reinforced scars in my chest. "Stop eye-fucking me, and tell me which is it? You're not happy about the car or the fact that you were going to have to face me in that house?"

"What?"

"You heard me." In two strides, he's in front of me, his presence invading. I've never been immune to him, and playing indifferent to my attraction at this point is ridiculous—not only that, he knows better.

"That was my second run today. You're not alone in what you're feeling." He glances at the car. "We can get rid of it, but I was the one who took it away from you, so I thought I should be the one to return it."

"It just surprised me, that's all. I didn't think I'd ever see it again."

"Right," he mutters in a dejected tone.

I grip his forearm when he steps around me, and he stops, shoulders tensing as he lifts amber-colored eyes to mine.

"I *love* the car," I say honestly, but we both know it's not the car I'm talking about. "I'm just . . ." Anger surges through me, and he reads the agitation taking over.

"Ready to *talk*?" He turns and moves in, causing me to take a step back. "*Fight*?" Another step. Nothing in his demeanor hinting of exhaustion, though he just ran for miles. He's pure wolf as he leans in, faint hints of citrus and spice invading my senses. "*Fuck*?"

When I remain mute, his shoulders sag. He presses a kiss to my temple before he dips to whisper. "More time, then. That's all we have, Cecelia," he reminds me before he makes his way into the house.

Chapter Eleven

CECELIA

"THAT LOOKS AWESOME," Marissa speaks up from behind me as I pull more of the fake web and tape it to the side of the window. Stepping back, I admire my handiwork and glance around the café, satisfied with the progress. After the morning rush, Marissa and I managed to transform the restaurant with monster motif. It's a bit premature with the holiday weeks away, but I needed the distraction.

"Looks good," I agree. I've never dreamed of being a shop owner, but I admit having a place like this is satisfying in so many ways—a place I myself would frequent as a patron. There are a few gathered around the cozy fire in the reading nook. There's a steady crispness in the air now as the leaves on the ancient oaks opposite the parking lot rapidly turn brilliant shades of pumpkin, red, and yellow, officiating fall's arrival. A season I used to loathe due to a few life-altering summers that I never wanted to end.

"Now," Marissa says sharply, "I'm going to whip us up some lattes, and you're going to tell me what the hell is going on. I've been patient enough."

Just as she speaks, a school bus pulls up and a few dozen

kids start filing out before heading toward the café.

"Oh, shit," Marissa says. "Did you know they were coming?"

"No idea," I reply, equally as taken aback just as Tobias pulls up in the parking lot, his attention shifting from me to the school bus of children piling into the restaurant. By the time he reaches the door, he's already rolling up his sleeves. He winks at Marissa in greeting before leaning in and pressing a brief kiss to my lips.

"Just tell me where you need me."

Chaos, utter and complete chaos would be how I describe the next hour. Rows and rows of school children fill every table and booth monitored by just a handful of teachers who look to be at their wits end. Though I relieved our third waitress after the morning rush, Marissa and I, along with Tobias's unexpected help, manage to do a decent job of expediting the food and drink orders—but the noise is deafening. Tobias zooms around with a bin, collecting plates like the job comes first nature, sweeping up spills and taking orders for the few stragglers who come in to dine.

"Goddamn rednecks make us all look bad!" Billy booms from the counter in reaction to something on TV, making me jump as I began to tally up the tickets to get the bus full of middle schoolers out of my café.

"Billy," I scold. "Little ears *everywhere*. Please try to watch your language."

"Sorry." He looks over to the mortified woman in an adjacent booth. "Sorry, ma'am."

She scoffs at his apology, and he takes immediate offense. "Lady, you live seventy years, and you can say anything you damn well please."

The "well, I never" in her expression as she tosses a look my way lets me know Billy's behavior is on me. "I'll take my check."

She collects her purse and begins to usher her little boy out of the booth.

"I'm so sorry, ma'am," I interject, handing it to her. "You didn't eat much. I would be happy to comp your meal."

"We won't be back," the woman snaps, handing me back her check expectantly.

When Tobias appears at her table, I see the immediate change in her posture as she drinks him in.

"Want me to bag this up for you?"

She shamelessly eye-fucks him before speaking. "That . . . would be nice, thank you . . . ?"

"Tobias. Avec plaisir, salope." *With pleasure, bitch.*

It's all I can do to stifle my laugh.

"Oh, that's beautiful. French?"

"Yes. Sorry, I forget my English sometimes," he drawls out, playing innocent foreigner. For a few seconds, I get lost in the sight of him in pedestrian clothes, standing in the middle of my café. Jutting his chin, he gestures over my shoulder with the knowing upturn of his lips as Travis rings the bell behind me. "Order up, *boss.*"

I narrow my eyes. "I'm aware, Frenchman. When you're done here, table three and six need bussing as well."

"As you wish," he concedes.

Turning to grab the order, I'm stopped by the heat in his voice. "Oh, Cecelia?"

I glance over my shoulder to see the smolder in his eyes as obnoxious laughter and cafeteria level noise sounds around us both. "Yes?"

"Je n'aime pas me réveiller sans toi. Je préférerais de loin me réveiller en toi." *I don't like waking up without you. I would much rather wake up inside you.*

"There goes that French tongue again," the woman scolds. "You know it's rude to say things that others can't understand."

Ignoring the self-important bitch, he keeps his focus on me.

"Tu as l'air un peu stressée. Je peux t'aider à te détendre. Avec ma langue, et ta chatte." *You're looking a little stressed. I can help you relax. With my tongue, and your pussy.*

Lips parting, I do my best to conceal my shock. "As-tu perdu la tête?" *Have you lost your mind?*

"Pas ce que tu avais en tête? Après tu décideras où ira ma langue." *Not what you had in mind? Then you will decide where my tongue will go.*

"We can discuss this at ho—"

"So, if you'll just bag that up," the woman interrupts, hating that I've stolen her thunder.

Her little boy, who looks to be around seven or eight, climbs out of the booth, watching our exchange with interest. Tobias leans down and whispers to him, and he giggles before he speaks up, mimicking Tobias perfectly. "Le pleck, le spit."

I toss my head back and laugh. Was it so long ago I was mimicking him the same way poolside at my father's house? Then we were at odds, fighting our attraction, denying our chemistry, the tension just as thick. When we were apart, it seemed like an eternity ago, but when he's this close, it doesn't feel that way.

"Tu m'as manqué, Mon Trésor." *I've missed you, my treasure.* The sincerity in his tone combined with the look in his eyes has my heart galloping, and visions swirling of the days he barely made it out of his Jag in my father's driveway before I was in his arms and our lips were colliding. A collection of days and weeks when our time was stolen, a time where we freed ourselves to openly love each other without uttering the words. A plate shatters behind me, breaking our spell.

"Did you just teach my son some sort of French curse?"

Without answering, patience thinning, Tobias grabs the loaded plate from her table. "I'll get this taken care of."

She eyes me suspiciously as he walks past. "That English seems to come and go so conveniently."

"Funny how that works," I agree, sauntering off and following Tobias through the double doors, zeroed in on his ass when I notice the label on his jeans. "Wranglers?" I can't help my laugh. "Planning on riding bulls anytime soon?"

"This is all they had in my size," he explains in defense as he heads into the kitchen. "Not much to choose from around here."

"You can't do that." I change the subject.

"Why should we let all that French you learned go to waste?"

"Not funny."

"I disagree," he says icily, dumping the contents of the woman's plate into a box.

"You didn't have to help, you know."

He cocks his head. "You know damn well I'm not irritated because I'm helping. I wanted to."

"Well, you don't have to play dirty to talk to me."

"You sure about that? Because we haven't had a real conversation since I got here."

"And now is not the time."

"When would be a good time?"

My silence only angers him further as he grabs a plastic bag and shoves the box inside.

"I'm adjusting, Tobias, and I'm thankful for the help, but need I remind you, you're a billionaire, not a busboy."

"And you're a millionaire, not a waitress. What the hell does that matter? I'm whatever you need me to be." He studies me for a second before closing his eyes and placing his hands on the metal countertop, seeming to muster up some patience. When he finally speaks, his voice is low, full of disappointment. "I'll be out of your way when I finish up with the tables." He gathers the bag, and without another word, walks through the double doors.

"Condom or knife?" Marissa nudges me, sidling up to me at the counter, my focus on Tobias, who's drawing with a little girl in the reading nook while he chats with her grandmother. We got a secondary rush after the kids left, a rarity. Despite our conversation, Tobias stayed to help us out, bussing tables without a word while running circles around Marissa and me.

"What?"

"Condom or knife. The ex-dilemma. When they first come back, you don't know whether to fuck them or kill them, am I right?"

"Nailed it," I chuckle, clearing the counter of some plates. "If you only knew." Which she doesn't and most definitely never will. That's the crux of being in a relationship with a man like Tobias.

Restless, I spent last night in my garden planting spring bulbs as he typed away on his keyboard in one of my patio chairs. Every so often, I would catch him staring at me, and I would return it. After I showered and dressed for bed, I found him waiting there for me. When I clicked off the light, he wordlessly pulled me into his chest. I knew he was there to help me combat whatever dream my imagination would muster up. I hadn't dreamlessly slept since he'd arrived.

"I've never seen a man that pretty in *real* life. It's like he's not even human."

"Trust me, he bleeds." I'm one of the rare few who knows where his scars are.

"So, are you glad he's back?"

"I want to be, but we're beyond complicated."

"Scared of getting hurt again?"

Tobias doesn't hurt. He murders hurt; he makes hurt seem like a trip on a merry-go-round, and I got off his ride eight months ago.

Latching a newly loaded napkin dispenser shut, I look to see him keeping rapid conversation with the older woman. "I gave him an ultimatum almost a year ago, and he's just now coming around."

"It's always like that, right?" Opening the register, she exchanges some of her tips for larger bills and pockets the money in her apron. That one simple act brings me back to a different time and place. Triple Falls, smiling Selma and her tortillas. A lifetime ago.

"It's always like what?"

"You finally get it together enough to get over them—live without them—and *bam*, they show up on your doorstep expecting you to feel the same way. My momma always said, 'Don't ever count on a man to realize his wrongs on your emotional timeline 'cause men always take way longer to come around and deal with their feelings. They're emotionally stunted.'"

"Never have more truer words been spoken." It's taken my stunted Frenchman too many unforgivable years to come around. That's what I'm having the hardest time with. More than that, I'm not sure my heart can handle another spin on his merry-go-round.

"Well, better late than *never*, right? I swear I've never seen eyes like that in my life. I don't know how you're handling this."

"Stop staring, or he'll know we're talking about him."

Not even a second later, his eyes lift, and he smirks.

Bastard.

We both burst back into motion, which makes us look even more ridiculous. "So, you're playing mouse with that lion? No offense, but it looks like he could swallow you whole."

I scowl.

"Sorry, but it's the truth. I feel the tension between you two, and you look like a geyser about to blow, and he . . . well, if a man looked at me like that, I would probably strip naked without being aware of it."

She nudges me, and I nudge her back—hard.

"Oh, testy. Yeah, definitely holding out on him. You don't look freshly fucked. You just look . . . fucked." She giggles, and I glare before winding up and snapping her with my rag.

"Ouch!"

"Tell me why I hired you?"

"For my sparkling, no-bullshit personality?"

"Yeah, well, since we're in the business of honesty, when are you going to put our cook out of his misery?"

She glances back to Travis and wrinkles her nose. "I can't go there. I dated his brother in high school."

When I wince, she misinterprets. "Exactly. I mean, how can you date a man's *brother* and then—"

"Marissa, order up," Travis calls, and I'm thankful for the interference.

I glance at Tobias, and he reads my expression. When I retreat to my office, he's right behind me before I get a chance to close the door.

"What's wrong?"

"Nothing. Look, our . . . drama is distracting the staff."

"Our drama is distracting *you*," he corrects and crowds me against my office door, so I'm forced to look up at him.

"Tobias, you're making it hard for me to work." And sleep. And think.

He nods. "We've established that. I was just about to take off. Just wanted to let you know."

"I'm sorry. I'm just . . . I don't know what I am right now."

"You feel ambushed. We've got a lot to sort through, but until then, I'm here if you need me to be. And—" he leans in, encasing me in his arms, his hands caressing the wings on my back—"we have a lot to look forward to." He brushes my lips with his. "I'll see you at home."

Home.

"Okay. Thanks again for helping today."

His reply is a brief kiss to my lips. Releasing me, he shoves his hand in his jeans and pulls a wad of cash from his pocket, folding my hand around it. "For Marissa."

That afternoon, I return home to see a note from Tobias that he went for a run. After a scalding shower, I stand in front of my mirror and wipe the moisture away, jumping when Tobias appears behind me, his eyes rolling down my naked form before returning to mine. His hair completely damp and disheveled, his shirt soaked, he leans in and presses a kiss to my shoulder before snaking an arm around my waist and pulling my back to him. Resting his chin on my shoulder, he runs the pads of his fingers along my stomach. "Small talk is stupid, don't you think? Especially when you need to have big conversations."

He pushes the bulk of my soaked hair to the opposite shoulder before pressing his lips to my exposed neck, laving up droplets of water with his tongue. The sight of the act draws me back, so familiar, so intimate, it has me weakening in the knees.

I re-live the first time he did this, kissed me this way. It was the first night we were intimate. I bite my lip, remembering the sight of his cock as he pushed into me; the stretch, the fit, the intensity of that moment, and the recognition in his eyes.

But it wasn't just the feel. It was the emotion attached to it, emotions neither of us wanted to acknowledge.

"But I know why we aren't talking, Cecelia. I can wait," he murmurs as our eyes catch in the reflection. "Because I'm not going to walk around here chatting about the fucking weather, or the café—a business you can run with your eyes closed—or about what you're planting in your garden because I really don't give a fuck as long as it makes you happy. I can wait for a lot—" he pulls his mouth from me—"but I'm not going to let you deny that *I'm here* much longer." Erection pressing into my back, he leans in again, biting the nape of my neck before soothing it with his lips and tongue. Thoroughly soaked and needy, I fight to keep from rubbing my thighs together. "I'll talk to you about whatever you want, as long as we're having a conversation. But I do hear everything you're not saying, too. I'll always hear you." He studies me, watching my expression and reaction to him, my body blooming fully under his touch before his eyes close, and a curse leaves him. His expression pained like he's just seen something he can't handle before he releases me and shuts the door behind him.

My heart lurches after him, but my mind refuses to allow me to move. For the first time since he arrived, a thought occurs to me . . .

What if I'm incapable of forgiving him?

Chapter Twelve

TOBIAS

Age Twenty

HEAVY BASS THUMPS from the club to my right as I walk through a cloud of cigarette smoke. I cruise by while taking note of a guy tongue-fucking a brunette he has plastered to the side of the building, his hand disappearing beneath her skirt. Envy eats at me as she tosses her head back before biting down on the shoulder of her captor. When she opens her eyes, her lips part when she zeroes in on me. The sight of the dare inside them, pure temptation.

Come and get me.

Ignoring the blatant taunt, I pass the club, irritated I can't indulge. I can't remember the last time I sated myself with a girl or did anything considered normal. Would it hurt, just once, to spend a Saturday night at a club? To reward myself with a long, thorough fuck to take the edge off?

It's then I recognize a fellow student from one of my classes. I keep my eyes lowered so he doesn't stop me, not that he would. Since I started HEC, I've made it clear with my conduct that no one should attempt to. Aside from my new slob of a roommate,

Claude, a roommate I was forced to take on due to finances, I haven't socialized at my new school. I make sure Claude is wary of me by silent communication and body language. He keeps the hours of a student, often away on the weekends, giving me privacy while I continually burn the candle at both ends.

With graduation years ahead, I have no plans of changing any part of my stance. No one can know me on a personal level. But a small part of me wishes that—like most students—the only pressures I had were passing grades and simple decisions of which party to attend and which pussy to devour. Since prep, I've made it my mission to remain incognito, and so far, there have only been a few coeds brave enough to challenge me in that department. Their reward was a rude wake-up call, which is necessary to ensure I remain just another faceless student no one can remember details about. But after years abroad, even in a city as large as Paris, it's becoming a smaller world.

Fumbling with the new cell phone Dominic overnighted me, the line trills as I step around another crowd lining the sidewalk. He answers on the second ring.

"You're supposed to be on a plane."

"I have exams," I lie.

"You're lying," Dominic argues. "How do you expect me to help you when you don't tell me what's happening?"

The almost six-year age difference between us used to seem like eons in maturity not long ago. Although, after my last visit to Triple Falls, it's clear I severely underestimated them— Dom especially—and because of that, it's almost impossible to get anything past him. Surrounded by firelight six weeks ago, I found out just how ready he was.

*

"What's going on in France?" Sean asks from his camping chair.

"School," I reply curtly.

"That's not exactly true, is it, brother?" Dom speaks up, looking between Tyler and Sean. "He left to find help. Everyone at the meetings got scared when my parents were killed, and all they do now is bitch." He kicks back in his seat. "My parents were revolutionaries at one point, extremists at another, and my brother here wants to enlist people who know what the fuck they're doing." He looks over to me. "Isn't that right, brother?"

He knows far more than I'm comfortable with. The idea that he's been playing oblivious for this long rattles me to my core. He's good at deception, too good. "Why have you played fucking ignorant this whole time?"

His firelit face remains impassive. "I find it helps to be in the know, without anyone else knowing."

A genius sort of deception. A manipulation that he even fooled me with, playing uninterested for the most part, and clueless at other times.

"I'm lost," Tyler says, glancing between us.

Sean speaks up, his eyes darting between Dom and me. "I believe the short version is: Dominic is done playing dumb."

I scrutinize my brother and then Sean. "This won't work if we're keeping secrets."

"Says the blackest pot," Dom adds bitterly.

While I've been away, Dom's been piecing it together. My secrecy has spiked his curiosity, and he's just made it clear he isn't about to let me get away with it any longer without letting me know he's onto me.

"Right now, there's nothing to tell. And this isn't going to happen overnight."

"But this isn't just a conversation anymore," Dominic says definitively. "And you know it. We can't help you if you don't tell us what's going on over there."

"What is it you think you can do?"

Silence is my answer.

"Exactly, you stay out of this until it's time."

"You're living in fucking France, alone. You think that's smart?"

"What is it you want me to do?"

He doesn't hesitate. "Take me with you."

"Not a fucking chance. You know why I'm there, so there's no point in arguing about it. We need to focus on what's important, and right now, that's money."

Dom breaks our gaze, his eyes drifting back to the fire. "I have an idea, but you aren't going to like it."

I didn't and still don't, which is why I refused to let him jeopardize himself in any way before his time. I want him as far away as possible from what I'm trying to accomplish here in France.

"I'm tied up with something I don't want to discuss now." Gripping my backpack tightly to me, I crane my neck, keeping my phone cradled to my ear as music bursts from an opening door. "Can we argue about this later? I've got somewhere to be. I just wanted to check in."

"Whatever." There's a dejection in his tone, and I know it's not only about me missing my flight. I've maintained my promise to fly back every six weeks up until now, but things are starting to move in the direction I need them to, and I can't afford to waste more time, literally. The trips are only getting more expensive.

"What's going on?"

"Forget it. I guess I'll see you whenever."

"Dom, I don't have the patience to coax it gently from you. Out with it."

"We're fucking broke."

Pausing my walk, I run a hand down my face. The last time I was in Triple Falls, I taught them how to 'borrow' what they needed from those who'd gained their standing by playing and taking from others less fortunate. It was a code I invented shortly after my run-in with the knife-wielding thief last year. They'd run with it, and Dom being Dom, had thought of a few ideas of his own on how to increase our take.

"It's time to make some changes."

By changes, he means it's time to incriminate himself in a way that can't be reversed if he's caught. My lesson in petty theft turned into me getting schooled by my younger brother on more efficient ways to get fast cash. It was both amazing and terrifying to find out just how much he knows bordering fifteen years old.

"I'll figure something out," I offer.

"No time for that, either." His tone is grave, but he's still young and becoming more arrogant by the day, especially with his innate knowledge of all the technological advances.

"If you fuck up—"

"Have some faith, brother." The excitement in his voice is more alarming than anything. But the fact that he's been waiting for the green light from me has to be enough. I have to trust him. I have to trust them all to carry the weight until I accomplish what I set out to do here.

"Do it. And Dom, don't fucking think I won't snatch the toy from your hands if you get stupid with it."

"As if you could. I'm outgrowing you."

"Maybe so," I say with pride, "but let's not forget the rules."

"I'll hit you up when it's done."

"You do that and keep your fucking nose clean otherwise."

"Trust me, brother."

"I do."

We end the call, and I turn the corner, leaving room for a guy standing on the edge of the alley.

"Auriez-vous une cigarette?"

"Non," I answer without bothering to glance his way.

"Sure?"

"Sorry."

"American?"

"Non."

"That's not true, is it, Ezekiel?"

I'm already sprinting, but it's too late. Within seconds, I'm hooded and riding in the back of a van. I remain completely silent as a barrage of questions in English and scattered French come at me from all sides while my backpack is ripped from my arm and unzipped, but I know I'm safe there. I've rid myself of anything that indicates I'm anything other than a college student, but these guys know better. I stuck my nose where it didn't belong, and I will either die for it tonight, or I'll be warned in a way I'm probably not going to like.

"Should have stayed in America," one of them grunts as I maintain my count, tapping my thigh with my finger.

"How is American pussy?" one of them fires from my left. My silence buys me a busted lip, but I maintain, clearing my head from their distraction and keep counting.

From what I can tell, there are two of them, aside from

the driver. Ignoring the noise, I tap my fingers on the leather behind me.

Tap. Tap. Tap.

Sometime later, we slow, and I note the noise of construction to our left, despite the time of night. I hear the distinct clang of a gate when one of them exits the van before we drive through. In the next minute, I'm whisked out and dragged through a gravel parking lot, a doorway, and hauled down some steep steps. When a door closes behind me, the overpowering smell of urine hits while the hood is ripped from my head. I'm blinking to adjust to the light when a man comes into focus a foot away; older, early-fifties, his more-salt-than-pepper hair neatly trimmed, face impassive, eyes dull. Just behind him stands Palo, the man I inquired about at the strip club last winter, and I see no recognition in his eyes for me. My attention flits back to the man in front of me as he inspects me carefully.

"You're better looking than your father."

I can only assume it's Abijah he's speaking of. Beau was far less radical, and I can't imagine him tied to the man standing in front of me.

"Speak."

"I don't remember Abijah."

"He was a good soldier. It's a shame his mind betrayed him."

"My mother hated him. I'm loyal to her."

"I was very unhappy to hear of Celine's passing. Tragic. She was beautiful."

"She was murdered."

His face remains impassive, but in his eyes, I see a shift.

He's sharply dressed, his taste expensive. I've never owned a suit, but if all goes well—and this isn't my last night alive—I'm determined to get one of my own. My thoughts drift briefly toward Dominic and the idea that that call may be our last conversation. I touch my index finger and thumb together.

Tap. Tap. Tap.

"Pourquoi es-tu en France?"

"Here for school. Just a student."

"Tell me what need a student has in recruiting my men?"

Tap. Tap. Tap.

"I didn't know they were your men."

"Ignorance is not an excuse."

"Je ne fais pas la même erreur deux fois." *I don't make the same mistake twice.*

He mulls it over as if deciding how he wants his steak cooked, but it's my life on the line. But it's traits like these—his body language, his ability to exude strength with presence alone, the consideration of his words before he speaks, and the even tone in which he speaks them—that keeps me fully engaged. That and his fucking suit—double-breasted, flawlessly tailored.

He's given me next to nothing, aside from the fact he was an acquaintance of my parents, and I'm willing to bet he's this controlled in every situation—threat or none.

"No. Not just a student. And from what I've been told, these plans you have—"

"Don't include you." The burn in my temple from the brute force of the gun lets me know interrupting him isn't a mistake I should make twice. Blood pours freely from my temple as I stare straight ahead at my captor, saving my wrath for the motherfucker behind me for a later date.

"So, you believe there's room for all of us, do you?"

"I'm not that ambitious."

"I think we both know that's a lie."

"La France n'est pas le pays où mes projets se réaliseront."
France is not the country where my plans will be carried out.
I consider my next declaration and decide I have nothing to
lose with the truth. "The man who murdered them owns the
town, the police. He is the reason I'm in France, to enlist
my family for help."

"You have no family left here."

"I know that, now."

He pulls a pack of cigarettes from the silk-lined pocket of
his suit jacket, lights one up, and blows the smoke toward
me. Blood glides down my neck as I maintain eye contact.

"You still haven't asked who I am." He cocks his head.
"I feel you are more Abijah than Celine's son."

I don't bother replying but briefly wonder if it's true.

"You're going to need to let me in on your plans if you
want my help."

"I don't want your help. This is a *family* matter."

"Everyone wants my help," he muses and glances at the
man at my back as if he's made his decision about me, but I
can't read it.

Tap. Tap. Tap.

My thoughts drift to Dom and how aggressive he will be
in coming after me, to Paris, to seek the truth about why I
disappeared by inserting himself into this same situation. Will
we all die out this way? At the hands of powerful men who
decide our fates—or can we become the same type of men,
change our fate, flip the script?

"As I said, I'm not interested in your help, but I would
love the name of your tailor."

*

"Slow down," Claude begs as I cut a hand through the air to silence him. After our conversation and ample warning, I was freed solely because I'm Celine's son. When the man tired of me, I was again hooded and set free two blocks from the Eiffel Tower. Dawn breaking, I ran the six miles back to my apartment to wake my roommate Claude and demand his car. He insisted on coming with me, and instead of wasting time, I allowed him in the passenger seat as I hauled ass back to the alley I was abducted from just hours before. Once there, I made him take the wheel and closed my eyes, demanding his silence, starting the slow tap of my fingers just as he hit the gas.

"Droite. Deux lampadaires. Gauche." *Right. Two lights. Left.*

"Où allons-nous? Que s'est-il passé?" *Where are we going? What happened?*

Ignoring the onslaught of questions, I concentrate on my task.

Tap. Tap. Tap.

"Droite."

Tap. Tap. Tap.

"Tourne à droite ici!" *Take a right here!*

He speeds down the narrow road as I open my eyes and search for any sign, praying I didn't miss a turn. Claude's remarks seem distant as I sift through the path that led us here, step by step.

"Tu es complètement taré. Tu le sais?" *You're fucking crazy, you know that?*

"Tais-toi! Arrête-toi ici." *Shut up! Stop here.*

The sight of a construction zone yards away, and the gate next to it elates me, and I exit Claude's car and nod toward the road.

"Go."

He glances around the abandoned street.

"Nous sommes au milieu de nulle part!" *We aren't anywhere!*

If you didn't believe in ghosts before you came here tonight, he is proof.

And for a second, I visualize what Claude sees. An abandoned street time has forgotten, not a building in sight.

"Go, now." His eyes shift in fear as he studies my bloody shirt and the raging knot at my temple. "Moins tu poseras de questions et plus tôt tu partiras, plus tu seras en sécurité." *The less questions you ask and the sooner you leave, the safer you are.* Guys like Claude need little coaxing when it comes to self-preservation, and he's as self-serving as they come.

"Je déménage." *I'm moving out!*

I slam the door as he speeds away and dial Dominic, who picks up on the first ring.

"'Sup?"

I rattle off an address. "I need details of what and who, and I need them *now*. Dom, dig deep."

"On it. I'll text you."

"You'll what?"

"Jesus." Dominic hangs up as I start a slow walk toward the gate, willing my phone to ring. If they spot me before he gets back to me, it might not be enough.

The more time that passes without a word, the more the hairs on my neck stand on end. Frantically staring at the cell phone he sent hours before, I begin to backtrack, knowing I'm a sitting duck without the information I need. Instead of ringing, the phone vibrates in my hand. I press the cue to get to the message that comes across the screen.

Relief fills me as I glance up at the gate just ahead, armed with the information I need. When I make it to the entrance, I lift my chin to the camera angled just beneath the top of the gate and lift my hands. My first text message might've just saved my life . . . or ended it. Time will tell, and I don't have a lot of it because seconds later, the flaming red faces of two men who assaulted me appear behind the gate, their voices booming as they approach.

"C'est quoi ce bordel?!" *What the fuck?!*

"Tu viens de signer ton arrêt de mort, imbécile!" *You just killed yourself, imbecile!*

Once escorted inside the gate, I realize looks are deceiving and see it's more of a compound—a cluster of one-story, red-clay buildings that once thrived in a different time. I find the idea smart, much like the street vendor game of shuffling cups to find the red ball. The tactic gives him ample time to escape if need be, but I can see the flaws. Scenarios flit through my brain as I'm led to one of three buildings fifty yards from the gate, and this time, I'm taken upstairs before being shoved into an office and onto my knees.

Behind an oak desk sits the sharply dressed man. He scrutinizes me as I do him. It's clear he's fatigued from a long night, and I do my best not to celebrate the mild surprise in his eyes. It's dawning on him at this moment that I fully meant to get captured last night. It's taken me the better part of a year to get this man's attention, and that was easy compared to finding out who he was because I never could until just moments ago—known for being unknown but so notorious in reputation that no one dares to seek him out. It's skills like this I need in order to carry out my plans to become a worthy opponent. Whispers and murmurs are all that exist about him and his organization, but no one really knows who heads it, and if they do see his face, it's the last thing they see.

The press of a gun being cocked at my temple brings that knowledge home.

Mother, greet me. Father, keep me.

After a minute-long assessment of me, he lights a cigarette and takes a deep inhale, his exhale clouding my face before he speaks.

"All right, Ezekiel. You found me. How?"

"First mistake, they faced me forward on the seat. From then on, it was a matter of tuning them out and keeping up with the turns, light counts, the time between them, and speed."

"Like you, I don't make the same mistake twice." He lifts a blistering gaze to the two men on both sides of me, and I know I might have cost them. He squares his shoulders, but I can see the sting in his eyes and some of the contempt I've earned with my stunt. "Ego can be dangerous. Maybe I should have asked who *you* are."

With the lift of his chin, the men at my side bring me to my feet before closing the door behind them.

Once alone, we stare at each other for several seconds, and I know my time is limited.

"It was your reputation that had me seeking you out. I don't sell people, drugs, or guns, and never will. Who am I? For the moment, I'm an orphan and penniless thief, and my ambitions don't suit yours. However, I'm thinking maybe we can help each other, Antoine."

* * *

Gunning the gas, I race down the deserted roads next to Cecelia's house, sorting through the details of that day and the decisions of the years after. Did I distort all our futures that night? That move was my first on a new board and gave me my first real taste for the game.

Was it the beginning or the end?

I was desperate enough to associate myself with dangerous allies back then, but I had no idea the true cost. The tradeoff.

Those who have trusted me in the past—who shared my vision—eventually ran out of loyalty for me, and it's no mystery why. I can't blame them, any of them, for their flailing allegiance, or Cecelia now for her mistrust. All I can do is try to believe the woman who came back to me, who once believed in me. A woman who, not long ago, fought me, challenged me to be the man I was. But that man was deceptive, destructive, and fucking dangerous to the people he loved. And when he lost them, he gave himself permission to run rampant. Now that I've been derailed again by the possibility of a different life, I'm being forced to confront his demons.

I downshift, the Camaro needle slanting past the hundred mark as I try to escape the ache, the burn of my mistakes. The image of Sean, Dom, and Tyler's firelit faces the night I told them about Roman—about the truth of what happened to our parents—and about my plans to bring him down. As their trusting faces come more into focus, I know no amount of speed will ever erase that memory.

Chapter Thirteen

CECELIA

AFTER ANOTHER SHIFT, I pull up to see Tobias washing Dom's Camaro in my driveway. Dazed by the sight of him shirtless, taut, ripped, he raises his head when he hears me approach and gives me the slight lift of his thick lips from where he squats, scrubbing mud off the side of the car. From the looks of it, he's put all the horses under the hood to work. But the idea of his joyride takes a back seat to any other thought when he stands covered in the afternoon sun. His skin is glistening, beckoning, his jeans riding dangerously low on his hips, showcasing his clear-cut V, just before it disappears into his dark-washed jeans. Exiting the car, I walk over to where he works, intent on his task.

"Hey," he greets me, his voice chalky as though he's been shouting for most of the day.

"Hey back," I reply, looking at the car. "I see you went for a ride."

"Yeah, it's been a while since I let loose."

Something's wrong. It's so clear to see in the light creases next to his eyes, the weight on his shoulders.

"Everything okay?"

"Yeah." He tosses his sponge in a bucket before pressing a kiss to my temple. Retrieving the hose from the ground, he pauses his spray and shakes his head in afterthought. "I mean, no, not really okay, not today. But can we table this particular talk for later?"

"Sure," I offer easily, leaving him to it just before he snatches me by the wrist and pulls me toward him. His eyes bore into mine as he crowds me next to the car. He dips and kisses me, and I allow it, my heart thundering into the moment. My body begs me to relieve it of the ache, but my mind still forbids me from stepping into the free fall I've allowed myself one too many times before. It's not a matter of falling, but a matter of making sure I know how to land at this point. Denying I love him, am *still* in love with him, is pointless. Denying he's here and sincerely wants this to work is taking effort on my part. But forgiving him, that's what's stifling our progress. It's still too soon to embrace it—embrace him fully. Yet in those few seconds, he separates my lips with his tongue, tasting me thoroughly, and I can't help but feed my greed. He kisses me for long minutes, and I drop my purse, my appetite begging me for a minute more before he pulls away and presses his forehead to mine.

"I said I wouldn't hide anything from you, and I won't. I have these bad days, sometimes."

"What's bad about them?"

He pulls my hand from around his neck and kisses the back of it before pressing my fingers to his temple. "Here."

"Does it have to do with Dominic?"

"A lot of the time, yeah. Driving his car . . . I don't know, I got lost in my head a little."

"I'm sorry. I just, I thought you might want to drive it instead of my Audi."

He shakes his head. "Don't be. Maybe it was good for me."

"Not by the looks of it."

All I can feel is the ache seeping from him and my instinctual need to comfort him. "Sometimes I wish—" he exhales. "Sometimes I wish I dreamed the way you do, so I could exorcise my thoughts that way, and maybe I wouldn't have these days."

"No, you don't, Tobias. I promise you that you don't." I dart my eyes away. "I should let Beau out. I need a shower."

He nods and releases me. Shutting the front door behind me, I push out a long breath. Being in the same space with him again, there's no denying the sheer force of what his presence does to me. I'm still breathless from his kiss, core throbbing from the need thrumming between us, but his pain overshadows all of that. So much of me wants to give in, hear his words, take them to heart and truly let go of all of the grudges so we can start to heal together—in a way that brings us closer.

I have to try. I have to give in, meet him halfway at some point.

It's clear we're living the opposite of what we collectively pictured after our reunion in the parking lot, and I can physically feel the disappointment in both of us every time we lock eyes.

I've barely let him touch me or given him a chance to explain himself. But I can't lose myself in him again, at least not completely. Getting physical with Tobias is not simply sex. It's close to a religious experience. I'm not in denial so much that I don't realize that I'm the one preventing our progress.

I head to the fridge to grab a water bottle and decide on something stronger. Maybe a drink will help relax me to the point of starting a conversation. Reaching for my whiskey tumbler, I open the freezer for some ice and see that he's grocery shopped, and not only that, he's zip-locked red grapes for me and frozen them. Visions of the days where I lounged by the pool at my father's mansion sucking on them while he swam laps run through my mind. Though our history was brief, we were together twenty-four-seven for weeks, studying each other's habits, learning each other's bodies, falling crazy in love. Then, he'd used *my* brand of toothpaste. And despite my resentment-filled comment, I do know him, his habits, his moods, and it was jealousy from my dream that told me otherwise.

The devil is in the details, and I remember my devil well. It's gestures like this that bring me back to that time he doted on me endlessly. The dinners he used to cook for me, the baths he drew that we took together, and our long talks during. The long hours playing chess, our time in the clearing drinking Louis Latour while stargazing. Making love for hours and hours, covered in sweat, eyes locked, bodies humming, before we fell into an exhausted sleep just to wake up and do it all over again.

Closing my eyes, I fight the urge to go to him, to bridge the gap. Every night we seem to call a truce, and he wraps around me, dragging me into his body, waiting for me to ask questions, to start a conversation, but I haven't. I'm still trying to give myself permission to be happy about it, to let my guard down, to embrace him here, permanently.

"Just one, okay?"

I jump. "Will you stop sneaking up behind me?!"

"I didn't sneak up on you. You've been staring into the freezer since I came into the room."

I shut the door. His eyes drop to the frozen grapes I hadn't realized I pulled from the bag. "You used to drive me crazy sucking on those while you were reading."

I toss a few into my glass along with some ice and turn back to the counter to pour my drink. "Why only one?"

"We have plans tonight, and I need you alert." He opens the back door to let Beau out. "I've got somewhere I need to take you."

"Where are we going?"

"A meetup," he answers simply.

I reel on him. "Are you fucking kidding me?"

"It's just to introduce you to those looking out for us here in Virginia."

Simmering, I toss back the whiskey. "I thought you said no one was looking for me."

"They aren't looking for *you*," he answers, his eyes conveying the rest. The fact that *he* needs protection should scare me, but it doesn't. "I was going to take a quick shower."

"Then I'll take a quick *bath*." By the time I finish my drink, he's already in the shower, no doubt to grant me space. Undressing, I see him watching me in the mirror from where he stands, lathering up his body. Eyes locked, I pull off my T-shirt and bra, my skin pinkening from the blush creeping up my neck. He smirks, and I lift my chin, taking my painstaking time to bend, lowering both my jeans and panties. I don't bother to look back because I know how cruel the act was. I can't help but bite my lips at his watered-down curse.

Stepping into my clawfoot tub, I admire him through the clear shower door as he runs a sponge down his body. The bathroom is the only room I fully remodeled when I bought the house because it was the size of a closet, and though now it's doubled in size, it still seems small with his proximity.

Ezekiel Tobias King is devilishly dark perfection, especially when wet.

And he claims he's mine. *Forever* mine.

Sinking into the tub, I watch him shamelessly as he discards his sponge and runs a handful of shampoo through his dark mane before lifting fiery eyes to mine.

Wet lashes accentuate the surreal color of his eyes. Through the stream of water, I see it so clearly. I'm twenty again and reaching for him just as he meets me halfway into the shower before kissing me senseless while impaling me on his cock. A cock that has stirred to life fully now as the seconds pass and we stare off, both engulfed by memories and coming unglued with need. He's engorged now, thick, veiny, the sight of his tip, mouthwatering. In an act of cruelty, he turns his back, letting the spray wash over the heavily inked wings stretched out along his shoulders. It's then I see the distortion, the clear interruption of the pattern I've traced with my lips so many times before. Exit wounds.

One just beneath his right shoulder blade and one above his right hip.

Instant tears emerge at the sight of them and what it means. He was gravely injured while we were apart. Hazy images of the night he took me so unforgivingly at my father's mansion emerge, and I can't at all recall feeling them, but they could have been there.

"Tobias," I whisper hoarsely, the blood draining from my

face, but he doesn't hear me. It's everything I can do to keep from going to him, to demand answers, but there's a partition far thicker than the glass and porcelain between us. He doesn't want to push me, and I don't want to be pushed. He seems just as reluctant at this point to get physical with me for a reason I can't pinpoint, and I'm not sure how I feel about it. As if reading my thoughts, he turns to me, weighing my expression before ripping his gaze away, another curse leaving him as he turns off the shower, grabs a towel, and leaves the bathroom soaking wet.

Chapter Fourteen

TOBIAS

FEAR.

That's all I saw through the glass door of the shower. That, combined with the fact that she doesn't fucking trust me, is enough to have me questioning my renewed presence in her life. That's the second edge of the sword that grates the most. And it's the sick feeling of that truth, a continual slow pour of the acid constantly churning in my chest, in my gut. The fear in her eyes isn't because she's afraid of me. She's afraid of what being part of *us* can and has done to her. Still, she holds her head regally high on her slender neck as she rides next to me toward our arranged meeting. Hair still wet, she glosses her lips before smoothing and securing it back into a ponytail. Staring out the window, she remains mute as I grip her hand and bring it to my mouth, pressing my lips against the back of it.

"We have to do this, Cecelia. But I'm hoping this doesn't encroach much on our life here."

"I know."

"We can't negotiate this."

"I know."

"I promised you would be *in the know* every step of the way."

"I want that."

I glance her way, briefly taking my eyes off the road. "Are you sure?"

"Yes," she says icily. "In the know is a luxury I *paid for* a long time ago."

"You'll have it, but it's not going to pay off the way you want, at least not at first."

She glances back out of the window, and I slow to a stop on the side of the road because I want her to hear me. She's trapped in the car this way, no escaping the conversation, which is where I need her for this confession. I want to be ready for whatever reaction she has. She frowns when I pull out my phone and compose a text, holding up our meeting. She watches me expectantly when I shoot off the message and face her.

"We're going to have to have one of those conversations now."

"Tobias—" She shakes her head. "I understand why we need security."

"There's more to it."

She bristles. "Goddamnit, isn't it always something?"

"Yes. That's my point. There will always be something. *Always.* No matter what, there will always be something, and you have to decide if being with me is worth this never-ending hassle and, more importantly, losing your life. *Your life*, Cecelia, because once you make this decision, there's no going back."

"I made the decision years ago, until you decided for me, remember?"

"Stop being so fucking flippant about this," I bark. "And maybe I'm thinking that it's still a decision for you because maybe you don't *feel* the same way anymore."

"I'm not being flippant. I'm adjusting. What haven't you told me?"

"Everything I need to because you haven't given me a fucking chance!" I clench my fists, trying my best to level out my temper. "And I get it, okay? I do, but this really is that serious."

She licks her lower lip, her eyes remorseful. "I'm trying."

"I know. Dom's body wasn't even in the ground before Miami retaliated."

Her eyes widen. "What?"

"They came from Florida guns blazing and declared all-out war, just as we finished cleaning up the mess at Roman's house. We were completely unprepared."

"Jesus."

I turn in my seat and fully face her.

"Within a week, they hit every fucking southeast chapter of the brotherhood and successfully killed a raven in *every single one*, including *Alicia's* brother. That's how we met, at his funeral. I was there the day they buried him."

She nods solemnly.

"But that's not when we got together. That funeral was just one of a dozen I attended in the month after you left, including Dominic's."

Her eyes fill with nothing but empathy, the reaction of a true queen, not a jealous ex, as she tries to wrap her mind around what I'm telling her.

"They came in droves, Cecelia, and all for. *My. Head.* You have to remember that only a few founding members knew of my association. Once I was outed by Miami, I became enemy number one. Sean and I split the chapters, amped-up security even though we weren't really on speaking terms. We weren't on any kind of terms at that point, but our dedication was unshakable, and we worked together, and both stepped up. That war lasted a solid six months before it finally started to die out. And it only reinforced my decision to keep you far, far away."

"But . . . I thought all of those defecting in Miami were killed that night?"

"Some got away, and when they did, they armed up and came back with a vengeance. Miami was one of our best crews for a reason. They were the largest and had the most connections. A few of them had mafia ties, and they were *not* fucking around. They went straight for the head, me, and it got bad. When that news spread after that shitshow at your dad's house, my authority and control was put into question by the brotherhood. Some thought I'd turned my back for personal reasons. News got muddled, and word spread fast. And it didn't help that we were losing brothers left and right. Families got pissed, and all of them blamed me. It was my worst fucking nightmare. I was sure we were all about to get exposed, and every time I lived past a new threat, I assumed it was about to be over. The longer it went on, the more funerals I attended, the more I tried to right the world of the families that got destroyed before the government stepped in and snatched me. For the first year, I was sure it was all over."

"But nothing ever came of it? No authorities caught wind?"

"The war was spread out across several states. Thankfully, we had enough feds with wings on our payroll to destroy the tie of the markings in the media, but as far as leaving a trail, as careful as we were, I wasn't sure about it because it was an all-out street war by that point."

She swallows. "How many died?"

"Too many." I stroke her cheek with my thumb. "Way too fucking many on both sides."

"Those scars on your back. They're from gunshots?"

I nod.

"When?"

"A year to the day I sent you away, to the day Dom died. Not a coincidence. I was finishing a run a block from my Charlotte office when I got gunned down on a fucking city street. Just more evidence that it wasn't over, which only convinced me I was a fool to think about ever coming for you."

"Did you—" her voice clogs—"did you . . ."

"Almost die? Yes. I was touch and go for about a week, from what Tyler said. And honestly, at that point, I didn't give a fuck if I did. It would have been a relief for me."

Her eyes water. Tentatively, she reaches out and cups my jaw. I cover her hand with mine.

"The aftermath of that night turned out to be far more than we could handle. I was in no position to drag you into that mess, no matter how much I wanted you back. I had eyes on you everywhere. So did your father up until the day he died. It was a silent partnership with my birds and his added security."

She winces.

"I'm not saying this to guilt you, Cecelia. I just want you to know they may seem like excuses, but they are good reasons for me, reasons why I couldn't contact you, couldn't come to you. It was way too fucking dangerous the first few *years*. Those still wearing wings, still dedicated to the cause, were heavily vetted during that time. To some others, the ones we weren't sure about, we made them believe the brotherhood was dissolving, becoming a thing of the past. Once all hell broke loose, we shrank in size, and in the end, Sean and I decided it was for the best. We knew what we were doing as far as you were concerned. It was safer for us to hurt you emotionally and for you to hate us for it. The more you resented us and stayed away, the better off you were."

She runs her tongue along her lower lip, her eyes searching mine before she pulls her hand away.

"After all this time, you and Sean really never . . . talked?"

"I tried," I admit. "Of course I tried. I tried to get him into the business side when his son was born to keep him safe, to keep Tessa safe. But no, Sean and I haven't been the same since the day they returned from France and saw us together."

Her voice is distant when she speaks. "All this time, I thought at least you had each other."

I shake my head. "I had my precious fucking club, and that was all I had left, and it was falling apart day by day. Everything I worked for went up in flames the night Dominic died. And I didn't care at that point, but it was the people who depended on me, on *us*, that kept me going. When the fog of war finally lifted, I got lost. I got lost in my head. And I guess in a way you could say—I went a little crazy."

"I'm . . ."

"Sorry? Don't ever be. It was only the first real taste of reaping what I've sown. I told you long ago I knew it would catch up with me at some point. I just wasn't expecting it to happen so soon. There's more, and it's coming, but they're waiting for us."

She nods as I turn the ignition and glance in the rearview at the necklace hanging from it. I reach up and pinch the metal wings between my fingers. "When I got here, Sean texted me, asking about you, and for the first time since Dom died, he asked about *me*. I think he's finally trying to forgive me."

Dropping the necklace, it sways back and forth as I put the car into gear.

"We'll never be the same, but I knew that when I chose you over him, and *that* was before." I exhale, and dread cloaks me as I fill her in on the rest. "Cecelia, they will *always* be after me, and I use the term loosely because the *they* is interchangeable. The night I came to you with that head wound? That was the result of another attempt on me that I wasn't fucking expecting. I put more holes in him than necessary to make sure that was the end of the threat, but instead of doing what I should have and erasing any more threats, I laid low and came straight to you that night."

"Who was it?"

"A house call from an enemy I made in France in my early days for an associate. And there's a really good chance that's not the last retaliation. There are long memories in this game." She mulls over my words. "With you, I continually broke my number one rule. With you, I wasn't thinking like I should have. I never really did after we got together, but I didn't want to be without you."

I stare at the open road before us.

"If we do this, really do this, you need to know, if they ever get to you, the most valuable thing in my fucking life, it's *game over* for me, Cecelia. End of. I can barely handle dealing with the possibility of losing you. I've only *survived* this long without Dominic, and losing you, and Sean, my respect, my purpose, I just stopped fucking caring about everything that mattered to me personally. I became someone I didn't recognize, and there was no one there to stop me from . . ." Flickers of the nights I let depravity consume me flash briefly, shadowing the rest of the light of day in darkness. I reach into those memories in an attempt to describe my state of mind. "I felt better not fucking caring, liberated in a way I have never been because I had nothing to lose. I had no one close to me anymore to worry about, and I was relieved. My head wasn't racing so much, and I wasn't . . ." I shake my head. "If they get to you now," I grit out, "they take *everything*. So, this meeting is more than necessary. But all of this can stop *right here, right now*. I can't walk away from you again, I can't push you away again, and I never will, but you can order me away. If that's your decision, I'll respect it, because Cecelia, there's a very real chance you could die for loving me, and I can only promise to *try* to keep you safe."

It only takes her a second to nod before she straightens in her seat. "Like I said, I made the decision a long time ago, Tobias. Let's go."

Chapter Fifteen

TOBIAS

Age Twenty-One

WALKING UNDER THE cover of the canopy of trees at the entry of the park, I shove my hands into my jeans, keeping a leisurely pace. A lone bird swoops in from above, catching my eye as it flies overhead before landing on one of the low-hanging branches. Eyes fixed on the bird, I feel his watchful return stare following my progress as I stroll past. My mind wars with the significance of its appearance as my gut tries to decipher if it's a warning or a signal to keep going. I decide on the latter, walking further along the outskirts of the park. It doesn't take me long to spot the group of men gathered in pairs at a cluster of tables, most of them older, mid- to late-sixties. All of them are situated across from each other, chessboards in between. Only one man sits alone, the pieces on his board scattered as if mid-game, the chair opposite him empty. Pulse kicking up, I take the last few strides, positioning myself amongst them before sliding into the vacant chair. The men surrounding us don't so much as spare me a glance, too immersed in their own games.

The man I'm sitting across from doesn't acknowledge my presence in the slightest when I survey him, his face etched with years of wear; deep lines in his forehead and around his lips. His thick, greying hair is on the longer side, and his worn clothes are slightly wrinkled—as if he gave no thought about his appearance and simply rolled out of bed. He situates the board pieces delicately, caressing each one with the pads of his fingers before releasing them as he sets them back to their starting position on the worn board.

Seeming satisfied with his ritual, he finally lifts his eyes— the color of mine—to sweep me with the same careful inspection. His lips twitch in amusement at the slip of my expression, due to our likeness, a clear familial relation.

Since I've been in France, and due to whispers about my birth father, I've grown more curious about the man he was before his sickness claimed him. I've discovered some sparse details from Antoine, who was, from what I gathered, at one point in time his associate when my parents were together. My father was, in essence, an executor of orders for the highest bidder. Many feared Abijah. Some respected him. As a thousand questions bud on my tongue, I don't dare ask them. I'm here on invitation, and I'm not about to fuck it up with my curiosity before I find out why the invite was extended.

He wasn't on the exhaustive list of contacts Delphine so carefully constructed for me—that consisted mostly of my mother's relatives—all of whom are former activists, and very few on my birth father's side. In truth, he's an unlikely ally. Skepticism takes hold for his motivations, but I know without a doubt I'm staring at Abijah's father, my grandfather. Someone I would never have considered to enlist help from in any form, the fear ingrained inside of me when I was young. The notion embedded deeply by my mother that Abijah was a man I should never be curious about or seek out in any capacity. Because of that, I've rarely, if ever, given much thought to his extended family.

As we study each other, some part of me recognizes the possibility that because my mother fled France—taking Abijah's only son while abandoning him completely for another man—it may have caused an indirect grudge for all involved, including me.

I weigh his expression closely for any trace of that grudge or resentment. Instead, I find something resembling joy in his eyes, as if he's been thirsty for the sight of me all of these years.

But maybe it's not me he sees as he stares back at me, but the ghost of my birth father, a son he lost to mental illness long ago. I can sense an inkling of that bond now as I stare back at him. A bond I had at one point with the man who raised me and that I now have with my brother.

The spring sun begins to beat down on our heads as the morning clouds part, lighting up the board.

"Se voir accorder le premier déplacement est perçu par certains comme un avantage. Je considère que c'est mon avantage. Avec ce seul coup, je peux souvent dire si mon adversaire est agressif ou non. Fais le premier pas, Ezekiel, je suis assez curieux de voir." *Being granted the first move is seen by some as an advantage. I consider it my advantage. With that one move, I can often tell whether my opponent is aggressive or not. Do make the first move, Ezekiel. I am quite curious to see.*

"Je n'ai jamais joué." *I've never played.*

Another twitch of lips and a flicker of what I perceive as pride shines clear in his eyes.

"La plupart répondraient, 'Je ne peux pas jouer.' Je préfère ta réponse." *Most would respond, 'I can't play.' I like yours much better.*

He takes a pawn and moves it two spaces diagonally before pulling it back in its starting place on the board.

"Tu ne peux avancer ton pion de deux cases que la première fois; une fois qu'il est en jeu, le pion ne peut se déplacer qu'une fois par tour. Lorsque tu retires tes doigts du pion, c'est joué, tu ne peux plus revenir en arrière." *Only the first time can you advance a pawn two spaces; once it's in play, the pawn can only move once per turn. Once you remove your fingers from the pawn, it's done, never to be pulled back.*

He draws his brows in question, and I give him a slow dip of my chin in understanding. He speaks clear English with his next words. "I was very unhappy to hear about your first move."

Antoine.

It's the only conclusion I can draw.

I barely have time to register the implications of what he's saying as he gestures back to the board. "Pay close attention, Ezekiel."

He moves down the line, demonstrating the horizontal and vertical movement rules of each piece until I've grasped a mild understanding of them. He does this silently for several minutes as I watch on, rapt, paying close attention to the way he regards each piece.

"Vous considérez le pion comme le plus important?" *You consider the pawn most important?*

"Cela dépend de la connaissance du pion et de sa position.

Et puis, l'union fait la force, n'est-ce pas?" *It depends on the knowledge of the pawn and its position. And there's a comfort in numbers, is there not?*

The question is directly related to my reason for seeking help in France, which lets me know just how long he's been aware of me and my quest here, and how deep his connections run. Shoving my pride aside, I admit the truth I've gathered through years of isolation here and nod. The time I feel most at peace is at home, surrounded by my brothers.

"Mais tu vois, s'il est correctement positionné, le pion seul peut devenir l'une des pièces les plus puissantes du plateau, et a la capacité de mettre le Roi en échec." *But you see, if positioned correctly, the pawn alone can become one of the most powerful pieces on the board and has the ability to check the king.*

He lifts the piece and turns it in his hands with great care, and I watch him, engrossed in his movement before he sets it back on the board.

A lesson in chess is not at all what I expected this morning. The irony strikes me that as much as I've compared my moves in my time in France to this game, I only know the basics, the essence of it, the central goal.

Awareness of the strongest kind overwhelms me, and I welcome it, thankful I trusted my instincts earlier on my walk here. There have been a few times in my life where I was certain about my path, by way of overall electricity that consumed me and told me I was exactly where I was supposed to be at a certain point in time. The first time was in the clearing the night my parents died. The second time it hit was the last night I spent in that diner with Preston. And I feel the same zing now as I lift my eyes to the man sitting opposite me.

"Tu m'as dévoilé ton handicap avec tes premiers mots; ce qui n'est pas une sage décision dans un jeu de tactique. Je sais déjà que je peux et que je vais te battre, mais ton avantage est maintenant le premier coup." *You gave away your handicap with your first words to me; not a wise decision in a game of tactics. I already know I can and will beat you, but your advantage now is the first move.*

He gestures toward me to begin, and I summon instinct, moving the first piece into play. His brows lift in mild surprise, and he gives me a slow nod.

"Do you play often?"

He kicks back in his seat, the metal legs scrubbing slightly against the pavement. We both know my question has nothing to do with the game.

"I retired long ago, but I dabble on occasion if I have good reason to." A silent communication passes between us until he lowers his eyes and makes his first move.

Chapter Sixteen

CECELIA

HAULING A BAG of groceries in, I deposit it on the kitchen table, curious as to why Beau hasn't pummeled me with his usual sloppy greeting. Surveying the back yard out the window, I come up empty for my two Frenchmen and begin to search the house. It's in the study that I discover them both occupied. Beau stands propped with his front paws on Tobias's thighs, nudging open his cupped hand to feed on potato chips, while Tobias sleeps practically comatose in my oversized, round chair. He's in nothing but black sweatpants and wool socks, a soft snore coming from his gaping mouth. Bags of snacks and candies surround him, and I spy a half-eaten tub of Ben & Jerry's peeking up from the end table. The TV blares next to me, muffling my laugh as Beau searches Tobias for remnants of more oil-soaked snacks.

It's both funny and sad, and it's clear my constant absence, along with the space I'm putting between us, is aiding in the creation of a French couch potato. Due to the state of sleep, it's clear he's eaten copious amounts of carbs that he used to forbid me from indulging in.

A splayed hand rests on his chest, and his legs are hooked

over the side of the chair. Beau busies himself licking the other hand clean.

It's evident he wasn't expecting me home so soon. Aching to go to him, to swipe the remaining crumbs from his face and lick the leftover chocolate from beneath his mouth, I watch him as he sleeps. When I bought this house, I never pictured him here, and if I'm honest, I never imagined him in any domestic capacity. Sure, I lived with him in my father's house, but then it was all fine dining, wine tasting, nights spent playing chess next to the fire, and sexy sessions that had us sweat-soaked and gasping for breath.

This dynamic is completely foreign.

Unease sneaks in that he's so bored already, filling his days eating crap and binge-watching TV.

That gnawing of guilt and the fact that this is how he's spending his time here only further reiterates my idea that he doesn't fit, that small-town living will bore him to the point of restlessness.

Even in his slob state, he's the most beautiful fucking man I've ever laid eyes on. And if I wanted to, I could go to him right now, swipe the crust off, and lose myself in him. I hate that I'm being so resolute, but my conscience demands it, and he's forced me to be like this because of his past behavior. It's been a little over a week since he showed up, and I'm determined to stick it out for my own purpose. He needs to know that any time he's spending frustrated with me for the space I'm keeping between us, I've felt a thousand-fold—fuck that, a million times over when he pushed me away, exiled me and belittled our relationship. All the while I fucking begged him to acknowledge us. Immature as it may be to hold that grudge, I suffered at his hands too much to just give in. And I won't. Not until I'm sure he understands I won't ever stand for that again.

It's not just the sins he committed and the lies he told in our time together that he never had to answer for, but his cruel denial months ago when I made a fool of myself. However, those combined are reason enough.

But the longer I watch him, the more drawn in I become, a little more helpless to the pull, a constant thrum of need for him, and only him.

Images of our past taunt me as I gaze on. A flash of me on my knees in nothing but panties as he fisted my hair and pushed his thick cock in my mouth, ordering me to suck. And I did, my reward . . . the stoking fire and satisfaction from the control I gave up evident in his eyes, in the grunts and murmurs from his mouth before he fucked me raw. I can indulge in the hellfire and draw that same satisfaction at any point in time, but sexual frustration will not be what breaks me. It will not be what has me giving in.

I honestly don't know what it's going to take, but I trust myself to know it when I feel it.

I'll always want him. That's a given. My body, heart, soul, all that makes me who I am, will forever ache for him whether he's near or far. That's a foregone conclusion my heart made long ago. But it's that same addict's heart that I refuse to give in to. For the moment, fuck my heart, I need peace of mind.

Beau finally finishes his meal, doing a half-decent job of cleaning Tobias up before he bounds off the chair to greet me. I bend and run my fingers over his ears as he bobs in front of me enthusiastically, telling me about his day.

When the TV blasts the introduction of a new episode of *Storage Wars*, Tobias jars awake, his eyes wild and on alert as he jerks into a sitting position. He searches the space, eyes widening in surprise when he sees me standing just inside the doorway. A sleepy, sexy-as-fuck smile graces his stubbled jaw before he realizes he's been busted grazing on the foods he'd once forbidden me from eating. He quickly snatches some of the bags into his fist before hanging his head, a sheepish smile gracing his lips. "You're judging me."

"Abso-fucking-lutely, yes, I am." I bob my head for emphasis.

"You're home early."

"Only by a half-hour." Beau whines at my feet. "I guess I should thank you for feeding the dog."

One side of his mouth lifts at my raised brow. "I'm deeply ashamed."

"Uh huh." I cut through the hilarity of the situation and inch closer in an attempt to read him. "Did you have another bad day?"

"No, not really." He seems to search his thoughts before his face lights up. "Did you *know* there is a show about treasure hunters who bid on stranger's storage rooms? Incredible what they find!" He slaps his thigh and widens his eyes with pure delight. "This we can *binge-watch* together." He's truly excited about this prospect, and it's all I can do to keep from buckling with laughter.

"You truly have been living on an alternate planet, Mr. King."

Flaming eyes rake over me, and he reaches out a hand, and I take it before he pulls me into him so I'm straddling his lap. "Too fucking far away from you," he murmurs softly, pulling off my beanie before stretching his fingers through my hair. "You're cold." He cups my face in his hands before sliding them up and down my arms, creating friction to warm me. Leaning in, he presses his lips to mine briefly before he nuzzles my neck.

Sinking onto him, I get lost in the feel of his olive skin, the taut and deeply defined muscles along his shoulders. "You're going to get a relationship gut and blame it on me."

"I wouldn't give a shit," he says, squeezing my hand when I run it over his carb-bloated belly.

"You are going to get some greys soon, too." I lean in with a grin and press my cold nose to his. "You're getting old."

"I've got plenty of prime years left," he scoffs, lifting me onto his lap so I can feel his growing erection, "and when the grey comes in, I'm going to let myself go. Eat fried chicken and drink *whole* milk."

"Ah, well, I have no say in this? I'll be stuck with a chunky chicken-fried Frenchman?"

"You will love me anyway," he says in his thick brogue, again nestling into my neck. "Even if I'm fat and grey."

I tug at his unkept onyx hair for another shot of amber, unable to stop the slight movement of my hips over his thickening cock, my words conflicting with my need for more. "I prefer we wait a bit longer to let ear hair be an issue."

He jostles me in his lap. "Oh, let's have fried chicken for dinner."

Narrowing my eyes, I glance at the end table and lift a brow when I see the little antique box. "You got into my emergency weed stash."

"Maybe." He lifts guilty eyes to mine, and though he's being playful, the sure tug of the truth of his new reality is starting to weigh heavily, zapping some of the ever-present sexual energy.

"You're bored here."

His brief hesitation only confirms it. He grips me tighter when my fingers relax. "I'm not."

"Tobias, you don't have to quit. I told you when you got here. I won't let you. The work you're doing is too important to the people who rely on you, and it matters to you."

"You matter more, and I'm on vacation," he insists, running his hands along my back where my wings lay. When his eyes flare and his hands begin to explore, I push at his shoulders.

"I've got groceries to put away." It's a shitty excuse for breaking the intimacy, but I use it anyway and feel the hesitance in his arms before he releases me. I stand and grab some of the trash, and he grips my wrist, my hand wrapped around a soupy pint of Cherry Garcia.

"I will clean up my own mess, Trésor, and it wasn't a bad day," he insists, before releasing me and standing to gather his trash.

"But it wasn't a good one, either. What's next, an Xbox and a headset? You going to turn into one of *those* guys?"

"Why the fuck not? I've earned it." He follows me to the kitchen, trash in hand, and tosses it in the bin.

"I'm not saying you don't deserve it."

He crosses his arms over his taut chest, his dark hair limp and slightly curled around his ears. "Why don't you just say what you want to say?"

"This isn't you."

"No? Fine, what would please you?"

"It's not about pleasing me."

"Isn't it? You seemed to have some preconceived notion

about me and this life with you. I guess I'm not living up to it."

"I have no notion. That's the point."

"And I'm telling you, I'm exactly where I want to fucking be."

"Well, pardon me if I don't believe you because I know better."

"Yeah, well, excuse me if I think the same about you."

I pause with a granola box halfway out of the bag. "What's that supposed to mean?"

He crowds me where I stand at the kitchen table. His eyes lit with animosity. "This isn't you, either. This is the life of the Cecelia Horner—who you might have been—before you knew what true living meant for you. You aren't exactly living the standard of the woman who ran a board meeting with spiked fucking heels eight months ago and spent her spare time taking down adversaries of her choosing."

"You're calling me a hypocrite?"

He presses in. "Yes. I saw you. I saw the victory in your eyes when you cornered your prey. I'm not faulting you for the life you've chosen to live, but it's not exactly suited for who you *really* are, is it?"

"I know who I am."

"Do you? Because the woman who left me eight months ago was far more fucking daring than the one I hold at night."

I slam down a box of angel hair pasta on the table, and he lets out an exasperated breath. He begins to stalk off but, thinking better of it, turns around and rushes toward me. "I'm not going to act like I'm not having a hard fucking time not being in control—or in the know—but the least you can do is admit to me that this isn't what you see for yourself permanently. You're hiding because I hurt you. Your confidence took a blow because I broke your heart, *again*."

"You don't get to credit yourself for the life I chose to live the minute I walked out of your office. You don't have that much sway over me, not anymore. You lost that right," I snap.

Jaw set, I see the sting I inflicted with my words in his eyes a second before I flit my gaze away and start unloading the rest of the groceries. He keeps his stare on me while I wordlessly finish my task, refusing him the fight he wants. I feel his disappointment when I don't rise to his challenge as silence lingers between us before he turns and storms out of the kitchen. The front door slams minutes later, and I know he's gone for another run.

Later that night, I feel the dip of the bed before he pulls me tightly to him, so I'm snug against his chest. Wrapped in his arms, I feel his apology, his need to make it all right with every beat of his steady heart against my back, but I stay mute with the burn of the truth he spoke. If the conclusions I drew were also the truth—which they were due to his bite—then we're both adrift for the moment.

Chapter Seventeen

TOBIAS

Age Twenty-One

"WHAT'S WITH YOU today, man?" Tyler asks, taking a chair as I toss another log onto the fire. Sean and Dominic finish setting up camp just as the sun begins to dip past the tree line.

I'm still jet-lagged from my flight in, on Paris time, the realities I'm living between worlds blurring as I scan the clearing. The burden of maintaining my roles in each is beginning to wear on me, but I refuse to let it deter me. Especially after today. Ten years ago, in this very place, I set out on a path to avenge my parents' murders, and being here grounds me, reminds me of how far I have to go to seek that justice. But my presence here, in this place I consider sacred, also lets me know how far I've come and how close I'm getting.

"I'll get to it," I tell him as I glance over at Dominic who takes his chair and meets my pensive gaze. I swat at the mosquito sucking on my forearm as Sean uncaps a beer. Fresh from his first school pep rally, Triple Falls' budding star quarterback is still clad in his jersey.

"I told you we aren't drinking tonight." I snatch the bottle from his hand just as he lifts it to his mouth.

Sean glares up at me. "You make it through a two-a-day football practice and tell me you don't deserve a beer. And newsflash, I have a set of parents. They live a few streets over from yours, and they've taught me right from wrong."

"As much good as that's done you," Tyler jabs.

"This is important," I snap. Sean's eyes flit to the confiscated beer in my hand before I toss it into the flames. This past summer was supposed to be my time to reconnect with my brothers, but I was absent, often flying back to France, and mostly because of Antoine's demands. But I still need him for the moment, so I'm stuck being his errand boy until I can find a way to be less dependent. He's been the resource I thought he would be, supplying me with damn near everything I've needed while remaining greedy with his wealth, so he's the only leg I have to stand on. It's the right move on his part to keep me contained, keep me reliant on him, but it's stifling my progress to the point I need to make moves to ensure I can sweep his legs if need be.

"Can we get on with this?" Tyler says, pulling my attention from the fire.

"You have somewhere you need to be?"

"Yeah, I do, actually." He darts his eyes away.

"He's been disappearing a lot," Sean supplies. "And won't tell us who she is."

"Because there is no *she*," Tyler snaps.

Sean grins. "Methinks the lady doth protest too much."

"Methinks you're going to lose some baby teeth if you don't shut your fucking mouth."

I ignore their exchange, eyes trained on Tyler.

"Anything I need to know?" He jerks his chin in reply. He's clearly hiding something, and it's personal from his bite. There most definitely is a *she*, and that's one of the reasons I've called the meeting.

Sean kicks back in his camping chair, and in a sudden move, Dom leaps from his own and shoves Sean's chest, tipping him over. Dom and Tyler both chuckle as Sean curses and stands brushing the dirt from his pants before fishing out a pack of cigarettes from his jeans.

"You broke my fucking smokes, dickhead."

"Shouldn't be smoking anyway," Dom says, pulling a joint from his backpack.

I lift a brow. "Are you fucking serious right now?"

"Serious enough, brother," he mumbles, lips wrapped around the joint as Sean strikes his Zippo.

"Just hold off on that a minute," I order.

Dom reads me and nods, tucking the joint behind his ear.

"What's the update on the garage?" I ask, between the three of them. "How close are we?"

"It's done. As soon as I get my settlement money," Dom says. "No other offers on the table because no one else around here has the money to buy it."

Tyler chimes in, his brows drawn tight. "What's the point of the garage with everything else we have going on? Is it just a front?"

"No," I say, gaze straying back to the fire. "It will be a legitimate business. We'll be fixing cars and taking money for it. The legal age for mechanics in this state is sixteen. But we'll need a few more in order to make a decent profit and handle overhead costs."

"I know someone," Tyler adds. "Name's Russell. He's been

teaching us how to work on the classics Sean's uncle left us. He's old enough. And he's fucking good."

"Trust him?"

"Yeah," Tyler nods. "He's good people and never been printed either." We have a strict no-print rule when vetting new birds for obvious reasons. We don't want anyone associated with us with fingerprints in any database—even as a juvenile—which makes it harder to find the type of recruits we need. We need smart thieves and good men, but in our neck of the woods and with the meth spike, they're hard to come by.

"Bring him in. I want to meet him."

Tyler nods. "I'll see if he knows anyone else."

My eyes drift back to the flames, and it's then I'm struck by the thought of my parents, locked in a room as similar flames surround them while they scream for help. It's no mystery why that image of them is weighing on my mind.

Picking up some kindling, I toss it into the fire. "I saw Roman up close for the first time today."

"Where?" Sean asks.

"The library," Dominic supplies, "when he came to pick me up."

I glance over at my brother, mildly surprised. He was in the far corner of the library, engrossed in his book when Roman strolled in, looking weightless, as if he wasn't responsible for ruining lives. But I guess he wouldn't be weighed down with guilt. Men like him consider my parents, "the help", no more than liabilities whose murder probably inconvenienced him more than anything else. He'll never know that my mother was the only woman capable of getting me out of my moods, of soothing my temper with a few words, of making me smile not just with expression but with my whole being. He'll never understand the notion of my stepfather's American dream. Or that my parents chose the town he's monopolized to create a better life for us—and for the woman he rescued from her mad husband and her bastard son. Even if he was made aware, I doubt he would care. Because it was evident by the way he treated his own daughter today, he's got no weaknesses of his own.

Dom stares back at me, irritated. "Did you think I wouldn't notice the man who murdered my parents?" He scoffs. "You think I'm still too busy playing video games and jacking off?" The look in his eyes is one of an old soul, not a kid inching toward sixteen.

"We aren't positive it was premeditated. And before we make a move, I want solid proof."

"The two fucking headstones at the cemetery aren't enough?" Dom snaps, underlying rage in his tone. He's angry—in the quiet way—which means he's been simmering about this on his own. Glancing out past the clearing it's then I notice some of the field has been unearthed. "What's going on here?"

"Speak of the devil, and he appears." Dom nods toward the newly vacant land. "Roman's decided to move into our neighborhood. He's building a fucking mansion where those trucks are sitting."

Seething from the idea that he's so close to my place—to our place—I curl my hands into fists. "Un-fucking-believable."

"Believe it. I've seen the blueprints."

I glance at my brother. "Do I want to know how you came across this information?"

"Building permits. He was approved for them last week. He owns everything now up to that flag post."

Fury sets in that I've had my head so far up my ass—in truth, up Antoine's ass. I've been so distracted carrying out his orders, I've dropped the fucking ball on my own agenda. My time in Paris now only takes away from my progress at home. I can feel some resentment coming from Dom as I soak in that realization. My priorities are in Triple Falls, and this is where I need to be—not playing errand boy for a French gangster. But even with the need to erase Roman from the board, the image of his little girl trailing behind him toward the parking lot today remains front and center. The look of defiance in her eyes with their exchange damn near makes me smile. That combined with the clear rebellion in her words and posture before she trailed behind him and I followed. I'd been in the know about his daughter for years, but she'd never been part of the picture until today.

In all my plans to bring him down, I never considered bystanders. I've seen the carnage that comes in wars like these, mostly territorial, and I refuse to let that innocent kid suffer for her father's mistakes. In a game made of criminals bordering psychopaths, many have no regard for innocents, especially when at war, but being a bystander myself, that man will never be me.

I wasn't sure if Dominic noticed Roman or thoroughly researched him to the lengths I have, but it's clear he knows a lot more than he's let on.

Even at their age, with no shortage of dick jokes and immature behavior, they seem to comprehend the importance of hammering out the details. After a lingering silence, I finally speak up.

"We're going basic with our strategy."

"Meaning?" Tyler asks.

"We've got to play this just right. The only way to defeat a man like Roman is to play sleeping giant."

"Think Helen of Troy," Dom voices, reading my line of thought before glancing at Sean and Tyler. "But it seems like a lot of trouble to go through when we can just eliminate the problem."

Alarm shoots up my spine as I weigh his words. "I know you're not fucking suggesting we kill the man in cold—"

"Eye for an eye." Dom shrugs. "Our parents burned to death. Don't you think that calls for aggressive action? You, yourself, told Delphine you were sick of all the talk. The meetings are a joke, filled with nothing but pussies who like to bitch while she refills their coffee. Might as well be a book club for all the fucking good it's doing." Dom looks straight at me when he speaks. "You know, if we boil down enough tobacco and dab the right amount of concentrate on his fucking car door handle, within minutes of it seeping into his skin, it's game over. Heart attack on the autopsy report. Presented with the right opportunity, it's a hundred percent untraceable."

All the blood drains from my face.

"He's not a smoker, so there's the first hole in that stupid idea, and that's not who we are," I grit out, terrified that these are the thoughts running through his mind. "And not who we will be, Dom. That's not what Mama and Papa wanted. There is a better, more diplomatic way to handle this, less merciful than death." I shake my head adamantly, "No, what we're going to do is change things for the better." I think of Antoine and how he represents everything I hate. He—like Roman—thinks himself indestructible. But I've learned a lot over the past year. More than that, I've learned what not to do. "Once we take Roman down, there's a hundred like him to take his place. They exploit people like our parents and discard them once they become a liability." I glance between the three of them. "What are we going to do about *them*?"

Sean shrugs. "Not our problem."

"We're going to make it our problem. That's the whole point of all of this. It's not just about our family, or this town, not anymore." I shove my hands in my pockets. "We're going to do this in a way that will honor them."

Sean produces and pops the cap off another beer. "This seems ambitious. I mean, come on, man. Look at where we're at—bumfuck nowhere."

"That's exactly the point," Dominic snaps. "You want to end up just another line cook at Daddy's restaurant? What's going to happen when they call in that bank loan?" He glances at Tyler. "Are you going to be a career soldier?"

"This is exactly why we're here," I interject, "to get our priorities straight."

"My priorities are perfect." Sean lifts his hands and begins to tick off his fingers. "Pussy, pussy, pussy, pussy, and . . ." he holds a finger on his thumb, "yup, I'm going to have to go with *pussy*."

Tyler and Dom laugh, and I reel on the three of them. "This is another reason why I called this meeting. You want a girlfriend? *Have one*, but pillow talk and this fucking club are never to go hand in hand. What the other birds do is not my business, but as far as we are concerned, women don't have a place at this fire, not yet. And not until they are vetted by me personally. *End of*."

"I thought you said women are a sanctuary." This comes

from Sean, who tests me with the lift of another beer, a smirk in place.

"They are. Away from *business*. Personal attachments are the greatest liability. And the first one who fucks up on that front will pay dire consequences—" I give each one of them a pointed look—"no fucking exceptions." I again snatch Sean's beer, just as he lifts it. "I'm not dealing with another fucking alcoholic."

Sean's smile disappears. "Since when is a sense of humor a crime? I consider it a necessity. And who the hell do you think has been cleaning up the puke off your aunt's fucking face for the last five years?"

Tyler snaps to, glaring at the side of Sean's head. "You aren't the only one looking after her."

"No, we all are—" he nods toward me—"but *he* sure as hell isn't."

With that admission, I dart my gaze between the three of them and wrack my brain for the right words, but they would all sound like excuses. In this moment, I don't have any good enough. I can't make up for what I've missed and will continue to miss. In a blink, they've gone from kids to teenagers bordering men. But if I can come through for all of them, there may be a chance of redemption. A chance they might see my sacrifice as worth it. It's all I'm working for. In the meantime, all they feel is my absence and a growing bitterness that comes with my arrival and the demands I make.

They need laughs, they need these stolen moments, they need to experience their youth in the way I couldn't.

"You're right," I admit, handing Sean his beer. "Just, take it easy, okay?"

Sean nods, cautiously taking the beer from my hand, mild surprise on his face.

Tyler stands and grabs some of the logs from the ground, his posture hostile as he tosses them into the fire. Something is . . . off with him, and I'll make it a point to take him aside and try to figure out what it is.

"So, if I'm getting this right," Tyler drawls, "we need a wooden horse to recruit an army to hide inside of it and the opportunity to slip into the city."

We all stare into the flames as he continues. "I'm going to be a third-generation Marine, it's a given, and if there's one thing I know how to do—it's build an army."

Sean speaks up next. "Me and Dom will cover the garage, and once it's up and running, I'll figure out a way to get us through the gate." He ruffles Dom's hair. "And we all know this asshole's going to Harvard or Yale or some shit."

"Guess that makes you the horse," Dominic adds tightly, his eyes on me. But his true irritation tonight is due to our earlier fight and my refusal to let him return to France with me. He's been begging for months, insisting he can follow in my footsteps at prep and finally join me there. I'd take him with me in a heartbeat if it weren't for Antoine. I want my brother nowhere within reach.

"No, little brother," I say, as flashes of my own blueprints flit through my mind, and I reveal the true reason as to why he's needed here. "*You're* the horse. And—" I give them all a pointed look—"as of this moment, *I no longer exist.*"

The three of them look back at me with unguarded surprise. But beneath the layers of resentment and mild confusion, all I see is blind trust. "From this point on, not one new recruit will know who the major players are. You can give them an impression, but our goal is to confuse them."

"We're going to confuse the men working *with* us?" Sean asks, unable to see the logic.

"It's the only way," I insist and glance back at the construction as the sky goes dark. "Leave Roman to me. With him, we're going to have to bide our time, and you're going to have to trust me."

"What about Helen?" Dom asks, joining me where I stand. We stare off for lingering seconds.

"We're leaving Helen *out of it*."

* * *

But we didn't leave her out of it, and it played out as I expected it would once she was brought in. Complete and utter fucking disaster. Despite my role of protecting her, Helen hasn't stopped punishing me for it.

Eleven days.

Eleven fucking days of flannel pajamas.

And just to pour salt into my weeping dick, she leaves the door open when she showers, when she changes, and when she slathers her insanely toned body in a scent so alluring to me, I get hard when she breezes by.

Well played, queen.

Most days, I wake up alone, and for the majority of them, I'm left hanging in the wind without direction—without any indication of how this will play out between us. Since I've been here, I've been stuck in a place of reflection, reflection I once managed to suppress with the constant aftermath over the years.

Now, in this silent place, without plans to make and orders to pass out, I'm helpless to the constant surfacing of all I've compartmentalized. Especially the most recent years, the agonizing years I forced myself to exist without her.

She wasn't wrong, but boredom isn't a word I'd use to describe my current state. It's more a combination of restlessness edging toward paranoia with every day I willingly forgo being in the know to sort out my relationship with her. She tried to tell me she's okay with me going back in, but I know that I can't do it halfway.

I'm an all or nothing man, and I don't know how to be any other way.

I keep hoping for her emotions to kick in and take over to help bridge the gap, but her sensibilities seem to be winning over her feelings. A skill I taught her—that emotions have no place for an objective player—a lesson she's clearly taken to heart and has turned against me. There's a hard edge to her that wasn't there before; in her scrutiny, in her voice, just throughout her that makes her even more alluring—but that much harder to reach.

When I do manage to catch her before she flees for the café and pin her with my lips, she's receptive, sometimes playful, but the look of fear I despise is still there. The look that lets me know she's waiting for the other shoe to drop. Apparently, assuring her that we'll be looking over our shoulders for the rest of our lives isn't enough.

And I admire and respect her so much for it considering the carnage she witnessed after living a mostly sheltered life.

Over the years, as I resurrected myself and what was left of my army, she's reinvented herself as an army of one—armed to the teeth. But I don't want her smoking gun anywhere near me. What I need is a long drink of her strength, of her love, and a little submission.

Fat fucking chance.

Without trying too hard, she's been dangling her sweet pussy carrot in front of me since I arrived. It's been eight hellacious months since I've had her, and before that—years, and I've never in my life been so hungry.

The last time we were together is not the way I want to remember having her.

I ridiculed her for loving me.

I shamed her that night for being the soldier I no longer was.

I did my best to strip her pride, to save her from this type of life, to selfishly save myself the worry, but she wasn't having any of it.

I left in awe of her, in awe of who she became without me.

Even more so, guilty for the way I couldn't step up.

She told me then that love makes the danger worth it.

I'm just going to keep believing her. Even if my biggest fucking fear is seeing it unfold all over again, this time with her as the sacrifice.

It's only a matter of time until we go head-to-head again, but it has to be the right time. I want no fear in her eyes when I claim my queen for good. I want her fighting back, and more so, I want her certain about me the way she was— of my place in her heart, by her side.

She's chosen her personal armor in the way of fucking flannel pajamas.

Grabbing my newly delivered dumbbells, I do another set of reps to try and rid myself of restless energy. Facing out her bedroom window, I note the painstaking lengths she's gone to replicate her father's garden. Between hedges and rows of empty vines is a reading nook. Above the wooden canopy hangs branches of deadening wisteria.

The sight of it brings me back to the morning in Roman's garden, where I all but blurted out my love for her. Dropping my dumbbells, I walk over to the window and reflect upon our shared past. It wasn't the first time I took her in a way that conveyed physically what I was feeling, but it was that morning in particular that I felt it most, that I knew I was irrevocably in love with my enemy's daughter. With a shared look and with a confession I felt to the depth of my soul, I broke my own creed and gave in to the deepest part of me, and my soul-deep ache for a connection with her. Within seconds of recalling those minutes, I surrender to the heat coursing through me. My arm braced on the window as I grip my cock in my mesh shorts.

Stroke.

Her exposed throat.

Stroke.

Her breathy moans.

Stroke.

The unguarded love in her eyes.

Stroke.

Her perfect tan thighs spread out before me, tight pink pussy glistening.

Stroke.

The feel of her wet heat on my fingertips.

Stroke.

Her pebbled peach nipples.

Stroke.

My first desperate thrust inside her.

Jaw tensing, spine tingling, heat emanating from my every pore, I'm just about to grunt her name when the bedroom door opens, and Beau comes barreling through with Cecelia behind him, her eyes widening when she sees me.

"Oh," she whispers, darting her eyes away before palming the handle to close the door.

"Don't you fucking dare," I hiss, which freezes her movement. I release my angry grip on my cock and stride toward her, leaving it untucked from my cheap sports shorts as her eyes widen a little further with every step I take. When I reach her, I crowd her at the door, gripping her hand from the knob and cover my raging dick with it.

"*You.*" I wrap her fingers around me, gripping her hand and lead it along my length to stroke. "That's what I'm thinking about. *You.*" I bend eye level as her breath picks up and her dark-blue eyes pool. "I saw the wisteria in your garden, and it reminded me of that day. Remember that day, Cecelia?" My cock jerks in her hand. I run her curled fingers along the length of my shaft, and we move together as her full lips part. I lick along her lower lip. "*You.*"

"Tobias—" She tries to release her palm, and I jerk my chin, tightening it around me.

"I didn't come here to play fucking roommate."

Inhaling her scent, I continue to guide her hand down my length, cupping her palm over the head before pulling it back down, a curse full of pleasure leaving me on exhalation as I show her my need.

"I know," she rasps out.

"Do you remember that day?"

"Of course, I remember."

"Have you come thinking about that day?"

"Yes," she replies hoarsely.

"Then you remember how good it felt the second I pushed inside you."

"Tobias," she whimpers as I lick along her lips, drawing

them into a responsive kiss. She grips me even tighter, eliciting a groan from deep inside of me as we get lost in the past, summoning that morning into her bedroom. Veins thrumming with the need to claim, possess, and destroy her hesitation. I rip myself away to watch the rise and fall of her chest before my gaze rolls down the rest of her.

"That's a nice outfit," I grit out as she strokes me without prompt, her purse still hanging from her shoulder. Fingering it off, I relieve her of it while doing my best to restrain the beast roaring inside of me. "You look beautiful."

"T-thank you."

I'm tempted to laugh at her reply, but I'm too fucking hard, too needy, and on the verge of making a fool of myself. Years of pent-up longing, of need, of lust, of devotion, of love, threaten to overtake me. I want her too much, I always have, and at this point, I want to punish her just as much as she has me, but it wouldn't be just. But when she smears the precum over the head of my dick with her thumb, I snap. "Sorry, I'm about to ruin it."

Before she can react to my threat, she's off her feet and in my hold. Slick with sweat from my workout, she glides her hands along my shoulders, pressing her forehead to my bicep as I walk her toward her bed. "Is it too much to ask to take things slow?"

Attaching my lips to her neck, I bite down. "At the moment, yes."

It's when I lay her on the bed, and her hair fans out behind her that my cock jerks in warning. She gazes back at me, waiting, no more protests on her lips.

Jerking her skirt up to rest on her hips, I groan when I see she's wearing leggings. More layers. Annoyed, I yank her sweater up to see lace-covered breasts and drag the flesh-colored material beneath her perfect tits, so they're drawn together in offering. Regripping my dick, I resume my strokes, and she gazes on, rapt.

At the sight of her drawing nipples, I increase my pace, and with a few more frustrated tugs, I groan out my release, coating her breasts, bared stomach, and leggings.

Disappointment flits over her features as her navy eyes drop.

Good.

"You're playing on a weakness we *both* have, Trésor." Lifting her foot, I pull off her Uggs one by one and toss them over my shoulder. With the beast partially satiated for the moment, I kneel at the end of her bed, pulling both her panties and leggings down. She watches, entranced, as I run my hands up and down her newly bare skin while she sinks further into the mattress. It's my voice that brings her gaze back to me.

"You want slow?" I run a finger through her soaked lips and am rewarded with the buck of her hips. "Fine, we'll go slow, though I don't see the fucking point because I'm not the only one you're punishing. But since we're laying down the law—" I press a thumb to her clit, massaging it briefly before taking it away. She hisses through her teeth, eyes flickering with impatience.

"*Lover, boyfriend.*" Leisurely, I rim her opening with the pad of my finger before I slowly push it in—knuckle deep. The sight of it, along with her neatly trimmed landing strip, threatens to ruin what restraint I have. My dick hardens, envious at the sight, as she clenches, wet and hot. Her eyes close when I twist it to beckon her G.

"Tobias."

"That will do, too," I say, blowing along her center, increasing my speed while using the ridge of my finger to fully prime her. "Not your fucking roommate." I lick her soundly from center to top, sucking her clit briefly to earn my first plea. "The man in your life, your partner, your soulmate, your other half." I dip again and jackhammer my tongue where she needs me most. She mewls in protest when I pull away.

"Tobias." Her voice is laced with years of ache, and I feel every single day of our separation.

Heart hammering its own plea and fully erect again from just the taste of her, I tamp down my own need because there's something I want more.

"I thought I would never hear that again. Dis mon nom." *Call my name.* Dipping, I nudge her clit with my nose, and she bows off the bed. She needs this just as much as I do. Flattening my tongue, I smoothly lick her again and pull away.

Tossing her head back in agitation, she slams her eyes shut as I press in a second finger, filling her before nipping her clit.

"Who am I?"

She lifts her hips, searching for friction. In response, I hook her legs over my shoulders, ignoring my greedy dick as it demands its rightful place. But it's greed I shove away, needing to feast.

"Who *loves* you, Cecelia?" I enunciate each word carefully, knowing they'll bring her back to the first night I brutally kissed her in that clearing, a place that has since become sacred to the both of us. I want her to know that even *then*,

I wanted her for myself. The way I *still* want her. I've been starving for her. But it's penance I'm paying, for then, before there can be a now.

My needs don't matter.

Not yet.

"Please," she cries out as I continue to run my finger along her G, feeling the telltale swell. She rips at my hair, thighs quivering and squeezing around my head. I reward her with another long pull on her clit. Pulling away, I gaze up at her, just as she sinks her nails into my scalp in retribution.

"Slow," I remind her. "I'm capable of slow. It requires patience. You think I haven't suffered through the lesson of patience while waiting for the right time to come back to you? Waiting all these months for the day I could finally and fully give in to what I feel for you? All I've got now is time." I savor the anger swimming in her eyes, her pebbled nipples, the flush of her skin, the swell of her body.

Rising from my position, I lift her top from her body as she pounds against my chest in protest, in an attempt to get me back to the task at hand, all traces of her own patience gone, her need taking over. I hover above her as she glares up at me, still covered in my release.

"You want to take things slow, Trésor? Is that what you want? All these years apart wasn't enough? If I seem eager—" I let her hear the jealousy in my tone as I lift my hand, spreading my cum on her chest before sliding my palm down her stomach. "If I seem eager, it's because I want to erase every touch that wasn't mine." I trail my hand down her body and press my essence between her thighs. At the moment, I'm at her mercy in every aspect of our situation, even in the bedroom. But it's time to remind her that I'm still the bad guy, and forever will be the tyrant she fucked and fell for—and on this playing field, we're equals. But her relent to let me dominate is a gift I refuse to let her take away. The vulnerability that shines in her eyes, the emotions she's feeling, the hint of helplessness is what I need solely for the purpose to let her know—in this physical way—she can still trust me as she has countless times before. Her pleasure is mine, and without it, I'm not the same man.

Fingers still thrusting inside her, I hoist myself atop her and press our bodies together as I gaze down at her with the culmination of the longing I've felt, hoping she can see.

"I love you," I murmur and instantly see her eyes soften. "I've missed you so fucking much, so much." Emotion threatens as I think about the collective seconds, hours, minutes, days, and years I forced myself to believe she could never belong to me again. Of how at one point, I knew I possessed her, that she was mine, and losing her cost me more than a broken heart. It cost me my sanity and my soul. "I can do slow, but don't deny me my rightful fucking place."

She grips the back of my head and brings me to her, kissing me with unspoken confession. Clasping her legs behind my back, she opens for me fully. Mouths molding, tongues dueling, we kiss for long minutes, and I rub my cock against her pussy and stop her just as she lifts her hips to allow me inside. Pulling away, I shake my head. "I'll wait for you, Trésor, as long as it takes."

Lowering back to kneel before her, I thrust my fingers in and suck her clit with fervor. Not long after, she calls my name, gripping the sheets in her fists. She goes completely silent as her body erupts, back bowing from the bed, her clit pulsing against my tongue with each wave of release, the glide of my fingers growing slicker and slicker as she floods my mouth. As another wave hits, my name bursts out of her, and the sheer force of it has my throat burning.

Fast breaths pump out of her as I milk the orgasm, savoring the taste along with the crash of emotion coursing through my chest. My act turns selfish as I seek more, feeding the rush. Only she can get me this high. Only she can make me feel this way. Only she can soothe the burn she, herself, creates.

I love her beyond limits because she loved me through what I forced her to endure. She loved me, though I made us impossible.

I was the one who forced our stars to blaze past each other. I was the one whose wrath made our path detrimental to us both.

And she loved, and still loves me, despite it all.

But even with the solidarity of that love, it's trust and forgiveness I seek.

It's when she goes limp that I go in for another, and she clamps her thighs against my ears in an attempt to push me away. Wrenching them apart, her dark-blue eyes shine with momentary surrender as I bow and resume my worship.

With a few more targeted thrashing licks, she's writhing again, and it's then I relent, pulling my soaked fingers from her, licking the sweet, tangy aftermath off my lips. Dick throbbing, I watch her come down, her eyes glazing over. Flushed and gasping, she looks down at me when I bend and kiss the top of her pussy, the sensitive skin of her thighs, darting my tongue out one last time to her center, spearing her with my tongue just to satisfy my own greed with one last taste. When I lift to hover above her, the sight of her takes my breath. She's a prism of beauty, glowing in residue as I flip her, caressing the wings on her back with my fingers. For the first time since I marked her, I can fully appreciate them for what they represent. Gripping her neck with my hand, I run my throbbing dick along her slit before lowering my mouth to trace the ink with my lips and tongue.

"Faite pour moi." *Made for me*.

I squeeze her neck, kissing every single inch of marked skin before collapsing to her side, refusing myself the chance to make my words a lie.

Slow.

The stars have managed to pave the way for us again, and I'm not fucking up another chance to collide with her.

It's taken me years to admit that the thing I fought the hardest brings me the most peace — as much peace as a man like me can have.

Turning her head, she looks over to me with eyes that hold heavily guarded affection, and I know I made the right choice by stopping myself.

"I won't pretend to know how I hurt you or what it felt like when I did, Cecelia. But I do know how much it hurt *me*, and that's enough to know I deserve your anger and caution. But right now, I need you too goddamn much to stay away when you're right fucking here in front of me. When you are who you are, which is, in case you're wondering, the other fucking half of me. I'm sorry for the things I've done, but it's time you let me show you how much."

She slowly nods her head, a lone tear sliding down her cheek. She's angry with herself for giving in, and I make a firm decision that I won't press her for more physically, no matter how much the space hurts.

Slow, it is.

We lay there for long moments before I speak again.

"Ask me *anything*," I whisper as she regards me carefully, mulling over her thoughts before she finally speaks.

"Is the truck . . . with your things, still idling?"

I dip my chin.

"Then have them brought here." Lifting to hover above her, I grip her face in my hand, searching for the sincerity in her words. "You're sure?"

"I'm sure."

"You know what you're saying?"

"I'm adequately scared, Tobias, and I'm not playing immune, but I like to think that my naïveté died a long time ago. I know who I am now. Next time, believe me—" her eyes flash with residual anger from the night her innocence was truly stolen, her tone sharpening with hindsight bite—"I won't hesitate."

She's finally on guard the way I need her to be, and that brings me partial relief. Leaning in, I draw her lips in for a kiss. She breaks it, her voice an icy warning. "I'm expecting huge fucking dividends on my investment, Mr. King, a big payoff. You break my trust, my fucking heart again, and I'll put a bullet in you my damn self. I'm still angry. I'm still trying to get used to the idea of you being here. All is not well with us, *yet*, but facts are facts, and the facts are, we're in this together, no matter what. There's a lot that hasn't changed and never will. And sadly, I do love you, too."

I can't help my chuckle, and I kiss her again, this time more aggressively, and she latches on, kissing me back because we both know time isn't on our side, never has been. These seconds are precious, and she lets me draw on her as much as I want because she feels it too. We're forever on borrowed time, our opponents faceless, a whole new board, but this time we're making all our moves together. When she finally pulls herself away, keeping closer to the edge from the free fall she used to allow herself when we got swept in our emotions for the other, I allow her the retreat. It's when she pauses at the doorway to the bathroom, looking back at me for lingering seconds with the same longing, that I feel a shift between us. It's small, but it's there.

And it's enough.

Finally.

Progress.

Chapter Eighteen

TOBIAS

Age Twenty-Four

PARLAY.

I read somewhere it takes three lines of solid income to make a man rich, six to make a man sustainably wealthy. Between the last few years of keeping tabs anonymously online—due to Dom's help—as campus bookie at HEC, the scraps of profit I take from Antoine's legitimate business deals, my cut of white-collar crimes my brother has spearheaded, and the fluctuating income from the garage—that makes four.

A rich man, I'm not. And sustainably wealthy is where I need to be.

As of late, we give almost as much as we take to keep our consciences clean and our hands heavy with loyalty. We're gaining strength in numbers, but it's not enough. Money and stature are the last hurdles I need to clear to get myself into a position to take Roman down.

With my masters earned from one of the best business schools in the world—as soon as I have the capital to start my company—I can declare war on my unsuspecting nemesis.

So, parlay, it is.

Today's the day, and I've been on this board far too long.

It all comes down to a wildly expensive bet. A gamble capable of setting me free of being a slave or victim to any other man's whims.

At this point, I stand to lose as much as I gain, having paid as much for the intel as I have to gamble with, but that's the nature of the beast. Money has always been an obstacle for me, a necessary means of getting from point A to point B. And while some men let it drive them, let the abundance or lack of it corrupt or destroy them, I refuse to become a slave to it. Instead, I'll obtain enough of it to wield its power, its sway, to open avenues and help level the playing field for men like me and my brothers, our parents, and whomever else's fate rests in the hands of men like Roman Horner.

With the clip of the price tag, I'm ushered into the jacket, the last stroke of the brush on the picture I'm intent on painting. Giving myself a once-over in the floor-length mirror, I school my features to hide my excitement as the tailor looks on, brushing the shoulders of my jacket.

"Not bad for a poor mixed breed who grew up in a dilapidated shithole in Nowhere, North Carolina."

With the furrow of his brows, it's clear my words are lost on the tailor who speaks little English, but he nods in agreement to please me. "Cela vous va très bien." *It suits you.*

Sorting through the bills from my pocket, I tip him and move to step off the pedestal. He stills me, kneeling and running a mildly soiled cloth along the top of my shoes. When I pull out another bill in gratitude, he waves it away, and I nod in thanks. "Merci."

Making my way out to my waiting car, I light a cigarette

and inhale deep, exhaling some of the threatening stress of the morning. Surveying the daybreak sky, I spot a flock of birds flying low in the milky clouds, wings extended in perfect formation, mimicking each other's flight pattern, a silent communication amongst them along the wind. The sight of it makes me envious.

This. This is what was missing in the order back home.

Frères du Corbeau *(Brothers of the Raven)* was my step-father's pipe dream. A dream to lead the revolt against the greedy leaders of corporate America—namely Roman Horner—to fight for the good of the common man.

The idea was good, but there was too much miscommunication amongst them—along with too many opposing beliefs and ideas about how to proceed in taking him down. And not one of them, my papa included, had enough backbone to move in any direction. They never could get it together enough to evoke any real change or take action against those who continually fucked them, especially Roman. The only person in that group who had any real gumption to carry out anything was Delphine, but she dulled her razor's edge with the drink over time.

It all comes down to my brothers and me.

I refuse to indulge in a poison of any kind that will dull my edge.

Whether it be drink or a woman, or any other threatening vice, I'm determined to abstain. I refuse to let any personal or frivolous need weaken me. When I think of the bigger picture, it's much easier to maintain.

I can make Papa's dream a reality while seeking justice and ending Roman, or I can backslide like the rest of the originals, becoming useless, another voice in the void.

Throughout the years I've been in France, I thought it a possibility on more than one occasion that I would fail. That this whole thing was pointless. But doubt breeds insecurity, and insecurity chips away at confidence, and I have no fucking room for it. It's time for bold moves. It's time for execution.

With that needed mental clarity, I slide into the back seat after my borrowed driver opens the door, mildly surprised to see his boss waiting for me. The driver, Luis, gives me an apologetic glance before leaving me with Antoine, who does nothing to mask the smug pleasure on his face.

I should have seen this coming.

"Allais-tu m'informer de tes projets aujourd'hui, Ezekiel?" *Were you ever going to inform me of your plans today, Ezekiel?*

I tug the cuff of my shirt. "My plans today don't include you."

"I could have helped."

"As I've told you, *repeatedly*, I don't need your help."

"But you borrow my car, my driver?"

"You offered it to me when I need it. And please don't insult me by acting like I haven't earned some courtesies for the years I've spent working with you."

I've practically rebuilt his army of thugs from the ground up using common sense they desperately lacked and implementing tactics I've studied for years. Unbeknownst to Antoine, I've been using his organization as a guinea pig to work out any future kinks for my own.

"Un tel manque de respect. Tu pensais qu'un costume cher ferait de toi un homme digne?" *Such disrespect. You think an expensive suit makes you a worthy man?*

I assess his suit. "Definitely not."

Before my blatant insult can sink in, I lift my chin to Luis waiting in the driver's seat. "Longchamp. Merci."

Antoine pauses his cigarette halfway to his mouth as we race away from the curb. "What business do you have at the horse race?"

I shrug, loving the feel of the expensive shirt linen on my skin. "Maybe I'm interested in the sport." His soulless black eyes narrow. "Business that doesn't concern you and has nothing to do with our arrangement."

He thrusts his index finger at me, the cigarette burning low between his fingers. "You are testing my patience, Ezekiel."

"I don't answer to you."

"Tu le feras si cela affecte mon business." *You will if it affects my business.*

"Tell me where I have not held up my end of our agreement, and I will gladly explain myself."

For years I've played shepherd for him, using his underground reputation to both grow and educate his army, herding to gather my own intel while siphoning less than a quarter of his recruits.

What Antoine doesn't know hasn't hurt him in the slightest, but it's greatly helped to elevate me to the position I want to be in. But the more I do for him, the less satisfied he seems to be. With my stint in France coming to an end, he's been searching for any possible angle to get his hooks in me. He wants me as his second, and it's never going to fucking happen.

"I have looked out for you, Ezekiel, have I not?"

"We've looked out for each other."

"Why do you feel the need to exclude me from something that's beneficial?"

"Who says it is?"

"Do you consider me a fucking fool?"

"I consider you a partner."

Reaching into his small bar, I pour myself a splash of gin. I'm already sweating, and I need to calm my mind. This is a setback I didn't fucking need so early in the day.

Antoine scrutinizes me carefully. He has a mistress in Pigalle, close to where his tailor is, and I know that's where he just came from. He reeks of cheap rose perfume. On the other hand, his wife is one of the most beautiful women I've ever laid eyes on. It's painfully apparent she's deeply miserable with him. Despite her efforts to get my attention, I haven't laid a hand on her, nor do I intend to.

Often—especially when I visit their home in Montmartre—I catch her staring at me. The attraction is mutual, but there is zero benefit in acting on it. She's in her late twenties and desperate for any man to take her away from the man sitting across from me. Sadly, I won't be that man, but I do catch Palo, Antoine's most trusted lieutenant, staring at her the same way. One day, I may be able to use that in a play against him.

Emotions, namely love, can make even the strongest man weak, giving opponents leverage. Leverage I never intend to let another have on me.

"Partners share information."

"Fine. I plan on hiring my own car soon to save you any future imposition."

"Ah, you're intent on being greedy?"

"It's greed that has you badgering me."

"I have shared with you."

"You've given me scraps, small ends."

"Only because you refuse to partake in any *real* business."

He keeps his voice even despite his temperament, a trait I've adapted myself.

"Because your real business is destructive. I've explained this repeatedly as well. I won't be in France full-time much longer."

He scoffs. "And you'll go back home to what, work in Roman's factory?"

Doing my best not to show my growing hatred for him and the fact I revealed far too much early on about my predicament, I wave the threatening emotion away and toss back the rest of my drink before speaking. "Don't trouble yourself over it. I'll find my own way."

When the car stops, I shift in my seat to get out. When the door opens, he grips my wrist. Glaring at him, I let the dare in my eyes speak for itself.

In an hour, I'll become financially independent, which will negate most of my use for him. I won't let him take this from me. Tilting my head, I drop my gaze to the gun in his holster.

I've made myself invaluable to him. I've proven myself time and time again over the years. He wants ownership of me, and he's not getting it, but the threat of losing me just might be enough to end my life. For now, he's still got the upper hand. Toying with me, he mulls over the decision, weighing the pros and cons of discarding me as he has so many other of his men, before unlatching his fingers.

"You're beginning to bore me with your laughable nobility," he mutters, averting his gaze before sliding back in his seat and righting his jacket. "You're no better a man than me."

"Always a pleasure, Antoine."

*

Tap, tap, tap.

Tap, tap, tap.

On the other side of the caged counter, the man stills his progress looking pointedly at my busy fingers. Averting my eyes, I rip them out of sight as he produces the life-changing piece of paper. I snatch it from where it rests and stalk away, neck heating.

Walking up to the bar, I place my order. When my gin is delivered, I stare into my drink as a familiar blanket of unease begins to seep in. I'm completely and utterly alone in this gamble.

One. Two. Three.

One. Two. Three.

Taking a healthy sip, I glimpse the mirror behind the bar, briefly admiring my suit before lifting my gaze to the clock above it. Five minutes. A woman sitting alone catches my eye at last glance, and I look to my right to meet her smile. Dark hair, cunning brown eyes, and beneath her form-fitting dress, a body built for punishment. Her painted lips lift further as I drink her in, and she reciprocates, her eyes trailing from my lips to my Italian leathers. Briefly, I imagine doling out that punishment, but grab my drink from the bar instead, seeing her eyes dull when she reads my intent.

"Vous allez laisser une femme boire seule?" *You're going to leave a lady to drink alone?*

"Veuillez accepter mes excuses. Je vous assure que si c'était un autre jour . . ." *Please accept my apology. I assure you if it were any other day . . .*

Her eyes rake me with determination.

"Je garderai la dernière gorgée pour la fin de cette course.

Peut-être qu'alors vous vous joindrez à moi." *I'll save the last sip until after the race. Maybe then you will join me.*

I pull a bill from my pocket and nod to the bartender to grab her another.

With the lift of her lush lips, I read the promise in her eyes that says she'll be waiting.

A step away from the distraction, I shift my focus to the paper safely tucked in the inside pocket of my jacket and amble outside. Veering from the bulk of the crowd, I take a vacant seat scanning the track just as my pulse elevates and my mind begins to race uncontrollably.

Stay calm, Tobias.

An overwhelming and familiar feeling engulfs me as I do my best to keep my shit together.

Two minutes.

Glancing around the horde of people, I'm all too aware of the leg up I've garnered in knowing what thoroughbred will cross the finish line. Keeping my eyes forward, I try not to think of the others who might've placed similar bets on the wrong horse—their own situation as dire as my own, and bat away the guilt.

One. Two. Three.

Sweat beads on my temple as I survey the track, searching desperately for something, anything to steal my focus and rob my errant thoughts. Inevitably, I come up empty knowing exactly what I need. Unable to battle the urge any longer, I pull out my cell phone and press send, on the verge of explosion. He answers on the second ring.

"Hey, brother."

"Dom." It comes out in a whisper full of emotion. I clear my throat of it and still find myself unable to speak.

I'm fucking terrified.

"What's wrong?"

"I just needed . . ." You. I need you. I need to remind myself why I'm doing this. For Mama and Papa, for us, for our future.

"Talk to me, brother." All bullshit aside, he's been with me, for better or worse, every step of the way, trusting me, believing in me. In taking this risk, I could blow it all. Even with the guarantee I paid for, there are too many variables. There's too fucking many.

Panic seizes me fully as I still my fingers and swallow the contents of my drink in two gulps.

Maybe I should have shared this secret with him. Maybe I should come clean about my involvement with Antoine and my fears that our ties will never be severed without dire consequences.

Maybe I've gone about this all wrong and made one too many risky moves so early in the game. But this fear, I don't want for him. This burden and the consequences that may follow—I'll shoulder alone.

"I just want to talk." Commotion breaks out in front of me as the announcer begins to alert everyone to the start of the race.

"Bullshit. Tell me what's going on." The clank of tools lets me know he's working at King's. Being a mechanic is a trade he enjoys immensely, and for that, I'm happy, even if it's just another way to get by for the moment. With his intellectual aptitude, he's got a bright future with or without me. He'll go far, even without my guidance. I respect him immensely for the man he's becoming, and he's only just cracked his knuckles, barely scratching the surface of his potential.

"Dom, just . . ." I close my eyes, "stay on the phone with me."

"What did you do?"

When the gates open, the onslaught is immediate, a thousand stinging needles in my chest. It's painful, but the gin circulating makes it bearably less so. Keeping my eyes trained on the number on the side of my horse, Dom remains silent, and I know it's because he's listening intently to the barrage of noise surrounding me, searching for clues. After a few seconds, he speaks up.

"What's our number?" he asks softly.

"Seven," I reply. The number of years I've been away from what's most important to me. The number of years I've been living dual lives. Years of hunger and humility, years of metamorphosis that changed me from a revenge-seeking orphan to a common thief, to barterer, brother, mentor, student, teacher and now . . . ?

"What did you bet?"

"Our future."

Cringing, I get nothing. Not a cross word, not even a harshly-exhaled breath. It's absolute trust, and it pervades me with an unimaginable feeling and a hell of a lot of guilt. It's on the tip of my tongue to whisper an apology for abusing it when I see our horse fall slightly behind. I can barely breathe with the intensity of emotions running through me.

"Tob—"

"Just this once, please. I need my goddamn brother," I whisper, tightening my hold on the phone.

"I'm here," he replies hoarsely, a rare fear in his voice. But it's not fear for his own well-being, and that guts me all the more.

Swallowing, I curse my emotions as more remorse surfaces on how I've wronged him. Of how I left him in that fucking cockroach-infested house with an unworthy parent, to fend for himself, to man up before his time. Just once, I want the sacrifice to be worth it. I want him to feel like the sacrifice is worth it.

Our horse takes the lead in the last quarter mile, and I can feel the hairs on my arms start to rise.

"Brothers first," I whisper.

"Always brothers," he replies softly, a second before our horse crosses the finish line.

Shock and adrenaline shoot throughout my body as I exhale a steady breath, and Dom speaks up. "What did we win?"

It takes several seconds for the panic to give way to exhilaration. Liberation gives a bounce to every step I take as I make my way back inside, forgoing my waiting date at the bar to collect my winnings. "Exodus."

* * *

"*And* look at you now, King, just a regular Joe doing everyday shit," I mumble, dumping two extension cords into my cart before pushing it along the aisle. "No bad guys to hunt down, not a suit in sight to negotiate billion-dollar deals with."

While I might have schemed my way into becoming a millionaire and smooth-talked my way out of *death* on more than one occasion, earning the *naked* trust of my former enemy's daughter might be the deed to outdo all others.

Our progression is *slow* all right because, day by day, she's fucking killing me gradually.

Twenty-one days she's held out on me, on letting me in.

Twenty-one days she's denied me entrance fully back into her heart.

Twenty-one days I've fucked my fist.

Twenty-one days of aching when I hold her while she sleeps in neck-to-ankle flannel pajamas.

Twenty-one fucking days.

Being the tactical man I am, I decided it's time to come up with a plan.

An average Joe's plan. Innocent enough.

Wine, dinner, seduction, *connection*.

Daily, she's managed to curb me at every turn. But somehow, someway, I will succeed in wrestling her back into some sort of submission.

Resisting the urge to punch the happy-go-lucky fucker who passes me, I smack a double stack of toilet paper into my cart.

All we need is the right setting to share one perfect night, and for that, I'm pulling out my entire arsenal.

It's all wrong, this space she so easily puts between us . . . we need something, something I can't pinpoint to get us back to where we were. When my phone rumbles in my pocket, I scramble to answer, hoping it is some sort of sign, anything to help me get past this crossroads.

"Talk to me," I wheeze out, glaring at another happy husband who takes one look at my face and turns to walk in the opposite direction.

Sean chuckles in greeting. "Just checking in, man. How's it going?"

"How's it *going*?" I can hear the contempt in my reply. "How's. It. Going?" I grit out. "Well, at the moment, I'm just crossing off the honey-do the Mrs. left for me and picking up toilet paper. And tonight, after I've scooped up enough dog shit, she might just reward me with a kiss goodnight after another day of pointless fucking living."

Collective laughter echoes from the other end of the line, and I press the phone to my ear, speaking through clenched teeth. "You have me on speaker?"

"Sorry, man, couldn't resist."

"Fuck you all," I snap, as peals of laughter ring out at my expense.

"Don't hang up. We're here for you, man," Russell belts out through a dying chuckle. "And don't get the cheap shit, chicks hate that."

I stare down at the label and second-guess my choice. "It's Charmin."

"You're good," Sean pipes up before I hear the door of the garage close.

"All right, talk to me."

"She's bleeding me dry, Sean. My tolerance, my patience, all of it."

"It's only been a few weeks. Hang in there."

"I have no idea what to do with myself here. I have no idea how to be . . . *normal*."

"There is no such thing, and you know it."

"Oh, but there is—" I briefly scan the store and lower my voice—"and I'm living amongst them." I pick up a box and scrutinize it before tossing six like it into my cart. "But don't worry, I plan to hammer and fucking nail my way back in by the stroke of midnight."

Another extended chuckle on his end.

"I'm so glad I amuse you."

"Right now, I fear for you both. Just do yourself a favor

and get out of a public place. It's not safe for others. It's just going to take some time to adjust."

"Adjust." The word is acid on my tongue. "That's a word she's used *multiple* times." The cashier eyes me as she rings me up, and I toss two bars of chocolate onto the counter before shoving half of one in my mouth and chewing slowly, daring her to judge.

"Have you been honest with her about *everything*?"

Canting my head away from the cashier, I lower my voice. "I haven't even been able to get past the rehash since she left Triple. She's . . . impossible."

"Just give her more time, and try not to think about what's going on here. Do yourself a favor and keep your business brain out of it. We've got it covered. Just concentrate on her."

I let out a pained groan. "If I concentrate any harder—"

"I know, man, I know. Tessa is just as fucking hard to crack when she gets pissed at me. Just do what you can. I'll call you back soon."

"When?"

"When, what?"

"When will you call me back?" I snap, swallowing down another mouth full of chocolate.

I don't miss the laughter in his tone. "You need a when?"

Again, I turn away from the cashier, who's doing a shit job of hiding her smirk. "Yes, Sean, I need a fucking *when*."

"I'll hit you up tomorrow."

I end the call and turn to pay the cashier.

"Flowers?" she offers a suggestion, nodding toward the buckets of bunched stems nearby. Though it's a typical gesture, it's not a bad idea. The woman loves a garden and spends endless hours doting on her own. Grabbing every single flower in the bucket, she nods in approval as I hand her my card.

"Thank you."

"If four dozen roses don't help, honey, you might want to think about something shinier."

"Noted."

The wheels of my shopping cart squeak on the uneven pavement beneath me as I haul out my load of supplies to the Camaro. Once unloaded, I close the trunk and pause when I see a familiar car parked a few rows down. The same rental car I spotted back at the gas station.

Not a coincidence.

Glancing back toward the store, I see a man standing, waiting at the side of the entrance, his eyes averted.

My phone rumbles in my pocket, and I lift it to see a late warning.

We're on him.

I type back a quick reply.

Let me handle it.

Pushing my cart back toward the store's receptacle, I dial Cecelia.

"Hey."

"How is your day going?" I ask.

"Well, considering I only got here an hour ago, okay so far. What's up?"

"I did call for good reason." The irritation of her remark

combined with the arrival of a new stalker is coming through my call, and I rip at my hair in annoyance before I lighten my tone. "A very good reason."

"Oh?"

The man casually inches to the side of the store, nearing the corner as I take my time, my gait slow and unassuming. Being on the phone helps the illusion. It's when I shove my cart away from me, crashing it into the others, and shift directions heading straight toward him, that I know he's as green as they come. It's fucking insulting with his skill set that he was the one sent to me.

"Date night," I say, picking up my pace.

"Date night?"

"Yes. Date night," I grit out, "a weekly ritual by couples to maintain intimacy. It's a thing."

I can hear the smile in her voice. "I'm aware."

"I'll go on a date with him," Marissa chimes in the background.

"So, we can have one?"

"What did you have in mind?"

"I'll take care of the details."

The asshole turns the corner, his body tensing as if he's ready to take off. It would be laughable—if I weren't so pissed.

"Ne me fais pas te courir après. Tu ne vas pas aimer quand je te rattraperai." *Don't make me chase you. You won't like it when I catch up.*

He pauses his walk. He's listening. And he's listening because he understands.

French.

Goddamnit.

"Tobias, who are you chasing?"

"An imbecile who took my shopping cart."

"Small town, Frenchman, first impressions are important. You just got here, don't make yourself a menace."

"I'll keep that in mind."

Hot on his heels, the man leaps into a sprint, and I burst into motion.

"Date night will be at home. Until then, Trésor."

After hanging up, I catch up with him quickly, my long runs paying off in spades when I grip the hood of the asshole's jacket and yank him off his feet at the side of the building. Airborne, he yelps before he lands flat on his back in a thud on the concrete. After disarming him, I drag him behind me, the material of his slicker good aid in helping with the effort while I keep my eyes peeled for passing cars.

Much to my delight, in a town with a population shy of two thousand, there isn't a single car coming in either direction—a perk of small-town living. My birds are already waiting behind the store in an idling sedan as I come into view, pulling the idiot behind me who grunts when I hit a patch of uneven pavement.

"Je t'ai dit de ne pas courir." *I told you not to run.*

Once we're safely out of view, I kneel down and search him for ID and credit him for having the good sense to leave it back at whatever hole he's occupying. I hit paydirt when I retrieve a cellphone from his jeans.

"Now we speak in English."

Silence.

"I know who sent you. I have everything I need from you already. Tell me why I shouldn't kill you right now?"

No response.

I cock his own gun before pressing it to his temple. "You've got one more chance to answer me."

"I have a message from Palo."

"No, you don't." It's then I know *how* he found me.

And that Palo is most likely dead.

Fuck.

Dread filters from the center of my chest, circulating through my veins as I keep my mask in place while the implications of what's next pummel me from within.

Pulling the man to stand, I lean in on him, pressing all of my weight against him. A pained whimper comes from his lips.

"It's broad daylight, and you have the audacity to try and shadow me? Did you not know who you were coming after?" I click my tongue.

"You were not supposed to know I was here."

"Passons au français parce que tu ne peux pas être aussi stupide. Tu devrais travailler ton anglais." *Let's switch to French because you can't be this stupid. You should work on your English.*

"Je déteste l'Amérique. Je ne reviendrai pas." *I hate America. I will not return.*

"Tu seras enterré ici si tu ne coopères pas." *You will be buried here, if you don't cooperate.*

"Je devais signaler où tu étais et avec qui." *I was to report where you were and who you were with.*

"Et tu l'as fait?" *And have you?*

Fear flashes in my incompetent assailant's eyes. It's too fucking late.

And that's the crux of the situation. As it always has been. If I had remained alone, there would be nothing to report.

This would have been another day at the office in my old life, but my circumstances are different now, and the stakes are much higher. This morning, I had time in abundance. Time to try and help her understand my reasoning for the decisions that led me to the place I'm in. And for the last three weeks, I took for granted the freedom of being an average Joe.

"Have you sent pictures?"

Another nod, and I do my best not to snap his neck as I keep him pinned and lift his phone.

"*Quel est le mot de passe?*" *What's the password?*

He rattles off a four-digit code, and I check his messages to see an active thread with a familiar area code. He's been reporting for the last two days, his most recent text sent minutes ago to which he got no response. I make a note of the frequency of their texts and pocket his phone. The image of the snapshot of Cecelia at the entrance to her café has rage taking over.

Using my elbow, I black him out to keep from getting rupture marks on my knuckles for Cecelia to inspect. Once he's unconscious, the two birds I trusted on watch, Oz and David, quickly drag him into their back seat. I scan them closely as they nervously load the car, each of them glancing over their shoulder to me. Both are dressed in plain clothes, with muscular builds, but Oz has a mohawk, which is eye-catching and distinctive in this town or any fucking other.

These are Russell's most prized recruits?

He should know better.

Just as they close the door on their unconscious passenger, I step up to them both, seething.

"Why was your text too late?"

Oz is the first to speak. "We weren't sure—"

"You weren't *sure*?" I clench my fists to keep from lashing out. "Captain Obvious has been here for *two fucking days*." I look between them. "I don't give second chances. Not at *this* post. ID him and bleed him of information until you're sure he's working here *alone*. Call Russell, get six more birds here, two to replace the two of you. I want them here *today*. I don't give a fuck how. He's in your custody now and your responsibility until I say so. Let me down on this," I snarl, "and you're fucking *out*."

Clipping wings isn't something I threaten often, especially when they've earned their ink, but this is a major fuckup, and one inked men should never make.

They nod, offering zero excuse, no doubt due to the murderous threat in my eyes. Once they're back in the sedan, I search for anyone who might've seen the spectacle before taking off back toward the Camaro. Behind the wheel, I feel the needles start in my chest and run my hand over my jaw.

The sun beams through a raincloud as a new arrival grabs a cart at the entrance of the store. He's probably here to pick up a power tool, nothing more, and carry on with the rest of the day—an average Joe.

Envy shoots through me as he strolls in with weightless shoulders.

For the first time in my life, I had a sense of normalcy, and I wasted it feeling sorry for myself. I had the freedom to live as an everyday man, no matter how temporary, and I didn't realize how precious it was to me until it was taken from me only minutes ago. It would be so easy to ignore the distraction, the impending threat, to ignore the danger a little longer, in an effort to win her back fully. But as of this moment, I'm running out of time.

Doing my best to slow my racing thoughts, I try to concentrate on the task at hand.

Date night.

She deserves the effort, it's what I promised her, and more than that, it's what I need in order to proceed with her. We have to get back to some semblance of us before we can take on any more. I won't let anything get in the way of more progress. One last secret, and for no other reason than to buy me time to win her over before we weather another storm. Between fury and worry, I lift my phone when it rattles with an incoming message.

> **Russell: I know I'm sorry isn't enough, man. I'm sending two straight from Tyler.**

I don't respond because sorry isn't enough. These are mistakes we can't afford to make anymore. Not this late in the game.

Once again, a decision has been made for me due to uncontrollable circumstances. Turning the ignition, I press my head to the steering wheel and take deep inhales.

I'll sort through the threats as they come. I have a day or two at most to come clean, and I'm going to use every second to make it right.

"Putain de fils de pute!" *Motherfucking son of a bitch!*

I slam my fist on the dash and immediately regret it, smoothing my hand over where I struck, thankful there is no evidence.

Chest tightening, I exhale slowly.

I've got a book to read, and a dinner to cook. I can do this, for her. The seize in my chest threatens to take over as I put the car in gear and gun the gas, peeling out of the parking lot.

I just need a little gin first.

Chapter Nineteen

CECELIA

ADDING UP THE day's receipts at my desk, I pull my phone from my discarded apron and see several missed messages from Tobias.

> Tobias: I hate this fucking book, and my calf is pregnant. Beau needs to be neutered.

> Tobias: There's no God in my life to choose over you, don't you get that?

He's never been so openly emotional in a text, and this is definitely not the way he's revealed any of his feelings in the past. Something is wrong, and it's been apparent in the last week with his excessive runs and increased drinking that the isolation is starting to get to him. Armed, he's been walking the perimeter of the house at night before he locks up, often peeking out the windows when he thinks I'm not looking, his face visibly relaxing only when he receives texts from the ravens at our post. There's clear fear instilled in him at this point. I don't know if it's protection or paranoia that has him acting like a caged lion, but I can only assume it's a mixture of both. It's evident he worries more than he sleeps. Two nights ago, he gathered me in his arms and whispered, "come back to me," on gin-infused breath. I didn't acknowledge I heard him, and I'm still feeling remorseful about it. And right now, he's alone at home reading a story I once considered a prophecy that slams a character I identify him with, no doubt hurt and insulted. Guilt gnaws at my conscience as I read more of his texts.

Tobias: This is not our story, Cecelia. This is not our fucking story!

I shoot off my own text in hopes of starting some damage control.

I'll be home soon. I'm cashing out now. It's just a book, Tobias.

Tobias?

Tobias?

When I get no response, I dial his number and am sent straight to voicemail. Panicking, I cash out and race to my Audi, dreading what I'm in for. I'd placed too much importance on the book—which clearly paints him as the selfish and egotistical villain—which is how I viewed him for so long. For the better part of the time he's been back, he's been fighting with something, something underlying that he hasn't yet put a voice to due to conversations I've refused him. His 'bad' days seem to happen more often than not, and I'm sure it's because of his isolation. That combined with the fact that he's all but abandoned the brotherhood, his purpose, the thing that's defined him and who he is for over two decades, to play house with me. All he's living for now is me, and I've given him next to nothing for it. No matter how strong of a man he is, this transition is getting the best of him. I told him I wanted a king, not a coward, but what if that demand has hindered his ability to be open with me?

Nothing gets to me more than seeing him this vulnerable. This once impenetrable man who I had to fight for full sentences from, for anything *other* than cruel indifference. It's not his looks or our sexual draw—though its potency hasn't waned in the least—it's what he's let me get glimpses of in the past, the romantic he revealed in the clearing, our resulting relationship after because of it. It's his love for his brothers, his dedication to his cause that drains my iron will, day by day.

It's his humanity, his empathy, his flaws, and the fact that I'm the woman he chose, the one he trusts to reveal this side of himself to that has my guilt multiplying.

But I demanded the man I met, and in a lot of ways, I'm not the same woman. Is it hypocritical of me to think that the last years haven't changed him? Because at this point, I sure as hell can't say the same. He all but told me he had closed himself off completely after Dominic died and became a sort of machine. But this openness, *now*, giving me this much in so little time, lets me know something is going on inside of him far more haunting than what he's revealed to me.

Speeding toward the house, my anxious heart pounding,

I make the last turn on my road when I catch sight of him, running in jeans and . . . Oh. My. God.

"What the hell?" Slowing to his pace, I roll down my window as Tobias runs like his ass is on fire in my kitchen apron, a hot pink ribbon secured around his waist. He's covered in sweat and what looks like . . . flour coating half his face and dusting his hair.

"What in the hell are you doing?"

He stops his run when I again call his name as if he's in some sort of stupor, hyper-focused on something that's not here and now. I pull over and exit the car, a gust of wind slapping me in the face. When I approach him, it's clear he's freezing, his olive skin tinged red from the bitter cold, and he reeks of gin.

"You're drunk? I thought this was date night?"

"I'm . . . Trésor . . ." he hangs his head and jerks me to him before burying his head in my neck. "I couldn't be there."

"At my house? Why are you drunk?"

"I'm not drunk . . . I am . . . a little. Doesn't matter."

"Get in the car, Frenchman, your skin is like ice."

He ignores my orders and releases me. "You compare me to this . . . *Ralph*," he grits out with disgust.

"Tobias, it's just a book."

"That's not us."

"I know it's not."

"J'ai été égoïste, mais j'avais mes raisons. Il y a une raison à tout ce que je fais. Et si c'est notre histoire, sache que je suis ici pour te donner, pour nous donner, une meilleure fin." *I've been selfish, but I had my reasons. There's always a reason for everything I do. And if that's our story, then know I'm here to give you, us, a better ending.*

Sulking, he walks over to the passenger side of the Audi and plops himself into the seat before slamming the door. Pressing my lips together to hide my amusement at his rare tantrum, I take the driver's seat and turn the heat on high, opening the vents his way. Full of contempt, he sits there like a scolded child, his jaw set, his eyes averted. Pressing my lips together, I put the car into gear as he speaks up.

"I never brought a woman into this for a fucking reason. First, it was too much to ask of any woman long-term. Period. And this, what's happening between us, the resentment you feel for me now is why. That's one of the reasons I punished them so harshly for dragging you into this."

"You're blowing this out of proportion and taking it too personally."

"I have no choice." He remains silent as I drive the few miles back to the house, but I can feel the war raging inside of him, the energy in the cabin dense and coming from every gin-infused pore. When we pull up to the house, he stops me from exiting the car with a hand on my thigh, bringing tortured eyes to mine. "The only reason I believe God exists is because you do. So many times, I wanted to come to you—"

"I don't want to hear it!" I explode, surprising myself with my venom.

"I told you why I couldn't!"

"It doesn't make it any better!"

He switches gears as if he's having too many thoughts. "Was Collin your Luke? In the book, Meggie marries a man she doesn't love. Alicia was my Luke. I didn't love her. I couldn't."

"He was in a way, but you can't generalize relationships like that."

"What do I know about *relationships*?" He slings the word with disgust. "That I tried most of my fucking life to avoid them? I know how to treat a woman, that's . . . common sense, how to fuck them, but I never allowed myself to have anything *real* for any woman . . . until you." He swallows and shakes his head ironically. "Instinctually, I *always knew* . . . that if I let myself get lost in a woman, how fucking detrimental it would be for all involved, and I was right. I was fucking right." His grip on my thigh tightens. "And then I *lost* you."

The sting and the soothe of his admission have my own tangled emotions about us surfacing. The sting begins to win as I fight the urge to lash out, but he's speaking the truth. That's the nature of us, of how we started and all the resistance that followed as we battled our desire and our growing need. But my resentment wins.

"You didn't lose me. You discarded me, cruelly, purposefully," I remind him. "You forced me out."

"I had to! I couldn't even protect myself!" He curses in both English and French, searching my face. "Am I too late?" He regards me for seconds before he slams a fist on the dash, eyes red-rimmed and losing focus.

"How much did you drink?"

"Not nearly enough!"

I flinch, and he shakes his head.

"Fuck, I'm sorry. Don't be afraid of me. Jesus Christ, stop being afraid of me!" He jumps out of the car and rounds it, yanking me from the driver's seat just as I grab my purse, his expression hopeful as he runs his hands over me. "I have a surprise."

And I have fucking whiplash.

Physically, I can feel the ache inside him, his desperation to turn it all around and not later, *now*. He's drunk as hell, but all he's feeling is visceral. I can sense his hurt, his guilt, his agitation with our situation, and my refusal to fully let him in.

And because of that, my newly returned King is coming undone.

He guides me into the house, and once inside, he presses me to the door and flips the lock behind me.

One, two, three.

He lowers his eyes with shame when he sees me take note of his actions. "It started when my parents died, and I had to lock Dominic in the house. I had to make sure he was safe. It's a false sense of security, and the logical side of me knows that, *it knows*, but it doesn't matter. Somehow, counting helps. When counting isn't enough, running helps exhaust my racing thoughts. And smoking helps me at times in between my run and my first sip of gin."

My heart is in the midst of exploding when he lifts volatile eyes to mine.

"Do you understand that?"

I nod, unflinching. "It's a nervous condition and nothing to be ashamed of. I'm sorry if I ever made you feel uncomfortable talking about it."

"It's . . ." he lets out a resigned sigh, "sometimes it takes over."

I cup his jaw, and he molds his hand over mine, seeming desperate for the contact, and my chest swells further with ache. "It's anxiety that stemmed from a very hard and very traumatizing time in your life. When I'm stressed the most, that's when the worst of my dreams manifest."

"It got . . . so much worse when I sent you away," he admits and closes his eyes. "Running, smoking, gin, nothing is helping today. Come." He grips the hand he's holding and drags me into my destroyed kitchen. Burnt veal cutlets sit on the counter, along with an empty bottle of gin and two Louis Latour bottles. Caked mixing bowls and utensils line the counters, and it looks like he fought a bag of flour and lost at one point. I wrinkle my nose as I survey the damage.

"Did you smoke in my kitchen?"

"I had one." He holds up two fingers.

"Don't smoke in my house."

"*Your* house," he parrots, and I feel the sting that comment causes him. He glances at the stove. "I made you dinner." He furrows his brows. "Well, I *burnt* dinner, but I've got this!" He reaches for an empty bottle of Louis Latour on the counter and pours three drops into a glass before thrusting it toward me. "Saved you some."

I eye it and bite my lips to stifle my laugh as he hangs his head in defeat. "This is not how this was supposed to go. Not any of this. Forgive me."

I glance at the newly shredded book, which lays just below a fresh scuff on my wall. He follows my line of sight.

"Another one bites the dust," I say through a sigh.

"That's not—" he shakes his head back and forth. "That's not us. That will never be us. I don't at all like your perception."

"All I see right now is a *very drunk*, very tired, very stressed-out Frenchman who had a bad day and needs to sleep it off." It's then I notice the absence of the other Frenchman in my life. "Did you leave Beau inside when you ran?"

His eyes bulge in fear before he races out of the room. A minute later, I hear an audible protest from Beau for being accosted. In the next second, Tobias carries my dog into the kitchen before presenting him to me in his palms like a trophy. "He's here."

I take Beau in my arms, and the confused dog licks my lips. I murmur my hello as Tobias snaps at the both of us. "I'm jealous. Of. A. *Dog*."

I shake my head, unable to hold in my grin, and glance around the kitchen. "Looks like you had a more than productive day. I appreciate the thought."

"I am *not* bored," he says softly. "I'm . . . *adjusting*."

He steps in front of me and runs his knuckles along my jawline. "I didn't think it was possible to miss you more than I did before I got here, but I do. And I want to fuck you *so bad*." The ache in that declaration and his tone is comical, but the sentiment hits hard.

"Wow. Okay. You get points for honesty."

He grips my hand, and Beau snarls at our feet. Tobias snarls back. "She was mine first, fucker."

I lift his chin with my finger as he stands off in a cock fight with my dog. "Think you might want to sleep it off, and maybe we can talk in the morning?"

He entangles our fingers. "I don't want to be your thorn, Cecelia."

"I know."

"I am yours."

"Yes," I muse as we stand in my obliterated kitchen, "in all your glory."

He frowns. "I fucked this all up. I was going to wine you, dine you, make you come," he murmurs, his thick lips tempting even in his state. "I was going to make you remember how good we are. I want to do things for you like I used to. You used to let me."

"I'd say you've done enough for one day."

"This has to stop. You have to face me."

"I'm looking right at you."

He places his palm over where his heart lies, his eyes intent, his voice urgent. "I'm sorry."

"I know." Eyes dipping to where his hand rests on his muscular chest covered partially by my fiery-pink, lipstick-kissed apron, I lift it to inspect a painful-looking grease burn. "Does it hurt?"

"Stop, look at me."

I do, and in his gaze, I see nothing but yearning.

"I want to live here."

"You are living here."

"I'm *existing* here, but we can make a life here if that's what you want. I'll give you whatever you want. Dream with me again, Cecelia. Dream a thousand more dreams with me, and I will make them all come true. I can give you promises. Promises I couldn't before."

"Tobias—"

"I don't want to be your goddamn thorn or the moon you cry for!"

When I jump due to his outburst, he closes his eyes, running his flour-crusted fingernails through his hair, coloring more of his onyx strands white.

My eyes narrow as I weigh his words, his actions, his desperation. "This is about more than the book. What aren't you telling me?"

Haunted. That's exactly how he looks. Even in the bright

lights of the kitchen, I can see the tortuous shadows of the past closing in on him.

"Tell me we're still possible, Cecelia. Tell me I'm not too late."

"Sleep it off. We'll talk when you're sober."

"It's hard for me to make sense of my life so you understand."

"You're making perfect sense."

He shakes his head as though he's not getting through to me. He pulls his hand out of my grip, sliding down against the cabinet onto the floor. "I want to tell you . . . so much."

"I'm listening."

"Your heart isn't open to me, and until it is, you won't truly hear me." He pauses for several seconds and closes his eyes. For a minute, I think he might've passed out until he speaks up and his eyes open to slits. "The morning, at Roman's house, the day I confessed to you, you said . . . that Dom said something about us, about you and me." He brings glistening eyes to mine.

I nod, tears filling my own eyes. "I'll tell you tomorrow when you'll remember."

"I can't forget anything. Don't you understand?" He grips his hair, agony twisting his features. "My mind does this to me." He chokes on emotion. "I can't ask you tomorrow," he whispers hoarsely. "Please understand I can't ask you again."

"Okay." I sink to kneel in front of him and survey his face. The face of a man in torment, not the confident man I collided with. "Then I'll tell you without being asked. But you should know he wanted you to be happy."

"Do you think it's possible?"

"I think that you're upset right now, and it's not a good time for us to talk," I answer. I grip his hand again and press a kiss next to his angry, blistered skin.

"You still love me," he whispers, watching my face intently. "But you don't want to love me anymore," he says mournfully before brushing his thumb over my lips. "Tu es si belle." *You're so beautiful.* "I never thought I'd find you, and when I did, you weren't mine."

I shake my head. "I hate how admitting it feels, and I wish you would stop making me, but I've always been yours."

"But you really loved them."

I nod. "Tell me what you need to tell me, Tobias."

"These things I think about? Trust me, you don't want to know."

"You promised." There's a warning in my voice.

"Which admission do you want?" His brows furrow into a deep v. "That I'm scared that every day I wake up with you, every time I fuck you or make love to you, I'll feel guilty. That every day I live this life with you, I'll hate myself a little more."

"You can't—"

"The more I try to let go, the more my head refuses to let me. There's so much you don't know. Most of my life I lived without you. Thirty-one years of life I lived without you, and my brother was there, my brother," he swallows, "he was with me for most of that time . . . I can't move on from that. Dom . . ." he chokes on his name, and it cracks my heart. He's still grieving as though he just lost him. "There's no escaping it."

"What are you saying?"

"How different would this have all turned out if I would

have just fucking listened to them?" His voice is tattered when he speaks. "You have to think about that. I know you do. About the future you would have had with one or both of them if I wasn't in the way. It kills me that you might still think about that. Dream about it. I can't . . . this feeling, Jesus Christ, this jealousy I still feel at times. It eats at me. I saw how you loved them, and I still did it, I did it. I forged my way in, purposefully, as the man in your life because that's how much I wanted you. Brothers be damned, everyone be damned. And you know what that did? It damned everyone, including us."

He lifts his chin defiantly, and it's clear his nemesis is staring back at him in the reflection of my gaze. "Maybe I shouldn't want your forgiveness. Maybe I need you to continue to punish me. Because I don't deserve the pardon, Cecelia. It's fucking wrong that I get you, while my brother rots in the ground." He gathers some of the scattered pages from the floor with his free hand and lifts them between us. "Maybe I hate this—" he crushes the pages in his hand— "because it's the truth."

"Did you finish it?"

"Yes." He shakes his head. "I want to give you a better story. I just wish I could give you a better man. My brother was the better man."

"Tobias—"

"Just tell me if I'm too late, tell me the truth."

"The truth? All the good admitting the truth got me with you before," I snap.

"It got me here!" he roars. "It got me here. But I want the ugly, Cecelia. I need it. Fucking tell me, so at least I know where I stand with you."

"You have never dealt with honesty well, Tobias."

"I need it!"

"You're drunk."

"I'm miserable! You called me out for being a coward. Pot, kettle, Cecelia. Stop backing away from this."

"You're unforgivably selfish! Is that what you want to hear? And maybe I don't want to forgive you for the *years* I spent crying for you, dreaming about you, or for the hell I endured eight months ago, begging you to see what was so fucking clear to the both of us. You sent me away to ease your own guilt, pain, and fears, never taking into consideration how much I suffered alone—or if you did—it wasn't enough to keep you from hurting me again. If you're unforgivable, it's for that. And what you're doing right now is equally as selfish."

"I know that, Cecelia, but there are no magic words. There are no gestures grand enough or deeds good enough to make up for what I've done to him, to you, to Sean. I couldn't figure out how to work my way around it *then* to get back to you, and I can't figure it out *now*. So, maybe I need you to keep punishing me," he chokes out. "Maybe it's the only way I'll be able to live with myself. I'll endure it every day for the rest of my fucking life just to be with you. I'll do anything," he chokes again, "and we can joke about this situation, but this is truly hell for me. I love you, Cecelia, but it fucking hurts." His eyes droop, and he lets out a defeated sigh. Scrambling for the words he just confessed doesn't make a difference. I inevitably come up empty as he lowers his eyes and studies the back of my hand, stroking his thumb along my skin before pressing his lips to it. "Will you lock the door three times if I go to sleep?"

"Yes."

Relief sags his shoulders as he sinks back against the cabinet and releases the pages, which scatter to the floor. "Thank you." He begins to fade out, his head lolling, as he slides further down the door.

"Tobias," I nudge him, and his eyes open briefly before they lose focus. "Oh no you don't. Good God, you crazy French bastard, at least help me get you to bed."

After much effort, between comatose steps, a few scary dry heaves, and some unintelligible French, I manage to get him face down on my bed before I set off to start repairing my kitchen.

On my way back from the bedroom, I spot the new chessboard in the living room sitting next to the fireplace. Dozens of roses in different shades are arranged in vases and mason jars throughout. His intentions for our night clear. He wants us back. And the stinging truth in my throat tells me the feeling is mutual, but after so many years apart—in a way, a lifetime—I still can't summon myself to open up completely after the way he let me leave so easily the last time we parted. Hovering over the board, I inspect the new pieces, the set almost identical to my father's. Setting the king back down, heart heavy, I make my way into the kitchen.

I'm halfway done cleaning when Beau whines to be set free. It's when I open the back door that my breath catches, and my heart bottoms out. Strung high above my garden are lights intricately woven across the yard and secured by wooden posts. And they aren't just any lights. They brighten and dim, an unmistakable twinkle in pale yellowish-green.

Fireflies.

His attempt to recreate our sacred place.

Somewhere between his racing thoughts, the last of his gin, too many glasses of Louis Latour, and his read of *The Thorn Birds*, his plans for date night went south. A book I'd entertained for far too long, which I thought resembled my life and our relationship. But he's right, it's not our story, and for the first time since he showed back up, I open my needy heart to the possibility that we may be able to write a better one.

The sight of the twinkling lights underneath a star-filled sky fills me with hope. Though we've just scratched the surface of our issues, the truth is, we were cut short, our unwritten pages ripped from us before we even had a chance to live them out.

Despite our losses, he still believes in it, in us, in magic, because I begged him to.

The rest of his sentiment rings clear as tears fill my eyes. I walk out further into the freezing night and envision my first dream. A dream I've long since forbidden my heart to imagine, the lapping of seaside waves on our feet as we walk down a shoreline, safe, in a faraway place I can picture so clearly because I've seen it. It's then I finally answer his question aloud. "It's possible, Tobias. It's possible."

After ushering Beau in, and with one last look at the lights, I close the door and flip the lock three times.

Chapter Twenty

TOBIAS

Age Twenty-Four

THE ECHO OF an obnoxious engine followed by the telltale "fuck you" of horns sound as Dom whizzes through the terminal. I manage to smother my budding grin with a scowl just as the sleek muscle car comes into view. He's spent nearly two years restoring it from frame. He skids to a stop a foot away, his dark tinted windows down, a menacing smirk firmly in place. Agitation fleeing just from laying eyes on him, I retrieve my duffle from the sidewalk, and he holds up a hand before lifting a poster board that reads **Giorgio Armani.**

"Hilarious," I snap, "and you're twenty minutes late." I step off the curb and open the passenger door, tossing my duffle between us before sliding in and surveying the interior, unable to conceal how impressed I am.

"This looks . . . fucking amazing."

Pride shines in his eyes at my reaction. "Just picked it up from the paint shop. That's why I'm late. You're the first passenger. I made sure of it."

Cupping the back of his neck, I pull him to me and press my forehead to his. "MIT. I'm so fucking proud of you, little brother." A rare but wide smile cracks his face as he sinks into the contact briefly before pulling away.

"I read a lot of books. They made me smart."

I return his grin. "You remember that conversation?"

"I remember *everything*."

"I'm still pissed I had to hear you got accepted from Sean." Like me, Dom keeps his cards close to his chest, only showing them when his hand is forced, an issue we've butted heads on more than once, but he's cut from the same cloth.

"It's not that big of a deal."

"Agree to disagree."

He rights himself in the seat before peeling away from the curb, cutting a taxi off in the process. I shake my head at his deep chuckle.

"You'll have this fucking thing impounded in a week."

"Sean predicts days."

"My money is with him."

He glances my way, his dark hair scattering in the summer wind. "Who in the hell are you trying to impress with those expensive ass suits, anyway?"

"It's called being a grown-up. You should try it sometime."

"We aren't allowed to wear suits—your rules."

And that's the truth of it, because dressing up thugs in suits is an outdated tradition that may command respect—but also draws attention. It's a uniform for men of a different breed with a completely separate agenda. We aren't fucking thugs or anything like that breed, despite the fact we have to make thug moves on the regular. Our motives are entirely different. My corporate dealings give me an excuse to dress the way I want, and it's part of my illusion. "You would be lost without your little black boots," I jab, "and I have something better in mind."

He lifts a brow, cutting off another car as he shifts and guns the gas. "What are you thinking?"

"You'll know soon enough."

"Are you spending the rest of the summer here?" The hopeful lift of his voice rakes my chest.

"Bet on it."

"Good, because in three months, I'll be in my own foreign country," he mutters.

"Boston isn't a foreign country."

"It is to me," he says contemplatively. "I've never been out of Triple Falls."

The truth of that eats at me—but he was needed here—and I think his resentment is fading because he knows it's the truth. Without him, we wouldn't have made it this far this fast. He seems to read my thoughts.

"I can skip it," he offers up easily, too easily. "You know I can. Tuition is expensive and—"

"No. The longer you stay in Triple Falls, the more you'll remain a small-town thinker. School is a jumping point for you; it will be uncomfortable at first, but it will do you good, and deep down, you want to go. Sean will survive without you for a few years. And don't worry about tuition, you leave that to me."

He gives a small dip of his chin.

"Look at me, Dom."

His eyes cut from the road to me.

"It's *your turn*."

A brief flash of anticipation lights his eyes before he flits them back to the road.

"While you're there, you ease up on your part-time job, and that's a fucking order."

"I'm being smart about it. And I have to admit—" one side of his mouth lifts—"what we're doing feels good. It's a rush."

"The best kind," I agree, my own lips lifting. "Just pull back some, so you can focus."

"Aye, aye, Captain." He gives me a mock salute. "How was Paris?"

"Nothing new."

Dom floors the Camaro the second we're on the highway, putting every bit of horsepower under the hood to work. I keep the paternal reprimand dancing on the tip of my tongue and indulge him, enjoying the ride as his brother. In the last year, since I've resided in Triple Falls more often than not, we've grown closer, strengthening the club while we set our strategy in motion.

Like Sean and Tyler, Dom's grown into his own man, maybe more so than the other two, a man I respect and admire. The fact that I still have to go back to France every six weeks to satiate Antoine and keep him at bay grates on me, but I've got my own reasons for being there. Our first international chapter continues to grow with the addition of a few relatives I managed to find who have proven their worth.

And Exodus business is fucking booming.

Studying my brother's profile, I'm amazed at the change in his build, no trace left of the little boy who was terrified of the chickenpox. He's become even more bold, fearless, cunning, and cocky to a point it's now an ingrained trait. He knows exactly who he is, and that fills me with pride because when I was his age, I struggled with a little identity dilemma. He feels my watchful gaze on him and glances my way, his next question more of a demand.

"Tell me about France."

"Nothing to tell. Don't get curious. And don't waste your time."

"What does he have on you?" It's a subject he's broached more than once that I've refused to entertain. But I have to give him something, or he won't leave it alone.

"My youth. He's nothing but a resource, one we may need down the line. I have him under control, but let me make myself clear, my business with him has nothing to do with us. Not a single fucking thing. This is *my shit* to deal with, not yours. If you ever step in, we're going to have a serious fucking problem. Leave it the fuck alone."

Dom's nostrils flare as seconds tick past, and I hate that we're already at odds. But I understand why he won't let it go, and I would be just as adamant if I thought there was any threat to him. He wants to have my back, but I refuse to let him have it on this. I kick back in my seat, changing the subject because I don't want him to know just how much this particular gamble weighs on me. Antoine's becoming more predictable at this point, which makes his presence in my life less worrisome. "What's the plan for tonight?"

He grimaces and glances over at me.

"What?"

"Sean and I have plans."

"With who?"

"This girl we're seeing—"

"*One* fucking girl?"

"We treat her well."

"You really get off on that shit?"

His jaw ticks, and I know we'll never see eye to eye on this. He's a different animal when it comes to women. For me, they're an escape, a short-term refuge. For him, I'm not sure what they are. But I get the impression for the moment, they are toys, and that's not the way I raised him to think.

"Do your thing, brother, but mark my words, you'll probably regret it one day. What's going on with Tyler?"

"Jarhead's driving in tonight to hang. We're lucky he's stationed so close."

"Yeah, we are, but I don't need a babysitter while you go get pussy."

He smirks. "What are you going to do?"

"I'm meeting Eddie at a bar downtown. We're going to check on the price tag."

"New clubhouse?"

"Something like that."

He shakes his head. "All work, no play. You're fucking boring. Maybe it's time for you to find a Helen of your own."

We exchange a long glance. "No Helen exists for me."

He shrugs. "If you say so. So, what's next?"

"We buy Boardwalk and Park Place and any other property Roman hasn't already staked a claim on. It's time to invest in some real estate."

"We're really doing this," Dom spouts with uncontained enthusiasm, briefly letting his mask slip. Over the last few years, he's adapted an air about him that's both intimidating and secretive, albeit necessary for our purpose.

"We are doing this," I agree, satisfaction swelling in my chest. "Just make sure you, Tyler, and Sean are free by midnight."

"What are we doing at midnight?"

The buzz of the tattoo gun starts up again as Tyler fists off his shirt and takes a seat in the chair next to Sean. Dom walks over to where I sit, his arm slathered in light ointment, the dark inked feathers lined with smudges of blood through the clear wrapping. He, along with Sean and Tyler, requested extra heavy on the ink. A twitch of a smile graces his lips as he glances down at his arm with evident pride. "You can keep the silk ties, brother, this I can fucking work with." He smirks, his eyes rolling over my new suit. "It's a shame you can't partake—"

"Tobias, you're up, man," Jimmy, the shop owner says, waving me over to the waiting table he's just sanitized. Dom follows me as I shrug off my suit jacket and loosen my tie.

"Isn't ink frowned upon at the country club?" Dom asks as I untuck my shirt and begin to unbutton it. Jimmy hangs the sketch in front of the two of us beneath a desk lamp, and I survey it carefully before nodding in approval and answering Dom.

"Only if they can *see* it. And I fucking hate golf."

He carefully studies the raven, wings outstretched, his lit expression dimming noticeably as he scrutinizes the distinctly different tattoo. To any other Raven, it would be misconstrued as pecking order—an indication of my position in the hierarchy—but Dom's too fucking smart, and he knows ego has nothing to do with it. I hoped I could get this part of it past him until we were all done getting marked.

Dreading the inevitable, I curse under my breath as Sean and Tyler sense the shift in the air and stop their chatter, turning their attention to the two of us as Dom starts to bristle with anger. "Don't start," I snap at Dom in warning as he begins to pace in front of me.

"That's going to be your ink, man?" Tyler asks, eyeing the outline. "It's fucking sweet."

"It's fucking *incriminating* is what it is," Dom says, refusing to back down. Tyler and Sean look over to me with drawn brows as I address my brother.

"This is not up for debate."

Dom shakes his head adamantly. "No way, brother, we're in this together."

Sighing, I lift my chin to the two guys running ink on Sean and Tyler, and the buzzing stops just before they clear the room to walk out front. When they both have lit cigarettes in hand and are safely on the other side of the door, Sean moves from his chair and lights one of his own, readying himself to get between us if need be. "All right, what the fuck is going on?"

Dom's dark gaze narrows on me as he lifts his chin. "I believe our brother is trying to deceive us with this grand gesture."

"It's not deception." I grab the bottle from Tyler that we uncorked an hour ago when I announced our plans. "This is a celebration, little brother—" I tip the lip of it toward him—"and you're ruining it."

"Bullshit," he snaps, anger seeping out of him. "This is your way of ensuring you're the one who pays the bill."

"It's *done*." I cut my hand through the air. "*End of*."

"Not fucking end of." Dom shakes his head as Tyler glances

back at the draft of my tattoo in an attempt to figure it out. It doesn't take long. "No, man, this is bullshit. If one goes down, *we all* go down."

Sean's posture bows when he too gathers the truth of what's happening and pins me with the same accusatory eyes. "What the fuck, man?"

"You designed it this way," Dom growls. "All of it was intentional."

Wordless, I take another sip from the bottle.

"Whose name did you put the bar in today?" he prompts, refusing to let it go.

"Mine," Sean speaks up, his tone just as accusing. "He called me in to sign the paperwork, and Tyler now owns the land for our spot."

"Got the deed in the mail last week," Tyler adds.

Dom pulls it all together in a matter of seconds. "You're using *Exodus* as the front, and you're putting all the legit businesses in our name in case you get cuffed."

"All good business decisions," I argue. "If anything happens to me—"

"Fuck no." He jerks the outline of my tattoo from where it hangs. "This might as well be a target on your fucking back. If there's ever an investigation, all arrows will point to *you*."

"Which makes you the sitting fucking duck if we dip in the wrong bag and draw heat," Tyler adds.

"Which also means you'll be the one doing the most time for racketeering," Sean gathers, clear fury in his tone. "That's why you wouldn't let us in on Exodus."

Tyler speaks up next. "No way, brother, no fucking way, Tobias. We make these decisions together."

"Except this one he kept us out of because he knew we would never agree," Sean adds, his fury apparent.

"It's done," I snap. "So, there's no point in arguing."

"Fuck that. You don't get to martyr yourself," Dom refutes, his tone lethal. He hates not being in the know, but mostly, he hates that he didn't figure it out sooner. "If we fuck up, we go down *together*," he declares adamantly.

"That's not the way *we designed this*, and you know it," I remind him. "And you need to remember that we have other people's livelihoods depending on *us*." I look over at my brother. "I haven't forgotten what hungry feels like, have *you*?" My argument stuns him silent, and I dig in, intent on making my point. "We have to be smart about this—things are about to kick up, and we need to be prepared for anything."

"Motherfucker!" Dom explodes, flipping a tray of ink over as he glares at me.

I can't help my grin. "You're going to have to work harder to stay one step ahead of me, brother. You're not quite there yet." I glance between them, my gaze lingering for a few seconds on each of them. "And this is all speculation. Just do your job, keep your head in the game, and don't fuck up."

The gin begins to warm me, the light buzz lifting my lips as they eye each other. "Have a damn drink and stop sulking like I just told you Santa isn't real."

"He's not?" Sean quips, but the delivery is lackluster, and no one laughs.

I decide not to coddle them. Those days are long over.

"*I trust you*," I say emphatically, and all three of them snap their downcast eyes to me. I know that declaration is just as important to them as it is to me. "So, don't let me down." I lift my chin toward the two inkers in wait, and they stomp out their cigarettes before making their way back inside. I don't spare a glance at the three of them as I take my place on the table. Tonight is about celebration, and I'm not going to let their fear ruin the faith I have in them. Nothing but exhilaration courses through me as the gun buzzes to life, and I feel the first prick of the needles in my skin.

Minutes later, the music's turned up, the mood lifting as they pass the bottle, and we resume our celebration.

We finish the last of it huddled around the fire, piss drunk, with the future buzzing heavily between us. I gaze on at each of them as the familiar inkling comes over me. It strikes hard, the hairs on the back of my neck lifting despite my drunken state, and with its arrival comes the knowledge we are exactly where we're supposed to be. It's time to make our first move.

It's been a long fucking time coming.

But for the first time in years, surrounded by my brothers, I embrace the present. When the chatter starts to die out, and they begin to pass out one by one, I shift my gaze up at the night sky, and the image of the flock that inspired me comes to mind. Though pitch dark, I can see them so clearly, just as the pieces start to move on their own. Turning toward the newly built mansion, I see a single light on in the house and briefly wonder what kind of thoughts keep a man like Roman Horner up at night. Soon, I won't have to wonder. Piece by piece, I'll steal chunks of his kingdom from beneath him until it starts to crumble around him. And then, and only then, will I reveal myself as the thief responsible.

"I'm coming for you, motherfucker," I whisper vehemently, tossing another log onto the fire just as the lone light clicks off.

* * *

My head splinters as the recollection of that night fades, and the heavy pulse of fresh hell sets in. Prying one eye open, I see Cecelia sleeping soundly next to me and wince through the invasion of morning light. Beau's nails click on the hardwood announcing his entrance into the bedroom, and he nudges the hand I have hanging over the lip of the mattress, beckoning his new bitch to escort him out for his morning leak. Moving far too quickly, my body reacts, my head screaming obscenities as I usher him out of the room and through the back door to relieve himself. Shivering in the onslaught of cold, I'm slapped awake by one thought.

One step ahead, Tobias.

Alarm shoots up my spine as I rush inside and gather both phones before heading into the bathroom to check them for missed texts.

Russell: New birds in the nest.

The text was sent at eight o'clock last night. I feel slight relief knowing we're covered with Tyler's trained birds, especially since I wasn't of sound mind. For me, blind trust is damn near hard to come by, but over the years, I've tried my best to return it. Still, with so much to lose and flying blind, I'm in the worst imaginable position. I'm no longer in control or calling the shots, nor am I aware of every move being made on the daily, and it's nearly fucking impossible for me to deal with that day by day. Blind trust is what I have to continue to give so I can navigate my way with Cecelia. But now? I'm not so sure I'm capable. Especially if Antoine's planning on making a move. I'm just not sure of what his motive would be or what his intentions are, other than to keep tabs on me. But if he took the time to send someone—in lieu of a fucking phone call—chances are something's brewing.

Hitting a separate text feed on my burner, I see a message from one of the two birds I kicked to the curb after my run in yesterday.

Oz: He's working alone. He came to report and nothing more.

You're sure?

Oz: Positive. He showed us his itinerary, and we cross-checked it with every single passenger on the flight and every other within days of his arrival. So far, everything checks out. We're combing the sidewalks now.

Wait for word from me.

Oz: 10/4

Furious with myself that I let my emotions and nerves get the best of me yesterday to the point I drank myself into a blackout, I switch phones to see the demand for a report on the idiot's cell. I'm relieved when I see the message was sent only minutes ago. The order short and to the point.

Quelle est la situation?

I mimic the previous text.

Pas de changement. *No change.*

Anxiety slices through me as I will the fucking phone to go off with a reply. A reply that will ensure me more time for damage control with Cecelia.

Adrenaline spiking, I wait with bated fucking breath and see Antoine's response time has varied anywhere from one hour to five. It's too soon to tell if Antoine's onto me, so I shoot off a text to Tyler.

I want two birds in the air. Now.

His reply is immediate.

Tyler: On it. Need to talk?

I'll let you know.

Cursing the situation and the fucking disaster I made of date night, I summon Beau back into the house before creeping through the bedroom and softly shutting the bathroom door. After a brief inspection with bloodshot eyes, I wash my face, brush my teeth, and rinse my mouth out before swallowing down a couple of Tylenol from her medicine cabinet. The reality of last night slams into me as I take one last look in the mirror. "Run for your life, Trésor."

Phones cupped in my hands, I quietly open the door and slip them both into my duffle before easing back into bed. Cecelia stirs slightly with the dip of my weight, and I slowly exhale a breath of relief when I fully make it back in without waking her.

She slept in today purposefully. I'm part relieved, part terrified because I can't remember much past finishing the book and emptying the closest bottle.

Brief images flash through my mind of what happened after that fatal sip and some of the verbal vomit I spewed. I'm positive an apology is in order at the very least.

Did she see the lights? Chances are with Sir Piss-a-lot, she did last night.

Hopefully, it was some consolation for the complete fucking fool I made of myself. But I know her, and I know her heart. What I don't know is if that heart has any more forgiveness in it for me at this point, especially now. I asked her for a date, and she came home to a fucking shitshow. Covered in it, I gaze down at her before gently pushing the hair away from her face for a better view. No evident tear streaks, no puffy eyes, and for that, I'm thankful. I'm sure I still reek of gin and desperation, but I don't want to miss her reaction to me when she finally wakes. It will tell me all I need to know. I don't have to wait long because a minute into caressing her, she smiles at me before her eyes flutter open.

Thank Christ.

"How are you feeling?"

I draw my brows. "Like I ran a marathon while on an IV of gin and wine."

Her deepening smile erases more of my anxiety. "Pretty much what happened."

"I'm sorry. I meant to—"

She covers my mouth with her hand. "You apologized a lot. Yelled a lot. Revealed a lot. And unloaded a lot of that baggage. Unfortunately—" she purses her swollen-from-sleep lips—"you don't know how to unlock your suitcases." Brow creasing with worry, she lifts a hand to my pounding head before gently running her fingers through my hair. "Do you remember anything?"

"Some."

"Well, to start, you gave the book a bad review," she says, her soft laughter echoing in the bedroom.

I wince, mostly from the pain in my head, some from humiliation.

"I had a plan, and it seems I'm not so good at executing them these days."

"Well, you are on vacation." She edges her chin on her pillow, moving closer to me, and I'm thankful I brushed my teeth. Gin-brewed sweat beads at my temple as I try my best to recall the details of my blackout.

"Forgive me, Trésor. I don't re—"

Her full smile steals my speech. "Remember that your calf had sex with Beau and that you're expecting in four to six weeks?"

I faceplant my pillow and then turn to her and grin, opening one eye. She runs her fingers through my tangled, flour-caked hair, and I rest in the touch, a hope igniting in me that I've been starving for.

Her eyes do a slow sweep down my face before her tone turns to one of concern. "You were brutally honest."

"I don't know how to make things right."

"I saw the effort you put in while I was cleaning my destroyed kitchen." She widens her eyes. "No more cooking drunk, okay?"

"You should have let me clean it. Forgive me?"

"For last night, I'll consider it." She runs her hand down

my bicep and arm before squeezing my hand and entangling our fingers. "The lights, Tobias, they are beautiful."

"I didn't want you to see them alone."

"I think I needed to."

"Meaning?"

"Meaning, I needed to *see* for myself what you haven't told me in all the years we were apart. You're . . . a lot to handle in a room sometimes. I don't mean it in a bad way, but you're distracting. And your guilt . . . it's eating you alive. It's been years, Tobias. Haven't you made peace with *any* of it?"

"With Roman, all of that, yes, but with . . . everything else, no," I close my eyes. "I don't know how to stop it."

"We'll get through this." She moves her upper half to cover me, and if it weren't for my pounding head, I'd be all too eager to try and make love to her until she forgets the ass I was last night and remembers the controlled man she met. The man capable of conducting himself.

"Je suis un putain d'idiot," I mumble, biting my lip.

"My idiot." She grips my jaw and uses her thumb to pull it free from my teeth. For the first time since I came back to her, she initiates a kiss. Heart rocketing, I cup the back of her head and latch on, keeping her close, and kiss her back through the protest in my screaming head.

"Tobias," she moans against my lips, and I have a vision of ripping flannel, of more moans, of burying my cock inside her.

Shifting to hover above her, I see the one thing I desperately need in her eyes, permission.

Fuck the headache.

Chest cracking wide, I reclaim her lips and grip her hair,

angling her head and plunging my tongue deep into her mouth. Our kiss singes us both, and we set into motion. All at once, I give into every part of me, with the freedom I haven't had for years as I begin to touch her, taste her neck, inhale her scent, indulge and lose myself in her while dragging moans and rapid breaths from her lips.

"Fuck, I missed you," I murmur, lifting the hem of her flannel top with an eager hand just as Beau barks, his alert breaking us apart as the sound of an approaching motor stops all our movement. Cecelia glances up at me and frowns.

"Expecting someone?" I ask, ready to murder whoever is interrupting us as my cock weeps in my boxers. There's no fucking way anyone would make it this close to our front door without my birds aware. Whomever it is, they've already been screened and identified if they made it into the driveway. I'm positive there is a text waiting with an arrival announcement.

Hovering above her, pulse hammering, hips still grinding, I pose a hopeful question as she gasps at the friction. "Mailman?" I ask, and she shakes her head.

"It runs in the afternoon."

Groaning in frustration, I spring from her and grab my Glock. By the time I'm armed, she's already got her Beretta, missing the swipe of my hand to block her as I give chase, tugging on my sweatpants, as I stumble after her.

"Goddamnit, Cecelia!"

"Chill, Frenchman," she snaps behind her as she heads toward the living room.

I'm halfway to where she stands at the entryway when she turns from the window and rushes toward me, paling with every step. Alarmed, I reach for her to get her behind me, and she stops a foot away before thrusting her gun toward me. Gripping it, and knowing she's aware of who's in her driveway, I search her face as the alarm drains from it and concern kicks in. "What's wrong?"

"Go shower, okay? I'll get rid of them, and then we'll have breakfast."

"Rid of who?"

"Tobias, please, just let me handle it."

I move to walk around her as a door opens and closes, and panic fully blooms on her face.

"Please!" she begs, jumping in front of me and placing a hand on my chest. "Tobias, let me handle this. *Please.*"

Jealousy snakes in, and I narrow my eyes. "Who. The. Fuck. Is. It. Cecelia?"

She twists her hands in front of her like a teenage girl. "Tobias, when you got here, I completely forgot about it. We made plans so long ago. It slipped my mind."

"I have a text waiting that will tell me exactly who it is, and I'm not fucking moving until I know, so out with it."

She lifts terrified eyes to mine. "It's my mother."

Chapter Twenty-One

TOBIAS

STUNNED BRIEFLY BY her admission, Cecelia leaps into action before I gather myself in time to stop her freak-out. Within seconds, she slips out the front door as I shuffle to ditch the guns and dress. Racing to the bedroom, I place them in the duffle, not bothering to check my cell, an oversight I won't repeat. It was both reckless and careless to ignore any potential warning. After yanking on a hoodie, I shove into my sneakers before charging back in the direction Cecelia fled. By the time I clear the front porch with Beau whining in tow, I'm able to hear harshly exchanged words of a hushed conversation at the back of a massive RV.

"Mom, please, just go, okay. I'll call you and explain later."

"You're being ridiculous. We just got here, and you know we've been coming for months. What's changed?"

"Everything, Mom. Please, just go, and I'll call you." Her plea is for me, to protect *me*, which only makes my love for her grow.

"That's not necessary," I speak up, stepping into view, laying eyes on both women as they turn to me with gaping mouths.

"Tobias," Cecelia says mournfully, her eyes closing as her mother's bulge.

By reaction alone, it's easy to see Cecelia never told her about us, as her mother rapidly pales, her eyes darting wildly between us.

I always assumed Cecelia kept our secrets—even from those closest to her—and the proof is standing in front of me, seeming to be on the verge of passing out. Cecelia kept her involvement with me from her mother even after her confrontation with her eight months ago. I never asked her for the details because I was too busy trying to accept her goodbye.

Cecelia looks back at me, sheer panic in her eyes when she sees me moving to greet her mother.

"Hello, Diane," I say, inching my way in as she takes a lingering look at her daughter before lifting mortified eyes to me.

"*This* is what you've been hiding for so long?"

It's not so much a question at this point, but the truth of it has knocked her sideways. Cecelia tries to stop me from reaching her, but I grab the hands meant to subdue me and squeeze them in reassurance.

"Tobias, I've asked her to leave."

Timothy, a boyfriend I've only read about in informative emails, emerges from the RV looking between the three of us, his eyes coming back to me. It's odd how I've kept such close tabs on all of these people over the years, feeling as if I know them, and to an extent, I do.

Diane turns to Timothy, her voice shaking with fear. "Timothy, honey, will you grab a carton of cigarettes from the suitcase? I'm out."

"Not before I give this little lady a hug." He walks over

to where we stand and pulls Cecelia into his arms before turning curious eyes to me. "Hey there, I'm Tim."

"Tobias King," I counter, thrusting out my hand. Releasing Cecelia, he takes it and pumps it eagerly. "So, I'm assuming *Mr. King* is what kept you from answering our calls last night?" Timothy asks Cecelia, sporting a clueless grin.

"Tim, please, my cigarettes," Diane rasps out, her eyes glued to me.

"All right, honey." He gives me a *'women'* look before walking off to do her bidding.

"I forgot," Cecelia says, dragging my attention back to her. "I swear, Tobias, it totally slipped my mind. I'm so sorry."

"It's okay, Trésor," I whisper sincerely, before pressing a kiss to her temple. I sidestep her to reach Diane, who's now visibly shaking.

"It's been a long time," I say softly as Diane rakes her lip with her teeth, her eyes shining with fear.

"I've wanted to reach out so many times since that day."

I nod as Cecelia intercepts. "You've met her? You've met my *mother*? When?"

"I was eleven. Dom had chickenpox, and she gave me a ride to the pharmacy." I turn to Cecelia. "She was pregnant with *you*. She almost named you Leann." I lift my eyes to Diane. "Guess I had some sway on that?"

Diane nods, a lone, guilty tear gliding down her face.

"You never told me," Cecelia rasps. The hurt in her tone has me attempting damage control on them both.

"I didn't get a chance to, when . . . that day in my office before you left," I offer, to indicate which day I'm referring to. "We never made it that far into the discussion." And those details and revelations didn't fucking matter because she was ridding herself of *me* for good. There was plenty left unsaid between us then, as there is now. And due to our own shit, I haven't gotten to explain much more.

Cecelia mulls the latest dropped bomb and turns to her mother in question. "And *you* didn't tell me you met *him*, either."

Diane looks on at me in the most unnerving way, and I sense the ill feelings rolling through her. She's transparent with her eyes, her expressions, much like her daughter. "It was only the once, and I didn't think to mention it, well, because I had no idea you two were . . . Oh, God." She runs a hand through her cropped, brown hair. "I'll go. We'll go. We'll go right now." She eyes me over Cecelia's shoulder. "I'm so sorry."

"Come inside," I say, and both women's heads pop toward me. The resemblance unreal, mortification on both their faces. "*Please*, Diane, come inside."

"Got 'em," Timothy says, exiting the camper with a pack of cigarettes in hand. "Almost couldn't find them in that death trap you call a suitcase," he jests, reading the expressions of both women before looking toward me to relay.

"I could go for some pancakes and bacon, Tim. How about you?"

He takes my easy out, his eyes darting between mother and daughter before flashing an uneasy grin. "My kind of man."

I look down at Diane as she cranes her neck to study me while I walk her into the house. "Breakfast?"

She nods, stupefied, as we clear the door before she glances over her shoulder at Cecelia.

*

"Well, damn, this is the best cup of coffee I've ever had in my life," Timothy remarks as he eyes the French press in my hand.

"Tobias is a coffee snob, and he rubbed off on me," Cecelia replies, on autopilot where she stands at the stove. She insisted on cooking but has been in a stupor since she started, tossing wary glances my way. I do my best to convey in my return gaze that I'm okay with the situation and see nothing but apology in her eyes. Her phone rattles where it rests in her apron on the counter, drawing her attention away. She pulls it out to read a text, staring at it for several beats before she starts to type a response.

All I want to do right now is gather her to me and assure her I'm all right, which surprisingly, I am. I often wondered how I would feel if I ever came face-to-face with the woman responsible for making me and my brother orphans at this point in my life. It's a surprise to me how little resentment I feel toward her, but I made peace with it long ago. When I look at Diane now, all I see is the tortured and very pregnant teenager I met. I can still clearly remember the devastation on her face that day and the constant tears she battled the entire time we were together. That, combined with my love for her daughter, keeps me from harboring anything dangerous. It's uncomfortable, but only because of the two women vibrating with emotions, feeding off each other.

Diane has practically turned to stone where she sits, and I do my best not to let my gaze linger on her, knowing she's just as torn now as she was then. Some part of me feels the need to comfort her, but I have no idea how to go about it with the way she's reacting to me. Timothy is clearly oblivious or playing blind to the ten-ton, red elephant in the room as he rattles on about the weather and his new RV.

Nodding every so often, I watch Cecelia closely, her shoulders tensing as she texts. She's due for work any minute and hasn't missed a day since I've been here.

"Everything okay at Meggie's?" I ask, and she nods her head subtly before Tim tries to lure her back into conversation. "What you've done to this place since the last time we were here is incredible, Cecelia."

"Thank you," she replies lifelessly, abandoning the pancakes to type a mile a minute. The next text that comes through has her smacking her phone against the counter. Standing due to her sudden change in demeanor, I walk over to where she's standing, and she looks back at me, eyeing me for long seconds before directing her scowl at her mother. "What's going on? Is that Marissa?"

"Everything's fine," she responds with a frosty bite. "One of my waitresses no-showed."

"Do you want me to head over and help?"

She bites her lips together and shakes her head. "Of course not. They've got it. Go sit down." She lifts her chin toward the table. "I've got this."

"Sure?"

"Tobias," she sighs as I circle her waist from behind, resting my chin on her shoulder.

"This is okay. I am okay," I whisper.

"Well, I'm not fucking okay," she hisses, tensing in my arms. She retrieves her spatula from the counter, flipping a perfectly round cake as I run my fingers along her stomach. "Look at me, Trésor."

Hostile eyes meet mine, and confusion sets in. I can't get

a clear read on her. I press my forehead to hers. "This was going to happen sooner or later." She bites her lip thoughtfully, seeming to finally focus on me before her eyes soften. "It's too much to ask of you."

"No, it's not. If you can forgive me, anything is possible, right?"

She dismisses me, pulling out of my hold with the sharp dip of her chin. Following silent orders, I reclaim my seat at the table, confused about what's going on inside of her. It's clear her relationship with her mother is strained, and our combined presence here isn't helping.

Timothy swallows, his eyes darting around as he begins to sense it and fidget, but being the man he is, he's opted to bullshit around it. After another sad attempt by him to break the foot-thick ice, Diane speaks up. "So how long," she asks in a weak tone, drawing my attention from Cecelia. "How long have you two been seeing each other?"

"That's a complicated question, but the short version is we were together briefly before she went to college and just got back together three weeks ago."

"Complicated," Cecelia harrumphs. "I'll say." She flips a pancake, a very, very angry cook, and I frown at her back before she turns to address me. "She doesn't need to know." She slams her spatula down and folds her arms across her chest. It seems she's on a fucking warpath now, and none of us seem to be safe. Timothy audibly swallows, his coffee halfway to his mouth.

"Well, I would *love* to know," Diane retorts, her eyes flitting from Cecelia to me.

"I'm sure you would," Cecelia snarks, hurtling the milk back into the fridge before slamming it closed.

"What's important *now*," I referee, "is that we're together, for good." Cecelia cuts off the burner, adding the last of the pancakes to a platter before setting them next to the bacon waiting on the table.

"*Orange juice*?" she barks in what feels like accusation at the three of us, and we collectively shake our heads in reply.

Timothy digs in, looking for any excuse to keep his eyes down and his mouth full. Diane ignores the food, staring between her daughter and me as I busy myself, piling cakes onto my plate and digging in, hoping to ease some of the churn in my stomach. Cecelia's focus remains fixed on me as she feeds some bacon to Beau.

"That bacon is yours," I scorn her. "Eat."

"I'm not hungry." I can't help my grin as a glimpse of the stubborn nineteen-year-old that ruined me for all others peeks through. "Trésor . . . "

"You eat," she snaps before her eyes again soften and dart between her mother and me.

"Please," I ask, nudging her, using her maternal concern for me to my advantage. She narrows her eyes, letting me know she's onto me but shoves a bite into her mouth anyway.

"So, I'm assuming you aren't coming with us now, due to company?" Timothy asks, now attuned to the chemistry at the table.

"Where were you headed?" I ask as mother and daughter resume their stare-off.

"Cecelia was going to camp with us for a few nights before we head out west. We're going to Colorado, Arizona, Utah, and New Mexico."

"Going to hit the four corners?"

Tim points his fork at me. "Exactly. Standing in four states at once. It's this camper's dream."

Cecelia is already shaking her head when I glance her way. Though two days may buy me enough time to get a handle on my situation, just the thought of parting with her for any amount of time gnaws at me. But if there's a chance, this disruption might be a Godsend if I can get her to go.

"If you want to go—"

Slapping her hand on the table, she points her cutlery in my direction. "Finish that sentence, King, and I *will* stab you with this butter knife."

I can't help my chuckle. "Well then—" I look between them—"you'll stay *here*. At least for the night? There's no need to cut your visit short." I turn to Diane, who's focused on Cecelia, her eyes glistening as she continues to grapple with it all.

"Tobias—" Cecelia starts.

"These are your *parents*," I say definitively, doing my best to make it easier on her, which wins me nothing but another scathing glare. I frown at her as she blazes her eyes down my frame before lifting her wrists one by one and straightening the cuffs on her pajamas—in *threat*.

She smirks when she sees me conclude that she knows *exactly* what she's been doing to me with those fucking pajamas.

What. The. Fuck?

Timothy clears his throat before finally commenting on the growing tension. "If we're imposing, it's no problem. We can just cruise on a little earlier."

"It's no imposition," I counter, making my stance clear as Cecelia sinks in her seat.

"Are you sure that's best right now?" Cecelia slings, insinuation rolling off her tongue. She seems to be prepping for war when all I'm trying to do is make peace. I'm tempted to pull her ass aside and redden it before I lick it or simultaneously do both. "Yes," I nod for emphasis, cutting my hand through the air. "*End of.*"

She narrows her eyes. "Don't you dare—"

"Cecelia," Diane cuts in with the voice of a patient mother, "why are you—"

"I'm done," she snaps and stands, hauling her plate to the sink and tossing it in before looking back to Diane. "And done pretending too. You haven't even told him, have you, Mom? Your new *husband.*"

"Husband?" I ask, surprised by the news and taking first note at the rings on their fingers. It must have been in one of my recent reports. In my defense, I've been busy the last eight months.

"Yes, *husband*," Cecelia clarifies, her eyes trained on her mother. I'm expecting blood-colored eyes and a moving crown of snakes to appear any second with how she's behaving. I make a mental note to see how far away she is from her sugar pill days in her birth control.

"Haven't you learned *anything*? How do you expect to get through a life with him with *secrets* like this?"

Timothy calmly sets down his silverware and eyes me. "Can someone please tell me what I'm missing?"

"Unfortunately, your wife and I share some tragic history."

A tear escapes Diane's eye, and Cecelia plays immune, but I know the strain in the relationship is hurting her, so much so it's metastasized to uncontrollable anger.

"He knows." Diane lifts guilt-sick eyes to her daughter.

"I told him on the drive home the last time we were here, after I signed the papers for the restaurant and the house, even though you refused to tell me why I was doing it." Her gaze flits to mine. "And also after you refused to tell me why you'd lost fifteen pounds *you couldn't afford* to lose."

Insinuation clear, that revelation strikes me where intended, and Cecelia fires back. "Don't play concerned parent. It's a little late for that, don't you think?"

"Never, you'll always be my child. And I had no idea what you were going through because you didn't share it with me."

"We all have our secrets, don't we?" she says, none of us safe from that jab.

"Look at me, baby." Cecelia lifts her blazing eyes to mine, so much hurt shining in them, I want to shield her with my body. "*What hurts you, hurts me.*"

She fists a tear from beneath her eyes. "Tobias, this is too much."

"It's not. I promise you, Trésor, it's not."

The slide of Diane's chair has us all turning her way as she offers a barely audible "excuse me" before she scurries out of the kitchen, grabbing her cigarettes on the counter before rushing through the back door.

Timothy stands to go after her, and I stop him with a hand on his shoulder. He glances over at me with clear apprehension.

"So, you're—"

"Yes. But more importantly, I'm the man in love with her daughter. Please, let me." Timothy studies me for several seconds before giving me a slow nod. I don't give Cecelia a chance to object before making my way out into the back yard.

*

I find Diane fighting with her lighter in the center of the yard before she manages a flame, inhaling her first hit deeply, eyes closed, tears staining her cheeks. Sensing me, she opens her eyes and faces me while I approach with my hands tucked in my sweatpants.

"Mind if I have one of those?" She nods, opening the box, and extends it to me. I pluck one out, and she lights it, her eyes heavy on my profile before I back away. "Thank you."

"I can't even begin to imagine how this happened."

I pull on the cigarette and exhale a stream of smoke, thankful for the slight relief it brings. "It's a very complicated story."

"Did you become involved with her to hurt her, because of us, because of what I did?"

"No. In fact, I went to great lengths to make sure she was kept out of it, but I failed."

Her tone sharpens. "I might not have a right to ask, but when it comes to her, I don't give a damn. What *exactly* do you mean by that, Tobias? You had plans for Roman because of what *I* did?"

"Initially, yes. Roman was my target until I found out the truth of what happened. But I had no intention of hurting her. Protecting her has always been a priority for me."

"Since when?"

"Since the first time I laid eyes on her."

"Which was?"

"When she was eleven."

"Jesus." She's visibly shaking as she takes a drag of her cigarette and studies me carefully. "You love her, that's clear."

"I do."

"Roman never told me you were involved . . . God, that man."

264

"He was good at keeping secrets. But he was very aware when Cecelia and I parted ways, years before he died, that our relationship was over. We worked together to protect Cecelia."

"I guess I have no choice but to try and believe you."

"I hope you do. I would never hurt her."

"But you have."

I nod because it's the sad truth. "But mostly to protect her."

Her gaze loses focus as her chest constricts and her shoulders drop forward before she speaks. "So many, many times over the years I wanted to reach out, to confess the truth to you, to Dominic, and beg your forgiveness, but *you* disappeared. And eventually, he did too."

It's then I know my assumption was right.

"It must have been hard supporting *three* children every month."

Her eyes drop. "I didn't want you to go without. I'd taken so much from you, and I saw how miserable you were in that house with Delphine."

I exhale, tapping the ash off my cigarette. "For years, I thought the boxes without a return address mailed to our doorstep were from friends and relatives of my parents. Boxes with hundreds and hundreds of dollars' worth of clothes and gift cards, toys, shoes. But no one is that generous, are they, Diane?"

She sniffs, wiping her nose. "Delphine hated me, and I knew she would turn me away, but I just couldn't let you go without. I know it doesn't make up for what I did."

"You made a mistake," I say pointedly, as her eyes cloud with tears. "Those boxes saved us, sometimes for *months* at a time. I can safely say that act of kindness inspired me to pay it forward in a major way."

A sob bursts from her as I take another drag of my cigarette, keeping just enough distance so she's comfortable but standing close enough to catch her if she breaks, which seems possible. From the minute I met this woman, all I saw was agonizing guilt, and knowing she's lived with it all these years only makes me want to convince her further to set herself free.

"You know, you and I have a lot in common," I confess, "we both suffer from the horrible plague of survivor's guilt."

"I c-can never tell you how sorry I am for what happened."

Tossing my cigarette, I grip her shoulders, seeing so much of the woman I love in the woman before me—certain that Cecelia inherited her heart. "It's tragically ironic how well I know your pain because maybe if I didn't, I wouldn't be able to look at you now and tell you I forgave you a long time ago. It was an accident. I *felt* how deeply you regretted it the day we met. Your mistake changed my life in an irreparable way, but it also shaped me into the man I am today—for better or worse—a man who loves your daughter. It's crazy that somehow, despite what you took away, both you and Roman gifted me the only person in the world capable of loving me in a way that fills me with so much peace. Cecelia is my home and my reason for trying to forgive myself, and she needs to be your reason too. From what I've gathered, you've punished yourself long enough, and it's affected you and your relationship with your daughter. It's not too late for either of us, Diane. Cecelia is making me believe it."

A telltale sniff just behind the lattice has me grinning. "Come on out, Mon Trésor, I know you've been listening."

Cecelia's red-rimmed eyes meet mine and drift to her mother as she steps in front of her. "*This* is why you had so many jobs, and we still struggled?"

Diane nods. "I couldn't let them go without, and I know you suffered for it."

"Roman didn't know?"

Diane shakes her head. "God, no, he would have been furious because it would seem like an admission of guilt. He was so paranoid. But I'm not sorry I did it. I'm only sorry you suffered."

"Mom—" Cecelia's voice lifts as she pulls her mother into her arms. "We did okay. God, I only wish you would have told me."

They start to speak in hushed whispers as I turn and head back toward the house to give them privacy.

I don't really believe words can heal as much as they hurt. But I so want to believe it's not too late for us—that truly living again without that jagged ache is possible. More hope sparks as I glance back at the two of them and see mild relief in Diane's expression a second before I close the back door.

Chapter Twenty-Two

TOBIAS

TIM SET UP their RV for the night, insisting they sleep in it, no doubt due to the drama that unfolded today. I helped him set up camp, and with Cecelia occupied with her mother, dashed away to check both phones.

Oz identified the asshole watching us and is digging further into his background at my order.

Tyler was able to execute my request for air coverage, and the ETA was a half hour.

And fuckwit's superior ordered me to continue my watch and report. After a tension-relieving shower, I spent the rest of my day satisfied with bought time, intent on figuring out Antoine's motives and intent.

I will have to utilize my time wisely to make more headway with Cecelia, and I plan to do just that as soon as our unexpected guests leave.

After dinner, we gathered around a makeshift campfire Tim and I managed to scrounge up outside their camper.

Cecelia, Diane, and I sip wine as Tim tosses back the beer he has stocked in his cooler. We are all a few drinks in when Diane speaks up, inevitably ending a day's worth of progress.

"You haven't mentioned Dominic," she asks, looking between Cecelia and me. "Where is he now?"

I stop the glass halfway to my mouth as Cecelia's expression falls, and she turns questioning eyes to mine. We've never been faced with the question together, and try as I might, it's clear on both our faces.

Diane looks between us, her eyes budding with fear. "Please tell me he's okay," she pleads with me as Tim grips her hand in his.

"He died six years ago," Cecelia speaks at the same time I do.

"I think it's time you know the truth." Cecelia's gaze locks on mine as I finish. "The *whole* truth."

"Tobias—"

"It's *time*," I stress softly before staring into the campfire.

"Tobias," Cecelia urges my eyes her way, and I gaze back at her, the fire lifting some of the red tint in her chestnut hair as she quietly assesses me.

"It's time."

After a few tense moments, Cecelia nods somberly. For the next few hours, we take turns talking, and I reveal a lot of my story, of the moments I've been reliving since I've been in Virginia, taking the opportunity to come a bit cleaner with Cecelia.

I leave out my history with Antoine, a secret I've kept for twenty years. As Cecelia and I recall the details of our sordid past together, Diane's eyes dart wildly between us while Timothy speaks up every so often with a question or a "*holy shit.*"

At one point, too much truth sends Diane into a tailspin, her emotions getting the best of her, especially when we relay the events of the night Dom died and the aftermath. Thankfully, she maintains enough composure to make it through the recall of Cecelia's return to Triple Falls leading up to me coming for her three weeks ago.

"And so now . . ." Diane eyes me, her voice hoarse, "what will you do?"

"I'm leaving that up to your daughter," I say honestly. "She'll be the one to decide."

Fear shudders through her physically as Cecelia swallows, refusing to answer her mother's question. It's clear she's raw and exhausted from a day of hashing out our past, and for the first time ever, speaking her full story. The sad part is, I still have too much to tell.

I'm not at all worried about hood secrets or any of our secrets being spilled, for that matter. For the most part, Diane has been looking out for the both of us since we were children. I feel safe in that knowledge and better for her knowing the truth of our reality.

"Is this the life you want?" she asks Cecelia. "Even after all that's happened, as dangerous as *it* is?"

He is, is what she wanted to say, but I can't fault her for it.

"It's my decision, and I've made it."

Diane bites her lip for several seconds before lifting her eyes to mine.

Timothy clears his throat. "I'm in awe, man. Truly. This is . . . what a fucking amazing story." He shakes his head and glances over at me. "I'm still amazed you went to prep school with the President, and you planned it—" he sips his beer. "Too fucking cool."

"We've hit quite a few bumps in the road."

"I never knew that part, either," Cecelia says, her voice filled with hurt and underlying anger.

"You don't know a lot of the details," I admit softly, knowing I'm in for it.

"No, I don't," she redirects, anger simmering in her voice.

"Ask me *anything*," I remind her of the times I've tried to reveal myself to her in degrees over the last few weeks. Her eyes flare before she darts them away.

"Except it's not . . ." Diane says softly. "It's not a story, is it, Tobias?"

"No." I tip back the rest of my wine, emptying my glass. "It's not."

Diane turns to Cecelia, her expression blank as she gazes into the flames.

"What—"

"Mom, don't, okay? Just—" she sighs—"don't."

"I can't help it!"

"Well, you're going to have to trust me. I'm not yours to protect anymore."

"That's . . . bullshit, kid. I'll always be your mother."

"This isn't that, and you know it." Cecelia stands and glances my way. "I'm tired. It's late." She walks around the fire to kiss her mother's cheek before palming Tim's shoulder. "We can talk more tomorrow morning."

Diane nods, barely registering her goodbye as I speak up in an attempt to ease her mind.

"Nine people are guarding us, watching this house, two of them safeguard Cecelia at all times, some are combing the streets of this town for any possible threat. There are two drones in the air right now scanning every square foot of this land and the land around it."

"Jesus Christ," Diane sighs.

"You're safe here. But if you feel more comfortable leaving, I'll understand." I scrape my top lip with my teeth, dreading my next confession. "And when you get home, I'll have the birds who've been watching you two for years finally introduce themselves."

Both of them whip their head in my direction, and I shrug. "I'm sorry, it was necessary."

Diane's eyes shine with a mix of shock and awe. "All this time, you've been *protecting me*?"

"I promised Roman I would protect his daughter, and that includes protecting you. And I have good reason to be equally invested in your well-being."

She gazes up at me. "I knew when I met you that you were special, but this is some major overachieving, don't you think?" It's her first joke of the day, and I'm grateful for it.

"I'll protect her with everything I've got."

"Apparently, she'll do the same for you. By the way, she gets her *badass* gene from *me*." Another smile, another joke, and I'm pretty sure the wine is responsible.

"Of course, she does."

"Tobias—" she starts again, her eyes softening substantially.

"No more tears, Diane, and no apologies. Okay?"

She nods. "I'll try."

"Goodnight."

They give me a goodnight in unison as I walk into the darkened house, the only light on coming from the bedroom. I have no idea what I'm in for, but I slow my gait slightly as I make my way across the living room.

What in the actual fuck, King? Grow a set.

Speeding up my walk, I find her in the bedroom, staring down at her comforter as if it's fascinating. I circle her waist and nuzzle her from behind. "I know it was a lot."

She steps out of my hold, reeling on me, her eyes shooting blue daggers.

"What?"

"You *met my mother*, one of a *thousand* omissions you casually left out. Or how about this one: 'hey, you know I'm the mastermind behind a secret society of vigilantes, but the President is a fucking part of it.'"

"I didn't—"

"You had *months* to tell me these *details* when we. Were. Together!"

"Well, in those *months*, the fucking club was the last thing I wanted to talk about for the few hours I got to steal and *escape* with you. Up until I met you, my whole life was work. With you, I was selfish. I told you that. I've admitted it, I've apologized for it. But back then, in that time, with you, I was just . . . myself, me, Tobias. Just a man in love with a woman and loving the freedom I felt because of it." I exhale. "I couldn't risk telling you those details about Preston, Cecelia. I'd already handed you my own demise. And we were still undefinable at that point, all the way up until the day we imploded."

"*Preston*," she scoffs. "Even so, you still haven't learned, have you? Secrets and omissions tore us apart before and will again." Fury radiates through her frame as I try and stop the hemorrhaging before it starts.

"I won't let that happen."

"Won't you?"

"I'm trying, Cecelia, so fucking hard." Pulling off my hoodie, I run a hand through my hair before gripping the back of my shirt, tossing it off. Her eyes immediately drop, *to the floor,* disintegrating any hopes I had of resuming the intimacy we shared this morning.

Tempted to drive my fist through the drywall, I clench it at my side instead, as my frustration threatens to boil over.

"What you did today," she says softly, "for my mother, was . . . indescribable, so . . . selfless, and one of the most incredible humane acts I've ever witnessed, which only made me love you more."

I step forward, and she jerks her head back up, her eyes filled with accusation. "And you *ruined it*! You ruined it by being the same jackass you've always been!"

"By being honest?!"

I step forward and invade her space, eager for this fight. Because she's fighting her emotions now, and they're winning, and to me, that's more important than the why of it.

"You ruined it by keeping me in the dark about the details. All these things, if I would have known even half of them, I would have had a better understanding of you, you fucking jackass!"

"You do understand me! You see inside me, you've been in places no one else has."

"Maybe so, but these things you consider details are vitally important to me, Tobias."

"Are you on your sugar pills?"

"What?!"

"Nothing. Keep your voice down. Your parents are outside." My head begins to pound.

Welcome to the bliss of domestic life, Tobias.

But it's not my own voice I hear. It's Sean's. "I didn't have time—"

"More excuses, not reasons." She shakes her head and scoffs. "Haven't you ever in your life blurted anything out? *Ever*?"

"Once or twice, but only when fighting with you. And you know better, I've trained myself never to do that, you should know—"

"Oh, I know! Trust me, I know, you stupid French ape!" Biting my bottom lip, I dart my eyes away.

"Don't you laugh at me! This isn't fucking funny! This right here is the why, Tobias. This is why a majority of our problems exist, because of your fucking secrecy!" She slaps her chest where her heart lay. "You want in here?"

"Yes," I clip, my blood boiling.

"You want back in here?" She says it again.

"Yes, goddamnit, that's all I want!"

She rounds the bed and steps up to me, and smacks the side of my head with her finger. "Then let me in here!" I gape at her in shock as she steps away, launching the next missile over her shoulder. "Until then, you're wasting your fucking time here."

"I was honest with you tonight!"

She balks at me as if I've slapped her before turning her back on me. "Just once—" she marches to the bathroom, clicking on the light—"just *once*, I wish I could make you feel what this is like."

"I think finding out that you were brought into my club and having a relationship with not one but *two* of the men closest to me is enough fucking surprise to last a lifetime." I hover by the bathroom door, and she pauses with the toothbrush in her mouth before tearing it out, the residue bubbling on the corner.

"That's not the same, and you swore you would never bring that up."

"Not to hold it against you, it was to make a point!"

"A choice point!"

"Fine. I'm sorry," I grunt, my entire body lighting with anger and frustration. "I just meant it was surprising enough. And just to make myself clear, I'm good until twenty years past death with fucking surprises when it comes to you."

"That wasn't a surprise *of my design!*"

"Doesn't matter. You've met your quota."

"That was then," she argues back. "I'm talking about *now*. Right now, at this *very* moment."

The idea of coming clean about Antoine gets tossed out the window as I step in shit, neck deep.

I'm fucked now, either way. If I come clean about our possible threat, then she'll only slam up her defenses.

One fight at a time, Tobias.

"I'm talking about being *blindsided* without a good reason when you've had time to tell me the truth!"

You're so fucked. Pack a bag for your ass and kiss it goodbye.

The man inside of me refuses to back down, the man who desperately wants to mend this bridge. He wants to crush her mouth, silence her with his tongue, and punish her severely with his cock. This is anything but progress, and I fear all my efforts the last three weeks are fruitless by how she's regarding me—which only enrages me further.

"I've had time? I've had *time*? Putain." *Fuck.* She pushes past me, refusing to meet my eyes, and I follow on her heels. "Between bussing tables and following you around like a second puppy and getting the door slammed in my face, I've *had time*, right?"

"Don't you dare! I haven't slammed the door in your face!"

She squares off with me across the bed as I unclasp my watch and slam it on her nightstand, unloading my pockets. "Might as well have. And believe it or not, Trésor, you are not the easiest woman to fucking talk to. If the subject would have come up—"

She rips her sweater off, and my eyes drop to the swell of her perfect tits atop her heaving chest.

"Eyes up here, *Pierre*, and pardon me if I don't ask the right questions pertinent to the secrets you're keeping at the time." She throws up her hands. "Who the hell knows with you!"

"What do you really expect from me, Cecelia? Did you expect me to come back to you a completely reformed man with all the answers, who makes all the right moves? I'm still the same man—the villain. And I'll *always* play dirty to protect you and keep you safe. I'll consider making any allowance you need to try and make this work, but you're truly fucking mistaken if you think I'll shy away from the ruthless, unforgiving, and cruel parts that still exist in me when need be. You asked for the man you fell for . . . well there's two sides to him, and neither are going anywhere." I cut my hand through the air. "*End of.*"

I swear I see smoke coming from her nostrils, expecting fire to follow as her eyes narrow. In a flash, she shoves down her jeans and unclasps her bra before pulling open her chest of drawers.

"Don't you fucking dare!" I boom. "I'd rather you take that fucking Beretta from your purse and shoot my cock!"

"Don't tempt me, King!" She turns, tossing the fresh pair

of flannel pajamas on the bed—same fucking pattern, this pair in light blue, and I've never in my life hated the sight of an inanimate object so much. She drops the fuzzy socks—the cherry on top—onto the pile, and I cup the back of my neck and stare up at the ceiling.

"You just want to hold a grudge," I huff. "We were getting closer this morning, and this is your way of fucking that up. You're cowering away, *again*."

Silence ticks by along with the small clock next to her head, just before she hurls it at me and misses me by an inch.

I take a step forward as she jerks the top of the pajamas over her head, and it might as well be a knife to the chest. It's clear I'm not the only one who plays dirty. "We just relived every bad fucking thing that happened between us, Tobias. I think it's best we just stop talking."

"Yeah, because that's been working out for us so far. And it makes your whole argument moot. More silence—that ought to help."

When she reaches for the pajama pants, I hit my limit.

"If you so much as stick a toe in those goddamn pants, you're declaring war, and all bets are off!"

She shoves a leg in as my patience snaps.

"Merde. Bon sang, femme. Tu me testes au-delà de mes limites!" *Fuck. Goddamn it, woman. You are testing me past my limits.*

She pushes her second leg in, pulling the drawstring tight around her waist to rub the salt into my gaping chest. "Well, welcome to the fucking club, Frenchman! Good to see we're finally on the same page!"

"Anything but. We're not even in the same fucking *place* anymore."

"Fine with me." She points to the door. "You know the way out."

She sucks in a breath, and I can see her immediate regret. The shred in my chest is barely manageable as I drop my gaze and grab a pillow from my side of the bed. "Well then, my treasure, I'll save you the trouble of showing me the door *twice*."

Chapter Twenty-Three

CECELIA

I SPENT THE majority of the night tossing and turning, knowing I could ease the too-familiar ache of missing him by simply taking his hand and guiding him back to bed. And once his arms were around me, I could take back the words I didn't mean. But a lot of those words I did mean.

His recalling of our story to my mother blew my mind and shed some much-needed light on so many things. That's all I wanted, but he was right. I've refused him at almost every turn to explain his reasoning for the things he's done. I've damn near made it impossible for him to confess anything by both avoiding him and his explanations.

Putting our own story into words reminded me of just how much we've been through, but it also reminded me of the reason we can't fully mend—all of the fucking secrecy.

He can't change his spots overnight. All things ingrained—bad habits included—have cemented his personality over time.

Secrets are who and what he is, because he's lived as a secret himself for countless years.

If I want this to work, I'm going to have to remember that and try not to resent him for the secrets he still harbors. Whether he's aware or not, he's still keeping them—selectively.

After letting Beau back in, I tread lightly through the living room before using one of the discarded throw pillows to kneel in front of where he sleeps. He's completely unguarded as he draws heavy breaths, his thick black lashes fanning over his sharp cheekbones. He's bundled in one of the patched quilts I bought from an antique store when I moved here. He looks wildly out of place on my short couch that he dwarfs with his sleeping form. My fingers are itching to touch him, but Beau beats me to it by licking the side of his face. He grunts in disgust, pulling the covers over his head as I muffle my giggle. I expect him to resume his snoozing, but his voice sounds beneath the thick blanket.

"Va te faire voir, connard. Je sais que tu as dormi avec elle." *Fuck off, dickhead. I know you got to sleep with her."*

Stifling another laugh, I run my fingers through his hair, and he lowers the covers to glare at my pajamas before remorse-filled amber eyes meet mine.

"Hi."

"Hi," he whispers, stretching his long legs past the confines of the arm of the couch before turning his body to fully face me. "You're finally fighting back. Does that mean you're starting to forgive me?"

Running my fingers through his thick black hair, I lean in, inhaling citrus and spice, the smell flooding me with memories. "Why can't we just hate each other?"

"Simple," he murmurs. "We love each other too fucking much."

"We survived our first trashy fight." I nod past my shoulder toward the door. "Complete with my parents in a trailer outside."

He draws his brows. "This is good?"

"I think so."

He lowers the patched quilt and cups my jaw, squishing my lips the way he did all those years ago in Roman's kitchen. "All I want, Mon Trésor . . . is to build a bonfire the size of Texas and burn all these goddamn pajamas. It's all I'm living for."

My laugh breaks his hold as he easily lifts me from where I kneel to straddle him. He brushes the hair away from my shoulders as he gazes up at me, eyes probing.

"I have a lot to tell you, and some of it may make you angry, but I've lived many different realities and hidden so much for so long, it's hard to distinguish what secrets I held and what lies I told and in which life."

"So, tell me everything." I blanket him, laying my head on his chest, and he wraps his arms around me, resting his chin on the top of my head.

"I plan to, Cecelia, but it's . . ."

"I know it's hard. And I will be as patient as I can be, *within reason*." I press a kiss to his chest. "I do want you here, Tobias. I do," I whisper, palming his chest where my kiss lingers to feel his steady heartbeat. "If it makes you feel better, Beau only got to first base." I burrow deeper into him as he rubs his palms up and down my back, chasing away the morning chill.

"It's hardly fair. He's got home field advantage."

"True, but this is your home too."

His body relaxes with my words as he lifts me, adjusting

me so we're face-to-face, his dick thickening at my thigh, sending a wave of need throughout my body. I bend to kiss him just as he lifts to meet it. The kiss is sensual, unhurried, as he slides his tongue along mine, arm circling me as he crushes me to his chest. He feeds me his apology with every slow swipe of his tongue, and I reciprocate, moaning into his mouth, the ache of last night slowly slipping away as we part, eyes connected.

"Remember when—"

"Everything," he says softly, flexing his fingers through my hair. "I remember *everything*, Cecelia. Every word you said, every look you gave me. Your three kinds of laughs, the details of your dreams, the way your nostrils flare when you're starting to get pissed. The sting of your slaps, the salt in your tears, the fit of your breasts in my hand. The feel of your mouth, the taste of your pussy," he murmurs, sliding his thumb along my jaw, "so which part do you need me to remind *you* of?"

Running palms down his arms, I start to lose myself in the feel of him as he pulls me back to his lips. Warm hands tentatively explore as his kiss drifts from my jaw and down my neck. Soaked and needy, my pulse kicks up as I slide my hand down his chest and over his stomach to cover his cock. His massive length jerks in my hand as I grip him through the material of his boxers. A pained groan vibrates my lips before I murmur his name, a request on the tip of my tongue just as a knock sounds at the door.

Tobias lifts, keeping me in his arms while letting out a string of French curses. I pull away just as perturbed but can't help my laugh at his reaction. "Guess they're early risers?"

I stand and yank the pillow and blanket from the couch and hand it to him as he stands, a full-sized tent pitched in his boxers, a deep scowl on his face as I nod toward his engorged cock. "Do something with that, will you?"

"Oh, I intend to," he threatens, his voice a mix of lust and fury.

Blowing out a harsh breath, his eyes roll down my body before he stalks off with his arms full, stomping into the bedroom before kicking the door closed with his foot.

Tobias and I wave my parents off after I've assured my mother of texts and phone calls every day for the rest of my life. Her concern is warranted, but it's my job now to protect her from whatever truths may come. It's a part of being in on the secret.

Tobias gazes on long after the RV disappears from sight, and I study his profile as the sun starts to tint the morning sky.

"What are you thinking about?"

"Roman." Stepping away from me dressed in running clothes—sweats, a thermal and T-shirt, and worn Nikes—he grips his foot behind him in a hamstring stretch. His massive build is becoming slimmer and more defined due to his vigorous runs, and I can't help my thorough appraisal of his efforts.

"What about Roman?"

"Of what a fool he was, of what he missed." Satisfied with his warm-up, he steps forward and cups my wings, my eyes falling to his full lips as he speaks. "Of how I wish you could have met *my* parents. But if they hadn't died, I probably

284

wouldn't have you." He leans in and releases a wary breath. "Of how I hate some of the ways you perceive me, and I'm going to change it."

"That's a lot to be thinking about at seven in the morning." When his eyes drop, I instantly feel guilty, but I'm drained from the whirlwind of the last twenty-four hours. Posture defeated, he steps away, retrieving his earbuds from his pockets and slips them in before flipping through his phone, tapping to start a playlist as he speaks.

"Just how my mind works—" he lifts his eyes to mine—"I thought you wanted that."

"I did, I do. I'm *sorry*."

He grips the back of my neck and pulls me quickly to him, brushing my mouth with a kiss that leaves me aching. It's then I recognize the opening notes of Archive's "Again," a song I know by heart, streaming through his earbuds. "See you after work."

Within seconds, he's jogging down the road in the direction my mother left, my heart lurching after him.

Chapter Twenty-Four

TOBIAS

Age Twenty-Eight

VEGAS.
  The devil's playground.

As far as devils go, I brought all my favorites with me. And tonight, I plan to let them reign.

Our mark?

Elijah Rosenbaum, a thirty-six-year-old VP who belongs to a small but webbed network of ambitious thieves. He robs his own corporation for sport while he spends his free time terrorizing women. His newest victim, Amelia, sits at his side, a twenty-three-year-old former cocktail waitress who left her station at a Boston bar thinking he would be her Prince Charming. Right now, she definitely realizes she needs a white knight, but she's going to have to settle for a few rogue birds.

It's becoming more evident to her by the second that abandoning her life was a catastrophic mistake. Her eyes dart around in fear as she sits, a new captive across from us in ringside seats Elijah will no longer be able to afford after paying our bill.

Since round one, Dom and I have had eagle eyes on them both, scanning for any security he may have that we might have missed. But it's become apparent Elijah has gotten away with his evil deeds for far too long to take cautious measures. At this point, he deems himself untouchable. And it's clear that's not just an assumption by his behavior as he revels in striking fear in the heart of his companion. Every time her eyes wander past the apparent six fucking inches he will allow, he checks her with a hands-on approach. Both times that he's hurt her, she's burst into pained tears, only to be threatened to keep quiet when she reacts to his methodic torture.

"Motherfucker," Dom growls next to me. "If he hits her one more time, I'm going to fucking kill him."

"Easy," I clip, glancing over at Dom to see his shoulders tense, his fingers flexing with his need to pounce.

We've been butting heads recently due to his temperament and use of more extreme measures. He's a ruthless renegade and a lethal one at that. Over the last few years, he's hardened his edges, his patience dwindling, his fuse becoming shorter. At twenty-two, he's nearly caught up to me in height—his build slightly smaller—but when he strikes, he makes sure the pain is unforgettable. I see a lot of myself in him, but we differ a lot in opinion on tactics, which has made our last few jobs more difficult.

"I'll make a deal with you, brother."

"I'm listening." His eyes are zeroed in on Amelia, who's frantically searching for a way to escape her bad company.

"You keep it together until we can get him alone, and I'll let you give him a thorough lesson in manners on how to treat a lady. It'll be your show tonight."

Technically, this job is Dom's find anyway, a tip-off from

one of Elijah's victims who was confiding tearfully to a friend at the MIT library. Not only did she spill about her ill-treatment, but she spent minutes recounting Elijah's reckless bragging about his corporate conquests and wealth—which perked Dom's ears. And because of that exchange, this mark fell into our laps. After some thorough research, we knew Lady Luck was on our side, which is why Sean and I met Dom in Boston to spend a few days with him before we followed Elijah out to Vegas for the fight. It's the perfect location, a remote city in the middle of the desert with no ties to Dom's life in Boston. Elijah will have no idea who to seek revenge on, not that he's capable.

Just fifteen minutes in a hotel room and we'll be half a million richer. The kicker? If caught, Elijah will take the fall no matter where the money lands or how it's spent. That's the perk of robbing thieves.

Elijah is precisely the kind of prick we target. His greed and misdeeds make him easy money and a job none of us will lose sleep over. Along with the half-million, we'll gain a list of contacts and co-conspirators that will secure us a new list of targets to smoke in the future.

Dom sits next to me, posture rattling, his eyes fixed on our mark as sporadic shouts sound around us for the two men in the ring. The reigning champ is a bit larger in comparison to his contender, Lance Prescott, an up-and-comer I read about with an impressive record—a wildcard with an evident chip on his shoulder, who seems to be dancing with the devil in his eyes. And my literal money is on him. Scanning the arena, I spot Sean as he strolls up with a fresh beer and takes his seat at my right.

"All set," he says, before sipping his beer, Elijah's hotel

keycard tucked away in his pocket as he eyes them across the ring. "Is he still fucking with her?"

Our view is obstructed by two women in spiked heels as they saunter past us, their eyes trailing over the three of us with blatant interest. I shift my attention past them to the fight as Lance nails his opposition with a sick combination, stunning him.

"Damn, man," Sean says, elbowing me, "are you fucking asexual now, or what? I haven't seen you with a girl since—" he snaps his fingers—"what was that chick's name?"

"Chesty-toria," Dom supplies with a smirk.

Sean closes his eyes. "Yeah, man. I remember those titties well."

I roll my eyes as Sean nudges me, the foam of his beer dangerously close to spilling on my suit.

"You were what, sixteen?" Sean goads. "Seriously, man, it's time to get a back scratch, at the very least."

"He's got a couple of girls in France he sees to itch it," Dom supplies, earning my glare as he cants his head to get a view of Sean past me. "You forget Christian Louboutin here is a double agent. Maybe he prefers French women."

"Maybe I prefer privacy," I snap. "End of—" I turn to Sean—"and you're annoying me."

"That's what little brothers do," Sean snarks. Ignoring him, I glance over at Elijah, who's focused on the fight, relieved that I won't have to pry my brother off him for the moment. Mark or not, Dom's not going to last much longer.

Sean lets out an exaggerated sigh, fidgeting next to me until I cut my gaze his way. "What?"

"We've been in Vegas nine hours, and you haven't had one taste of that pathetic girl drizzle you call a drink."

"I don't drink on the job." I eye his beer. "You should try it sometime."

"Live a little, man. Don't you think we deserve it?"

"I've got plans for later."

"Oh, yeah? Did you schedule your first smile?"

My glare lands on the side of his head, his smirk disappearing in his cup before he obnoxiously gulps down his beer. "Ahhhhh, delicious." He sloshes the liquid around. "I would offer you some, but you're probably allergic because it tastes a lot like a good time."

Dom chuckles next to me and shakes his head.

Spending time with Sean and Dom is completely different from dealing with Antoine in his pit full of vipers. As relaxed as I am with the two of them for the most part, it's sometimes hard for me to acclimate from one role to the other.

Here in the States, I'm not constantly on guard the way I am in France, but the stakes are just as high.

Sean plants his elbow on his knee, cupping the side of his face as he gazes over at me, batting his lashes. "I just can't at all understand how you don't dazzle the ladies with your glittering personality. Wait, *Dom*—" he palms my chest, brushing my nipple with his thumb, and I slap his hand away—"I think I saw the twitch of his lips." He lets out an exaggerated sigh.

I snatch his beer and tip it, smiling into the cup as Sean's own smile vanishes.

"Anyone else noticing a pattern here?" He looks between the two of us as I down his drink, and he narrows his eyes. "Every fucking time I have a bottle, you take it away," he growls when I hand him back his empty cup. "Do you know how fucking long I had to wait in line for that, asshole?"

"Appreciate it."

Dom chuckles next to me, and I glance over at him, noting the rare smile on his face. At twenty-two, his future is so much brighter than mine, his worries fewer these days, making all of my efforts worth it.

It was all worth it, just to see him thrive. Dom looks back at me and draws his brows.

"What?"

I shake my head as Sean again palms my chest. "Three o'clock, T. Brunette built like a brick shithouse. Damn, is she smoking, and she's only got eyes for *you*." He turns to me. "She's jonesin' for some of that *mean* man meat." He chuckles, and his brows pinch. "Aren't you even going to *look* at her?"

"Roberts," Dom clips.

"Yeah?"

"Shut the fuck up."

Sean kicks back in his seat, restless as usual, the mirror image of Tarzan, who'd been forced to comb his hair and told to sit still.

"Here's an idea," I say, "why don't you watch the heavyweight fight taking place feet in front of you?"

"I've had haircuts more entertaining than this," he whines. "These are boring until they stop waltzing in the third or fourth round and really start throwing. I don't even know why we're here anyway. We've got everything in fucking place. We didn't need to waste cash on this bullshit."

"Because we have a job to do," Dom growls, growing as irritated as I am, "but if you're a good boy, I'll let you get a lollipop after."

"Can it be stuck to the ass on that one?" Sean gestures

toward a woman walking past us, this one a stunner with mile-long legs. "We've gone over this a thousand times. Seriously, how often do we get to do this? Never. We're in *Vegas, together*, and we're watching a boring-ass boxing match."

He rambles on next to me as I press my shoulder to Dom's. "What the fuck is going on with him?"

He eyeballs Sean past me and flicks his gaze to mine. "He got his feelings hurt."

"I told you that shit was going to backfire."

"You know, assuming makes you an asshole, right?" he retorts. "We've only shared a few, and I live in Boston at the moment, remember?"

"He didn't tell me."

"Why would he?" Dom's eyes roll over me. "You don't bleed like *that*."

His words sink in as I turn my attention back to the fight with more patience than I had a minute ago. Despite being the quintessential ladies' man, and though he jokes a lot, Sean has a lot of depth, and he takes life a lot more seriously than he lets on. With Dom in Boston for college and Tyler serving in the military, when I'm not in Charlotte or France, I spend my time with Sean and the rest of the chapter in Triple Falls. In that time, we've become closer, talking about mostly everything, a lot about life and shared philosophy. And the fact that Sean's acting up because he's hurting, and he didn't feel like he could tell me, cuts deep. Not that I can blame him; I don't do relationship talks. The sad truth is, I can't really identify with their reality most of the time. I glance over at Sean and inspect him more carefully, and now that I know, I can clearly see the sting in his eyes, along with the ache coming from him.

Sean's smile slips considerably when he glances over to me. "What?"

"You all right?"

His eyes harden past my shoulder at Dom for snitching before his gaze slowly travels back to me. "Can't put a lion on a lily pad and expect him to roar the same way, right?"

We stare off for several seconds before he looks away. It's then I understand, it's the club, *my rules*, that caused this, along with the expectation that they remain just as focused and unattached.

Guilt latches on, and after a few seconds of watching Lance throw, I bump my knee with his. "We can talk about the rules. Maybe make a few changes."

Sean shakes his head. "It's not a bad idea for others, but it's too late for me." Subconsciously, he runs his hand along his shoulder where his ink lays beneath. "It's better this way. I'm not ready to nest yet. But she was . . ." he shakes his head. "I'm good, man. It is what it is."

As Sean predicted, the fight begins to gain momentum as Lance starts to dominate the round. I dart my attention back to Elijah, who's in Amelia's face, berating her as she glances around, humiliated and terrified, just before her features twist in pain.

"Fuck this — " Sean stands suddenly — "I'm getting another beer." I tap my wrist to remind him of the time.

"Yeah, yeah — " he musters a grin — "all work and no play makes T. a very boring boy." He playfully smacks my chin, empty cup in hand, as he walks past the two of us in the opposite direction of concession.

"Where the fuck is he going?" Dom asks, as we both trail his gait, which becomes sloppier with every step he takes.

"Is he high?" I ask.

He shrugs, his eyes latched on to Sean with concern. "No more than usual."

Confused, I watch him as he begins to stumble into the rows of people surrounding the ring, reeling back as he's pushed off a few, lifting his hands in apology, before he ambles around the corner. It's when I see him closing in on Elijah that I realize his intent.

Dom curses, catching on when I do, pulling his cell from his pocket and furiously texting Sean. Sean stumbles around the ring, his drunken gait impressive, especially when he subtly taps his pocket in the midst of his performance, letting us know he's ignoring Dom's texts before subtly flipping us the company logo.

"Tell me this is not happening." I clench my fists as Sean stumbles his way toward our mark.

"I'm afraid it fucking is, brother."

"I'm going to kill him," I growl as Sean gets into position and sets the bait, feet away from Amelia, his eyes trained on her, waiting, a signature grin in place.

"Motherfucker," I growl. "Text him again."

"It's too late." Just as Dom says it, Amelia spots Sean and on instinct beams back at him, just as Elijah catches onto the exchange. I curse as Amelia's face blanches, and she burst into tears.

Dom goes to stand, and I grip his arm and yank him back in his seat. He turns to me, his posture drawing tight, his eyes darkening, livid. "He just fucking elbowed her in the stomach. Why isn't anyone helping her or saying anything?"

Sean ambles to the side as if the ground is moving beneath

him. He's already starting to gather attention, odd looks from some of the front row, and it's only a matter of time before he draws the attention of house security.

"Sadly, it's human nature, brother, and you have to keep a lid on that temper and wait for the right time to strike, or else you're just another dumb fucking thug looking to get caught,"

Sean remains idle as I fight to keep from aiding him myself, just as his gamble pays off and the entirety of the arena jumps to their feet. In the ring, Lance has managed to get his opponent on the ropes and is doling out punishment with a series of blows, raining hell with his blurring fists. With all eyes on the ring, Sean leaps into action, stumbling straight toward them before he fakes a trip, his head landing in Elijah's crotch. Elijah grips Sean by the arms in an attempt to push him away; just as Sean lifts and head butts him so hard, Elijah's mouth goes slack as he sinks down in his chair. With Elijah half-conscious, Sean manages his recovery by artfully fumbling over his feet and face-planting in Amelia's cleavage. Her eyes widen with shock as he nuzzles her a split second before he stands, apologizes, and saunters off. Amelia smiles in the direction Sean fled just as Elijah slowly comes to before searching for the freight train that just hit him.

Dom shakes in hysterical laughter next to me, and I lose sight of Sean, who slips into the standing crowd. It's the roar of laughter that spills from Dom's lips, a rare sound, that has me turning to face my brother, and at his reaction, my anger fades, and I'm unable to help my smile.

"Fuck, that was priceless." Dom's chuckle begins to slow as he claps a hand on my shoulder. "That's our boy," he proclaims proudly, his smile cracking his face wide. "That shit alone was worth the money we paid for these seats." Both our pockets rumble with an incoming text, and we check them at the same time to see a text from Sean. It's a real-time picture of us, Dom laughing, me smiling at him.

"Slick motherfucker," Dom muses, sending a reply as I gaze down at the picture to get an idea of where it was shot. Looking in the same direction, I scan the crowd, spotting Sean sitting a few rows back from Elijah and Amelia, a pride-filled smile on his face. Grinning, I lift my chin to Sean as Elijah and Amelia walk past him toward the exit, and he lifts his back before standing to follow.

"Let's do this," I say to Dom as he gets to his feet.

Dom stops me with a hand on my arm. "This one is his."

Half an hour later, after trick-or-treating and disposing of our Michael masks and plastic gloves, we were half a million richer and had a new list of marks to target. Thanks to Sean and Dom, Elijah became a thumb-sucker, and Amelia was set free to make better life choices. By the time the sun rose the next morning, Sean had managed to forget about his broken heart. But I didn't. And by the time Dom got back from college, we had new rules in place for birds looking to nest. A specific mark meant to protect them. A mark Cecelia now bears.

Dicing some onion, I glance back at the pile of shit I bought for the night and wince about the fact that it might be overkill. I was assured Cecelia would love it. Itching to take another drink of gin, I forgo it as the sunlight begins to fade and glance at the time on my cell. The café closed an hour ago. She should be home. I shoot a text to the new birds on watch.

What's her twenty?

Café.

I swallow back the sting she may be avoiding me and resume my chopping.

Chapter Twenty-Five

CECELIA

STRETCHING MY NECK to relieve it of some of the tension, I sit on one of the sofas in my café gazing into the fire while my phone charges.

As soon as it powers up, I see a missed text from Christy. A picture of her boys in the hand-sewn Halloween costumes she worked on for months. I heart the image and shoot a return text.

Awesome. Love you.

The bubbles start and stop, and I know why. I haven't called or FaceTimed her since Tobias showed up, and I know she's angry with me. When I got to Virginia, I called her daily, and being the friend she is, she talked me through setting up in a new life, my heart freshly re-broken.

The fucking usual.

Her texts have become shorter, more abrupt as of late because mine have become non-existent. She's put up with years of this shit from me and doesn't deserve it. If anything, she deserves a better friend, and I've abused our friendship to the point she should be seriously pissed at me. The truth is, I'm tired of lying.

I've been doing it for too long, and it's shortchanged our relationship.

She's my constant, my family, and she deserves better, but it's all part of the cost of loving Tobias. If I tell her I'm with him again, I know I won't have her support. And worse, if he breaks my heart all over again, I don't know if I can handle the "I told you so." So, for now, I'm hiding instead of lying.

This morning, I was ready to give in to what I feel for him, but soon after we were interrupted, I was struck by a gnawing fear that doing so could land me right back to a starting point I've been pushed back to one too many times before.

But I love him. And I want him, *badly*. The craving is getting harder to ignore. We've been sleeping in the same bed for nearly a month, and I haven't once permitted myself to get lost in him.

"Earth to Cecelia."

I glance up at Marissa to see her shaking her head. It's then I realize she's been standing in front of me with the deposit in hand, and I tuned her out the whole time she was trying to get my attention.

"I'm sorry, what?"

"I said I'd take the deposit if you want to head home." She shoulders her purse and smiles down at me. "Boss, please know I have your best interests at heart when I say this."

"*Okay?*"

"Put yourself out of your misery and fuck the man, already." She lifts a brow as my lips part. "First and foremost, I've *seen* him, and not even the Messiah himself will blame you for fornicating sinfully and often with him. You can think it through all you want, but combine sexual tension, old hurts, conflicting feelings, and what-ifs, and you two are going to be hamsters on roller skates for some time."

"Isn't it a hamster on a wheel?"

"Which do you think is harder for the hamster?"

I laugh and shake my head at her. "You're nuts."

"You're still punishing him."

"Trust me. I have reason to. But I'm . . . I want to let it go."

"So—" she nudges me and grins—"go home and mount that fucking lion, mouse."

"I'm not a *mouse*, and that's what I need to make him understand."

She nods. "Then get persuasive. Fight him if you must, but do it in your laciest *thong*." She grabs our cups. "I'm going to rinse these and take off."

I stand. "I'll leave with you."

I set the alarm, and it starts to beep as we head toward the door.

"You could take a day off, you know," she adds, "we can cover things here."

"I just did yesterday, and I'll see you *tomorrow*."

Marissa chatters on about her Halloween plans as I lock up, spotting the two ravens in the sedan parked a few stores down. I lift my chin in both greeting and thanks as Marissa and I step off the curb and she rounds her SUV.

"—I didn't think I'd see him again after that day, but he's got potential. I don't know, we'll see."

She opens her car door, and her chatter ceases. "My God, woman, it's like talking to a wall."

I wince and look over at her. "Sorry. I'm just . . ."

"Distracted. It's okay, girl," she offers patiently, adding a wink of support. "See you tomorrow, boss." She starts her Jeep and backs away, just as a mother of two steps out of the minimart a few doors down, passing out two freshly purchased orange pumpkin containers from a plastic bag to two eager costumed Minions. She catches me on the sidewalk noticing them, and smiles, and I wave before she sets to work securing them in the back of her SUV. I imagine her life is similar to Christy's in the family dynamic, and can clearly see their night playing out. A rushed dinner, followed by trick-or-treating, before wrestling their sugar-high kids into pajamas and later collapsing into bed sharing a high five.

A normal life.

I could have had that. I had every chance to have normal. But with Tobias, normal will most likely never be part of the equation. And the truth is, I resented normal when I did have it, my whole-being rejected it. I wanted him, a life with him. And he's *here*. He's here because he wants me too, and the rest of it just doesn't fucking matter.

Remorse courses through me as I picture the exit wound on Tobias's back while he was showering.

"What are you doing, Cecelia?" I scold as tears threaten.

My heart cracks in understanding of the time I've already wasted, begrudging him for mistakes he's already paid for ten times over. And he's still punishing himself daily, his heart continually breaking. And instead of forgiving him and trying to put his pieces back together, I'm ripping the possibility of a second chance away from us. While he's been fighting for what we had, I've been weighing him down with expectations.

Every minute counts, every second I'm with him is a gift, and I'm fucking wasting it.

"I remember everything, Cecelia. Every word you said, every look you gave me. Your three kinds of laughs, the details of your dreams, the way your nostrils flare when you're starting to get pissed. The sting of your slaps, the salt in your tears, the fit of your breasts in my hand. The feel of your mouth, the taste of your pussy, so which part do you need me to remind you of?"

"Shit." Eyes burning, throat tightening, I unlock my car, get behind the wheel, turn the ignition, and put it into gear before racing out of the parking lot toward my broken king.

Stepping into the house fifteen minutes later, my world is transformed when I see dozens of soft tealights flickering throughout the house. My ears perk up as I try to identify the filtering music—old, melodic, and slow.

Beau greets me with a lick on my hand, and I bend down to scratch his ears before racing through the living room, following the sound of light clatter in the kitchen. Stepping in, I'm met by the sight of Tobias cooking, his muscular forearms on display as he drizzles olive oil into a pan before turning his sunset eyes to me, his lips lifting in greeting. "Late day?"

My eyes water as I picture him in Roman's kitchen all those years ago. "Yeah, sorry, m-m-my phone died, and I don't like driving home in the dark without it charged up, just in case. I mean, there's a charger in my Audi, but I'm used to driving D-d-the Camaro."

He frowns as I stumble through my excuse, my heart pounding as the elation I felt weeks ago from seeing him in that parking lot comes flooding back in. He studies me, looking completely relaxed, an untouched drink on the counter next to him. He walks over to where I stand and takes the purse from my shoulder, tossing it onto the counter before stepping closer and turning me in his arms to untie my apron.

"Wait," I say, pulling a bulging jack-o-lantern bag of candy from my apron, my cheeks flushing when I turn and thrust it at him. "Happy Halloween."

He gazes down at it, and his lips lift. "Thank you."

"It's silly, I know."

"Not silly." He nods over his shoulder, a sheepish smile playing on his own lips as I look over to the kitchen table full of . . . everything imaginable, most notably two pumpkins ripe for carving.

"You want to do Halloween with me?"

He nods emphatically, turning back to me, a frown in place when he sees the tears in my eyes.

"What's wrong?"

"I love you," I blurt out. "I'm sorry I've made this so hard on you."

He searches my eyes. "No, Trésor, I deserv—"

"To be happy. We both do."

He cups my face in his hands, relief in his eyes as I throw my arms around him and kiss him. He groans in surprise as I amplify the kiss, showing him just how hungry I am, and he tilts my head, diving deep as we stand in the middle of my kitchen and explore, a low moan leaving my throat as he gives in and grips the back of my shirt while pulling me tightly to his chest. He closes our kiss before I'm ready and turns me in the direction of my bedroom. "Go shower. We've much to do and a chess game to start. Hurry up."

Taking his cue with a light slap on the ass and a little bounce in my heels, I walk through the living room to see he's cleaned the house spotless and vacuumed. There's not a thing out of place. The fire warms me as I walk by, the ambiance relaxing me further as I pause at the door of the bedroom to see that my desk has been cleared of clutter, the books shelved and organized. On top of my desk lays a leather-bound journal with freshly written script and a pen sitting next to it.

Cher Journal,

I met my grandfather, Abijah's dad, when I was twenty-one at a park in Paris. He sent me an invite to join him at his table by way of messenger. He'd been watching over me for the years I'd been in Paris, something I took great comfort in after the fact. Before we met, I spent years searching for my mother's relatives to help me and got the door slammed in my face due to being Abijah's son. This was not the case with Abel.

My grandfather never once treated me as anything other than his beloved grandson. And he never once begrudged me for my mother's abandonment of Abijah, either. After our initial meeting, he spent every Saturday with me for months, teaching me the game he held most dear to him while relaying to me everything he knew about life and the strategy of chess. I've always been a believer in the saying "listen to your elders", and though he fit the criteria, he was far wiser than any other man I've encountered before and after I met him, with one exception—my brother.

With Abel, I felt a kinship close to that of my bond with my stepfather, Beau, and maybe a little bit more so, due to the blood relation.

I've always felt guilty about that.

But after years of living mostly in solitude in the city, I had someone, a friend by way of family.

He was an odd man and laughed about things I often didn't understand at times without him explaining them. He lived on a diet of French bread, cheese, apples, and the strongest coffee imaginable and often demanded I bring all before playing our game.

It was fall of that year that I showed up at the park, a bag of his favorite things in hand, to discover our pieces still in play from the week before.

And I knew he was gone.

But what he left me with was a sense of family I hadn't felt from anyone but Dom since my parents died. I cherish that time we had together. More often than not, I sensed he'd been a major player at one point in his life, and he'd alluded to it often without much detail, though he never really confessed. However, it was clear that there were many aspects of his life he was deeply ashamed of. The most haunting, that he was a militant father. Maybe I was his way of dealing with his grief in losing his only son, my company a reprieve for some of his pain. But for whatever reason he reached out—it was worth it to me just to know him.

I can't remember his last words to me. And as a man with an extensive memory, that ironic and cruel fact baffles me to this day. I'm certain his goodbye that day was filled with warmth and subtle advice. Because despite the man he might have been, he died a kind man, a man I admired, and honestly, a man I began to love like family.

When I attended his funeral as his only living relative, I felt the strength of that lie and decided that, one day, I would seek out my birth father to try and get him the care he needed to honor Abel. I don't know if I believe in the afterlife, but I want to because I don't have a close living relative left, and it's comforting to think they all may be reunited somewhere and waiting.

I like to think that if an afterlife does exist, Abel rested easier when I finally found Abijah, knowing that he was cared for and wasn't alone when he died. And maybe now, they both have peace.

It's a question that plagues me often, the existence of the afterlife, and has since my

*parents died. A question I struggle with daily,
mostly due to guilt.*

*Because if we are truly looked upon, and
those who've passed are able to hear us, my
confession is this—*

*I haven't spoken a word to my brother since
he died.*

*Every day I wonder if he waits for word from
me.*

*And even with the guilt that he might be
waiting, I can't find the words. I don't know if I
ever will.*

With a lump swelling in my throat, I sniff and see a shift in my periphery and look over my shoulder to see Tobias watching me, his arms crossed, leaning in the doorway.

"Is this what you want?"

In his head, it's what I asked for.

I nod. "Yes."

"This I can do."

"I'm so sorry."

"It was a long time ago."

"It didn't seem so long ago when I read it. Did you ever ask about Abijah?"

"No, I never could muster the courage because I think it was too painful for him to talk about."

I turn my attention back to the journal and run my hand over the page. "Thank you."

"This is the only time I'll watch you read it. Whether or not you read my confessions is up to you. And *Sensodyne*."

"What?"

"The toothpaste I like." He shrugs. "I have sensitive gums."

I can't help my laugh as I sniffle back the rest of my tears. "I love you."

"I know." He shoves his hands in his pockets. "I'm sorry that's such a hard task."

"Not so hard." I walk over to where he stands, and he cups my face, his eyes glittering with affection.

"You want another confession?"

I nod, captive in his hands.

"I never had a *real* girlfriend until you. You were my first and *only*." His eyes are earnest, his words ripping at my heart when he speaks. "A flirtation, dinners, sex, but nothing more, and Alicia was . . . a distraction. She was kind and tried to take care of me no matter how much I resisted, but it wasn't real; we didn't share a life—" he runs his thumbs along my jaw—"not carving pumpkins, or a turkey, or picking out a Christmas tree, meeting the parents. And I never thought I would ever want these things, but I do. And I want to do these things with you."

"You want to do *normal* with me?" I ask as tears I can't help spring and spill.

"I do," he murmurs, wiping them away. "Why are you crying again, Trésor?"

"Because I'm okay with being a mouse . . . *sometimes*."

His brows pull into a deep V. "What?"

"You don't have to understand it."

"Okay, well, I love you, too, *mouse*." He dips and kisses me again, and I feel the strength of it down to my toes as he pulls back, and uncertainty crosses his beautiful features. "I don't know if I'll be a good boyfriend."

"You were when we were together, aside from, you know,

the *lying* and *manipulation*, and you still are, so very good at it."

"Trésor, I want to Halloweenie with you and Thanksgiving with you, and Christmas with you, but—"

I can't help my giggle. *"Halloweenie?"*

"Yes, with *you.*"

"Hallow-*weenie.* That's what you're saying, right?"

"Yes." The line creases in his forehead. "That's what I said."

"Tobias, there is no Hallo*weenie.*"

"Yes, there is," he insists. "My mother said it all the time."

I snort. "Tobias, it's just Halloween."

He looks at me like I'm ignorant. "It's the event, an occurrence, you know, what you do the day of—" He releases my face, tossing his hand in his explanation. "There's Christmas carols and caroling. Halloween, and Halloweenie—" He frowns as if it's starting to sound odd to him.

Laughter erupts from me as I cup his face. "Ah, you poor man, I think your mother lost that one in translation. You had just moved from France, right?"

He nods slowly.

"You're thirty-eight years old. How is it possible you still believe that's the right verbiage?"

"I don't celebrate holidays, so it's a rare conversation," he says dryly. "The woman at the store didn't correct me today."

"Maybe it's because you're a scary, mean-looking foreigner, and they're terrified to."

I swear I see his olive skin tint. "Tobias, my love, I'm sorry, but there is no *act* of Halloweenie."

"Whatever," he huffs. "Are you going to let me talk?"

Lips quivering with threatening laughter, I nod.

"I want a temporary truce."

"As in?"

"No club talk of any kind, just you and me. Just us, Cecelia. That's why I came here, for us. This isn't about the fucking club or the part it plays with us. And that's what we can't seem to get past."

"For how long?"

"We can take it day by day?"

"Halloweenie by Halloweenie?" he growls, and I laugh. "Sorry, but it's hilarious."

"Keep it up. I may strangle you tonight."

"Ooooo, a Halloweenie reenactment." I waggle my brows. "Are we going to play dress-up?"

"Yes," he draws out in monotone. "You're playing lumberjack."

"What?"

He darts his eyes to the waiting pajamas on my bed.

"Har, har."

"So? Can we agree to a ceasefire?" His expression shifts, the look in his eyes imploring.

"A temporary truce sounds perfect to me."

"Good. Take a shower. We've much to do. A list of Halloween rituals, and I'm making turkey chili. Deanna said, it's a good Hallo—" he stops himself, and I press my lips together—"*ween* meal for a cold night."

"Who's Deanna?"

"She's my cashier."

"You have a cashier?"

"No, well, I go to her line." He bites his lip. "Every time."

I lift a brow. "Is that so?"

He nods. "I trust her."

"Should I be worried?"

He rolls his eyes. "She is young."

"Now I'm really worried."

"Her boyfriend, Ricky, works at the liquor store, and they have two kids."

"You sure do know a lot about her."

"She helps me," he explains vaguely.

"Helps you what?"

"With you," he says softly, and my heart seizes at the fact he's taking relationship advice from a checkout girl.

"Well, you should trust her. You did good." I push up onto my toes and brush my lips against his. "You've already beaten every single first date I've ever had."

My sentiment touches him, and he kisses me, *really* kisses me before releasing me too soon. His eyes trail over me before he turns and heads back to the kitchen and I bite my lip, staring after him until he disappears with Beau on his heels.

Chapter Twenty-Six

CECELIA

WATER STREAMS FROM Tobias's face as he triumphantly lifts the apple with his teeth. His eyes are dancing with victory as I clap for him while he shakes the water out of his hair like a soaked dog.

"Good job, King. Bobbing for apples, *check*," I say through a laugh, "but you didn't have to put your *whole* head in."

He pats his face dry with a kitchen towel. "I don't see the point of this."

"Me neither, really. It's just a thing."

"I think we'll skip it next year," he says as he runs the towel over his neck, and my heart warms at the idea of another year. He tosses the apple onto the newspaper we have spread on the floor, just as my curious mutt interjects himself between us, dipping his snout into the large tin of apples.

"Non," Tobias snaps, and Beau jerks back before gathering a pile of pumpkin spaghetti guts in his paws and dragging it off with him.

"Ah, come on!" I cry as Beau tries to escape. Tobias manages to catch him, wiping his feet off before letting him out the back door. I trash the newspaper as Tobias lights the candles in our finished pumpkins. I walk over and click off the kitchen light as he sets the lid back in mine, and join him where he stands as we survey them both on the table.

"Well, I believe you win," I say, admiring his raven-littered pumpkin. "It's awesome."

"Yours is terrible," he retorts, looking at my gap-toothed jack-o-lantern.

Laughter bursts from me as I weigh his serious expression.

"All right, boyfriend 101, even if it's terrible, or I look fat in my jeans, lie to me."

"Now you *want* me to lie?"

"You are such an ass."

"Come on," he orders, picking up his pumpkin. "We have to put them on the porch to scare the bad spirits away."

Grinning, I gather my terrible pumpkin and follow him out to the porch. We sit them side by side in the freezing, star-filled night. Wrapping his arms around me, he pulls me back into his chest as we survey my front yard. The trees lining the driveway are nearly bare, but the view is picturesque due to the size of the yard and the distant moon beaming high above the field across the street.

"It is peaceful here, Cecelia."

"But?"

"No but, I have *adjusted*. Come on. It's cold."

Just as we turn to walk in, I see a dark object racing toward us and scream as it comes into full view, eye level, and hovers just feet away.

"Don't be afraid," he chuckles. "It's just Tyler, saying hi." He lifts his hand and flips him the bird.

"That's a drone."

"Yes."

Yeah, just your average, normal, everyday Halloween, Cecelia. But no part of me resents it.

"Since when do we have drones?"

"I told you."

"No, you didn't. I'm pretty sure I would remember you telling me we have drones."

"Oh," he recalls, "I told your *parents*."

"Well, it sure helped that *they* knew." I glance back at him, and he flashes me remorse.

"Sorry."

"This is a prime example of why you'll forever be in the doghouse, King." I turn back to where the drone is and wave enthusiastically to Tyler before I start to blow kisses.

Behind me, Tobias growls, before jerking me back inside the house and pinning me to the back of the door. He flips the lock three times, placing his palms next to my head, eyes narrowing. "You don't give those away."

"No?"

He jerks his chin. "No. Not negotiable."

"Such a jealous man. It's a good thing I don't want to kiss anyone else."

"Non?"

"Non," I whisper and bite my lip, anticipation thrumming through me when he lifts his finger, tugging it free from my teeth before running his thumb along it, his eyes pooling. He leans down and places a brief kiss to my lips, his gaze drifting down to my pajamas before he steps away.

And now I'm starting to hate my own flannels.

"What's next?" I ask, following him back into the kitchen.

Twenty minutes later, after sharing a joint, caramel apples

setting, we cue up *Halloween* and take turns shoving popcorn into each other's mouths. Amazed at the turn this day has taken, I study him through the flicker of tealights and the flashes of light from the movie. I watch him watch the slasher flick for the first time.

I'm his first girlfriend and his only love. The truth of that sinks in as I stroke his chest through his thermal.

Being a part of his firsts will never get old, no matter how big or small. It's painfully obvious he's missed a lot of living, and because of that, there's a sort of innocence about him that's still there, despite his age and the type of life he's led up to this point. It wasn't purposeful. It's just how it happened. And the truth of that is so alluring that I can't help but burrow deeper into him, pulling him closer to me.

He deserves this vacation just to be able to experience a little life without the club's expectations. The same way he did in those short months we were together, but even then, he was working. He's a free man now, and I'm determined to make it good for him. What he needs from me is so fucking simple. He needs me to assure him that it's okay to live for himself, for his own happiness, because he doesn't know what living is if he's not doing it for someone else. It's a habit I'll be hard-pressed to break, even though it's one of the most incredible things about him, but he's suffered enough for it. And in truth, it seems an unbreakable habit seeing as how he's done it most of his life.

But any small victory for me will be a sweet loss for him. However, in time, I will force him to make decisions based on what he wants—to be a little more selfish with his own needs. He runs his hand along the wings on my back as I press a kiss to his throat. His eyes dart to mine as the familiar serial killer track starts to play, his muscular arms tightening around me as he flicks his attention back to the screen and absently strokes me with his fingers.

Best Halloweenie ever.

Chapter Twenty-Seven

CECELIA

A LITTLE AFTER midnight, I peek out of the bathroom and spot Tobias in his black boxers, perched against the headboard where he's worked on his laptop since we came in from walking Beau. Shutting the door, I turn on the faucet and pull the box from beneath the bathroom cabinet where I tucked it away earlier. Tugging on the bow that binds it, I gather what I need and stuff it back beneath the sink before stripping and running juniper lotion over my skin. My nipples draw tight in anticipation as I redress, loading my toothbrush before scrubbing my teeth.

A thousand butterflies swirl in my stomach as I rinse my mouth and run my fingers through my hair. Checking my appearance one last time, I click off the light and open the door. Surveying him where he sits, I drink in every inch of his muscled body, pulse kicking up as my thirsty eyes devour him. His onyx hair is tousled. His sleek features are drawn tight in concentration as he types, intent on his task. His muscular forearms flex, lifting the pillow for a glimpse of the deeply etched V that starts at his hip. Wetness gathers between my legs as I linger in the doorway, growing thirstier by the second. It's only when I move to stand at the end of the bed that he pauses his fingers over the keys, slowly lifting his eyes from the screen to where I stand. A hundred emotions flit through his smoldering eyes before they blaze over the negligee he bought for me years ago.

My belly dips when he slowly closes his laptop as I stand in wait, skin buzzing, heart thundering, as he adjusts himself on the mattress with his fists, edging to the end of the bed. In seconds, I'm between his spread legs as he presses his forehead against my stomach, running it back and forth along the silky material.

"Cecelia." My name comes out strangled as he lifts his eyes to mine, setting my skin alight. Lifting his chin to rest on my stomach, he palms my calves in the gentlest of caresses before he slowly starts to work his way up.

"I was tempted so many times to throw it away," I confess on a whisper. "I did once or twice—the bow has a ketchup stain on it," I rasp out, his touch electrifying, sending goosebumps over my flesh, "but I never could bring myself to part with it." I pluck his hair as he gazes up at me, his hands slowly working their way up as his fingers ghost along the back of my thighs. "I used to sleep in it on hard nights and tell myself that maybe if I wore it . . ." I struggle with the memory, "maybe it would be the night you came back for me. It's . . . stupid, I know, but that's how much I missed you."

"Not stupid," he whispers hoarsely, sliding his palms over the curve of my ass to find me bare. A soft curse leaves him as he strokes my skin, spreading wildfire throughout my humming body.

"Soft," he murmurs, his palms lifting the material to bare me to him. "Sensual." He bends, running his tongue along my slit. "Delicate," he continues, repeating the words he seduced me with the first time he slipped the nightgown down my body. "Beautiful, so beautiful." He draws me forward with beckoning hands, tilting my hips as he sucks the whole top of my pussy with fervor. His dark lashes flutter closed as he spreads me with an explorative tongue, whispering it over my throbbing clit.

"Tobias." My needful moan fuels him, and he stands, gripping my face before crushing our mouths together. He licks into my mouth as I slide my palm down his muscled stomach. I match his thirsty licks, reaching into his boxers and grip his thick cock in my hand, rubbing the precum off the fat crown with my thumb.

His groan vibrates in my mouth as I squeeze him from root to tip. Hunger taking over, I break our kiss and drop to my knees, taking his boxers down as I go. Clawing his ass, I grip him firmly, flicking my eyes up to his before licking my lips and taking him to the back of my throat.

"Putain." *Fuck.* He fists my hair in an effort to control me as I go feral, taking him in deeper, choking on his girth as saliva dangles from my lips.

"Cecelia," he hisses as I suck his veined length to the thick head before again diving, my eyes never straying from his. It's when I start to leisurely explore, licking along the side of his massive shaft that he snaps and jerks me from my knees. In a flash, I'm pinned to the bed by his kiss alone as he dips his thick fingers between my thighs, stretching them to ready me. And in the next breath, he's on his back, lifting me easily before positioning me to straddle his face, his tongue plunging into me with meticulous licks as he grips my wrists, pinning them to the tops of my thighs.

Lust takes over as he devours me, his tongue assaulting while keeping me at his mercy. I feel every single thrust as he eats me, his groan vibrating my lower half before he finally releases my hands.

"Lift," he orders, and I do, tilting forward to prop on my palms on the mattress. He adjusts me to hover where he wants me before using his fingers and tongue until I'm trembling with the onslaught. He jackhammers his tongue against my clit, never stopping as his fingers probe, stretch, fuck. The build intensifies until I'm stuttering between begging and rapid breaths. He lifts his head to delve deeper, his black hair tickling my thighs before he sucks the whole of me between his lips, kissing my pussy just as thoroughly as he does my mouth before condemning me between torturous, relaxed licks.

"Dois-je te laisser aller?" *Should I free you?*

His breath hits my clit before he flattens his tongue along it, robbing me just as I start to crest.

"Tobias," I plea, grinding against his mouth for more friction, so close I can feel the early tremors of my orgasm. He gazes up at me, the hem of my negligee dancing along his face and neck, and I lift it to get a better view of him beneath me. His eyes hood as he circles his finger, nipping my clit before pulling away.

"Dois-je être indulgent?" *Should I show you mercy?*

Another tortuous lick as he runs a skilled finger along my G, and I cry out in frustration as he edges me. "Tu n'en as pas fait preuve envers moi." *You've shown none toward me.*

"Let me come," I hiss, ripping at his hair as he thrusts his tongue inside to replace his finger, cupping my ass to go deeper.

"Please," I beg as he runs his palm over my silk-covered breasts, molding and squeezing, his mouth working me into a frenzy until I'm wound so tight with need, I can hardly breathe.

His growl sounds a second before he closes his lips around my clit and sucks, and with the beckoning of his finger, I detonate. He grips my hips as I ride it out, running me back and forth along his heavenly mouth as I shatter, nearing a scream when I call his name. Soaked and shaking in the aftermath, he continues to lap me up until my high has partially subsided.

And then I'm on my back, as he groans against my mouth, his eyes demanding. Hovering, he parts my thighs with his palms, hitching my legs up high before running his thick head through my folds in a wicked taunt.

"Please."

My core aches with dire need as he teases me, massaging my clit with his crown until I'm writhing beneath him.

"Look at me," he commands. I lift my eyes to his molten depths as he drives into me with one earth-shattering thrust. My back bows as I gaze up at him, mouth parted, breath ripped from me just as his eyes close.

"Putain. Mon Dieu." *Fuck. My God.*

Choking from the invasion, my pussy pulses painfully, stretching around every inch of him just as his eyes flame open.

"Forgive me." He grips my throat, draws back, and mercilessly drives in again. I shout out as he tears through me with abandon, my thighs shaking as he pistons his hips and fucks me like I'm about to disappear.

Strokes unforgiving, I dig my nails into his chest as he

lifts to his knees, pushing my thighs further apart, his gaze dipping to where we connect as he drives in again. I follow, becoming equally transfixed on the sight of us connecting.

"Ma chatte. Mon corps. Ma femme. Mon cœur. Ma vie." *My pussy. My body. My woman. My heart. My life.*

His words tip me into a free fall, another orgasm paralyzing me, overpowering me until I burst into fast breaths with the rush. Rippling with aftershocks, he dips his head, kissing me frantically, thick lips brushing over every inch of exposed skin before he sucks my silk-covered breast into his mouth, pulling down the material to suck the other. He begins to shake above me, his kisses becoming frantic, his fucking just as hurried as if we're running out of time.

His chest glistens with a thin sheen of sweat as he ravages me, unrelenting, until I feel the shift, feel him falter. I kiss his Adam's apple as he swallows a grunt and scoops me beneath my arms to cup my shoulders, hands spread over my wings as our chests brush.

"I'm sorry," he croaks softly, slowing, gently rolling into me, capturing my mouth and thrusting his tongue to match his pace. It's then I taste the salt in his kiss, as desperate sounds begin to pour out of him. My eyes sting as I try my best to soothe him.

"Tobias," I murmur as he lowers his mouth peppering apologetic kisses along my neck.

"Je t'ai perdue," *I lost you,* he rasps out as he lifts his head, the rawness in his gaze grabs hold of me, fisting my heart so tightly I whimper at the loss of the last of the protection I held so dear. This isn't fucking or making love. It's the reunification of two souls ripped apart at the peak of discovery. And I know that's what he feels now as awareness flows between us and we again become one, leaving no trace any space existed.

We move together effortlessly as he trembles above me, gripping the edge of the mattress and rocking into me with deep thrusts—filling me again and again as he murmurs his love, his devotion, his apologies. I map his chest before running my fingers along his biceps. His eyes no longer search but probe deeper into me, navigating easily to the place inside only he is capable of reaching.

The renewed connection between us feels molecular, and it hurts as it heals. I'm certain that if God granted me only one minute of life on this earth, I would want it to be *this* minute, this moment with him, where I know exactly why I'm alive and who for.

Gazing up at the love of my life, I accept him fully back into his place in my heart, giving in to the one thing I've never had control of, and never will as long as his own heart beats.

Because it's mine.

"I love you," I murmur.

And with one last thrust and my whispered words, he comes.

Chapter Twenty-Eight

CECELIA

TOBIAS CRADLES ME in my clawfoot tub after hours of the most intense sex of my life. He's already hard despite our last exhausting session where our only words were softly delivered 'I love yous' between pleasure-filled moans, grunts, and desperate breaths. We've wasted ourselves with our greed while attempting to heal each other with our bodies, lips, and needy hands. When he lifts a warm, soaked rag and runs it along my shoulders, I tilt forward, giving him access, my hands braced on his muscular thighs.

"Do you think we're cursed?" I ask, and he stills the rag, mulling over my question before running it down the center of my back.

"I think we're our own worst enemies at times, and we've allowed too many outside forces to rip us apart. Me especially."

"Star-crossed," I whisper.

"I don't disagree."

"What about the other outside forces? Where the hell were our fairy godmothers when we needed them?"

He grunts in agreement. "They did a terrible job."

"Cupid?" I ask.

"He shot one too many arrows into you."

"Well, he's fucking fired too. Did no one show up for us?"

"Non."

"The saints?"

"Not one," he whispers, running his fingers along my stomach as I lay back to rest on his chest. "Not Lady Luck, not Father Time, none of them."

"Assholes," I harrumph. "Who else is supposed to be looking out for us?"

"Well, there's God. But I think I pissed him off before I was born."

His statement tugs at my heart. "No, you didn't, Tobias. Just remember, Job was a favorite, and He took everything from him, his riches, his family, everything he had before He plagued him with disease to prove a point to the devil. He put him through hell, so maybe it's not so great to be God's favorite."

"Well, in that case, maybe I am a favorite."

I run my nails along his legs. "You're my favorite and the best man I've ever known."

His fingers still.

"After all *I've* put you through, you believe I'm a good man?"

I turn in his arms and straddle him, and he laces his fingers at the small of my back, his brows creased.

"You're an incredible man. You revealed your true colors when we were together before. In recent years, your actions were mostly due to pain, and you're still in pain, my love. I'm not going to start pointing out all your flaws because fuck that, I have my own, but the core of you is made of pure gold, and nothing you ever say or do will convince me otherwise."

Wordless, he cups the back of my head, running his palm down my soaked hair.

"You say you don't like my perception of you, Frenchman, but my perception isn't skewed. I love all parts, all sides of you, good and bad. This thing between us is still new. We aren't going to come out perfect straight out of the gate. But all of you gets all of me, my stubborn King, *always*."

His eyes roll down my body, warming me from the inside. "We may not be perfect, but you are."

"No, I'm not, but I'm over the fact that I'm not going to get my way with you at times. Tantrums need to fall to the wayside at some point for what's important."

He bites his lip briefly. "Is it weird to say you sound like Sean?"

I shrug. "Is it weird to say Sean sounds like you?"

He glances down. "Is it weird that people sit in bathtubs full of filth, thinking it makes them clean? I can see scum floating on the top of this water."

"No, you French prude, but baths are good for a woman who was just bent like a pretzel and jackhammered until she nearly passed out. And don't knock my housekeeping skills."

"I'm not, Trésor." He rubs his thumb and pointer finger together in inspection. "You have absolutely none."

"Or maybe you're just too high maintenance."

He lifts his hips, running his erection along my center, hitting my clit just . . . so.

"Maintenance appeals to me very much." His eyes flare, and I shake my head with a grin as he traces my nipple with his finger, bringing it to a stiff peak.

"Tell me something I don't know, Frenchman."

"What do you want to know?"

"Anything I don't know, which is apparently *a lot*."

He gathers the hair on the side of my neck and bites down on the skin of my shoulder before soothing it with his lush lips.

"Talk, King. I'm going to look beaten at work tomorrow."

"You're not going to work tomorrow."

"We'll see."

"One day. You haven't taken a single fucking day for *me* since I got here."

"What will we do on this day?"

He pulls at my hips again, and I groan. "Tobias, I can't."

"Then let me." Even in the water, I feel myself slicken as he rubs a finger along my clit before curling it inside of me.

"We didn't use a condom," I point out. "All *four* times." His finger stills before he pulls it away, bracing both hands on the side of the tub.

"You're on birth control. I saw it in the cabinet. You take it religiously."

I nod.

"So, is this conversation necessary?"

"Isn't it?"

His jaw ticks, but his question comes out pained. "Have you been with anyone since me?"

I shake my head. "No, Tobias, no, of course not."

I pose the same question without words.

"Cecelia," he sighs. "No, fuck no. That night I took you so roughly . . . and the weeks after you left, I couldn't even look at myself."

"I thought as much, but—"

He shakes his head, cutting me off. "Even when I was a bachelor, I never really indulged much in women," he confesses. "And I had plenty of chances."

"With lingerie models," I add dryly.

"And one French movie star," he chimes in with a wink.

"Fuck you, King," I move to get off his lap, and he pins me easily, a satisfied chuckle coming from his lips. "There's my jealous bébé."

I wrinkle my nose. "It's not healthy for either of us."

"It's who we are and how we feel when it comes to each other. And so we really don't give a fuck, do we?"

I hang my head. "We're going to end up in couple's therapy, and with our tempers, we probably need it."

He pinches my chin and lifts it. "I'm addicted to you and have been since the minute I touched you. In the past . . . sometimes I would go . . . a very long time without any human contact at all. I was so focused for so long, it wasn't a priority for me—until you. One hit of you and I was like a fucking fiend. Now I'm positive that I was waiting for the right woman, for you. And it's a good thing I saved what little patience I have *for you*, or I'd be a dead man."

"Har, har. And you think you're so easy to deal with?"

"Non. I'm the devil you chose."

"And who am I?"

"You're the angel who constantly stabs me in the ass with my own pitchfork."

"Okay, you've avoided my question long enough. Tell me," I insist, running my palms down his muscular arms. Because I can. Because he's mine.

"Something you don't know?" The glint in his eyes dims.

"Shelly almost had me committed, and there's no punchline. I went fucking crazy when you left, when I let you leave."

"I wanted to hate you."

"I tried my best to make sure you did, but you called my bluff, stubborn-ass woman."

Neither of us smiles because the pain of that truth hurts too much.

"You were so much safer in that life, Cecelia."

"I wasn't happy. I would have never been fulfilled."

"Nor me. I totaled my Jaguar the day you left my office, left me, left Triple Falls."

"What?" I jerk back in his arms as he lifts some water and cups it over my shoulders.

"When they lost you—" he shakes his head—"fucking idiots, I knew you'd done it purposely and had no intention of being found. I had nothing to go on. You ditched your cell phone, everything. You even left your Audi in impound. I knew I was fucked the second they called, and I think I blacked out because I don't remember the minutes that led up to the wreck. I just went . . . fucking crazy."

"And you totaled it?"

He nods.

"I'm sorry."

"You gave me every chance to stop you." He rests his head back on the lip of the tub. His eyes fixed on the ceiling. "God, Cecelia, I've never in my life been so fucked up. Just thinking about that phone call." He lifts his head, his eyes demanding even with his plea. "Promise me you'll never do that again."

"Tobias—"

"I'm begging you, Cecelia. If we fight, if we are at our

worst, no matter how angry you get, this is all I'll ask of you. Our biggest fights are going to be about security, I know it. But please just let me protect you for my own sanity, my own peace of mind, even if you feel you don't need it. I can't take it. I can't fucking take it." He looks so damn beautifully tortured, his features twisted with pain, his lashes darker from the dripping water. If this life is really mine, if in time Tobias proves his intentions sincere, I can't imagine a better way to live.

I press my forehead to his. "I promise."

He grips my jaw and backs away an inch, still intent on getting his own way. "Always?"

"Yes, you pig-headed sonofabitch."

"This promise above all others," he insists, "above everything."

"I promise you, Tobias."

"Merci." There's nothing but relief in his tone.

"And what about me protecting you?"

He draws his brows, and I scoff. "Maybe I don't like your perception of me. Sometimes I see the reflection in your eyes, and I know you still see the naïve nineteen-year-old you met. You obviously forgot who you came back for." He rakes his teeth over his lip as I grip him firmly in my hand, digging my nails a little into the silky skin covering his cock. "It's past time I remind you." His eyes flare and follow as I lift my hips and slowly sink onto him.

Chapter Twenty-Nine

TOBIAS

Age Thirty-One

INCOMPETENCE. IF THERE'S one thing I can't fucking stand, it's the fact that I have money and resources at my disposal, and fuck them both for all the good they're doing me now.

My search for Abijah has proven fruitless. His last whereabouts reported on the very street I'm walking. But the man doesn't frequent the same places, ever. He's as elusive as they fucking come, and the fact that he's evaded us for this long is wearing on me.

My phone rattles in my pocket as I change directions and head toward the bar at the end of the street, intent on one drink before I shower to scrub off the failure of another day.

"Oui?" I bark, answering my cell, and am met by hesitance on the other end of the line.

"Tobias, it's Matt, Virginia."

"I'm listening."

"I'm sorry to be the one to tell you this, man, but you were right."

"How so?"

"They brought a girl to the meetup not long ago, and I really didn't think anything of it."

Motherfucker.

For the last few months, Dom and Sean have become oddly absent, only reporting the minimum, and have become harder and harder to reach the last few weeks. I assumed they'd taken on a new pet project between them, up to old tricks, and I was fucking dead on.

"My sister met her that night. Said she seemed like a good girl, but not exactly the type for the club."

I run a hand through my sweat-slicked hair, scanning the street one last time, my irritation growing. Leave it to my brothers to drag an innocent into the mix, and for what? At the most, she's a chew toy. I swore I would be patient about this when the time came. Obviously they aren't taking nesting seriously, which only pisses me off because at least that would be a good reason for their distraction.

"She said her name is Cecelia."

I stop mid-step, crimson snaking through my vision as Matt continues. "But she didn't get much more than that."

It takes every bit of restraint I have not to hurl my phone at the building next to me.

"Can you repeat that?"

"She said she seemed like a good—"

"No, the name. Are you sure it's Cecelia?"

"Yeah. Cecelia, right?" I can tell he's talking to his sister. "Yeah, man, that was her name. Said she was reluctant to drink or even hit a joint. That's not exactly the club type."

Ignoring the urge to correct him that you don't have to be a joint-smoking alcoholic with low moral standards to be in my club, I opt for a pressing question. "When was this meetup?"

"I want to say a month and a half, maybe two."

"Which is it?"

He holds the phone to his chest, no doubt consulting with his informative sister. "Alicia, that's my sister, says two. We haven't been to a meetup since, but I can try and find out if she's been to any others."

"You shouldn't be able to find that out, should you, Matt?"

The whole club is based on anonymity, as in you had to have *been there* to know what went on. Loose lips aren't tolerated, and his hesitance tells me he knows better. "Both this favor and my interest in this information are restricted to only me, am I clear?"

"Crystal."

Two months.

Two that I'm aware of. Two months of a summer that I resigned to stay in Paris, trusting Dom and Sean to run the club while I dedicated my time chasing down my birth father. Months of brokering deals so they never have to worry about their financial future. Months where I've taken the risks, put my name in ink on the paperwork, my life on the line. Months where I've had to barter my way out of doing unspeakable acts to keep Antoine from ripping the remaining humanity out of me.

The kicker? Dom's gone off the radar on more than one occasion when I desperately needed his help, leaving me open and vulnerable. My brother has never left me open and vulnerable, and because of that, I got suspicious and enlisted the help of one of our originals.

"Do you need me to go down there?"

"No. I'll handle it. Thanks, Matt."

Ending the call, I summon my driver, and in seconds, I'm in the back of my car, my laptop open as I look up the reports from the Raven in charge of keeping eyes on Cecelia Leann Horner.

"Où allons-nous, monsieur?" *Where are we going, sir?*

Tapping into my email, I shake my head. "Je ne sais pas encore." *I don't know yet.*

Their reports have been coming in weekly, like clockwork, with no change in frequency, and neglectfully, I haven't checked a single one in months. In truth, I haven't had a reason to. Cecelia and Roman's relationship has been non-existent since I saw her last, ten fucking years ago.

It's when I open an email from a month ago that I feel the brunt of Sean and Dom's deception. As of a month ago, Cecelia was still reported as living in Peachtree City.

Dom.

He would easily be able to manipulate this, as he's done countless times before. It's child's play for him.

"What about Helen?"

"We're leaving Helen out of it."

Roman's. Fucking. Daughter.

Anyone but her. Anyone but Roman Horner's fucking daughter.

Literally, any woman but her.

And worse, they've chosen her over me.

If it were a move to gain ground in taking Roman down, they would have told me. But Dom . . . if I had his loyalty and trust, why would they keep this from me?

Betrayal courses through me as spiked needles begin ripping through my chest. Uncapping a bottle, I pour a drink with shaky hands as my driver eyes me while I rip off my jacket and loosen my tie, feeling my world closing in.

Why? Why would they do this? I'm so close to bringing Roman down. Years of waiting, years of making moves. They know this. They know how close we are. Sean left the garage to go back to the plant to try and dig a little deeper to see if we missed anything before we make our move.

We're months away, at most, after fucking years of waiting. It doesn't make sense.

Resisting the urge to call either of them only to be fed more lies, I palm the burn in my chest, my back trickling with sweat.

"Tout va bien, boss? Avez-vous besoin d'aller à l'hôpital?" *Are you okay, boss? Do you need a hospital?"*

I shake my head in reply before I toss back more gin, my head spinning with only one question—why?

There's only one way to find out. And I'm fucking dreading it because somehow, I know, it's already over. I shoot a text to Palo to let Antoine know I'm leaving.

I'm going stateside.

His reply is almost immediate.

Tell him yourself.

Though our relationship dynamic has changed for the better over the years, Palo is a moody fucker, a bit unpredictable. But he's had my back more times at this point than he hasn't. And I can't blame him for being the hateful bastard he is, with the company he keeps. His growing hate and resentment toward Antoine I'm already using to my advantage. He's closing in after years of pining for his wife, which I know

335

will be the final step in securing an alliance. I just have to bide my time.

With my father just out of reach, and my brothers slipping through my hands, anger I've never felt builds inside of me. They turned my own tactics against me, making me the outside fucking man, pushing me out of the circle—one I had cemented us all in. From this moment forward, I don't know if I'll ever trust my brothers the same, no matter their reasoning. The ache that thought causes has me rubbing my chest.

Tap. Tap. Tap.

After all the sacrifices I've made to bring Roman to justice. After all the opportunities I showered them with, all I asked for was loyalty and trust, and they couldn't even give me that?

My own fucking brother has turned on me, for a woman—the daughter of our enemy.

And I never saw it coming.

"You know, assuming makes you an asshole." Dom's words cross my mind, but what else can I believe? They've been lying to me, worse than that, purposefully *deceiving me*, for at least two months.

Does Dom want control? Is he willing to hurt me for it? Is this some sort of lateral move to knock me off the board in an attempt to gain power?

If so, I won't fight him. He can have it. I live solely for what we've built together, for the possibilities of sharing in what we can do in the future. It's enough for me. As ambitious as I am, it's enough.

Have I not been generous enough? Supportive enough? Have I been more boss than brother? Is that why it is so fucking easy for him to betray me like this? Betray our parents?

"Jesus Christ." Ripping off my tie, I unbutton my collar before snapping at my driver. "À la maison." *Home.*

I glance out of the tinted window to a new world, one where I feel more alone than ever, with absolutely no one on my side. I search the street desperately for a kind face, a sign, a goddamn bird to let me know I'm thinking irrationally. And that's when I catch sight of him—a familiar face, one of our first fucking Triple Falls recruits, turning the corner, chin dipping as he lifts his cell phone while I pass.

Dom is having me followed?

He's the only one that knows of my whereabouts at all times.

My brother. My blood.

All the years of struggling, of self-deprivation, years of sacrificing, pushing away my needs, ignoring my wants, all the years I spent on the sidelines watching my brothers live fully while I worked tirelessly to build this dream alongside them.

And for what?

For what?

My cell rings, and I curse as I lift it, his voice coming out in a hiss the second I answer.

"You aren't going anywhere, Ezekiel."

"I don't like your tone, Antoine."

"I don't give a fuck," he snaps. "We have business."

"I'll brief Palo. He can handle it."

"Don't test my patience, Ezekiel. Your plans are going to have to wait."

*

337

It took me three weeks to get home. Three weeks I needed to get Antoine off my fucking back enough to escape his clutches and handle my own shit. Three weeks I spent digging further into the lies and deceptions I've been fed in bits and pieces by the hands of the men I trusted most.

And I've gathered enough by now to know it was all intentional. They'd even gone so far as to publicly humiliate her in front of a few chapters to try to get word back to me and throw me off their scent. A weak attempt at best that reeks of desperation, and I know better. Which also tells me they know I know. Since then, I've cut all communication with them in hopes of striking fear into them. And from the countless texts they've sent since, it's working.

It's always matters of the heart that bring men like me—like Roman, like fucking Antoine—down, and for that reason alone, I've steered clear.

It's always matters of the heart that turn solid statues back into pawns to be easily flicked off the board. Love and emotions have always equated to weakness. And they knew it when they decided on her, chose her. I made sure they knew it. I advised against it at every turn but knew that eventually—when they grew into their most comfortable skin—there would come a time to make allowances for whatever partner they chose.

I was prepared for that. It was inevitable.

But this?

There's no preparation for this.

Anger has taken hold now, and it's the anger I can't get control of as I head from the airport toward my clearing. For the first time as an adult, I want to strike my brother, yet I know I won't forgive myself if I do.

It's a good thing I left my heart scattered all over Paris because with it here, I'm liable to make a fucking fool of myself. But this anger, I've never felt anything quite like it. It's a mixture of wrath that is limitless and liberating for the surge of power it brings that frees me from all liability from the damage I could inflict, and it's fucking terrifying how good it feels.

Before I can face them, I need *something*, anything, a fond memory to reflect on so I don't react so vengefully. Even weeks after that call, I'm still so fucking raw, aching in a way I know I'll never be able to repair.

My only brother.

My friends.

Fucking Tyler, of all people, played along in this deception.

All of them. My club, my birds, my brothers.

Every single one of the Triple Falls originals. Men I trusted with my secrets, my life, my fucking fate.

They've all betrayed me.

All of them.

I'm completely and utterly alone in this world.

Slamming my car door, I head toward the clearing as rage surges through my veins. Any lies I've told or omissions I've made have only kept them safe, kept them from seeing the blood on my hands.

Just as I make it past the first row of trees, the sound of guitar music stops me. Pausing, I scan the forest, ears perking up for the source before I again stalk toward the clearing— the melody drifting into the woods becoming clearer as I reach the break in the trees. It's when I get to the empty field that I notice the absence of life, the tables gone. I stand in utter confusion as the song starts up again, the repetition gnawing at me as I begin to absorb the lyrics. The source of the music is coming from Roman's house, that much is certain. I start to walk toward his mansion under the cover of the trees before shooting a text off to the Ravens on his post for his twenty.

Charlotte.

Which can only mean one thing.

Cecelia is the source, and she's home.

Making my way onto the grass—knowing my birds control the cameras—I come upon a large set of speakers pointed in the direction of the clearing.

Either they told her, or she figured it out and my place has been compromised. My place, my fucking place.

It's then I know the reason for the music. It's a summons from Cecelia.

A summons for Sean and Dom.

And it's clear they've ghosted her.

Too late, too fucking late.

"Goddamnit!"

Furious beyond comprehension, I charge in my Italian leathers along the slick grass, walking the last fifty yards across Roman's perfectly manicured lawn. I've never once been this close to his palace, and I vow I won't ever be this close again.

The summer heat singes my scalp, only aiding in my irritation as I take long strides through the garden, the lyrics surrounding me deafening but clear in delivery.

This girl is in way over her fucking head.

Squinting due to the sun while burning up in my suit, I manage to make it to the deck and freeze when I spot her, *topless*, in a lounge chair.

Enraged, I stalk toward her and no longer recognize the little girl I saw in the library ten years ago. In place of the gawky girl lies the body of a woman in nothing but a bikini bottom, her tan skin glistening, face flawless, features serene. Sensing me, her lush lips lift in a siren's smile just before she slides her hand over her perfect breasts, flattening her palm on her stomach inching toward her bikini bottom. My eyes follow as intended before she lifts her hand to shield her eyes. The hair on my arms spike despite the heat, and I immediately start to panic as the familiar feeling consumes me.

No. No. No. No. No.

An electric shock of awareness hits me, a jolt so powerful it renders me helpless, speechless, and utterly incapable as I fight it with everything in me when she speaks.

"Nothing to say?"

When I remain mute, her eyes slowly open and widen, and it's then I'm damned by the second jolt.

Years of reports on her progress—progress I've mapped as closely as any other mark until recently. Years of knowing her history, of seeing her growth in black and white. Years of refusing to look at pictures and apparently for good fucking reason. She was just a child when I saw her, and she's anything but now as she lays beneath me, perfectly ripe and just within reach. For years I've denied digging too deep, but the details I've avoided rear their ugly head at me now as I stare down at my own demise, the only name in my mind repeating on loop as I clench my fists and try to will it away.

Helen.

Just as I allow myself the thought, she identifies me with the same shock.

"*You're* The Frenchman."

* * *

Gin bottle empty, I release it, and it cracks somewhere on the pavement. Its full contents necessary to keep me subdued to the point that adrenaline is the only thing keeping me standing. I lean against the hood of my Jag as Dom's headlights appear before they pull into the parking lot. Lowering my gaze, inhaling a drag off my cigarette, I wait until the car doors close and their boots appear in my line of sight.

"Before you say a fucking word, let me tell you how I want to hear this." I can't bring myself to look at either one of them yet, and I can feel fear and tension coiling away from them, which brings me mild relief.

This was never an intentional move to overthrow my position or take my place. After my run-in with Cecelia and the overwhelming urge that accompanied it, I had to drink myself into denial, especially after hearing her pleas for them.

But the truth is, there's no relief.

Because it wasn't just her devotion for them that shattered me, it was the fact it existed at all. They have the love of a beautiful woman, a woman who would risk it all for them. The same devotion I thought they had for me. And they've wronged her just as fucking badly. Tarnished her by passing her back and forth like the bottle I just emptied while putting her in danger. And in doing so, they ruined something sacred to me. As I unscrewed the cap to the bottle just an hour earlier, I had to admit to myself that she was the face of innocence I've been protecting.

* * *

"I want you both to tell me exactly when you decided to betray me and destroy my trust—both of you. Then I want you to tell me the details of how you did it, one by one. But first, I want to know how long you've been doing it."

I look up to my brother first, his eyes flashing with rare fear. "Three months."

I nod and nearly stumble when I take a step forward but manage to keep myself upright.

Three months.

Three.

The number of times I locked the door to make sure you were safe.

I can't help my smile at the irony. "It's always been my number."

"Tob—"

"*Three* brothers I trusted here, which gave *three* chances for one of them to come clean. Three months." I swallow and tear my eyes away from Dom to peer at Sean. He looks just as mortified as Dom, and it brings me no comfort.

"Well, allow me to inform you both right now, your sentence is three fucking times as much. Nine months. Let's add another for good measure."

"Tob—"

I glare at them both, and it buys me silence. "Say another goddamn word, one more fucking word. I end it all! All of it. I still have the power to do so, though you both obviously

343

regard me as fucking useless. I'll dissolve the whole fucking club in a matter of days. I'll move to France permanently and live my fucking life. Because it seems all I've been living for here is a lie."

"We never meant—"

"Was that three words?" I ask, staring between them. "Or am I hearing things?" I run a hand through my hair, swallowing several times, my voice raw when I speak. "No exceptions. These are the rules. This is the time. Accept it and serve it, or you're both out, and that's me being generous. Take it or leave it."

"Where?" The question comes from Dominic, and I can hear the remorse in his voice. It's not enough. It's not nearly enough.

"Where, you ask, dear *brother*? Where else? The place that *made me*. You've always wanted to go to France. Here's your chance."

He kicks back against the hood of his car, his face crestfallen. "Where will you be?"

"Wherever the fuck I want to be."

"You're fucking serious?" Sean asks, and I cut my gaze to him.

"You put everything I've worked for, that *we've* worked toward for fifteen years in jeopardy to get your dick wet. So, you tell me, Sean, *am I serious*?"

"That's not—"

"You going to lecture me about *love*, Sean?" In a flash, we're nose to nose, and I clench my fists tight, my nails digging into my skin to keep from striking my brother. "Because if that's where you're going with your line of thought, you don't know the first fucking thing about it."

"We do love her," Dominic speaks up, and it's like a kick in the chest.

"I don't give a fuck." I'm hollow. "Nothing matters to *me* right now, and you're going to have to convince me to care again if you want to keep what we built because at this point, I really fucking don't. I really—" my voice cracks—"I really fucking don't care."

"I know you're hurt, man," Sean says as I step away, his profile backlit by the headlights closing in as Tyler pulls up and jumps out of his truck, scanning the three of us before his stare lingers on me.

"You too? *You too*, Tyler?" I rasp out, my heart shredding as I look between the three of them. "After all we've been through?" I swallow again and again and slap away the weakness clouding my vision as I look on at Dom, whose eyes fill before he darts them away. "You fucking look at me!" He locks his gaze to mine. "This was for Maman and Papa, Dom. We were so close, brother. *Why*?" I croak as Dom expels a pained breath, his eyes spilling over.

Tyler steps toward me, and I shake my head, stopping him.

"Tell *me*, brothers, *word for word*, how you deceived me for three months. Tell me every single thing you did, every purposeful lie you told, every move you made to betray me this way, to keep me in the dark, and then," I rasp out, "tell me how you love—" my voice cracks again as my eyes drift to Dom—"tell me you love *me*."

Faltering, I cup my face, and Tyler grips my arm, ducking his head beneath it to keep me upright. Tossing my cigarette down, I lift my eyes to my brothers. "I suggest you tie up whatever lingering club business you have and do it quickly because the time doesn't start until you touchdown in Paris. And don't worry, I broke it to her *gently* that you won't come calling anytime in the future, and if you so much as contact her, *we're done*."

"Tob—"

"I can't even fucking look at you!" Dom gasps as I push past him and stumble forward. Tyler catches me as my mask slips fully while I bleed out in front of them. Needles thundering in my chest, Tyler manages to get me to the passenger door of his truck and hoists me inside, taking off just before I pass out.

For eight months after, I felt like an outsider in my own club, the only place that ever felt like home. For eight months, the remaining men whom I trusted, whom I loved like brothers, looked the other way when I walked by—disappointed in me, in my actions for sending Dom and Sean away, as if I were the one in the wrong.

And during those eight months, between checking on their welfare and progress in France and keeping close tabs while protecting the woman they deceived me with, I resisted temptation to try to uncover the mystery for myself in what they saw in her. A true to life Helen of Troy capable of breaking apart the kingdom I built with my bare hands.

For eight months, I closed in on her father, making my last moves to ensure the minute my brothers got off the plane, their final act to regain my trust was to aid in bringing Roman down.

I had absolutely no intention of ever laying eyes on her again. But when I could no longer handle being an outcast in the club I built, I went back to the place where it all began—to remember why we started it, to try and forgive them, make peace with their mistake and reclaim the place back as my own.

As I breached the trees, intent on gaining perspective, only to hear her calling for them, I knew without a doubt if there was a God, I'd pissed Him off somehow, arranging my life the way I had without consulting Him with my plans. And the most brutal kick in the teeth was seeing her drenched in moonlight, calling desperately for them. It was then I knew I was too far past the point of *His* redemption.

The proof shone down on me—by way of her—the minute I again set my eyes on temptation. Her innocence taunting me, crippling any decency I had left in me to the point I wanted to erase it and set fire to her love for them. Because she wasn't innocent; she'd singlehandedly destroyed everything by existing, and the evidence was glinting around her neck.

The minute she pushed back against my anger, just as furious, lips parting, eyes wide, I knew that I was being taunted for what I'd denied myself a hundred times or more. After years of resistance, of shoving compulsion aside, for them, for us, of keeping all the weaknesses I was susceptible to at bay, I wasn't going to deny myself another fucking minute.

And with one taste of her, I discovered freedom.

* * *

The same freedom I feel now when I open my eyes to see her mouth surrounding me, her deep ocean eyes full of silent demands.

My strongest temptation and undoing. The only woman capable of satiating me. My nemesis and equal, my torment and love.

Unraveling with her has never felt so fucking good.

Wrapping my fist in her hair, I revel in the stretch of her lips around my cock and the moan vibrating in her throat.

My trésor has never been easily sated, no matter how often I do my job. She chokes on my girth undeterred and bobs her head, jaw clenched in determination, earning a groan from me. I sink into the feel, the perfect pressure of her wet mouth, propping my hand behind me for a better view. She releases me just as I thrust up, her lips lifting in a sultry smile as she fists me in her hand.

"Good morning, Mr. King."

I can't help the return lift of my lips. "It is."

She claws my thighs, taking me to the back of her throat, and I drop back on my pillow, denying myself the buck of my hips, doing my best to restrain myself.

"Putain." *Fuck.*

She dives again, and I grip her head and gaze down at her. The sight alone has me close. She's completely naked, straddling one of my thighs, her perfect tits in view, nipples peaked as I run a hand over them before tracing the stretch of her lips.

"Tellement sexy." *So fucking sexy.*

We're back sexually, and I won't last long this way. She sucks me to the tip before releasing me and again pumps me in her hand, her eyes expectant.

"Something on your mind, Mon Trésor?"

"Fuck me," she says, her voice raw with desire. I run my fingers through her silky hair, unable to hide my smirk. "Collecting more dividends?"

"Precisely, and I'm not in the mood for conversation, King."

Chuckling, I lift her to my chest and claim her hungry

mouth. A growl escapes my throat as I get lost in our kiss, in the feel of her tongue as it brushes against mine.

Any kiss we exchange has never been short of perfect, no matter the emotion behind it. She feeds me exactly how I need her to, without instruction or prompt. We've mapped each other's bodies on an expert level, and reacquainting them fully the last two days has been nothing short of fucking paradise. The look in her eyes lets me know I left her hungry for far too long, a need I'm all too happy to remedy. Lifting her atop me, I stroke her wings as she runs her slit along the ridge of my cock before she guides me inside, sinking slowly until we lock.

Dominant need pulses through my veins, but it's control I hand over as she bucks on top of me with the perfect amount of friction, just enough so if I thrust up, I'm rewarded in the best way.

"Tobias." She licks her lips, placing her hands on my chest as she picks up her pace, long hair tickling my thighs when she throws her head back, the arch giving me the best imaginable view. Gripping her hips, I succumb to her tight, wet heat as we work together until I can't take another second.

Flipping her, I see the satisfied spark in her eyes for getting the best of me as I hitch her thigh around my waist.

But she always has.

Life, as I knew it, was over the second I laid eyes on her. All former versions of me were erased when I exchanged hate for love. It would have been so much easier to hate her. At one point I did, and at times I still do because of what she's capable of doing to me. But it's the surrender that changed my life, changed me as a man, eased my mind, and filled my soul.

Loving her has ruined me, wounded me beyond comprehension.

Loving her has also changed my perception of what matters, of gravity, of my own personal truth, and for better or worse, aided in creating the man I've become.

End of.

Slowly I begin to burn through her, her moans fueling me, her lips worshiping, her eyes void of fear as her heart pounds beneath the flesh I cover with my kiss.

There's not a breath of separation between us anymore. I don't feel any space, just whole and fucking thankful. Thankful for my undoing, for the heart that pounds beneath me that makes breathing easier, eases the tension, and releases me from the trap of my mind. Chests together, I drive into her as she gasps out my name, pulling my hair with her fingers as her eyes stay locked with mine. My heart knocks back against hers just as steady, but it's no longer begging for readmittance. The door is already open. With another call of my name, I grunt out my release inside her, pressing my jaw to her heaving chest, as I come down, and I feel it, the recognition of a destination I never thought I would find again: *home.*

Chapter Thirty

Tobias

Beau whines from where he lays at my feet, just as an icy gust of air slaps my face. Palming the mattress next to me, I come up empty as the cold wind whispers throughout the room, fully rousing me. It's when I open my eyes and see the source—the bedroom window wide open—that I jerk to sit at the edge of the bed, my feet hitting the freezing hardwood as I reach for my Glock. In the next second I'm struck, the sting lingering on my jaw as I realize by what.

Snow.

Relief covers me as I release my gun back in the drawer and narrow my eyes as a mittened glove appears briefly on the ledge. A second later another ball sails through the window, smacking me in the chest—the malicious act followed by my Trésor's maniacal laughter.

"You scared the fuck out of me, thanks for that. Your *ass* is *mine*."

"Sorry," she calls from just outside the window.

"Not sorry enough."

I glare down at Beau, who begins lapping up the ice from the floor.

"You're useless," I scold, "go eat her!"

Her laughter echoes through the bedroom as I walk over to the window, just as glittering dark-blue eyes clear the bottom of the frame. She smiles up at me from where she stands just below it, and I do the same just before I slam the window in her face and lock it, cutting off her, "Heeeey," protest before I make my way back to bed.

And wait.

Not long after, I hear the telltale creak of the back door before soft booted footsteps pad through the house. Beau gives her away fully when he joins her where she lingers at the bedroom door, no doubt locked and loaded.

"I am sorry," she says sincerely. "I wasn't thinking like that."

"You have to think *like that*," I scold, "at all times, and you know this, and only today will I forgive you, but fair warning, Trésor, you throw one of those at me, I'm going to consider it a declaration of—"

I'm barely able to shield from the three speeding balls being hurled at me in rapid succession. I'm instantly on my feet as she screams, dropping the rest of her arsenal before turning on her booted feet and launching herself out of the door, hysterical laughter pouring from her lips. I can't help my own chuckle as I chase her through the house, catching up with her in the living room and tackling her into the couch. She yelps as she falls back and struggles against me, her eyes shining with mischief.

"You are going to pay for that, *dearly*," I say, unable to help my smile as I gaze down at her.

"I let you sleep in long enough."

"You aren't going to work?"

"You should know, as a southern raised man yourself, that a quarter-inch of that white stuff," she says, nodding toward the window, "gives southern cities the chance to play ignorant to what it's made of and shut down."

"That so?"

"It's so," she nods, her porcelain skin flushed pink from the cold. Her beauty robs me momentarily as I press myself against her, and she paws me with freezing mittens. When I jerk against the discomfort, she giggles.

"We're going to have a proper snow day, Frenchman. There's enough for a good fight, a decent-sized snowman, and if you're a really good boy, I'll make you a *snow cream*."

I wrinkle my nose. "What is a snow cream?"

"It's a treat for good boys, you'll see."

"What does being a good boy entail?" I dip and press my lips to what skin I can reach beneath the layers she has on. "Will you settle for a skilled tongue? You know that's a lot to ask of me."

"Just going to have to give it your all, Frenchman."

"My all is ready," I murmur into her neck, grinding as much as I can into the quilt-thick clothes she has buttoned around her.

"Cool off, cowboy," she says, gliding her snow-crusted mittens down my sides, making me flinch.

"You want to battle me? You should know better."

Her eyes narrow at my challenge. "I can take you," she taunts.

"Think so?"

"Know so."

353

Abandoning the search for more skin, I pull myself away from her and the couch and lift my chin in acceptance of her battle. "Five minutes, Trésor. And you better hide *well*."

My four-legged henchman sniffs her out in the garden within the first minute, and she screams like a banshee, tossing an arsenal of poorly made snowballs at me before darting around the house to the front yard. Gaining on her, she makes it all of two steps into the foot-deep blanket in her front yard before she loses her footing and faceplants.

I can't help my laugh as she lays there, her body shaking with laughter and defeat when I reach her and roll her over to see every inch of her outlined in snow. "The shortest war in US history lasted thirty-eight minutes, Trésor. I'm so disappointed in you."

I dust her off as she giggles beneath me. "Oh yeah, which war was that?"

"Anglo-Zanzibar, 1896."

"You're such a nerd, King," she coos beneath me. "I thought you'd be happy the war is over."

"If you're referring to *our* war, I'm more than happy. In fact, I'm willing to accommodate all demands for *your* surrender. But we're going to have to work on your tactics. You couldn't even evade my henchman." I nod over to where Beau lifts his leg, dotting the white powder with a line of bright yellow.

"*Beau*," she scolds as he looks over at the two of us as if to say, "what?" She shakes her head, looking back over to me. "I don't think he likes it."

"No man likes being balls deep in ice. But those balls, we

need to clip, and soon," I say, pulling her from the ground. "He's getting way too comfortable with my calf."

"Shhhh, he'll hear you," I swear Beau whines in agreement before trotting away from us, his curiosity getting the best of him. Cecelia pivots when she stands and tangles her leg with mine in an attempt to take me down. I balk at her shitty effort to get me on my back before I give in and take her intended fall.

"You let me win," she pouts, landing on top of me, knocking some of the air from me as she folds her mitted hands over my chest, her smile beaming. I pluck some of her newly wet and matted hair from around her neck and toss it over her shoulder.

"I find it's best to let you win at times. Makes life a lot easier for me. And you need a lesson in self-defense," I add.

She raises a brow before making a show of pulling a mitten off. "Do I?"

"You do."

In the next breath, I'm cursing as she strangles my cock in a vice-like grip through my jeans.

"You were saying?"

"Not to be messed with," I grit out as she briefly tightens her hold before letting go.

"It's a shame that men are so vulnerable there." She bats her eyelashes. "And I fight *dirty*."

"As do I," I remind her, pulling her to her feet and surveying the whiteout.

"Beautiful, isn't it?"

I nod. "I thought it was going to be just a dusting."

"A cold front came in, and so we got a lot more than anticipated."

I nod.

"We deserve a good snow day after the last one we had," she says softly, bringing me back to the day I confessed all in her father's back yard as heavy snow fell around us. The guilt resurfaces as I picture her, freezing, tears falling as she begged me to acknowledge us, to admit what we both knew was true. And I refused her, breaking apart the whole time, knowing I wouldn't outlive the truth or that memory.

"I'm sorry," she says, reading my reaction. "I didn't mean to play that dirty."

"I thought about that day the whole time we were apart." I slowly lift the hem of her knitted cap, pressing a long kiss to her forehead before tugging it back down. "We'll make this day far more memorable, so you'll never think of that one again."

She nods, the clouds in her eyes slowly dispersing as she slinks down to the ground, a curve to her lush lips as she gathers snow in her hand.

"Revenge is a dish best served cold, right?"

"Don't even think about—"

She slaps the ice to the side of my face before she turns and makes a good showing of trying to get away. This time she makes it *five* steps.

Chapter Thirty-One

CECELIA

TOBIAS TURNS HIS nose up as I pop open the top of the sweetened condensed milk with the triangle tip of the can opener. He scrutinizes the label as I separate the snow into two bowls and drizzle the milk on top before grabbing two spoons out of the nearby drawer.

"I told you, Trésor, I'm not eating snow." He wrinkles his nose in clear distaste. "That can't be . . . sanitary."

"The top few inches are clean."

"No, thank you." He moves to walk off, and I stop him and swivel us, pinning him between me and the counter.

"You will try this," I demand, but he's already shaking his head.

"No, merci, but no."

"This isn't optional, King," I say, lifting a spoonful toward his mouth.

He turns his head. "I'm not eating *that*."

I shake my head. "I swear I just had a flash of the future, trying to feed a French brat, a little replica of *you*."

His eyes immediately drop to my stomach, and he slowly lifts my sweater, covering the flesh with his palm before lifting

357

a questioning gaze to mine. There's a deep sorrow etched there, and I put my threatening spoon back in the bowl, concerned by his reaction.

"What?"

"Do you want children?"

Alarm buds in my chest at his wary expression. "I haven't given it that much thought. I will admit that the idea of carrying your baby . . . there's something sexy, greatly appealing about it, and being a mother . . . I mean, I'm not opposed to *eventually* becoming a mother. Still, I don't feel like it will make me or break me. Why do you ask?"

He lowers his eyes to watch the glide of his fingers along my flesh in lieu of an answer.

"Do *you* want children?"

"I never thought I would . . . But the idea of you, pregnant with my baby, fuck." He licks his lips, his eyes blazing with desire. "Maybe, with you. Only with you."

His reply warms me just as the cautious side of me speaks. "Okay, so what's wrong?"

"Nothing."

"Don't lie to my face, Tobias. Is it the danger?"

"Some of it, yes."

"Okay, then we can talk about this down the road. We're in no hurry, right?"

"Right."

Too quick. I press in.

"What aren't you telling me? Is there . . . something wrong with . . ." I lower my eyes.

He jerks his chin. "No. I can give you children, Trésor."

"Okay," I sigh. "Give me *something* here."

He nods toward our bowls. "Your snow cream is melting."

I groan, frustrated, but decide this argument can wait. I'm in no hurry, and it's too hard to retrieve what he clearly doesn't want me to see.

Reloading the spoon, I lift it to my mouth and moan when the sweet cream hits my tongue. His eyes flare with a little curiosity as he watches me.

"One bite, for me?"

He nods, his knuckles still faintly caressing my stomach before he lowers my sweater. When I lift the spoon to his full lips, he opens, taking a mouthful, his eyes widening a little in surprise.

I can't help my victorious smile. "*Told you.*"

Without hesitation, he grabs his own bowl, and we head to the couch, our discarded coats and gloves hanging on a rack next to a roaring fire.

He shovels his snow cream in, as I try not to gloat, and then speaks up around a mouthful. His words imperceptible.

"What was that, King? Did you say 'nom nom good'?"

His eyes narrow. "I neef to go see Mawk," he mumbles, inhaling his treat and gesturing urgently for me to eat mine, as if I didn't just have to force the spoon in his mouth.

"You need to see Mark?"

He nods.

"Who's Mark?"

He swallows, dishing up another huge bite. "At the hardware store. For snow day supplies. He's my cashier."

I press my lips together as he cleans his bowl.

"You're getting around quite a bit these days, aren't you?"

He nods. "He's agreed to give me five percent off my purchase."

Laughter bursts out of me. "Won't Deanna be jealous?"

He shrugs. "Different store."

"You whore," I jab as he slurps back the rest of his bowl and gestures for me to share mine. When he opens his mouth expectantly, I make sure to cover his lips with the remnants of the sticky milk from my spoon. He scowls as I set down my bowl, still eyeing what's left in longing until I grip his shoulders and push him back onto the couch before thoroughly cleaning his lips. In seconds, he's forgotten my abandoned snow cream and opts to lick *me* instead. Lips swollen, wetness pooling, I pull away and gaze down at him. "I love domesticated Tobias."

"Do you?"

"Don't get me wrong, I love the salty, bossy, suit-dressed Frenchman too, but I love this version of you just as much." I press my lips to his jaw and feel him settle beneath me, his arms wrapping around me. "Maybe more."

Hours later, we stare into the fire as we lay comatose on the couch, half buzzed from wine after a long game of chess while the forecast hums in the background during the evening news. Tobias sits on one end while I lay opposite him as he massages my wool-covered feet. According to the weather report, our snow will be gone tomorrow, which makes me a little melancholy. It's the next segment of the news that snags my sleepy Frenchman's attention, halting my foot rub altogether. He turns up the volume as brief but grotesque footage is played and recapped by the anchor, snapping us both out of our stupor. Those responsible for it proudly proclaim themselves the culprits, a new terrorist organization, and it might as well be the fucking bat signal by the way Tobias is reacting—his posture going rigid and his jaw ticking. The hairs on my neck start to rise as Tobias bristles next to me, his reaction much the same. He's a closet empath to the core.

On instinct, he reaches for his cell, something I would have found odd years ago. His goal has always been corporate warfare, but since we parted months ago, his stake, his place, his say, and any future move he makes will be next level. A purposeful, calculated advantage I'm not sure he's been able to utilize yet.

The reality of that sinks in a bit further as he palms his cell and thinks better of it, glancing over at me before setting it back down. "They're already on it. Tyler and Preston," he clarifies.

I nod. "I'm sure they are. But make the call if you want to, Tobias. I'm not stopping you. And I didn't ask you to quit."

He clicks off the TV, his eyes back on the fire as he absently resumes my foot rub. As much as I've tried to tell him that I'm okay with him staying in the loop, he's refused, making sure I know our relationship is his priority. And I know with him, it's all or nothing. He's not the type of man to sit on the sidelines. I've resigned myself to the fact that it's his decision. I glance out the window gazing at our perfectly constructed but faceless snowman and grin. We got distracted when we got to that part. Our new snow day has definitely outdone any other I care to remember, and that makes me hopeful.

"I don't understand that type of man," he speaks up next to me, drawing my attention back to him. "The type of man who can kill innocents for any fucking reason to prove what evil they're capable of." He sinks back in the couch. "It's nothing new, and yet the more that comes out, the more desperate they become to outdo those who preceded them."

"It's not your job to understand them. You do enough by trying to stop them."

He shakes his head. "I have to try to understand them in order to stop them, so I can catch them."

I reach over and run my fingers through his tangled hair. "Be glad you don't understand them, Tobias."

"I've done horrible things," he admits. "But always to protect those I love, protect our cause, but I don't really lose sleep over it."

"You shouldn't."

"Maybe I should. Maybe I have a lot more of Abijah in me than . . ." he shakes his head. "I've heard stories about the ruthless man who created me. They're not good, Cecelia."

"How was he when you found him?"

"Gone mostly." His gaze loses focus as he speaks. "In my rare visits with him, he was only lucid a few times. Oddly, he was kind both times, but when he wasn't coherent, most of his talk was vapid nonsense. And his temper was . . . malicious."

"Tobias, you decide who you are, you know that. You taught me that."

His eyes drift over to me. "I saw you once in Paris. Your sophomore year of college. I'd just killed a man."

Shock. Utter and complete shock keeps me stunned silent as he speaks.

"He was a filthy motherfucker, handsy with children, cruel to his family, a horrible human being. One of Ant—" he cuts himself off, only fueling the hurt and anger surfacing. "I didn't hesitate a second pulling the trigger. Not a second," he whispers. "After I watched him die, I went to a bar I frequented. I had just drained my first gin when I got the text you were headed in my direction, and I knew you were coming straight for me. I only managed to get a block away when I saw you turn the corner, your hair blowing around your face, obstructing my view before you stepped in." His eyes lift to mine. "I knew you were in Paris. I always knew where you were, but it felt so much more intimate when you were there. I knew you were missing me because you were frequenting all the places we talked about when we were together. All the places I hoped to take you one day. I knew, in a way, you were searching for me." He gives me a sad smile as the first tear glides down my cheek. "And you nearly caught me," he whispers, his hand stopping on my foot. "It was like you were haunting me, and then you were there."

When he gauges my reaction, I close my eyes.

"Please don't get upset."

"How can I not? You saw me, and you didn't fucking—" I shake my head, my hurt taking over. "How—"

"I couldn't, Cecelia, I couldn't. I'd barely healed from being shot, and the painful stretch in my skin as I walked away from you was reminder enough of how dangerous it would be to drag you back in. If you only knew how bad that hurt. I could kill a man without hesitation, but leaving you there felt so much fucking worse. Jesus, if you only knew how much I wanted to walk back to that bar, just to get a glimpse of you through that fucking window. But I felt like a monster. And back then, I was far more monster than man." He shakes his head. "Knowing you were there, so fucking close and wondering if you sensed me there. I wanted so much to go to you, to touch you, even with fresh blood on my hands. And I felt . . . punished. Thoroughly punished and confused by how I could feel so fucking little about taking a life but so torn apart for needing you. It was complete chaos for me, both sides fighting for dominance and both wanting the same thing—you. And so I ran, I ran from you, chasing the monster far, far away, so he couldn't touch you with his bloody hands." His features twist in pain. "I started to hate Paris after that, hate everything about it. Being there felt like a betrayal of a future that we could never have." He closes his eyes. "It took everything I had to walk away from that bar. Everything I fucking had left, and that wasn't much at that point. I was more vengeance than human being, but you reminded me I was still flesh and blood that day . . . you reminded me. It was one of the worst nights of my life because I've never felt so alone."

Hot tears stream down my cheeks at his admission. Anger for the time we lost, for the relief we could have found in each other and never got due to his fucking overpowering need to protect me.

"It was always the job that cost me you. It's always been the job. I have to be a monster to catch the other monsters, and the job, in essence, is fighting a lost cause. Mostly, because men like that are never going to stop coming." He lifts earnest eyes to mine. "But there's only one you . . . and—" his eyes flit with emotion—"I've been alone my whole goddamn life. I don't want to be alone anymore."

I launch myself at him, wrapping so tightly around him, I refuse him any space. I breathe in his spicy skin, surrounding him, covering him, as he grips me just as tightly. "You're not alone, Tobias," I say softly. "I'm not going *anywhere*, not if I can help it."

He grips my head and gazes up at me, the sorrow I saw seconds before replaced by a sort of peace. He cements our lips together and separates them with his tongue in gentle exploration. Drawn in, I kiss him back, feeling every ounce of love in his kiss while feeding him my own.

Not long after, we get lost. He lifts from the couch with me wrapped around him, carrying me wordlessly to the bedroom. And with each step, I feel his decision.

They can wait. For just a little longer, they can all fucking wait.

Chapter Thirty-Two

CECELIA

PULLING UP FROM another exhausting day, I find Tobias in the front yard with Beau, his smile warming me as the dog leaps at his feet, eager for something in his hand. I catch the tail end of their conversation as I exit my Audi.

"Devrions-nous montrer à Maman sur quoi nous travaillons?" *Shall we show Mama what we've been working on?*

"Oui," I reply as Tobias reaches over a dancing Beau to grip me in his hold and kiss me breathless.

"Salut, Maman." *Hello, Mama.*

"Bonjour, Frenchman." *Hello, Frenchman.* "What are you two up to?"

Tobias's gaze glitters over me, his smile reaching his eyes. "I have a surprise." He gives Beau a stern look before he barks out his first order.

"Assis." *Sit.* Beau immediately sits on his haunches.

"You can't take credit. I taught him that," I taunt.

"Roule." *Roll.* Beau immediately rolls over, and I clap with glee as Tobias rewards him with a treat.

Beau pants, waiting for his next order as Tobias lifts the treat up to eye level.

"Pattes en l'air." *Hands up.*

I laugh as Beau raises on his hind legs putting his paws up in surrender.

"Ah, ah." Tobias keeps him in the air, right before he converts his hand into an imaginary gun. "Bang, bang."

Beau goes down in a rehearsed heap.

"Oh, my God!" I exclaim as I kiss both men furiously while giving them praises.

"How long have you been working on that?" I ask as Tobias ushers us both inside.

"A few weeks."

"You could be a dog trainer."

"I can barely tolerate him," he scoffs, giving me a snobby side-eye.

"You love him."

"He did give me a mercy fuck when you wouldn't," he shrugs, and I slap his chest. He grins, making quick work of retrieving ingredients from the fridge.

"How was your day, Trésor?"

"Just a day," I say, darting my eyes toward the bedroom, anxious for another journal entry. For the last few weeks, he's given me huge glimpses into his life, recalling bits and pieces of the years I've missed. Sometimes he'll expand over dinner on what he's written, and other times he refuses to discuss anything more in-depth. But his story is by far one of the most fascinating I have ever read. The day at the track, where he bet everything he had to start Exodus being one of my favorites. Every paragraph gives bits and pieces of his, Sean, and Dom's pasts, eliminating some of the mystery behind them, while only making them more intriguing. Every detail I savor, which only makes my love and appreciation grow.

"I'm going to shower," I say as Tobias closes the fridge and grabs me by the hand, jerking me back to him.

"Why so eager?"

"You know why, don't be a shit."

His lips twitch. "You like my stories, Trésor?"

"I love them." I palm his face. "*And you.*"

He reads the eagerness in my face and frowns. "I'm afraid I'll disappoint you today."

"I don't care."

He presses his lips to mine. "Trésor, this one will upset you."

The last few weeks have been a dream—more than that, a honeymoon of sorts. We haven't argued . . . much. It's like we've resumed our life back in Triple Falls. The brief sad looks we share over our past are overcome easily by the victory of the new reality we're creating.

We fuck like bloodthirsty animals every morning and make love every night. My bad dreams are getting scarce, and when I wake up, he's with me, kissing me, inside me, chasing whatever remnants remain away. Sadly, his anxieties haven't eased, and I know it's because of the secrets he keeps close. Day by day he continues to bare more pieces of his history, leaving me temporarily satisfied.

Once, I came close to beating him at chess, and I gloated for far too long because he punished me that night for a good half hour before he let me come. And as our old habits of stargazing and drinking Louis merge with new habits we've collected here in Virginia, we've hit a stride I didn't think was possible so soon in our new union. With one week left until Thanksgiving, it seems as though the worst of our struggle is behind us.

"Whatever it is, we'll deal with it," I say, fully confident that's the case.

He gives me a nod and goes back to his task of cooking, something he looks forward to and takes painstaking effort daily to do—in which I reap the rewards.

With one last reassuring kiss, I rush into the bedroom, tossing my purse onto the bed and take the seat at the desk.

Cher Journal,

Over the last weeks, we've become closer, closer than we were before, but there is still a space between us, and we both know why.

I'm hiding something from her, and she knows it. But this confession I've kept close for years, and when I finally tell her what it is, I'm afraid she won't understand it the way I need her to. I want so much to tell her, but the more time that passes, the stronger we become. Sharing this with her could change everything between us again. Neither of us wants that, but I need her to know I'm waiting to tell her this for a reason. A selfish reason, because for the first time in years of endless war in head and heart, I'm close to content. I don't want my fears to become hers. So, I need her to wait just a little longer. I can only hope she will understand.

I've known for a lot longer that he's been hiding something from me, and I needed no confirmation by way of his daily confession.

Anger surfaces as I read through his words again and slap

the journal closed. If I have any grudge or resentment left, it's because of this.

Knowing I'm in for a fight and completely unable to let it go, I stand and forgo my shower, walking back to the kitchen to find him missing, chopped vegetables abandoned on the counter. Opening the back door, I pause when I hear hushed conversation as Beau barks somewhere in the garden.

"This isn't just going to go away. You have missed two calls with me."

A woman's voice.

He's on FaceTime, and I step closer to get a look at her. Jealousy singes me as she comes into view, and of course, she's fucking beautiful. She looks to be early- to mid-thirties, dark hair and eyes, a melodic French lilt in her voice.

"I'm aware, Sonia. I've been preoccupied."

"I can't keep making an effort with you if you won't speak with me or return my calls."

"I understand. I'll be in touch soon."

"I urge you to make me a priority, as I have *you*."

He nods. "You have my word."

Her eyes find mine behind him, and she gestures to Tobias, who glances back at me, either already aware or being made aware I'm standing behind him. I can't tell which. They end the call, and I wait for an explanation, standing just behind him, my blood running hot.

"Exodus business," he says simply and stands before he faces me. The lie too easy to detect.

"Right," I say, turning on my heel and slamming open the back door.

"Cecelia," he grits out, following me inside, a soft curse leaving him as I whirl on him.

"You thought I was in the shower," I snap.

"I'm not hiding anything."

I scoff. "You just lied to my face."

"Cecelia—" he grips me by the arm—"it's a confession for a later time."

"Are you fucking her? *Have* you fucked her?"

"Jesus, no." He releases my arm. "Trust me, you'll know sooner than later. We called a truce, remember?"

"Fuck your truce," I snap, my jealousy winning over logic. He didn't shy away when caught, but it's not good enough.

"Is she part of what you're hiding?"

"Yes, but don't, Trésor, don't jump to conclusions." The timbre of his voice more mournful than fearful. "It's nothing like what you're thinking. This explanation you will get in great detail. She wants to speak with you."

"Well then, get her back on the phone, King. *I'm all ears.*"

"Not yet."

"Only when it's convenient for you, right? Like you won't tell me why you're pacing at night instead of sleeping and checking in with the birds on watch more often than necessary. Or why you get so lost in your head sometimes, you stare right through me. Maybe you'll tell me, maybe, or maybe you'll run away from giving the explanations I deserve like you did in *Paris*. Trust you, right? Trust *you*. How can you ask me for what *you* won't give?"

I stalk off and slam my bedroom door. That night, he wraps around me wordlessly. His silence festers, keeping me awake.

*

Cher Journal,

This morning we got into a fight, and it was a nasty one. She thinks I'm an "overbearing, arrogant, caveman with a God complex, who needs to loosen the reins a bit." I yelled at her in English and cursed at her internally in French for two hours before I stormed out of the house and ran until my legs gave out. But I'm not sure she understands the fear that drives me to act the way I do. I'm not sure she understood me clearly enough when I said I wouldn't survive losing her. Maybe I'm selfish, but I want more of this life we started together. I'm too afraid one wrong fucking move will end it all. I need her to listen to me because my fear is real. And I can't temper it no matter how hard I try.

I wish so much that she could experience this fear for just a few seconds if only to help her understand. That I could let her witness the catastrophe that continually rages in my head that leads to the needles that turn to knives stabbing my chest to the point I suffocate from it. If only she knew how it felt, then maybe I wouldn't be such a "chest-beating moron." Or perhaps I should just man the fuck up and tell her I'm sorry. But even doing that, I know I'll only act this way again. No matter how much I want to trust her instincts, and no matter how much I'm beginning to fear the Beretta in her purse because I swear, I saw murder in her eyes mid-fight.

> *So, my confession is this—I will always act*
> *this way, feel this way, insist on my own way*
> *when it comes to her protection, to keep these*
> *feelings from taking over. To keep her with me.*

I read his entry again and shoot off a text.

I'm sorry, too. Come home. I love you.

On my way.

* * *

Went for a run.

He's upped his runs to three a day. For the last week, he's been more and more on guard. On good days, when I get home from work, I find him waiting with a breathing bottle, usually in the kitchen, before he delivers a breath-stealing kiss. After dinner, we play chess, often until the late hours, talking, laughing, and exploring each other's bodies until we exhaust ourselves. On Thanksgiving, we dined alone together, stuffing our faces and splitting the wishbone, his win, before target practice gave a whole new meaning to a Turkey Shoot.

Though the secrecy is nothing new, it's been gnawing at me constantly since his confession, and I've been patiently waiting for him to finally reveal what cards he's got plastered to his chest. Often, I catch him in a daze, features twisted, eyes haunted, completely immersed in his thoughts, and I've given him ample time to come clean.

And he continues to fail me.

More than once, I've witnessed him drink himself to the point of passing out, an apology on his lips when I manage to get him to bed. And it's infuriating that even the drink that's loosened his lips in the past hasn't aided in bringing forth his confession at all.

His drinking would worry me more if he didn't take such immaculate care of his body. For now, I allow it because of his admission. It helps to stop his errant thoughts and calms him to the point he's able to sleep, which as of late, he's been doing less and less of.

If he came clean now, I could ease his burdens. He would keep his promises to me, but he hasn't, and odds are, he won't.

As of now, our watchful birds are becoming relentless, often dining at the café, and as of a few days ago, they started flanking me when I run errands, walking me to and from my car. They're on high alert, and I know why. They're becoming just as agitated as their boss.

It's infuriating for me to know that's the truth of it, and he's still hiding behind our truce to keep from telling me.

It's not hard to keep myself guarded when the deception at this point is so blatant.

Secrets tore us apart, and I have zero doubts they'll do it again—if *I* let them.

But while he's been sharpening his flock, readying them, I've made some decisions of my own.

I have to force his surrender so we have complete transparency.

It's the only thing that will fully heal us.

Until I get that, I won't stop seeking the truth from him.

On this, I won't break. I won't waver, no matter how much his kisses beg and his eyes plead.

So, for now, even with our truce in place, even as we draw closer than ever before, we remain in an unspoken stalemate.

I'll keep him just a breath away from where he so desperately wants to be from fully regaining my trust.

This is war. I'm not just fighting for the truth anymore — I'm setting boundaries for the future.

This time, I'm determined to break my king before he breaks me.

Chapter Thirty-Three

TOBIAS

Age Thirty-Three

OCEAN-BLUE EYES GAZE back at me as she hovers above me, fireflies dancing around the tall grasses surrounding us, the moon translucent between the trees. Warmth snakes into my arms, making them heavy, almost impossible to lift, the soothing rush circulating through them threatening to pull me back into the dark. Still, I fight it because she's here with me, whispering to me, kissing me, her presence soothing, like no other comfort I've ever felt. Straining, I can't hear her whispers as I fight to stay with her, the moon behind her glowing brighter now, rising high above the trees. Her lips move again as she reaches for me, but I can't make out the words she's speaking. The menacing orb hovers just above now, its glare brighter than the sun, threatening to take her with it.

Beep. Beep. Beep.

"Don't go," I beg as I fight the warmth and reach up to caress her face. She tilts her head in confusion, disappearing briefly as the overpowering light again obstructs my view.

Beep. Beep. Beep.

A distant voice sounds from beyond the trees, but it's not hers.

"Fight it, man. Come on, T."

I'm safe here, lying beneath her, her dark-blue eyes beckoning me to stay, just a little longer. But the moon threatens, and now she's fading, still smiling as she whispers to me. It shifts again as I call to it, asking for a little more time, and the man inside mocks me with his smile, betraying me by fully stealing the sight of her. I cry out at the loss, and it glows brighter and brighter until I'm blinded by it—until it's all I can see.

All at once I'm thrust into it as it burns my eyes, and pain takes over. Pain from the loss of her, everywhere, it's all I can feel.

She's gone.

"There you are." A face appears, the face of a young woman, blocking out the light above, but it's not hers.

"Ce—" I croak, but I'm unable to speak, my throat raw.

"She's okay, man." I recognize the voice as a masculine hand grips mine. "I swear to you. We've got her covered. She's okay." Tyler. His shadowed face becomes clearer as he stands above me, worry etched in his eyes. "Don't fight. Don't fight, man. Let them do their thing." His eyes dart to the woman, who isn't her. It's not Cecelia.

Furious, I struggle against him. I need to get back to her.

"Tres—" my tongue is coated in copper, my words blocked as Tyler curses and a picture flits through my mind—a memory, my feet pounding on the pavement, as Eddie Vedder sings about a sun in someone else's sky. I've just lost everything that mattered in my own. My sun, my moon, every fucking burning star between them. I want the moon back, even if it mocks me, and it won't matter to me, because at least I'll be with her. But I wasn't . . .

I was running. I was running when . . .

Awareness drives into me like a freight train as I jerk back into reality while Tyler stands above me, his hand pinning me back as the girl speaks to me in an attempt to calm me. But she's not Cecelia.

Cecelia wasn't here.

She was never here.

My eyes blister with the truth as I close them, feeling the full weight of it as hot anger leaks out of me, and I let out a soundless scream.

Those bullets failed me.

"Jesus Christ, man," Tyler croaks. "Please, brother. Please don't." He hovers above me, his red-rimmed eyes filling as he reads the truth in my own.

I don't want to be here.

Anywhere but back here. Not anymore. Not without Dom. Not without her.

Cecelia.

I was in the street as a group of strangers gathered around me, their faces a blur as I fixed on the cloud-filled blue sky behind them, relieved. Because I didn't have to force the lie of living anymore as I bled out on that sidewalk. Relief was coming. Maybe Dom would meet me. Maybe my parents.

But those bullets fucking failed me. They fucking failed me. And I'm back here, without her. I'm breathing again without a reason to. I don't want this life. I don't want any life. Enraged tears sting my eyes, and I stop struggling, utterly defeated as he presses me back against the bed.

"Fuck," Tyler rasps out hoarsely, his eyes darting over to

the side of the room where I know Sean is sitting, looking on at me with the same pity. I avert my gaze because I know they see the truth. I'm not the same man anymore. I don't know who I am. And I don't care.

Those goddamn bullets failed me.

* * *

Pearl Jam's "Black" fades as I pull my earbuds out, and walk down the driveway, the memory of the day I woke up in the hospital fresh in my mind. I exhale to try and clear my head, bracing my hands on my knees as sweat rolls down my temple. My heart rate starts to even out after another attempt at facing what haunts me. I was listening to that song when I got shot. At times I force myself to relive it, hoping eventually its hold will lessen. And for the most part, it has. The irony is, it doesn't lessen the memory of the heartache it evoked when I came to at the hospital.

But now the moon rises in my favor. Now I can reach out and touch her, and I don't need morphine or disillusion. She's with me, in my arms, every fucking night. It's no longer a dream. It's our reality.

That acknowledgment is cut short as Julien's phone rumbles in my pocket. Trepidation seeps in as I pull it out to see the same text I've gotten the past three and a half weeks.

Quelle est la situation?

I wait the appropriate amount of time before I shoot off a reply.

Pas de changement.

I add two pictures I took, similar to those sent in the past. One of Cecelia working through the window of her café, and one I had a bird shoot of me walking out of the hardware store, hoping they satisfy him, and I fucking hate it.

It only takes a few minutes for a response. Immediate dread circulates through the rest of me as I read the reply—a time and flight number. Antoine wants him home.

Any control I had is now slipping through my fingers. Control is what I need in order to function, in order to protect her, to keep my sanity.

The minute I put him on that plane, I'll be flying blind, with no idea what his plans are or how to proceed.

Whatever he's decided, it's clear he's not going to let me finish my life out in domestic bliss with Cecelia. And I've felt like this once before, the night before Dom died, hours after Cecelia and I were discovered by Dom and Sean. The night my brothers shunned me, turned their backs on me.

George Michael's "Father Figure" filters through the trees, a clear message for me as I pace the clearing, utterly torn on what to do. She's had the song on repeat, blaring it through her commercial-sized speakers out on her balcony since I showed up here an hour ago, attempting to come up with the right words to explain my deception. She knows I sent them away and lied to her repeatedly, but she doesn't understand the full extent of why I went to such extremes. Her emotions due to my actions will make it impossible for her to fully grasp the why of it all or understand the years of sacrifices I've made, some of them to keep her safe.

And with the way she looked at me earlier, I'm not sure I

can get through to her. I've lost any chance I had at earning her trust, and all I want to do is grab her and flee. Take her away from everything that's threatening to come between us. She's already packing, to flee from me, from the situation, minute by minute, convincing herself that what we had was just another lie. Every minute I hesitate in explaining myself is a minute lost.

Have I lost her already?

What will her reaction be once she wakes to find she's marked?

Maybe this morning, she would have taken the mark if I asked her to. But she's still so young, and the truth is, she can still get out of this.

She can move on from here as planned and live as though this time with me was just a blip on her way to something else, a safer life, nothing more.

I could push her out, force her to flee, and maybe with her absence, I can salvage my relationship with my brothers, and the club can recover.

From a business perspective, it would be so much easier to let her go. However, not for one second can I imagine living the next without her. It took me so long to find her.

Flicking the cap off the bottle, I'm thankful for the burn of the gin in my throat, praying it will quiet my racing thoughts for the right solution.

We could leave, flee together until the smoke clears, until I can give them time to deal with their anger and come back and test the waters. I dismiss the idea as soon as it occurs to me. I've never abandoned them, and I won't add to my own betrayal by doing it now, no matter how appealing it is to just whisk her away and keep her.

It's selfish, and that's what got me in this situation.

Dom will see the logic in marking her for one purpose only, for protection. Sean won't see it as anything but a possessive play on my part.

Both of them will be right.

But is she truly mine?

The look in her eyes this morning told me that is the truth of it, and I still feel it. She's mine, made for me, the only soul on this earth I've ever felt matched with, safe, home. The feel of her when I took her only hours ago, the lust-drunk slur of my name leaving her lips, and love-filled look in her eyes as she tightened around me convinced me nothing else has ever been so true.

She is mine. I still feel it with every fiber of my being, despite the way her heart broke upon seeing them again and the betrayal she felt for loving me back, for knowing she belongs with me.

This has gone too far.

Lighting a cigarette, I draw the tobacco in deep and exhale before taking back more gin.

Tick tock.

Every second is like a lash to the chest. I've already given the order to mark her. The minute she's asleep, she'll be branded as mine.

I've made bold and calculated moves since I was young, but the stakes have never been so high. My heart may have decided, but my mind is in fucking shambles. I'm utterly torn and have no idea which way to move.

The look on Dom's face, the rage in his posture, the hurt in his eyes, and Sean . . . I close my eyes and clearly picture his ravaged expression and the tears he freely shed, something I could never have anticipated.

I completely negated the depth of their feelings due to the nature of their relationship. And the truth was so blatant today. She loves them. The look in her eyes when they discovered us and the emotions whirring between the three of them is tearing me apart.

Every one of my gambles in the past has paid off. But like the others, once in motion, this is something that can't be undone.

I can't. I can't do it.

Pulling up my cell, I quickly tap a text to execute the order, my finger hovering on send.

She needs this mark. Anyone who saw her at the meetup knows her importance. She became leverage for any enemy of the club the minute she got involved with them. And from what I've gathered, Sean flaunted her all over Triple Falls when they were together. I still can't fucking comprehend what either of them was thinking, and instead of giving them a chance to explain, I'd acted as judge and jury and passed sentence. They'd served it, willingly and without much of a fight, to appease me.

And in return . . . I destroyed us.

As much as I want to regret it, I can't. Despite how we happened, her love is the purest thing I've ever known.

And I'm about to punish her for it.

I hang my head as the lyrics of the song wrap around my heart, feeding me a desperate sort of hope. Father Figure. Is that how she sees me? The lyrics cut jaggedly down the center of my already tattered chest as I try my best to think of a way to get to her.

If I go to her right now and give her my reasons and the absolute truth, will she believe me? Or will I be fully at her mercy to the point she won't listen to what's important?

"*Goddamnit!*" *Ripping off my jacket, I toss it onto the ground and stare up into the night sky. This place is where I've come since I was a child to find my answers, where they came to me through dancing rays of moonlight. But there's no moon in sight. Those rays are non-existent when I need them most. It's as if whatever gift I've been granted knows I've betrayed my path by falling in love.*

The festering in my chest increases tenfold as I try to imagine life without her. I've always dealt in black and white with decisions, emotions never a consideration.

No emotions, no mistakes.

When the song begins again, I stare down at my phone, my finger still hovering above send as it rings in my hand.

"*I don't have time to talk,*" *I snap.*

"*What was our agreement, Tobias?*" *Antoine hisses in reply.*

"*I did your fucking bidding. I just left Paris. I saw to it the deal was in motion—*"

"*Do you want to be the one to tell my sister her only son died tonight?*"

"*I told you not to move in without me,*" *anger surges, desperate for an outlet.* "*I told you not to send him. That he wasn't ready.*"

"*I don't take orders from you,*" *he bites back.* "*And now I have a dead nephew, and you cost me. This was your deal.*"

"*I told you I would be back in a few—*"

"*You've broken our agreement.*"

"*I told you to wait on me!*" *I roar into the phone, my palms sweating as needles begin to prick the skin of my chest.*

"*And you've wasted too much of my time with your little vacation home.*" *He keeps his tone even, and it's then I know he has an agenda.* "*I'm afraid this oversight is going to cost*

384

you a lot more this time, Ezekiel." I pause when the music drifting from the house is abruptly cut off, and know I have minutes to send the text to cancel the order, to free her of my mark, to rid her of this life, especially since I know that by being here, indulging her, I've just indebted myself to Antoine.

"We need to have a long discussion about our future."

He doesn't give a fuck about his nephew. And I wouldn't put it past him to sabotage his own deal to get what he wants from me—my allegiance. I take comfort in knowing he doesn't give a fuck about my club. It's control he's after—that I can give him to stave him off.

"I'll go to my Charlotte office and wire you the money. I'll personally make sure your sister has my sincerest condolences."

"I'm afraid that's not going to be enough."

I hang my head, knowing that he's got me. Not once have I failed to deliver, but by being absent, I gave him an opportunity to entrap me. And his next words only confirm my suspicions.

"I'll expect you home within the week."

"France is not my fucking home!"

"Maybe a compromise, then. I'm not an unreasonable man, and I've always been curious about the place you consider home, Tobias."

Tobias.

He's never once called me by that name.

That itself is threat enough. He's found some leverage in my so-called fuck-up, and he's not letting go of it.

Over the years, I've fed him bits and pieces about the club through Palo, spoonful by spoonful, to give him the illusion he's in the know, but it seems that tactic is starting to backfire.

I can't afford to have him involve himself in any way in my life here, especially now.

"You're crossing a fucking line." I feel the pulse in my temple pounding.

"I, too, am offended by your disregard. He was my only nephew."

I start in the direction of Roman's house just to lay eyes on her, to gather some comfort just from her presence, despite the hostile reception I'm sure to get, and make it just a few steps toward her when her bedroom light clicks off. Stopped halfway between the clearing and Roman's mansion, I stand in a state of utter indecision as defeat starts to seep in. There's no way around Antoine, and my priorities have to shift now if I want to get ahead of him and keep him far, far away from what matters most to me.

"I'll call you in a few hours when I'm back in my office, and we can discuss our future."

I have to get to my brothers to try and stop the hemorrhage before it ruptures any further. I need them sharp and focused if Antoine's threat becomes a reality. That realization has me stopping just a hundred yards away from her and changing directions to get to my Jag.

Every second I let my emotions make decisions is a second we can't afford to lose.

I can hear the satisfaction in the sick fuck's voice with his parting words.

"Don't keep me waiting, Ezekiel."

The line goes dead as his threat hangs heavy in the air, and I start at a dead run past the tree line, all the while paralyzed inside. I carefully go over every possible move, knowing that I'm fucked in every direction.

Once behind the wheel, I pull up the text, and my finger hovers for seconds before I slowly backspace until I've deleted it.

The decision's been made for me.

She'll need protection from the club moving forward. She'll wake up marked, and she'll hate me for it. Another unforgivable deception I'll have to live with.

Hours later, I slam my phone down on my desk and sink into my chair in my Charlotte office, where I've been since I left King's Garage, in an attempt to do damage control with Dom and Sean. I've spent nearly the entire day negotiating with a fucking madman in the bed I made years ago. I wired a significant amount of lunch money to keep the bully at bay, to keep him as far the fuck as possible away from my brothers, my club, and the woman I love.

And in doing so, I agreed to a new arrangement, one that will have me under his heel for some time to come. But it's not my newly forced allegiance to him that's eating me alive. If I can manage to get my club and relationships under control, then I can better figure out a way to deal with Antoine, even if it means declaring war and bringing him down. It's the fallout with my brothers at our garage just hours ago that has me feeling defeated in a way I never imagined possible.

No matter what I do from this point, I already feel like I've lost everything.

She woke up hours ago, no doubt feeling violated in a way that's incomprehensible to her. And I wasn't there. I wasn't there to attempt to explain myself or my reasoning for doing what I did. And at this point, I know they won't matter.

Swallowing down the guilt, I scan the Charlotte skyline, my hands tied in a way they've never been. The helplessness

Kate Stewart

I feel is inescapable, my fate and future sealed as Shelly comes in with another cup of coffee.

"Honey, you look like hell. Drink this." She places the offering on my desk as Sean and Dom's condemning words circle my mind, my jaw sore from the punch Sean threw as their parting words to me rip my insides apart. Shelly lingers at my desk, and I can feel her concern, her hesitance before she finally speaks. "I know this isn't the time, but you have a call—"

"Take a message."

"He said it's urgent, regarding someone named Cecelia."

Every hair on the back of my neck stands on end as I head straight to the blinking light on my desk and lift the receiver. "Did they give a name?"

She nods. "Roman Horner."

That phone call and the hours after I've replayed so many times at this point, I re-live it vividly. From the meeting with Roman that changed everything I thought about him, to the two terrifying hours I spent speeding back to Triple Falls to try and get to her. To the minute Dom lay dying in her arms and down to the second our eyes held just after I ordered her never to return. In twenty-four hours, my life exploded, and a war began.

That night I truly lost it all. Every bit of my control, along with my brother, Cecelia, my club, *everything* that fucking mattered to me because I hesitated when making decisions due to my emotions. I can't make that mistake again. I can't hesitate. I can't lose her because of it. I have to let the emotionless soldier—the monster that dwells inside me—take over if I want to gain the upper hand with Antoine.

I can't let love make a single fucking decision for me.

There's a storm brewing, and it's one I can't see, but I can feel it, just like I felt it all those years ago. I have to fucking figure out his intentions—his plays. And more than that, I have to be several moves ahead of him.

Without Palo, I'm a sitting duck. A phone call with Antoine isn't going to convince me one way or the other. And without a word from him for the last month, I know it's just a matter of time before he comes calling. This time, I'll be ready. I've spent the last six years satiating his demands while trying to clean up my own fucking mess. My plans to rid myself of him are taking a back seat to the recovery of the club. I was intent on keeping him at bay while we rebuilt, and with Cecelia's sudden arrival and my efforts to get back to her, I waited too fucking long to move in on him.

I never make the same mistake twice.

Because of love, I've made that declaration a lie.

And I'm a man in. Fucking. Love.

If it's war this motherfucker is after, my peacekeeping days are long over.

Decision made, I stalk toward the house, and twenty minutes later, I speed out of the driveway in the Camaro.

Chapter Thirty-Four

CECELIA

"ORDER UP, CECELIA," Travis calls, just as I shoot off a text to Tobias. He's been quiet all morning, which has me slightly on edge. I left him sleeping this morning and snuck away with a brief kiss to his lips, which he returned while attempting to pull me into him, still submerged in sleep.

"I've got it, boss," my new hire, Alena, announces as the distinct sound of a familiar engine sounds in the parking lot, drawing every eye toward the source of the noise. A second later, Tobias pulls to a screeching halt just in front of the doors and the hairs on my arms rise and panic sinks in. Too far from my Beretta, I scan the restaurant for anyone who might seem a threat. In the next second, he's out of the Camaro looking both tortured and devastating in dark-washed jeans, a black T-shirt, and matching cardigan that showcases every inch of muscle in his tension-filled shoulders. But it's the purpose in which he walks and the expression on his face that has me on high alert. When he charges through the door, all chattering ceases. I nearly jump out of my skin when Marissa sounds up behind me.

"Oh shit, girl. What did you do?"

He's pure intimidation. His fire-filled eyes find mine across the counter as he prowls toward me, jaw set and hellfire running rampant in his eyes. He stalks toward me and rounds the counter, no fucks given about the spectacle he's making. Swallowing, I brace myself for a fight when he reaches me, his eyes flitting with emotions I can't pinpoint. Chest heaving, he looks like he's about to burst at the seams as he stares down at me, demanding explanation but asking for none. I nearly flinch when he holds out his hand.

"Come with me." His voice is hoarse as if he's been screaming the entirety of the ride here.

"Tobias, I'm working."

He nods over my shoulder to Marissa, and I follow his line of sight to see her grinning like a lunatic.

Traitor.

"She'll be out for the rest of the day."

"Tobias," I begin to protest when he grips the back of my head and bends so we're eye to eye, his tumultuous gaze tearing a hole right through my resolve. This isn't the same man I kissed goodbye this morning. This is the very man who tore through my soul with a kiss the second time we met.

"Not debatable." He scoops me off my feet in a fireman's hold as more objections fly out my mouth and light laughter echoes around us. I'm barely able to sputter out quick orders as Marissa assures me that she's got it handled while he carries me out of the restaurant. Opening the car door with ease, despite my weight, he deposits me in the Camaro, and a second later, we're tearing out of the parking lot. Locked into the seat by speed alone, I can't help but admire the sheer beauty of his profile and the power he exudes as he transitions the car easily from one gear to the next.

"What the hell is going on?" My words come out a muddled mix of fear and demand.

He jerks his head toward me, cutting off my protest, his jaw set grimly, his eyes swimming with resolution. Though the picture of control, I can feel him coming apart next to me.

He takes a curve at neck-breaking speed and then a quick right onto the road that leads to my house. He remains mute as a thousand or more scenarios behind his upset race through my mind just before he skids to a stop in the driveway. Before I can blink, he's pulling me from the car and leading me into the house with his hand on my wrist. I fumble with my words as he unlocks the door.

"Tobias—"

Once inside, he presses me against it and gazes down at me.

"Explain yourself, right now, King. What happened?"

"What happened?" His tone is gravel. "I lost you. *I fucking lost you*. And I won't do it again."

I search his face for any clue as to what brought this on when my attention falls on the packed duffle bag sitting just a few feet away. He follows my line of sight and turns back to me, his intent clear.

He's ready for this fight.

"DON'T YOU DARE LEAVE ME!" The voice is mine, the plea is from me, but it's not my heart speaking. It's my soul that's screaming now.

"I have to. It's just a few days. I'll be back—"

"No!" I shake my head furiously. "No!"

"Trésor—" his voice wavers slightly—"please, look at me." He's fully intent on leaving me. I turn my head as the blow penetrates so deep, I'm unable to breathe. But something inside me cracks as I manage to find my fight, my body blistering with outrage.

"You promised we would make our decisions together. You promised never to leave me!"

"And *you* promised to let me protect you. A promise above all others."

"No! A promise to you above all others *I've made*, not the promises you made to *me*. You're not getting away with this. If you walk out this door, we're done. You walk out this door. I won't *ever* let you back in. Not ever."

"I have to. I have to. And you have to trust me."

I shake my head, incredulous. "You're never going to stop breaking my heart, are you? You're never going to stop lying to me!" I feel it then, the walls threatening to go up, and he can sense it too because I hear the pained grunt escape him as he presses in to try and get the response he wants.

"I have no choice, listen to me." It's an order. An order from the man who forced himself into my heart years ago. It's my resurrected King speaking. It's him who's seeking an audience now—the man who's planned and plotted his way around his whole life. The same man I took on years ago, and it's the very same man I glare at now as he gazes down at me, his mind made up.

"I'm done listening, as long as that packed bag exists. Fuck you, Tobias."

"Stop it, Cecelia," he scolds, but I'm not having it. Not this time, and not any other.

"You leave, and we're done. It's that simple."

The intensity and emotions rolling off him are far too potent to look away. It's only the slap of my hand against his skin that brings relief, the pain I'm inflicting that releases the anger. I want to tear him apart for what he's doing. Bitter tears spring to my eyes as he grips my hair in his fist, bending so we're eye to eye.

"You have to trust me. I'm doing it so we can have *more* of this life together."

"I don't trust you. You haven't earned my trust back yet. Not even close. And if you walk out this door, you'll never have it, and you'll never have me. Not fucking ever!"

He forces my eyes to his with his grip, and I close them, a tear rolling down my cheek as I start to shut down, bit by bit. "Don't do this," I warn. "If you do, you put a bullet in us. I'm not bluffing, Tobias. I'll give you *anything* but *this*."

Recognition seeps into his gaze, and he knows I mean it.

"You're the one who has to trust, Tobias. You have to trust *me*, and you just can't, can you? After all we've been through, you can't trust in *us* at all. You refuse to believe that no matter what happens, whatever comes our way, whatever danger we face, we can face it *together*. But you've hardwired yourself not to. But hear me, I won't bend on this. I won't forgive this. I'll never look back if you break us this way."

"Look at me, Cecelia."

"You don't want me to look at you right now, Tobias, because all I'll see when I do is a fucking liar who continually breaks my heart—and his promises. And up until ten minutes ago, I saw a man who I would walk through eternal hell for. This is the one thing you can do that will end us for good."

I slam my palms against his chest. "So close. I was so fucking close. I guess third time is the charm for you, isn't it?"

"Cecelia—"

He's really going to do it. He's leaving me.

"This is it, Tobias, of all the decisions you've made, this will be the one to make or break us. And it's yours to make. I made mine. All you have to do is trust *me*. There's no other way around it. I'm not waiting for you to come to the right conclusion, and your time is already running out. You made a fucking promise to me. And you already broke the first two by refusing to tell me what's going on. You think I'm ignorant to the fact that you're hiding something? You think I'm fucking ignorant to *you*? You can't hide from me!"

"I don't know what's going on," he explodes, "and that's the truth! I can't give you a truth I don't have! I don't know what's going on, and I can't protect us if I'm in the fucking dark."

"But you know *something*, right? *Enough* about something to know *where* to look, *right*?" I counter, his eyes lower, and more tears slide free.

"You're ruining this. We just got each other back, and you're ruining this because you refuse to fucking trust me!"

His eyes flicker as he keeps me pinned to the door. I'm not sure who's blocking who anymore, but while my hope shrivels, my goddamn heart is still fighting, and I know without a doubt I mean every word I'm saying. This I can't forgive. This I refuse to forgive.

A pained grunt leaves him as he claims my mouth in a searing kiss, and I jerk away, snapping at his lips, which only earns me a pleasured groan. I push at his chest. "You'll get no farewell kiss from me, you sick bastard. You always did love the taste of the tears you cause."

"Oh, I'm fucking sick, all right. Sick of being afraid of

what I can't see! I can't do anything if I don't know what's happening! I can't protect you if I don't know what's coming!" He shakes his head as if I'm clueless and spins me, using his weight to press me to the door. I scream out in frustration, furious that I'm unable to move, furious he's using his strength to restrain me. He's too strong, and I'm powerless against him. "I hate you." It comes from deep within as he presses his full weight into me, anger rolling off his frame.

"Je t'aime," *I love you*, he says, pressing his chest into my back, laying his forehead against my shoulder. "Don't shut me out, Cecelia. Wait for me."

"No!"

"Don't shut me out. Don't do it. I'll come back. I need two days. Two days. Can't you give me that?"

"You don't even have two minutes. If you take longer than that, we're over, regardless of if you stay."

"Cecelia—"

"No!"

He crushes me with his chest, trying to exert his will into me, his heart pounding erratically beneath my shoulder blade as his arm snakes around my stomach, and he unfastens my jeans before ripping them down my legs.

"Stop it!" I yell as he pulls my sneakers and socks off. I buck against him as he easily pins me back to the door with one hand.

He grips my shirt, and I cross my arms.

"Stop it! You aren't getting me fucking naked right now!"

He slams his fist into the door, the frame rattling.

"You promised me, Cecelia!"

"And you promised me!"

"Don't you get it? I can steal your time, your attention, and even your body, but I can't *take* what I came back for!"

"That's right, and you're not getting it. Not if you do this to me again! You walk out of this door—there's no coming back."

He lets out a guttural roar and flips me in his arms, ripping my shirt from me as I claw at his shoulders in an attempt to push him away.

"Stop it, King! What the fuck are you doing?"

Undeterred, his patience evaporated, he strips me, yanking down my bra and panties until I'm completely bare.

"You don't get to do this and get *any* part of me." I go to move around him, and he lifts me easily as I scratch and claw at him until he deposits me next to the couch. He jerks me by the arm to face the back of it before hooking both my arms behind me with one of his. Struggling beneath him, I buck as he keeps me hostage and completely at his mercy.

"You fucking monster!"

His voice is even when he speaks. "Only when I have to be, and for you, I will be."

I jerk against him, my struggle futile as he keeps me immobilized by his strength. Anger like I've never known courses through me at his betrayal.

"You're going to pull this bullshit, then you fucking face me, you coward!"

"Why bother? You hate me for who I am."

"I hate you for what you hide!"

"I'm not hiding now." He leans down, folding his body over mine, and whispers in my ear as furious tears cloud my vision. His voice is filled with venom when he speaks.

"This rage you're feeling, the helplessness you feel *right now*, the fear of not knowing what's coming, feeling exposed in a way that fucking humiliates and infuriates you, leaving you powerless," he grunts out, each word more pained in delivery, "is exactly what *I feel* every time you're threatened, and I don't know by what or who, and yet you refuse my fucking protection."

His words settle in just as he releases me, and I whirl and slap his chest, his face, his neck, unleashing hell. He takes every blow without so much as flinching, his eyes blazing with rage while I exhaust myself. His words barely register as my fight weakens, the desperation seeping into his eyes zaps some of my rage as I slam my palms against his heaving chest. He looks like he's on the verge of explosion. "I just wanted you to know what your win feels like for me," he swallows, rage controlling his voice while his eyes shine with defeat. "You win, Cecelia, I'm letting you fucking win, and I don't know what that means."

"I hate you," I croak, all strength leaving me, my eyes overflowing with anger.

"For every single thing I've done or will ever do to you, I have a reason. And I'm sorry if they're not good enough, but I don't give a fuck as long as your heart keeps beating, and there's a chance you will forgive me for making sure it does." His voice cracks with every word. "But if you take this away from me, I have nothing. You leave me with nothing."

The rest of my anger leaves me as the gravity of his sacrifice seeps in, and I grip his face in my hands. Furious, he jerks away from my touch.

"You have me," I assure him as I grip him more firmly and his eyes dart away. I press a kiss to his jaw, his throat as he swallows repeatedly, vibrating with rage. Gripping his shirt, I push off on my toes and lick along his throat. "You'll have my trust. You'll have my devotion. You'll have *all of me*."

"Love isn't going to save us," he snaps.

"Maybe not. But love and trust are the only things capable of saving *you and me*. You have to trust me, Tobias."

He curses, a caged bull, as I do my best to soothe his anger, pressing my body against his while sliding my hand between us, up and down his chest, before gripping his erection. He grips my wrist to stop me, making me wince, his fire-filled eyes scathing as he batters me with a look.

"Tobias, you have me," I murmur as I press in. He jerks his chin in refusal and steps away, putting space—I refuse—between us.

Intent, I step forward, hands roaming as he looks down at me with nothing but disdain, and I feel the line thinning between love and hate as we edge along it. But I know this edge, we've ridden it before, and I know what wins with us, what will always win.

His eyes roam my skin, his breaths coming faster as his anger festers and familiar, potent need spikes between us.

"Damn you," he grits out, his voice growing thick with fury as he slaps my hands away, his eyes smoldering with the promise of delivering a different kind of hell.

Stepping back, he shrugs out of his cardigan, his eyes licking heat down my body as the sweater falls to the floor. He fists his T-shirt, the hem sliding up his chiseled torso before he tosses it onto the pile. Amber eyes blazing, he toes off his boots and unzips his jeans, and I watch, entranced by the sight of him as he discards them along with his boxer and socks. His cock bobs heavily between us as my mouth waters at the sight of it. Naked and panting, we take the other in, souls bared, hearts raw. Within my next breath he pins me, denying my kiss and again facing me toward the couch before he lifts my knees to rest on the thick edge.

Slowly and painfully fisting my hair, he glides his free palm down my stomach, tucking two fingers between my legs as a low moan escapes me. A groan escapes his chest at my back when he feels how slick I am before he begins to fuck me ruthlessly with his fingers. Gasping with the sting of a bite, I spread my legs wider as more wetness gathers at my core.

"You hate me? Maybe I hate you, too," his whisper is venomous, and I shudder with the arrival of a threatening orgasm as he pulls his fingers away from me. This is punishment for my win, and I'm all too ready for it.

"Then hate me."

He grips my ass with his roaming hand, spreading me as his erection brushes between my cheeks and tension coils in my belly. From behind, his fingers again plunge into the wet heat gathered at my center, a pained groan leaving his throat as he stretches me further, my heart rate skyrocketing as my clit throbs in anticipation. He slides a palm up my back before snaking it around my throat and squeezing, my back arching with the movement as he pushes the tip of his cock into me, drawing the back of my head to his chest until our eyes connect and he's glaring at me from above. The second we lock into place, he drives into me completely, and my body goes taut with the invasion as his eyes close.

"Putain." *Fuck.*

Within the first few thrusts, I tighten around him and start to come apart, my thighs shaking uncontrollably as his hand again tightens on my throat and his eyes flame open, his gaze unwavering as he peers down at me.

Invading.

Claiming.

Furious.

Gripping the back of his neck, I brace myself against him as he fucks me with punishing thrusts. His eyes flare as I stiffen in welcome, an orgasm unfurling throughout my limbs as he keeps our eyes locked and drives in, tearing through me.

With the next thrust, I detonate, my body convulsing uncontrollably as he continues at a maddening, purposeful pace. I've never been fucked so savagely in my life, and I can't get enough.

With every few thrusts, I quicken, my back arching further, as I come undone again, and again, and again as he stares down at me, a man possessed, the desire in his eyes his only tell as the rest of his features twist cruelly, his intent clear.

Punishment.

When I again crest down in a wave of ecstasy into familiar ashes, I go lax in his arms only to be met with a violent slap on my ass.

My whole body latches onto that pain as pleasure seeps through my every pore. His lips part as he loses himself briefly, and I arch my back further, lifting my ass to take more of him in as liquid fire drips from his gaze. Within seconds, I'm coming again, the orgasms crashing through me, wave after wave on the heels of the last, as he fucks me viciously, channeling all of his anger into his movement.

"I get everything?" he taunts, his finger invading the

forbidden, the threat hanging in the air as he presses his finger in.

"Yessss," I hiss before I explode around him, my thighs threatening to give out as he picks up his pace, his fingers tightening around my throat as if in indecision. I see a flash of satisfaction as he denies me breath for several seconds, which leads to yet another explosive orgasm, this one far more intense.

He curses when I go lax from the weight of it and pulls me from the couch. In the next second, the hardwood bruises my knees as he grips my hair in his fist and pushes his engorged cock between my teeth until I'm choking on him. With a few thrusts of his hips, he grunts, filling my mouth, his release hitting the back of my throat. I take it all, savoring every second, my body filling with renewed desire as I lick him from root to tip, sucking every inch of him clean. He watches, rapt, his eyes flaring with mild surprise. When I finally release him from my mouth, I lick my lips with only one request.

"More."

He lifts me from the floor with the same punishing grip before taking me to bed and giving me exactly that.

Chapter Thirty-Five

TOBIAS

Age Thirty-One

I PULL UP to the garage in time to see Sean speed off in his Nova, not sparing me a glance as he whizzes by—but I can feel his anger just the same. Parking next to his Camaro, the garage light clicks on, and I'm relieved Dom's alone. But I know it won't make a difference in the way this will go down. Whether it's one or both of them, the outcome will be the same. I never had any intentions of them finding out this way. Thoughts still racing, chest aching from their expressions when they saw us in Roman's back yard, confessions of love pouring from our lips, have me walking through the lobby and straight into the fire. Dom stands in the middle of the garage, staring into space. Long, tense seconds tick past, and I prepare myself for everything. When I reach him, he turns to look at me with the eyes of a man I barely recognize, our connection nowhere to be found.

"If you're expecting me to hit you, fight you, you're fucking pathetic." He shakes his head, his eyes black with rage. "You didn't see me as your brother. The one fucking time I needed you to see me, to hear me as your brother, you couldn't stop playing parent. You couldn't take me seriously. You assumed I was fucking around. Nothing new. Dominic being Dominic. But I saw it the minute you believed me, and it wasn't ten months ago when I asked you to. It was back there when you realized it was too late. That was better than any punch I could throw. Fuck you. Get out."

I remain mute because I have zero defense I can think of, and with his words, I don't want any. I want his wrath because for now, it's better than indifference. As long as he's fighting me, there's a chance for us.

"Get the fuck out," he repeats, clenching his fists.

"I can't."

"You're fucking worthless to me now," he says, moving to his toolbox and flipping it open.

"I have been for some time. You're your own man now."

"Nah, that's not what you saw in me. You needed me as an excuse to play warden, to keep control."

"I witnessed it all, Dominic, from day one, I've been there—"

"You're not my fucking father!" He approaches me at full height, his eyes flaring, his teeth bared. "You barely share my blood. Get out. I'm not asking."

"I can't."

"You'll get no absolution from me."

"I know."

"Then what the fuck is there to say? Go to her. She may listen to your fucking lies tonight, but it won't be me."

"Dom, I'm in love with her."

"Sounds familiar." He strikes then, both hands to my chest, and pushes me up against a truck perched in the bay behind me. I don't fight him as the war rages in his head. The same war I battled months ago before I sent him away, refusing to listen, refusing to believe his feelings for her were real. It's then I hear the squeal of brakes and the give in the gravel just outside the doors.

Fuck.

Dominic glares at me, eyes full of contempt and condemnation. It's then I wonder if my brother will ever look at me the way he used to, with respect and admiration. I felt the snap in him the minute he realized what was done. "I can't even ask you if she's worth it. Because I *know* she is. You got what you wanted. She's yours. You knew exactly what the consequences would be, the damage it would do to us, to Sean, to her, so what the fuck do you want from me?"

"I'm marking her tonight. I wanted you to be the first to know." It's then I see Dominic eye Sean past my shoulder.

"You're what?" Sean seethes from where he stands, and I glance over to see his fists clenching and unclenching at the threshold of the garage. He wants to end me. It's so fucking transparent. He won't forgive me anytime soon and never will once I've made it clear what I'm about to do.

"I'm marking her for obvious reasons and for her protection. Order's already out. It's done."

"The fuck you are!" Sean charges me, and Dominic steps between us, his head tilted as if he didn't quite hear me right.

"You're going to take it this far?" His tone is lethal, and I feel the second strike of betrayal emanating from his frame.

"I have no choice."

"You have a fucking choice," Sean explodes, "and so should *she.*"

Dominic reads my posture, my intent, and nods. "Yeah,

you do that. You fucking mark her. You better bold that shit, and then you can *live* with it."

"Dom!" Sean barks, incredulous. Dom shakes his head, turning back to him. He knows my reasoning, but Sean's too broken to see it.

Sean steps up to the two of us, the picture of aggression. "You're going too fucking far to prove a point. It's not enough you fucked us all?"

"Not for me," I counter as Dominic turns to face me with a smile so fucking wicked with intent that I know I've earned some of his hate. My brother hates me, and it's deserved.

I will hate, maim, or fucking murder anyone who tries to take her away from me. Anyone, but my brothers who love her just as fiercely, but what's killing them both is she's no longer fair play.

"I didn't lay a hand on her until a few months before you came back," I tell them both because it bears being repeated—although it's still not a defense.

Sean charges for me but stops a foot away, his eyes blood-thirsty, the devastation harder to see now that it's masked by fury, but I know it's there. "Yeah, well, you also stole our ability to fight by keeping us gagged in your fucking zoo! And I'm willing to bet we had a chance to get her back until you stepped in!"

"My orders didn't stop you from leaving a necklace," I look between the two of them, and neither speaks up, but neither seems surprised I know, either. "I'll fucking apologize for loving her the minute you do. But what I did—" I shake my head—"I don't expect your forgiveness."

"You won't get it. And you don't deserve her," Sean clips.

"And you do? You two idiots parading around like men,

like soldiers, when you don't know a fucking thing about sacrifice. And with her, you sacrificed nothing! Not a fucking thing! Until you know what that is, you aren't capable of being the man she needs." Jealousy boils over as I condemn them both. "And you know all too fucking well that you lost her the minute you shared her—" I look over to Dominic—"and chose this life over her."

"And you didn't manipulate your way in?" Sean shakes his head with disgust. "The only thing I'm sorry for was that I ever believed your bullshit." He spits on the ground, inches from my shoe.

"I brought her in *fully* and told her the fucking truth because it was safer for her, all the while knowing she could take me down, take us all down! This isn't about me, or you, or our fucking agenda right now. This is about her." I step up to him and can feel the tension coiling, the raw violence radiating from his frame. He's torn between striking his brother while determining me his enemy. "You pulling out, Sean? If so, leave your wings at the door. Tonight, I'm here on business."

Sean gawks at me. "You dare say this shit to me?"

"Yeah, I am. I need to know how far you're going to go with this."

"Who the fuck are you?" His voice is raw with pain.

"I'm the man who would step in front of a bullet for either one of you, no questions asked, but I'm also the man who held your fucking hands before I shaped them into fists. I'm the same man—up until I met her—who put you both above everyone else. But right now, who am I right now? I'm the man who loves her enough to not let *anyone or anything* in front of *her*."

Sean's voice shakes with hate as he looks over to me. "You playing I saw her first?"

"Yeah, I am. And I think you fucking knew what line you were crossing, or else you wouldn't have hidden her from me."

Sean rears back, his right catching me in the jaw a split second before Dominic pushes me back, relieving me of the brunt of the blow. Dominic rights me and glares back at Sean before turning to me. "You didn't believe me, brother, but I believe you, now. Cecelia may be yours, but The Triple Falls chapter is *mine,* and as long as she's here, she's under *my* fucking protection. I've been running things here since you've been globetrotting, and if we're going by rules, and business is business, you best goddamn mark her for no other reason than that. If you need anything from us from here on out, you're going to have to ask *nicely*. Until then, we're both done with you. You listening, big brother? We're done with you on the *non-business* front. *Get. The. Fuck. Out.*"

The lividity and finality of his tone rips a place inside of me that can't be repaired. My relationship with my brother is never one I would ever have put into question a year ago. It's the one place I had peace, solidarity, consistency, and I've ruined it with my actions. But amongst the wreckage, I found a different place, one that I never believed could exist for a man like me.

Exhaling, I cup the back of my neck, and I find myself leveling with him in a way, a plea to hear me—fighting for his attention over his anger and hatred, a barter I never imagined I would have to make with my own blood. With the boy I raised and the man I shaped. But I can feel the shift, and it's crippling. It takes me several seconds to speak before I look between them. "I've never asked you for anything, and I'm not asking you to forgive me, not now, but I feel I've given enough to ask you both this. For her, not for me, for Cecelia. You both brought her into this, and I'm keeping her in it for her safety and for my greed. I love her. And no matter what happens from here on out, I need your word that when the time comes, *she* comes first. And make no mistake, I know what part I played, but the truth is, we *all* made this more than business." I turn to Dominic, knowing the truth about that day at the library, knowing full well he saw her and was always aware of her. "You brought her in when I told you to keep her out of it. I told you what would happen. I just didn't know how it would play out. We're all to blame. All of us."

Dom charges toward the back door and slams his way through it. I stare after him, the hole he left in me burning as I run a palm down my jaw. I can feel the world we created slipping through my hands as my need to get back to Cecelia increases ten-fold.

Am I losing her right now for the same reasons? My greed, my need for her, for something for myself. For the first time in my fucking life—and with her, in those precious weeks we had where our walls disappeared entirely—I felt liberated, like the version of myself I would have been had I not gone down this path. All I want now is to discard all of it for more time with her. With this knowledge, I have a clear understanding of why I deserve their wrath. Maybe she created the same sanctuary for them.

Maybe Dom and Sean became the more desired versions of themselves with her. We all have sacrificed in some way for this life. Maybe she was their sanctuary. And I hate it if it's true. If they found the same pleasure, the same belonging

I have. I dismissed their feelings because I couldn't wrap my head around the fact that they fucking shared the woman I moved heaven and earth just to steal weeks of happiness with. And together, they passed her back and forth and took pieces of my treasure, pieces I can never get back.

This is my price, my penance for being the thief I've become. For falling in love, for stealing her. For living my life, for once, for myself.

But I have consequences to face that will complicate things far more than what's going on here.

Resigned this is just the beginning, I face off with the man I've loved like a brother since the moment he crash-landed into our lives. In seconds, my hurt shifts, and I'm grieving for the boy that he was and the man he's become and meant to me. We'll never be the same. None of us will. It takes all my energy not to let the anger be front and center, though every fiber of my being screams for flesh and blood. But this blood I can't have, and my greed for her will never be sated.

The agony of that truth has me seething as Sean steps up to me, his eyes a mix of rage and the same type of ruin. "Why?"

"You know why. You're right there with me! But I'm not fucking sharing her, not with you, not with my brother, not with a goddamn soul! That's where you fucked up, Sean, and you know it. Her place is with me. End of."

"You think so?" His condescending smirk has my blood boiling. "I wouldn't be so fucking sure. I know what I saw today, and maybe I can't fight a lost cause, and that's my cross to bear. But I also know what you laid witness to as well back in that yard. I saw the fear in your eyes. Fear for the parts of her you'll *never* have. The part that belongs to *me*, the other to your *brother*. Claim her all you want, mark her, piss all around her, but you'll never have her fully. Not. Fucking. Ever. You'll always be sharing her with us, no matter what you fucking do. You'll never possess her the way your thief's soul needs to own her. And you get to live with that. We *all* get to live with that." He shoves his way past me, and I slam my fist down at the hood of the truck.

"Sean!" I swallow hard, the burn making my voice raw and unrecognizable to me. It's agony knowing it's true, but I push through it for what's important. "For her. For her. Not for *me*. I'm asking for this. She comes first."

"Jesus, man," he scoffs, "the fact that you still need assurances is pathetic. Using her as an *in* was the excuse I came up with for *you* mere days after I met her. This has always been about *her*."

Seconds pass, the howl of the wind outside shakes the bay doors. "Why didn't you claim her?"

His eyes slice. "Because none of us were worthy of doing so with the lies floating between us. And those lies existed because we had your back. Because we believed in you and our cause. And until she knew the whole truth . . ." He shakes his head. "Doesn't fucking matter now, does it?"

"None of us deserve her," I state honestly. "None of us."

"You least of all, you selfish fucking prick." I feel the slam of the door behind him down to the marrow in my bones.

* * *

Retrieving a bottle from Dom's trunk, sweat pouring from my forehead after my midnight run, I forgo the house, walking around to the back porch to collapse in the lounger, my heart cracking from the memory I re-live *daily*.

Staring at the bottle, I know cracking it open won't erase a single word we exchanged that night or make the heartache any less intense.

It's the definition of insanity.

Even after an exhausting day of fighting and make-up fucking with Cecelia, even with the knowledge I've reclaimed her heart, even with the closeness between us I've longed for since returning has sealed some of the hole that's been there over half a decade—I can't shake this.

And I knew it would happen.

I knew that no matter how happy I got here with her, that this haunt wasn't leaving me. The contentment ripped from me because of my long, cruel memory. Thoughts of our fallout the night before Dom died plagued me nonstop tonight, making sleep impossible. I stared up at the ceiling for hours after Cecelia drifted off, sprawled naked over my chest, her thigh hooked around my torso while she dreamed. I let her sleep, no matter how badly I needed the distraction of her body to try and ward the ache away. But it's not on her to wrestle my demons.

This battle I fight daily, and I've never won once.

But I'm still weak with need to go to her now. To rouse her, fuck her, and lose myself in her, basking in the safety of her love, her arms, my sanctuary. I stare at the blue bottle of Bombay, knowing it's a shitty fucking alternative.

Tonight, all I feel is restless.

Maybe it's because of the battle I lost today, but even in losing that, I'm a little relieved. I never wanted to leave her, but I didn't have any other game plan.

Not even the fresh blueprint I managed to conjure up after I lay in bed with her hours later, before shooting off a text to Tyler, brings me any peace.

The night air begins to cool the sweat on my skin and my breaths even just as the back door bursts open and Beau dashes out, licking my knee and darting off a second before Cecelia's red-rimmed eyes find mine. It's then I realize just how badly I fucked up.

"I didn't leave a note."

A tear slips down her cheek as a sob bursts from her lips, and the sight of it kills me. Reaching out, I grip her hand and pull her into my lap, the relief in her so apparent, it only breaks my heart further.

I press my face into her neck, inhaling her scent. "I'm sorry, baby. I'm so fucking sorry. I wasn't thinking." For the first time since I got here, she needs consoling due to fear—fear *I instilled* in her, and it's on me.

I cup her face as she shakes in my hold, more tears gliding down her cheeks. Stilling her quivering lips with the long press of my own, I use my thumb to stroke away her tears. As strong as she's become, I managed to scare her in an unforgivable way by being too immersed in my own shit.

I trace the tiny divot in her chin with my thumb. "I've lied and broken promises to you one too many fucking times for you to believe me. But I wish you would believe I could never do that to you again. That's why you won, Trésor. I surrender. My white flag is yours."

"I f-f-f-ucking . . . h-h-ate you, King," she says through another hitched breath.

"You should. I'm sorry, Trésor. I'm not leaving. This I *promise you* above all others."

She blows out an exasperated breath, and I wait until her body relaxes against mine. No words I can say right now are good enough. Over time, I'll prove myself. I press my face into the side of her neck and inhale. "I'm sorry I can't stop this. This is my shit. I will get better for you."

Drinking in her juniper scent, I eye the bottle I discarded on the table. Maybe she's all I need. She seems to read my thoughts.

"Don't." Deep-blue eyes plead with mine, "Talk to me instead."

"It's not a problem. I won't let it be. I won't waste my life like that. This I know about myself."

She regards me with tear-soaked eyes. "Well, you may not need one, but thanks to your late-night run, I do." She lifts the bottle from the table and unscrews it, taking a long drink before dipping to kiss me. I savor the taste of the alcohol, sucking on her tongue and earning a moan until she breaks the kiss. "Please talk to me. Tell me what hurts you so much."

I nod, scraping my lips with my teeth.

"After I left you in that yard—the day Dom and Sean discovered us—I gave them a few hours to cool off a little before I went to them. A lot of hours, actually. I came back and paced your back yard. I heard you playing "Father Figure," for *me*. It stung so fucking bad. I knew how hurt you were. I ended up going back to them before I came to you, and you know I never made it."

"Why?"

"For the same reason I'm surrendering. I've made one too many bad decisions that put the people I love at risk. It's made me paranoid, and sometimes I don't know when my instincts are right, or it's the paranoia. It's getting harder to distinguish which. I really needed this fucking vacation."

She nods and runs her fingers through my hair, waiting patiently for me to speak. I want to give this to her, and more

414

than once, I've torn pages out of my journal recalling that night, but I could never get through it. I take another long pull of gin and set the bottle down, giving her my full attention as I relay every detail I can remember about that night, save the call from Antoine. She listens attentively, drawing closer to me with each word, her grip on me growing tighter, her eyes shining with empathy when I finish.

After a bout of silence, she situates herself on my lap so she's fully facing me before she speaks. "You know a judge passes a sentence for crimes committed in order of the severity of the degree of the crime. How much time do you plan on serving, Tobias?"

"It's not that simple."

"No, it's not, but do you think he would want you to live the rest of your life a slave to your guilt? Guilt for actions you regret with your whole heart and being? You know the answer. As hard as he was, that's not Dominic's heart. That's not who he was at all. He was the same impenetrable man operating on love, a mirror image of you." I bite my lip as she palms my jaw, forcing my eyes to hers.

"I've never felt like I just lost my brother, and I know that may seem weird. But I feel like . . ."

"You lost a son," she whispers. "It's not weird. You took on that role. You were both."

I nod. "I *know* that love, Cecelia," I confess, "a father's love. For the most part, I was Dominic's father, despite my title." I shake my head, unable to see her now through my pain. "And the day before he died, I took the *one thing* he wanted most in the world away from him. He died *in love* with you. I thieved from him and broke his heart, his trust. What reason did he have not to step in front of those bullets?"

Her eyes widen, and she shakes her head furiously. "You can't possibly think that. I know you can't think that."

"Maybe I do."

"You're lying to yourself, Tobias." Her navy eyes demand mine. "Frères pour toujours." *Always brothers.*

She repeats Dom's last words to me, and she might as well have taken a sledgehammer to my chest. "*You* were the reason he took those bullets. He saved us both by saving you *first.*"

"Don't," I begin to come undone, the rawness in my chest burning my throat. When I lift the bottle, she takes it from me.

"Don't do this to me—" I shake my head—"*please.*"

"'I've never seen him light up like that with any woman.' That's what he said to me that night. That's what you wanted to know when you were *sober.*"

I avert my gaze, but she presses in.

"He smiled when he said it, Tobias. I wish you could have seen that smile because if you had been there—if you had seen it—you would know without a doubt that he wanted you to be happy, even if that meant losing me. What we had was beautiful, but you're placing too much importance on the *wrong* relationship, and I can see in your eyes, you know it's the truth, but admitting it means admitting he died for *you*. And he did saving *you*, Tobias."

"Cecelia," I beg the burn in my throat causing me to choke.

"He loved you just as fiercely and unconditionally as you did him. He was angry but just as protective of you and your happiness, and that's why he *saved* you."

"Goddamnit!" I snap, and she pins me where I sit, steadfast and pressing in further.

"The truth is, he pushed *you* out of the way that night

416

before he caught any bullet to shield *me*. He gave his life for *yours*. You refuse to accept that, and that's what's hurting you most." She pulls me into her chest as I begin to tremble as grunts pour out of me. She wraps around me, refusing to let me free as she whispers the truth, a truth I would do anything to forget. "It's past time you face it and accept it. I'm not the only one he saved that night, Tobias. You have to accept his sacrifice. Even if you're angry about it, you have to accept that his love for you was just as strong, and you have to accept that he forgave you and loved you enough to want you to be happy. You have to unshackle yourself from this guilt, or you'll never be able to accept the rest of the gift he gave you."

I press my face into her chest and shudder with the onslaught of the truth I've been avoiding since the life left his eyes. From the time I held him as a baby in my arms, knowing he belonged to me, to the day he looked up at me and faded away, he was mine.

"Je suis désolé. Je suis désolé. Je suis vraiment désolé. Je suis vraiment désolé." *I'm sorry. I'm sorry. I'm so sorry. I'm so fucking sorry.*

"You have to thank him by living," she murmurs as I exhaust myself while soul-deep remorse rolls through me. It doesn't feel like punishment. It's rawer than that. It's blood-letting, implosion, and at the same time, a strange sort of release. I don't want that so much, because if it happens, if I forget one single detail of any memory, I won't get it back.

Falling apart in her arms, she murmurs to me, running her fingers all over my skin, through my hair, smoothing her hand down my back. I'm unsure of how long we stay in that chair when I finally come to, her murmurs constant, her tears pelting my skin as I come back into myself, into my present, exhausted but far from empty. It's not a flood of relief, but it's the cusp of a little release.

Shaken by what just transpired, I bury my face into her neck and inhale, her scent calming me to the point I can take full breaths. Lifting my eyes to hers, she shakes her head as I open my mouth to speak, so fucking raw from emotions I can barely manage.

"Don't you dare apologize to me," she says softly.

"I don't know if I'm the man you fell for," I confess. "I don't know if I ever will be again."

"I know."

"I've never been a king, Cecelia."

"That's where we disagree. You don't see what I see. Maybe you never have. All you seem to see are your mistakes, and I'm determined to change that. But to me, you're everything."

The uncomfortable feeling threatens, but I ignore it, knowing I'm completely exposed. But with her, I always have been, whether it be the unchecked desire she draws from me, my darkest thoughts, my truest truths, or my unrelenting need for her. She's always managed to peel me apart, layer by layer, cracking my foundation to get deeper than any other has ever gone.

From the little girl with mischievous eyes to a woman with nothing but fire in her heart—she stole *me* first, and that's the truest truth of this thief's heart.

We sit for several moments just listening to the noises of the night, the sweat drying on my skin as I breathe in her scent again and lift my eyes to her.

"Juniper," I grin, my eyes half-mast from exhaustion. "You are aware, Trésor, that *gin* is made of *juniper berries*, right?"

"Don't flatter yourself, Frenchman, that's pure coincidence. I've been wearing it since I was sixteen."

"It's not a coincidence." I run my hand down her wings, her eyes hooding a little more with each caress. "Nothing about us is a coincidence. You should know that by now. Life may have a fucked-up sense of humor for pairing us together, and all outside forces may have deserted us, but if there was ever evidence of two people fucking fated to be together, star-crossed or not, it's us."

We stay silent for several minutes on the verge of sleep until the crunch of gravel sounds from the driveway. Cecelia spikes to life, and I tighten my arms around her to keep her from springing from my lap.

"It's okay. We're expecting company."

"It's close to three in the morning. Who is it?"

I nip at her lips as she pushes at my chest, impatient for an answer.

"Our ride."

Chapter Thirty-Six

CECELIA

Tobias slides into a freshly tailored Tom Ford that arrived sometime after I slept by way of bird messenger, no doubt for this very reason. He tugs the cuff of the shirt to button it, his eyes catching mine in the mirror before a smirk graces his face. I'm turned on beyond comprehension as he surveys me in nothing but my black lacy bra and panties while I run a hot iron through my hair. I'm indecisive at the moment on whether to fuck him or kill him, but I'm pretty sure this will be the norm as long as we're together.

But the reason for my fraying nerves at this moment is because I'm readying myself to travel to D.C. to meet. The. President.

He played me, yet again with his plotting and scheming, making more plans I wasn't aware of, and disguised it as a "surprise."

"This isn't deception," he assures me, his voice even. "This is my plan B, my Hail Mary."

"It feels a lot like manipulation. And you have *yet* to tell me what's going on."

"You locked the door on me," he says, gathering his cufflinks, "so I'm opening a window."

"Meaning?"

"You'll know soon enough." My eyes drift down to his fingers as he secures his cufflinks and lifts a brow. "Is your hair supposed to be smoking?"

I pull out my hot iron and am relieved to see my hair didn't come with it.

"Stop distracting me," I snap.

His lips twitch. "Trésor is *cranky* when she hasn't gotten her full eight hours."

"Don't blame it on sleep deprivation, Frenchman, I haven't had a full night in weeks."

"Those were moans that kept you awake, not objections."

"You smug bastard."

"Ton salaud." *Your bastard.* He moves toward me, the fit of the suit enough to have me salivating. Though he's denied it, he's still every bit the arrogant King I fell in love with. The buzz in my veins no longer exists due to gin or the endless orgasms from hours earlier.

It's him.

This buzz is all him, *us.*

He reaches me in two confident strides and slowly lifts the form-fitting dress I chose from the hanger, unzipping it for me to step in. I do before he pulls it up and lifts my hair to press a kiss to the nape of my neck.

"This is just a house call. Don't think too much. I'll explain on the ride in." He turns me in his arms and backs me into the dresser, his eyes dipping.

"Don't even think about it," I warn.

"Against this dresser or in the back of that limo, your choice."

"Dream on, pal, back in the doghouse you go."

"It's a surprise," he reminds me as I grab my purse. He follows me out of my bedroom, tipping his chin at the raven charged with housesitting Beau. There's a spring in his step, and if I'm honest, in mine too, but I refuse to let him see my elation because once again, I have no idea what his plans are.

After locking the front door, I turn with Tobias at my back to head toward the limo, and he stops me, blocking me, his eyes intense.

"You locked it."

"Yeah?" I stare up in confusion.

"You locked it three times," he rasps out, emotions swirling in his eyes. "You locked it *three times*, Trésor. You didn't even realize it, did you?" He pushes me into the door and presses his forehead to mine before exhaling and looking down at me, swallowing repeatedly.

"Tobias—"

He shakes his head gently, running his nose along mine. "I'm . . . fuck, Cecelia. I asked you if you thought being happy was possible for me, but that wasn't fair, and you couldn't answer that," he says softly. "But I can. I am. You make me happy."

The emotion in his voice brings me to fast tears.

"I would get on my knees right now and ask you to marry me if I could."

Gaping at him, he grips both my hands in his. "Sometimes, I wish I could be as selfish with you now as I was before."

"What do you mean?"

"Nothing," he says softly. "But I do want to say this, and I never thought I would ever say this." He exhales a slow breath and peers down at me. "I'm glad that you loved him, and I'm glad he knew what it felt like to be loved by you before he died, and it's because of the *way you love*, Cecelia."

"Tobias—" he captures my lips and kisses me until I'm gasping, then he pulls away. "Nothing above you," he assures with brief eye contact before he grabs my hand and whisks me toward the limo while my head swims with his confessions. When the driver opens the door, Tyler steps out, a blinding smile on his face as he surveys the two of us.

"Oh my God, you've been *here* the whole time?"

"Hey, beautiful girl," he says as I leap into his open arms. "What the hell took you two so fucking long?" he asks, his chin digging into my shoulder before he releases me. "I was getting too pissed off to properly surprise you."

I nod over my shoulder. "Blame him. He's the one who took half an hour to dress."

Tobias cuts his eyes to me. "I spent *fifteen* of those minutes spelling my name with my tongue, first, middle, and last," he announces unabashedly as my cheeks heat.

Tyler shakes his head with a chuckle as I glare at Tobias. "What are you, a fifteen-year-old boy?"

"Would you two freaks get in the limo, please? We're going to be late."

Tobias ushers me in, and I hear their hushed exchange, their legs still in view.

"Guess things are going better?" Tyler muses.

"Thank God. I was this close to starting on a Dad bod and researching lawnmowers."

"I heard that," I snap, and they both pop their heads in the limo to see my narrowed eyes. I can't help my laugh at their collective "busted" expressions before they slide in. I'm thankful I'm in the seat opposite Tobias so I can admire him in the suit. Not only that, I'm graced with the sight of Tyler, who only gets better with age. His warm brown eyes are slightly jaded by a lot of living, the small crinkles around them not doing a damn thing to detract from his appeal. All of his boyish good looks are gone, sculpted features taking their place, but his dimple still peeks out when he smiles, and for that, I'm thankful. There's more wear in his muscular posture since the last time I saw him.

Seeing them together like this is jarring. Added with knowledge of who they are, where they've been, and what they've accomplished together makes it all the more fascinating.

If the world knew their story, they wouldn't believe it. I still have a hard time believing it.

"Don't be nervous," Tyler speaks up as I fidget. "Preston will love you. So will Molly. She's good people. You look beautiful, Cee."

"Well, I was about to say the same to you. You look incredible. Are you seeing anyone?"

Ignoring the flaming jealous glare my compliment and my question earns me, I keep my eyes on Tyler. He shakes his head slightly, his eyes dulling with a flash of pain. "No time right now."

He's not ready. Even after all this time. It's been years since Delphine died, and he wants no part in trying to move on yet. Sadly, I understand it, because I felt the same. He lost the only woman he considered his true love and not by choice, not due to selfishness, fear, or any other idiotic reason that keeps people apart. A long silence ensues. I share a look with Tobias, and I know we're thinking the same thing.

"You two finally realizing what idiots you've been?" Tyler chimes in. "Because I seriously fucking begrudge you both for it."

"We are," Tobias says, keeping his eyes on me.

"As long as we know who the *bigger* idiot is," I point out.

"Glad to see you two so happy," Tyler interjects. "You deserve it." He gives me a pointed look. "I was charged with checking in on you every so often. I was pissed you didn't come back raising hell a lot sooner."

"Should have told me I had a good reason to come back."

"Couldn't. I had a psycho for a boss."

"Eh? What are you going to do?" I shrug, and we share a sad smile. "But we aren't the only ones who deserve to be happy."

He winks in response, but I can feel the plea in his eyes not to press the conversation any further. I don't want a loveless life for his future, that much I do know. I hate the thought of it.

After a few minutes of chit chat, Tyler rolls up the partition and checks the clock. "We have about eighty minutes until we pull up."

"Speak freely," Tobias says, and Tyler nods.

"I can tell you pretty much everything, but I'd rather Preston explain it, so you don't have to hear it twice."

"Please don't make me wait," I ask between them, noting the fact that Tyler calls the President by his first name. The reality is, I'm on my way to meet the leader of the free world. The President that my gorgeous soulmate and lover helped put into office with a scheme they cooked up when they were teenagers. And I'm afraid I won't be paying close enough attention to details once I get there. I don't let my nerves get the best of me often, but this is a big fucking deal. Eyes roving from Tobias to Tyler and back, I can see the hesitation.

"I'm going to legitimize us," Tobias says simply.

"What?" It's the last thing I expected him to say.

"To an extent," Tyler adds.

"Meaning?"

"Meaning no more hiding from 'Big Brother' and we'll no longer be at risk for doing felony or *any other* type of time."

I dart my eyes between them. "You're serious?"

They both nod.

Tobias leans forward and takes my hand in his as I speak up. "This is your plan B, your window?"

"It has to happen, Trésor."

"But . . . this goes against *everything* you stand for. Why would you . . ." I shake my head, "Oh, no, *hell no*, you don't get to use *me* as an excuse to do this."

"I'll do whatever it takes to keep you safe."

"But this is . . . Tobias. This is *conformity*!" I shriek. "No." I snap at him before turning to Tyler with another emphatic, "*No*."

"Told you she would hate it," Tobias says, a barely perceptible smile on his lips.

"Monroe is only going to be in office for seven more years at *most*," I remind him, "and then what?"

Tobias shrugs. "Then we'll have a lot to accomplish during that time. This can't last forever."

"And what about the others, what about—"

"They'll come around, or they can kick fucking rocks," Tyler speaks up. "This isn't selling out, Cecelia. This is next level. It wouldn't be a new CIA or anything. Don't jump to conclusions. But if there's a way for us to evolve without further risk, then it's worth exploring. We *want* to change and work with a government we can trust. That's the whole point of all of this. And if it's temporary, which history guarantees it will be, we'll do what we can, while we can. If I didn't think it was a good idea, I wouldn't have put it on the table. Right now, we're in the position to write our own rules."

"I don't understand. Why *now*?" But I know the answer. I look to Tyler, widening my eyes at him, and mouth, "what the fuck?" His features remain impassive as he stares back at me.

"It will work out. Trust me."

I shake my head and turn my attention to Tobias. "Don't do this. You don't have to."

"We do have to, Trésor."

"I'm not a fucking treasure, or a delicate rose, or a shrinking violet or a damsel in distress, or a fucking mouse! I'm just as capable as either of you and as soon as I'm able, I'm going to kick both your asses!"

They burst into laughter as I cross my arms, fury rolling through me.

"Spoken like a true queen," Tobias muses.

"Please don't do this *for me*," I beg. Angry tears threaten. "Neither of you will be my fucking hero for this."

"Again," Tobias points to his chest, *"villain."*

"Yeah, such a horrible man. How much will you lose for me?"

"Everything," he says without hesitation. "But this isn't about losing."

"Please don't put this on me."

"Okay, I won't."

Hope springs inside of me.

"I'll do it for Sean. He's got another baby on the way." All my objections cease. He didn't deliver the news with the intent to hurt me, but the long look we share tells me he's afraid it might.

"Cecelia," Tyler says, taking my attention away. "I promise you. This is a good thing."

I swallow and stare at the two of them, knowing it's happening with or without my support.

"You've worked your whole lives—"

"To change the rules," Tobias states. "And we are."

I chew over his words as we ride in amicable silence before Tyler speaks up.

"You're all grown up, Cee."

I look over to him and see him staring at me with warm eyes.

"You're just . . ." He shakes his head. "When I met you, well, you were . . . it's just wild, the changes."

"I could say the same about you."

He turns to Tobias. "Are you going to put a ring on this woman or what?"

Tobias gazes on at me, completely silent, without any intention of replying. He asked me if I wanted children, and not even an hour ago said he would marry me if he were selfish, which only confused me further. Breaking our gaze, I stare out the window. "He's barely managed to get through six weeks of domesticity, Tyler," I smirk. "Let's cut him a break."

Chapter Thirty-Seven

CECELIA

BUTTONING HIS JACKET, earpiece in place, Tyler exits the limo and leads us into an underground entrance. We walk down a long, lifeless corridor and enter the elevator. Minutes later, we step into the Oval Office as the President hovers over his wife, who seems to be giving him hell from where she sits on the couch.

"—you stubborn ass."

"Baby, don't be rude—" he glances up, his politician's smile firmly in place—"we have company."

The First Lady directs her attention to us, her scowl giving way to a playful smile as she stands. The President's eyes land on Tobias a second before they rush toward the other, doing the man clap thing and holding their embrace for a few lingering seconds.

"It's been too long," the President says as they break and take a seconds-long look at each other before his eyes roll over Tobias in appraisal. "Nice suit. You look good, brother."

"And you look like shit," Tobias quips.

"Goes with the job. I'm projected to look mid-forties by the end of my first term."

His wife speaks up. "I've told you a thousand times not to pay attention to that bullshit."

The President's sparkling eyes find me, and I'm so flustered by the sight of him that I flush.

"I can see why you have taken an interest in Virginia."

Tobias turns, pride in his eyes as he reaches for me and introduces me to them both.

"Mr. President—"

"Cut the crap, King," the First Lady says.

"This is Cecelia Horner."

"So nice to meet you, sir," I say, pumping his hand, my voice shaking at the reality I'm currently in. Mere hours ago, I was in Virginia, fighting with Tobias in a closet as he ripped my panties off, licking me senseless while demanding I pick out a dress. Now I'm standing in the Oval Office.

"Call me Preston."

"And I'm Molly," his wife adds, her eyes sweeping me. "So, you're the one that got away."

"I didn't run far enough, apparently."

Her eyes light with her laugh. "I hope you're giving him hell."

"She is," Tobias chimes in.

"It's truly an honor to meet you both," I say, allowing myself the moment. Molly Monroe has been a sort of idol for me since the campaign trail. No bullshit in her delivery, both on and off camera, and she constantly rains hell on the media. She's very much "what you see is what you get" in an "in your face" way. She seems to truly care about the work she's doing, has amazing fashion sense, and doesn't seem to give two shits about outsiders' opinions.

"You'll have to excuse my outburst when you got here.

My jackass of a husband seems to think calling my bluff on quitting time is a good idea. He's under some notion that *he's* boss."

Preston looks our way, his eyes wary. "I had my pick of debutantes from every state to choose from, and I happened to pick the sassiest, most stubborn woman alive to badger me until death do us part."

"Which will be a premature death if you keep jacking your jaws," Molly tells him off without sparing him a glance, and I can't help my laugh. Tyler signals to all of us that he'll be back and gives me a wink before he shuts the door.

"I've got a helicopter ride, a little air tour of D.C. set up for us girls, while the boys talk business."

I hesitate because I don't want to be outside of the room when it happens, but this isn't a club meeting, this is the United States government, and I just have to try and trust that my boys will keep me in the loop.

"That sounds incredible," I say honestly.

"Don't steal her away just yet," Preston speaks up before taking a seat on the couch.

"You up for a mimosa?" Molly asks, lifting two flutes from a ready tray. "I know Preston woke you up early, but I've got a boring as hell day ahead, and I could use a little numbing."

"Sure," I say, glancing over to Tobias, who stares back at me like I'm the most important person in the room. I can see the clear "I love you" in his eyes and have to dart mine away when our connection gets to be too much for the situation.

"Wow, that's refreshing to see, isn't it, Pres?" Molly asks, a hint of her Boston accent sneaking through as I take the offered drink.

"Sure is, take notes," he snarks, gripping her wrist just as she lifts the flute to her lips. "Only one for you," he instructs before looking between Tobias and me. "We're doing IVF. That's why she's lost her damn mind lately. I'm pretty sure she's about to start challenging our guys to arm wrestling."

They've been open about their journey to start a family in the media, but to see them talking about it so openly has me a little awestruck. It's painfully apparent they want to become parents so badly to resemble the true definition of a First Family, and I hope with all my heart it becomes a reality.

"If I've lost my mind," she quips, "it's because I married a man capable of running a country but has zero hang time."

"*Gives*, baby, let's be careful with the verbiage, gives you zero hang time, lately," he corrects pointedly. "Let's not poke holes in my manhood today, tiger. And rest assured, I'm going to put a baby in you *tonight*," Preston fires back, his voice heating. "And five more after, so you have six replicas of me to deal with on the daily."

They share a hopeful look, and I can see some of the heartbreak in Molly's eyes when she turns to me.

"It's our fourth try. But it's going to happen this time," she whispers. "I can feel it." She snatches another mimosa off the tray and dares Preston to object. He squeezes her knee in encouragement as he kicks back and crosses one leg over the other. I can't help but take in how beautiful he is in person. The camera truly doesn't do him enough justice.

"I can't believe you two went to school together."

"Good times," Preston says. "I bet he never told you about the night he saved my life."

"That's a stretch," Tobias says.

"The hell it is," Preston retorts.

"I guess I owe you, Tobias." Molly shrugs. "Or *do I*?"

"Keep it up, woman." Preston smiles at his wife, his eyes thirsty as he rolls them over her, giving Tobias and I another peek inside their private life. Tobias grips my hand in his, and Preston clears his throat when Tyler walks in.

"Ready to do this?" Preston asks, standing.

"To hell with that, you're going to eat your breakfast first, then business."

"Molly—"

She turns to him, her stare murderous, and he bites his fist before shaking it at her. And it's then I fall for them both.

Tobias bursts into laughter across the table from Preston, and the sound of it has me pausing mid-conversation with Molly. I haven't heard him laugh like that in years, if *ever*, and I dart my gaze between the two of them, a little awestruck.

"We're lucky, aren't we?" Molly asks, sipping the orange juice she switched to after her second glass. She looks between the two of them as they talk. "We're sitting with the two most powerful men in the world, but that isn't what makes it so special. If anything, it makes it harder to love them, not to respect them, but to love them, doesn't it?"

I nod.

"But that's what makes *us* special," she continues. "This isn't just a courtship of boy meets girl. They fall in love, yadda, yadda. This is a lifelong commitment to men who aren't satisfied living ordinary lives. It sometimes seems more of an obsession than a mission. One that can test a woman to her absolute limits." She grins over at me. "But for him, for *that man*, I'll do it. I'll be there when he fucks up so badly he can't celebrate how good he is or what he's done. I'll be there whenever he doubts himself and our relationship suffers because of those doubts. I'll be there with my hair done, and my lipstick on, in my best heels, with my head held high on his darkest days, because that's what he needs. And I don't want him changing. I don't want him to stop being who he is, not ever, not for me, and not for any baby we make." She turns her gaze to me. "But I will use the tips of these heels to pierce and pin his brass balls down if he ever stops giving me what *I* need." She winks and takes another sip of her OJ, and from the sparkle in her eye, I can see it might not all be juice. Heat licks my profile, and I know he's watching me, curious about our hushed conversation.

She glances at Tobias, a soft smile on her lips before she turns and zeroes in on me. "Do you have a good set of heels, Cecelia?"

"Already wearing them," I assure her, taking a sip of my drink after we clink glasses.

Standing in The State Dining Room of the White House two hours later, I look up at Healy's portrait of Lincoln hanging over the mantel and marvel at the fact I'm here. I'm exhausted but running on adrenaline due to all that's transpired and the fact that I have the First Lady's personal cell phone number. I gaze up at Honest Abe, wondering how honest he really was and curious if he ever got his hands dirty—or had a similar monster, one remotely close to the one my man deals with. I stare on entranced until I feel *him*, a different kind of man, one far more aggressive in his approach to seek justice as he circles my waist and nuzzles me.

"How did it go?"

"Really well."

"You mean that?"

"I'm surprised at how happy I am."

"Good." I swallow. "I'll drag the details out of you soon."

"I'll give them all to you after some sleep. You'll be in on the next meeting. I made sure of it."

I nod and turn to him. "You know it's not fair," I say softly.

"What's not fair?"

"You deserve recognition for what you've done the same as any of these others. I know they've all gotten their hands dirty at one point. Maybe they had their own monsters. None of them are innocent. You deserve . . . so much more. You deserve to be recognized for what you've done, Tobias."

"I didn't do it the honest way," he says easily. "And even if their hands weren't clean, they gave the impression they were. A lot of them were good men weighed down by others. And I don't give a fuck about notoriety."

"I knew you would say that."

"Because it's true. The only opinion, the only reflection I care about, is looking right back at me. And as long as she's staring at me the way she is, I consider myself both validated and *recognized*."

"I see you. Even what you hide."

He pauses before kissing me briefly, eyeing Abe behind me. "As sexy as it may seem to christen the White House, and for a moment, Trésor, I briefly entertained it, there are far too many dead men with watchful eyes here."

I laugh and hug him to me as he whispers sweetly into my ear. "Let's go home."

"Lead the way, my King."

Chapter Thirty-Eight

TOBIAS

PARKING JUST OUTSIDE the motel, I glance around to see a few cars passing by before approaching the door. Before I can lift my hand, it opens. Oz greets me with a nod as I zero in on the asshole sitting at the table. There's an array of untouched vending machine snacks sitting in front of him. He lifts his eyes to mine, and in them I can't see a flicker of fear, but it's clear in his posture he's unsure of his fate by the way his arms are braced on the table. Taking the upholstered stained chair across from him, I put my Glock on the table and nod toward Oz and Dave before they leave the room.

"Quels sont ses projets?" *What are his plans?*

He shrugs. His posture is still rigid, but there is clear contempt in his eyes for the fact he's been holed up here for weeks, and he would probably rather die than be a prisoner in a run-down hotel.

"All right, Julien, let's cut the bullshit. You know that I know who you are. A born Frenchman who grew up in an affluent family in Côte d'Azur and graduated top of your class before doing a brief stint in the military. Shortly after, you were recruited into Antoine's ranks which, to be perfectly honest, might be my fault because I told him what to look for. You're also fluent in English, Italian, and Spanish. You had a shot at a decent future, until you joined him, up until this very moment. But I am curious as to why you played ignorant with me."

Another shrug.

"So, you hate America?" I say, placing my palms on the table.

He nods.

"What exactly is it that you hate? And please don't say our arrogance, because that's also a French trait. I should know. I'm both."

Silence.

"I'll tell you what I don't like about America—*greed*. This country was stolen and established by materialistic men. It's an illness that's plagued us for hundreds of years, giving the illusion of opportunity and freedom. And it is, but only for those who have the balls to take what doesn't fucking belong to them. For those men, it's a free for all. Have you ever heard of Al Capone?"

He dips his chin.

"One of the most notorious gangsters to ever live. The mere mention of his name could strike terror into the hearts of countless people while he reigned. Most know how he lived, but do you know how he died?"

A quick shake of his head.

"In a shit-filled diaper due to neurosyphilis. I'm sure you'll agree it's an undignified end."

His eyes widen slightly.

"It surprised me as well. I could give a hundred more

examples of assholes just like him, but none of them have good endings. Very few like him die comfortably in their sleep with peace in their hearts." I sneer down at him.

"Can you imagine what being lost in the mind of that sort of evil would be like? I don't want to. I'm not him. I just learned from his mistakes and dozens of others like him because, in the end, no one wants to be that motherfucker, do they?" I pull the return plane ticket from my pocket. He doesn't so much as glance at it.

"But America isn't the only place that greed exists. Our planet is infested with it. France is no exception. I believe there was a hundred-year war forcing young gents into disfigurement because they practiced with bow and arrows day and night to prepare themselves for a war that they were too young to fight—a hundred and sixteen years of fighting. A couple of hundred years later, another war was declared by an overly ambitious French bastard. Can you tell me his name?"

"Napoléon," he says as though he has a bad taste in his mouth.

"Another greedy man, and so on and so forth. I think you get my point. We all do what we have to do at the end of the day, don't we? Because even if I'm willing to fucking share what I earn, it won't be enough. Greed doesn't understand the concept of enough. But these unspeakable acts we take part in are all necessary because we made up our minds on what lengths we would go to the minute we decided to play this game. I can be a virtuous man all fucking day, but I couldn't have gotten to where I am if I refused to fight the residue beneath the surface. And that's *business.*"

I bend so we're eye level. "But this is my personal life you've been ordered to fuck with, and in doing what *you* had to do, you just lost your future. Rest assured, no matter what hole you skitter back to in France—the *American-made me* is fucking coming for you. At least then, you'll have a good reason to hate it. But I will grant you this, when I find you, you'll die at the hands of a fellow *Frenchman*."

Everything inside me wants to end him now, but if I do, my message won't be delivered.

At this point, I'm prepared to face Antoine's army, and I'll be damned if I let that fucking thug steal any more of my peace of mind. This charade has gone on long enough. If it's war he wants, I'll do what I have to do to win it. Even as I dread the idea, there's a side of me that hungers to get back into action.

"Tu veux mourir? Et laisse-moi être clair, si tu hausses les épaules encore une fois, tu le seras." *Do you want to die? And let me be clear, if you shrug one more time, you will.*

"Je t'ai dit tout ce que je sais." *I have told you all I know.*

This I know to be the truth. The texts are too vague for this asshole to be Antoine's most trusted.

"Tu n'es rien de plus qu'un putain de chien de garde, et tu n'es même pas bon à ça." *You are no more than a watch dog, and you're not even good at that.*

His eyes flare with anger, but he remains mute, swallowing his temper. And because I'm the bastard I am, I want more. "It's a waste of your skills if you ask me. You should have demanded more for yourself." Rolling my eyes down his frame with clear disgust, I bait him for any excuse to strike.

"Tu n'es même pas digne d'être Français." *You're not worthy to be a Frenchman.*

His answering sneer is barely perceptible, but it's all the ammo I need. Gripping my Glock, I toss the table aside and hover above him, pressing it to his forehead. To his credit, he doesn't flinch. Gripping him by the throat, I dig my fingers into his Adam's apple and bend so we're eye to eye.

"Dis-lui que le temps ici est parfait." *Tell him the weather here is perfect.* I lean in as he struggles for breath, eyes darting toward the motel door. "Et que l'eau est prête." *And the water is ready.*

Resisting the urge to crush his skull with my Glock, I storm out, lifting my chin to Oz, who's waiting outside. "Put him on the plane."

Twenty-four hours. Twenty-four hours until Tyler sends his finest—until we've got the protection of the Secret Service alongside my birds. It's just enough time. And in that time, I have to come clean about every detail, starting with my history with Antoine. I have ten of those hours until Julien gets to France, and after that, the real clock will start ticking. I have zero doubts it will be another fight with Cecelia, but I also know it won't break us to the point we can't recover. Even with that protection on its way, I'm unsure of what's coming. That alone has me hastening toward her, intent on keeping us as close as possible. Not only could my confession drive a fresh wedge between us, but the fact that I'll refuse her any personal space from here on out is going to be just as fucking nightmarish. She wants my trust, but when it comes to the unpredictable, I can't give it, and on this, I won't budge. Pulling up to the café, I don't see her Audi and frown before shooting off a text.

Where are you?

When I don't get a reply, I reason with myself as best I can as I try to ease my rapidly pounding heart.

Chill, Tobias, she probably went to make a deposit.

She usually does before she comes home, typically carrying a bank bag with a receipt in her apron. I walk into the café to see Marissa at the counter, cleavage on display as she dotes on a customer. She lifts her chin in my direction, her eyes shining in welcome, as the man sitting behind the bar does the same, a distracted smile on his face before his eyes connect with mine.

Mr. Fucking. Handsome.

"Hey, Tobias," Marissa chimes in nervously, drawing my attention from him. "She just left to make the deposit."

"Is she coming back?"

"She didn't say."

"I'll wait."

"Want some coffee?"

"I'm good."

Glancing down at my phone, I see no message from her and try not to panic. I shoot off a message to my birds, lingering in the doorway as Greg stands and pulls out some bills.

"I'll get your change," Marissa drawls out in a tone better suited for the bedroom.

"No need."

"I'll be off in a few hours," she says, and he nods. It's obvious they've got something going on. Cecelia's mentioned seeing Greg a few times back in the café and assured me he no longer had eyes for her. His new prey leans over the counter again just as I lift my gaze back to my phone before shooting off another text to Cecelia.

She's probably driving, Tobias.

Mr. Handsome leans over in my peripheral, no fucks given and suggestively whispers to Marissa, and I only manage to catch the ass end of it:—"about the company you keep."

Frowning, I lift my eyes as he drapes his coat over his arm before strolling toward the door, whistling. He stops when he reaches me, giving me a 'I've fucked her wink' and the dip of his chin. "Tobias."

Blatantly ignoring him, I look back down at my screen.

"She probably went on home," Marissa sounds up. "She usually does after she makes the deposit."

I nod. "Okay, see you later."

"See you soon," she beams, her eyes drifting back to Greg, who's making his way toward his BMW. Marissa begins to wipe the counter, and as the newest member of his fucking fan club, starts whistling his departing tune.

Irritated, my hand on the door, I freeze as an image of a hotel room in Paris shutters in before fully blaring into my headspace. I picture it so clearly, knocking over a half-empty bottle of Bombay on the nightstand as I scrambled for the remote. I was ripped from sleep by singing, only pausing when I recognized the woman belting it out as Ann-Margret, the same woman who starred in an Elvis movie that Beau used to watch when we were kids. But the reason that memory stuck with me is because of the song Ann was singing.

"Bye Bye Birdie."

Chapter Thirty-Nine

TOBIAS

BURSTING THROUGH THE glass door, I manage to catch sight of Greg just as he pulls out, his window down, his eyes fixed on me, and this time, there's a dare in them, along with the smug fucking twist of lips. "See you at home, *birdie*."

In a second flat, I have my gun trained on him, but he floors his Beamer, and I curse as I'm forced to give chase. Frantically dialing, while I turn the ignition, I get no answer as panic like I've never experienced races through me.

Ditching the phone to concentrate, I manage to catch sight of Greg's tail and downshift, gunning it to give it everything under the hood. It's when I get stuck behind an old Civic and Greg slips just out of sight that I lose it, veering off the road and honking the horn in warning before tearing through the tread to catch up with him. Scanning mentally through the routes I've taken in the past few months, I know there's no shortcut that will get me there faster. It's when he makes the few turns toward Cecelia's house that dread engulfs me fully, and I go full-on road rage. Mr. Handsome will die tonight, this much I know. No matter my fate, he will die.

And I hadn't seen it.

Has he been acting alone? And what is his connection, if any, to the French fuck I just put on a plane?

I replay the conversation we had the day we met.

"She's beautiful, isn't she?"

"Am I that obvious? I've been here every day this week."

"That so?"

He nods, before lifting his cup in salute. "Greg."

"Tobias."

"That a French accent? You sure are a long way from home."

"Fuck!" Heart pounding, hope plummeting, I do my best to catch up with Greg, but he's too far ahead—in every way that counts. I blow out Dom's engine making good time, but it's not enough. By the time he's on Cecelia's road, he's got me by six car lengths.

"Please, be okay, Trésor, goddamnit!" I lift my phone to see nothing, not a single message from any bird or her, as more fear slams into me. What I do know is that I'm driving straight into a trap, and I have no fucking choice. If they've taken her somewhere remote to deal with me, I have no fucking chance of saving her. But I could see it in Greg's eyes: he's a monster of a different breed; he's hungry, and he wants this to hurt. And he knows she's the way. "Be here, baby, please be here, God, please not again, not again!"

The sun has fully set by the time Greg speeds into her long driveway, and my stomach dips when I see the house is completely dark. The streetlight at the end of her yard isn't enough to see what's ahead or who, but mild relief covers me when I see her Audi.

Odds are she's breathing.

Please God, this one thing I'll ask of you. One thing. Nothing more.

Forgoing the driveway, which the piece of shit decides to use, I tear through her trees to make up time, shredding her yard. I slam to a stop just feet away from her door, effectively pinning him just past the entrance as his first shot hits the passenger side of the windshield. Confusion mars his features as a shallow hole appears but doesn't puncture, and I grin back at him because my brother wasn't a fucking idiot.

"Bulletproof glass, motherfucker."

I already know by the pitch black of the house and radio silence, Greg isn't working alone. Somehow, he's managed to goad my birds away or distract them at the very least. My only hope is that Tyler is watching and can see the fucking spectacle I'm making with Dom's car. And from the way Greg just baited me, it seems he wants me for himself. He hasn't slipped into the house yet for cover, which tells me a lot. And he's either a horrible shot, or he's just playing with me.

Bring it on, bitch.

Camaro idling, I open both doors and glance over the dash to see his eyes darting between them to see which route I'll exit. Instead, I press in the clutch, put the car in reverse, and floor the gas. The car whips into motion, effectively shutting the passenger door as I rotate fully, facing him to get a clear shot. He lunges over the hood as I unload a clip to get him away from the front door. I can't afford to take him out yet. I gun the gas, correcting the wheel as he scurries to the side of the house and speed toward the gate, again pinning him. He turns back and shoots on instinct, which has me chuckling until he jumps on the hood like some kind of fucking commando and begins raining bullets on the windshield, the holes he's putting in clouding my vision.

Our eyes meet just above his last shot as he reaches for a new clip from his slacks as I roll down my window. "You've got a horrible fucking tailor."

Before I can position my hand enough to get a shot off to immobilize him, he's on top of the car, his footsteps above me. With no choice, and time running short, I jump out, Glock upturned just as his tasseled loafer lands square in my jaw.

And as the black spots fade, I realize fast that someone has sent a JCPenney-dressed Jackie-fucking-Chan-reject for *me* in small town Virginia.

My mind mercifully slows then, and tunnel vision kicks in as he practically dances off the trunk while I visually weigh him up, and he does the same, his smirk still in place.

This motherfucker thinks he can take me.

I discard one of my Glocks a few feet away, and he does the same, then I toss the other. I know I made the right call when he shakes out his hands in preparation.

Just as I'm tempted to play along and give him the fucking Bruce Lee come-hither wave, he lunges for me, and I slam an elbow into his stomach, robbing him of breath. The blow lifts his body, throwing him back enough for me to land another in his gut and one below the belt that has him gasping for God.

He was expecting a valiant fight, an opener by way of a fist to dodge.

He grips his balls, his face twisted in pain as I move in.

"You went there first, motherfucker. Where is she?"

I know his type, entitled from an early age, just like the

fucking brats who made fun of my accent when I landed myself in the Triple Falls school playground—spoiled, threatened by what they don't know. The type that would rather give a verbal or physical beatdown than hold out a hand to help someone new. I've met very few of the type of man who would. Greg is the type of man Preston would have become if he didn't have a good heart and decent soul. But I guess I should be thankful for fuckers like these. Because of them and often being outnumbered, I learned quickly how to street fight—rule-free, relentless, and fucking dirty.

He regroups too quickly and lifts his chin.

"It's just you and me out here, *birdman*." He flexes his fingers, and I rush him. He manages to get another punch in before I grip him by the collar and deliver a head butt so brutal he damn near collapses on me, blood gushing from his nose as his legs give out.

With a growl of frustration, he recovers, darting his eyes to the ground for a gun he's not getting back.

"That was your only chance, bitch, and you lost it." Knowing he's about to tap into his reserves, I rain down my fists in his face. The more time I deal with this fucking piece of shit, the more time I lose getting to her. His uppercut narrowly misses me, and that's when I go feral, letting my rage take over temporarily until he gasps and gurgles beneath me. I have to force myself to stop, still unsure of what or who waits inside.

The piece of shit sputtering beneath me is my only chance of knowing what I'm up against. Scanning the yard for the birds who should have already fucking been here, a genuine fear sets in.

Where the fuck are they? Backup should be here by now.

There's not a single sign of anyone, not even the drones. Wracking my brain, I know I'm fucked because I left my cell in the car. I have no way of getting word out or knowing who's coming and when.

Greg whimpers beneath me as I tuck his gun in the back of my jeans beneath my hoodie and retrieve my Glocks.

He begins to fade out as I glare down at him. "No, no." I slap at his face, and when he doesn't rouse, I press my finger into his destroyed nose. A shriek of pain leaves him as he comes to, groaning in agony as I drag him toward the rain drain where I have another gun and some extra clips. I stash them where I can fit them in both my jeans and hoodie.

"Who's inside, Greg?"

Greg coughs and sputters beneath me as I press into his nose again, digging around the busted cartilage through the massive gash with my thumb. He screams, and I cover his mouth, knowing those inside heard it.

"I'm only going to ask one more time, dickhead."

An outraged noise comes from his throat, something that sounds close to a laugh, just before I feel the metal in the back of my head.

Fuck.

In seconds, I'm gripped by two shadows after my Glocks are stripped from my hands, and we're both lifted from the ground and ushered inside. The silence once we get through the front door has my heart clanging against my ribs. If she's gone already, I can't feel it. She has to be here.

Not knowing is killing me, and I resist the urge to call out to her to show the extent of what she means to me, to hide the fear in my voice. It's when the hairs on the back of my neck begin to lift that I know, I just fucking know, I've been bested.

It's confirmed a second later when Antoine's voice sounds from the living room.

"How long are you going to make me wait, Ezekiel?"

Chapter Forty

TOBIAS

EYEING THE TWO shadows just inside the entryway as I am hauled in, I spot a few more in the kitchen before I'm released at the doorway of the living room. My eyes immediately land on Cecelia, who's standing on the opposite side just outside her bedroom. She is dressed in her pajamas, her hair still wet from a recent shower, her Beretta in hand. A dead man lays just feet from her—and from the looks of it—died by her hand.

"She was quite insistent on keeping her gun," Antoine muses from where he sits opposite her in the high back chair next to the roaring fire—the only light in the room. Antoine sits relaxed in the chair as if Cecelia doesn't at all pose a threat with her gun, and from the looks of our situation, she doesn't, because standing on either side of him are two familiar, armed men.

Palo and Julien.

Are David and Oz dead? Did they even make it to the airport?

I move to stand next to Cecelia to get a clear view of the three of them and meet Palo's steady gaze; he gives me absolutely nothing. I can only conclude he's again switched allegiances. If I had any hope at all, it was that I still had his. Then again, I haven't heard a fucking word from him in weeks, which is indicative enough of where we stand.

The problem with buying men is that they can be bought.

They've allowed Cecelia to keep her fucking gun because they find it laughable. I study Cecelia, and her expression remains stoic as her eyes trail over me with relief and mine do the same.

She's breathing. She's unharmed and armed. It's more than I could have asked for, and yet we're still fucked.

Too soon. It's too soon for us to be over. We didn't have enough time. We've been robbed of it from the start. The reality of that rakes at my chest as I begin to mourn the loss of us and mouth, "I'm sorry."

She subtly shakes her head as I turn to face off with Antoine.

Where the fuck are my birds?

This can't happen again. This can't fucking happen again.

I glare at Antoine, who's impeccably dressed, his frame frailer than the last time I saw him due to his age. Greg joins his side, a towel full of blood in one hand as he retrieves a vial from his pocket with the other and thumbs the cap off.

Coke.

Which explains a lot. The man can't fight for shit, but the drug made him a believer. I grin at the fact that I've ruined his tool for consumption, and he glares at me as he tosses it to the back of his throat.

"I told you," Antoine says, giving Greg a side-eye, "that you were running a fool's errand."

"He's fucking here, isn't he?" Greg snaps, his eyes

drifting between me and Cecelia, whose gaze is zeroed in on him.

"Jerry's estranged stepson," Cecelia clarifies for me, loud enough for the room to hear. "He's here for *me* because *I* cost him his inheritance. *Oops.*"

I glance over at her, fury coiling through me; she caught it, and I missed it due to jealousy. But by putting a bullet in Roman's old business partner before I got here, I set off this chain of events and helped put this into motion. In my haste to get back to her, I left a loose end.

One too many, it seems.

Greg chimes in. "I suppose I should thank you for putting a bullet in the fat fucking pig's head," he says to me before turning his eyes on Cecelia. "Or should I thank *you* now that my mother lives in a mental hospital? And the cherry on top? I'm now power of attorney over a *bankrupt* empire." He bites his lip, his eyes on Cecelia, his intent clear. "We could have had some fun, you and me, and we were going to until your fucking thug boyfriend showed up and told me your little love story. Thankfully for me, stepdaddy dearest wasn't at all concerned about his trail. Once I found his contacts, and Antoine and I had a little chat . . . it made it a lot easier to put the pieces together." He takes a menacing step forward, and so does Cecelia, hand steady as she keeps her gun trained on him.

Greg scoffs. "You going to shoot me, sweetheart?"

"Yes," Cecelia replies without hesitation.

"And then what?" Greg looks around the room, knowing he's got us.

Cecelia shrugs, her intent clear as she inches forward, her hand steady.

There are guns aimed at us from every adjoining room, except her bedroom, which is where it appears she came out, gun blazing.

One fucking day, we needed one fucking day for our protection to kick in.

Think, Tobias.

"Cecelia," I warn, and she doesn't so much as glance my way.

With the lift of Antoine's hand, Greg steps back, but Cecelia remains where she is, and I join her.

"Common enemies, Tobias, you advised me on that," Antoine jeers. "Between you both, I would say you're gathering quite the list . . . well, that is until you started ticking them off before you got here—"

Cecelia cuts him off. "Some random asshole with a pretty face shows up to my café out of *nowhere* four days in a row and takes an interest specifically in me? It was *amateur*." She clicks her tongue at Greg. "I was onto you day two, and certain by day *four*," she says, projecting her voice to me, "gotta love Ryan."

"You called fucking Ryan and didn't tell *me*?" I grit out.

"He's my partner in crime, good at finding out who the leeches are, and you and I have had quite the failure to communicate on this front, haven't we? But don't worry, your old business partner has introduced himself."

"You hid her well, Tobias." Antoine's eyes rake over Cecelia, who stands stoic beside me, alert and ready, before she returns her gaze to Greg, a defiant lift to her chin. Antoine's eyes drift back to me.

"Let's save each other some time by stating the obvious. You were expecting me."

"At some point, but I was hoping you would spare me the headache. However, I knew you would come when you found the right leverage."

"My leverage is beautiful." He sickeningly assesses Cecelia, and it's all I can do to keep from lunging at him.

"She was never a part of our arrangement."

"Ahh, that's where you're wrong. My body may be turning against me, but my mind has not, Tobias. I remember our conversation well. You broke our agreement a long time ago, and my trust."

"Our business has been over for some time. You aren't here because of broken trust."

"No? Then do enlighten me. Why am I here?"

"Because you're close to your expiration date. Because you have nothing left to live for now, other than your bitter grudges, and you're inventing them at this point."

His eyes flash with fury as Cecelia bristles next to me, her hostile eyes on Greg, who only smirks.

"I'm disappointed in you, Antoine . . . after all I've done—" I look toward the men standing behind him—"*this* is the best you've got?"

"You shouldn't be so smug. It was far too easy to get through your front door and Cecelia's been such a good hostess—well, aside from those first few minutes." He glances down at the dead man at her feet. "For you to go to such lengths to keep her from me all this time tells me all I need to know." He clicks his tongue. "The daughter of your sworn enemy. You went against everything you believed."

"Worth it," I swallow. "And you can end me right now. You can end me right now by taking her away. I'm not denying it."

"A punishment that seems fitting of the crime."

"What crime? You've always been so fucking delusional, and that's why you never got my allegiance. I've broken no arrangement. I owe no debt to you. Why is *she* such an insult to you?"

"Because my nephew and men died while you indulged in her all those years ago. I had wondered what kept you. Now it makes sense."

"A nephew and men you cared nothing about. I've never crossed you. You've lived a long life, and your safety was never my priority. But here you are, alive and breathing because of *me*. That should tell you enough."

"You're so quick to point out how you educated me and my men, yet you let your dick make your decisions, which is *fucking pathetic*, according to you."

"And what would I have to live for if I would have taken my own advice? I realized the error of my ways. And my number one goal was never to become a clone of you. No one to remember me. No one to take over my legacy. No reason to fucking live other than for the game, and later, to exist alone only to reflect on my evil deeds. I chose a different way. You take this from me, and then what? Who will you go after? Is this what you truly want?"

"Don't insult me with your bleeding heart, Tobias. You know I can't be persuaded."

"Do you want me to beg for her? Because I'm not above it."

"Tobias, don't," Cecelia whispers softly, as Greg's lips curl into a fucking feline smile.

I pull Greg's gun from the back of my jeans—a gun they didn't bother to check for after securing my Glocks—and know that there are at least six others trained on us. Four in the kitchen, and the two I passed in the entryway. Even if we get a few shots off, we're going to lose this fight. Rage thrums through me at the idea that this is how it all ends. I've been bested by a man I detest, an unworthy man, and he's about to take the one thing I can't live without.

"For her, I'll give you every cent I've earned. I'll hand it all over. Take my money, take my life, but let her go."

He scoffs, "There's that nobility. I'm afraid it's going to cost you a lot more this time."

I keep my ready insult to myself, hoping that at least I can somehow negotiate her to safety. If I can just get her away from this house, there's a chance she can make it to my birds, but I see no option, no chance of that.

Antoine has always been merciless when doling out his punishments, and that's one thing he'll always have over me.

Hope disappears as resolution covers me. I've got nothing, absolutely fucking nothing. There's no scenario here where one or both of us doesn't die.

"If you take her, my wrath would be welcome, wouldn't it? One last thrill, old man, before you go?" I lift the Glock to my temple and Cecelia gasps my name. "I won't let you have the fucking satisfaction, and if you even so much as look at her again, I die, and you won't get what you came for. Care to fucking test me?"

His eyes light up with surprise. This was always going to happen. Always. No matter how much space I put between my past and present, Antoine was always the thread between them.

I became useless to him—to the game—when I gave in to my own needs for the first time in my life—when I stole those months with her. I knew then I'd lost the upper hand over any enemy past, present, or future.

I've always been right about emotional entanglements being a downfall. Just this once, I wish I was wrong.

For Antoine, it's jealousy and greed that brought him here along with the tasteless state of his life now.

At one time, I saw his present as my own future. The future I agreed upon when I started all of this, one I accepted for myself more than once, until she came back into my life and reminded me that I had a choice. I sacrificed our happiness over and over to ensure this confrontation would never come to pass. But she and I have always been ill-fated, star-crossed in every imaginable way. In the end, I chose her, instead of suffering the wait without her. Emotion threatens and I swallow it back, my rage boiling over as I press the gun into my temple as Antoine keeps his gaze on mine.

"Just let her go."

Antoine scoffs. "So fucking scripted. Who's pathetic, Ezekiel?"

I saw Cecelia's future as well, as she pleaded for me to love her back those long months ago, as she begged me to see what we could still be, all the while imagining what her life looked like through Delphine's bloodshot eyes. By sacrificing our hearts, neither of our lives would be worth living. Mine as an emotionless and hollow man, and hers as a loveless woman. And even through it all, I know I felt it and she would say it now if given the chance: worth it.

Gun to my head, I stare off with Antoine in a dare. It's me he wants, and I know despite his threat, I'm the real bargaining chip. I have to believe that he'll attempt to talk me out of taking his prize away and spare her. It's my only move.

"It was worth it, Trésor. So worth it," I say, squeezing the trigger just enough to have Antoine gripping the sides of the wingback, his eyes fixed on me. He's starting to believe me.

"Fireflies," Cecelia says softly, and I turn my attention toward her.

"That's our outside force, Tobias. They were the ones that looked out for us." Her eyes water as she studies the gun pressed to my head. "Wouldn't you agree?"

I nod, my own eyes stinging as I weigh her words.

"We were never alone, Tobias," she murmurs softly, her tone curling around my heart. I can see the resolution in her own eyes as we step to the edge of the cliff we'd thrust ourselves upon. Even now, while on the precipice, I can feel the conviction of that truth between us. Worth it.

"Heavy is the head, my love," she murmurs as if we're alone, "just this once, let me save you the burden."

She turns her gaze back to Mr. Handsome and I do the same to see red lasers beaming through every window of the house just as I realize her intent.

"Cecelia, no!" I lunge for her just as she pulls the trigger.

Chapter Forty-One

Cecelia

Tobias has me pinned to the floor behind the couch as countless pings shatter the glass and both doors burst open. In seconds, the house is filled with blurred movements as Tobias curses in a mix of English and French, his eyes and hands searching me frantically for injuries.

"Trésor," he croaks, his hands coming up empty as he palms every inch of me. Glancing over, I see Antoine deathly still—in the wingback chair I plan on burning—multiple lasers covering him from head to chest. Lights go up in the kitchen and surrounding rooms as Antoine's men—those left standing—are secured and pulled to their feet, their fearful eyes darting around. Mr. Handsome lays dead just a few feet away, his eyes wide and lifeless. Shifting, I look up at Tobias and cup his face as he continues to murmur to me, his face panic-stricken as his palms roam up and down my body.

The fear and confusion in his expression have my heart aching and my love multiplying past the point of love—or whatever word represents what I feel for him—something that transcends it, something indescribable, something there will never be ample words for. When he sees I'm unharmed, his posture goes rigid as his gaze flits to Palo and Julien.

"What the fuck are these two not doing in cuffs?" he yells at the men securing the few left in the kitchen. I grip his face from where I lay on the floor beneath him.

"It's already over, my love," I inform him, as he briefly lowers his gaze to me and regrips his Glock. Intent on getting through to him, I cup his face in both hands as he struggles in my grip.

"Tobias, look at *me*," I command in a tone that has his eyes moving slowly back to focus, "*it's over.*"

Lips parting, he gazes down at me, the truth of it not quite getting through. "I love you, Ezekiel Tobias King, so fucking much," I murmur, "even if you force me to prove myself to you time and time again. I told you I wouldn't fucking hesitate, and I meant it." His brows crease into a deep V. "You *made me* a *Raven*. You *gave me* my wings, so I took it upon myself to use them."

"What?"

I call out to the man standing next to Palo. "Julien, s'il te plait," *Julien, please*. Julien comes forward, kneeling so he's eye level with Tobias before discarding his Glock on the carpet. Tobias bristles atop of me until Julien unbuttons his shirt and slowly rolls it up to reveal fresh ink.

Tobias's jaw goes completely slack as he faces off with one of his own and realizes the implications of the hell he put him through.

"He got it last night," I say with a grin. "It's the least I could do after the brain damage you nearly cost him. Julien has been a raven for almost six years."

Antoine curses and shoots a death glare at Julien, whose

lips twitch with a smile. Palo remains silent, but I can see the amusement dancing in his eyes. Tobias studies both of them for long seconds and then shifts his gaze back to me.

"Thank you, Julien," I dismiss him, and with a nod, he retrieves his gun and moves back into place. Tobias goes to speak, but I press my fingers to his lips. "But the fact that you *challenge* me is probably one of the reasons I love you most. Knowing you, loving you, and understanding you helped shape me into the woman I am."

He swallows, my sentiments hitting him as he examines each word carefully.

"A few weeks in," I explain. "I knew something with you wasn't right. And I couldn't figure out what it was. I already had Greg on my radar and thanks to my old partner Ryan, he checked him out, and we concluded his game was weak. Let's face it, Greg never had a fucking chance." I lower my voice to a whisper. "But I had to find out what or who had *you* so on guard. I had to know what unspoken threat was bothering you, a threat you *repeatedly* refused to tell me about, even after you promised you would. I was so furious with you at one point because I knew you'd fallen into old habits again, keeping me in the dark, so I called Sean."

"*Sean* is in on this?"

"He had his suspicions, but we sent Julien in to make sure he was right."

His eyes widen. "You . . . baited me?"

I keep my voice low as the commotion sounds around us. "Yes. Antoine was never aware of me. Never. You covered your tracks, *our* tracks, perfectly. He would have never discovered us. But I didn't care if Antoine was a threat at that point. I wanted him gone regardless because of the state you were in. So, when I found out about Greg, I *fed* him bits and pieces to lead him to Antoine. But Antoine came at *my* invitation. I brought the fight here."

He gapes down at me. "You fucking *what*?"

"To kill two birds, no pun intended." I tilt my head as it sinks in. "This was inevitable. I just sped up the process, *my way*."

"You lured him here?" he rasps out, his features twisting in fury.

"I did. And you damn near put a kink in my plans by legitimizing us with condition of protection from the Secret Service. I *really wanted* this to be an *in-house* job to show you the strength of your own club, but, luckily, I knew a guy. We worked our way around it."

"You knew this whole fucking time?" Realization takes over as his flaming eyes narrow on me. "*This* is why you nearly castrated me the day your mother came . . . you found out I was keeping secrets. It was the day after . . ." he turns to Julien and then back to me.

I nod. "I got so angry when you didn't tell me about your run-in with Julien, who was reporting to *me the whole time*— by the way, nice photos—and when you didn't come clean, I was furious. So I used your past secrets and our issues as an excuse to yell at you for it. That anger wasn't fake. And the longer you didn't tell me, the angrier I got. Because . . ."

"I promised no more secrets," he finishes, hanging his head briefly, his eyes filled with apology when he lifts them. "Cecelia—"

"Shut up, King. And try to keep up," I scold as I run my hand along his jaw. "My next step was all about picking the size of the spoon."

"The spoon?" I stroke his face with my palm and lift to press a brief kiss to his lips before I look him right in the eye. "To get that medicine down. *Checkmate,* my love."

Complete and utter disbelief. The look on his face is priceless, making this moment one hundred percent worth the effort.

"So, Palo?"

"Not dead," he replies from where he stands feet away, and I can't help my giggle.

"Clearly," Tobias snaps, turning his head to look up at him catching his smirk.

"Sean can be convincing." He shrugs, his lips lifting briefly.

Tobias narrows his eyes at Palo. "What's in it for you?"

"A wife. *Antoine's* wife, to be exact," I answer for him. Antoine's face turns beet red due to the evident restraint from the guns trained on him.

The house starts to go quiet as the rest of Antoine's men are taken away, zip ties securing their wrists as they struggle, cursing in French and promising retribution. Tobias looks down at me, his old world tilted on its axis as his new world comes into focus.

"You're exhausting. You know that? Between the secret meetings I held with David, Oz, and Julien, working with Sean and Tyler to get Greg to lure Antoine here, and persuading the rest of the boys to jump on board so they wouldn't face your wrath, I've barely had a moment's rest to make sure you got your *vacation.*"

"Tyler, Russell, they all *knew*?"

"We all agreed it was the only way you would ever fully trust me."

"*All* of this was a setup?"

"Aside from Greg, every bit. We even anticipated you dismissing the two birds that day Julien purposefully drew you in and played incompetent. Tyler had backup birds ready. He knew you wouldn't let a fuck-up like that slide."

"How did you know about Antoine?"

"Ask Sean."

He shakes his head in retrospect. "*This* is why you went to work every fucking day?"

"I had a big job to do. My part was to distract you by playing wounded, pissed-off, jaded ex-girlfriend, which honestly was no big stretch. I thought you might be onto me a couple of times, especially that day you stormed into the café after deciding to play Rambo. The café was the only place I could keep in regular contact with the boys without you catching on. For the first time ever, *I* was in on it, and *you weren't.* My *blueprint, my plan.*" I can't help my pride-filled smile. "Now swallow that medicine, King, and let it settle in."

After a few lingering moments, he rests his forearms on the floor and lifts my head, cradling it with both hands. "My God, woman . . ." he shakes his head, nothing but awe in his expression. "That was *brilliant.*"

"I learned from the best. But like I told you, you forgot who you came back to. I know who I *am,* Tobias, and it's time you remember who *you* are—a man who built a worthy army but fought too many battles alone. We have *you.* Have had you," I say softly. "It's time you trust *me* . . . trust us."

My words strike where intended as realization sets in. "You're a protector, my King. It's who you are, who you were born to be, and I can't seem to stay mad at you for it. But I am a protector too, my love, and it's time you see that."

He buries his face in my neck, tension leaving his shoulders as his chest begins to pump, and I realize it's laughter.

"You aren't angry?" I ask.

He lifts his head, a beaming smile on his face. "I'm fucking *furious*."

"Ezekiel?" Antoine rasps from where he sits on the other side of the living room, his tone filled with desperation.

Tobias doesn't even spare him a glance as he brushes lazy thumbs along my cheeks before another smile overtakes him. "That was one fucking hellacious speed session of couple's therapy you just put me through."

"And totally necessary," I murmur, "no regrets."

Amber eyes bore into mine, and I can see the sincerity in his love-soaked expression. "I will never, *ever* keep you in the dark about anything, *ever* again."

I snort and roll my eyes. "I've heard that before."

He winces. "I just . . . wanted—"

"I know why you did it. And you're still wrong in doing so. It's going to take a lot to train you on the boyfriend front."

"Never again, never again," he assures me.

"Uh huh—" I purse my lips—"until the next time."

His lips quirk up. "What am I going to have to do to convince you?"

"A lot. It's a good thing I have the patience you so clearly lack." Adrenaline rushes through my veins as I stroke the curves of his biceps, and oddly . . . I'm turned on in a way I can't describe. He reads my expression, lips lifting further as he continues to stroke my jaw with fiery promise in his eyes.

"We'll get to *that* as soon as fucking possible."

Just as he speaks, our names are called from the front door.

Oil-stained yellow boots and faded denim appear in our peripheral before Sean squats down next to us. "Are you two fucking serious right now?"

"*Very*," Tobias quips before we both shift our attention to Sean, whose complexion is blistering red as he scratches his golden mane with the hand holding his Glock. "Someone mind telling me what the fuck is going on here with the Secret Service?"

"Tyler didn't update you?" I ask, eyes bulging.

"No, and I damn near had a fucking heart attack when they stopped me before they identified themselves. I thought I wouldn't be able to get here in time. Since when are we in bed with the government?"

"Since about ten minutes ago," Tyler chimes in as he strolls into the room, appearing out of thin air.

"How long have you been here?" Tobias grunts, standing and pulling me to his side from the floor.

"Long before the *fireflies*, and just in time to see you take your medicine." He winks at me, and I can't help my victorious smile. Tyler ushers the four of us into my bedroom and closes the door before turning to Sean. "Sorry, bro, but this was *my* part to play. And since this has been my mission for fucking years, I thought it should be *me* who gets to pop the champagne."

Sean looks ready to pummel him. "Maybe a little heads-up not to shoot at the Secret fucking Service next time?"

"Test run, won't happen again," he assures. "Good thing you're a terrible shot."

"Fuck you, and I could do without the prison time with a wife and three kids."

"You'll never see the inside of a cell," Tyler assures, clapping a hand on his shoulder. Sean's eyes immediately widen and then shift to Tobias, who slowly nods.

"What did you do?" He glares between them and reads their expressions. "Tobias—"

"Amnesty, for all of us, for you, and for your son," Tyler announces proudly. "If Dom ever decides to ink up." Sean's eyes drop, and I know he's trying to rein in his emotions, but they get the best of him as he lifts his eyes to Tobias, and they share a lingering look.

"See, worth the wait," Tyler whispers to Tobias with the subtle lift of his lips, "just to see the expression on his face."

"Fuck," Sean exhales harshly, running a palm down his jaw. Physically, I can see the tension leave him. It's obviously something that's been plaguing him for years as a family man, something he's prepared himself for if it ever happened, and now something he'll never have to worry about again. His hazel eyes drift back to Tobias, and Tyler speaks up. "We'll talk about the details later."

Sean nods, his eyes never leaving Tobias as he bobs his head several times.

"So, what now?" I ask, turning back to Tobias.

Tobias shrugs, a slight lift to his lips. "Don't ask me. I'm not in charge."

Tyler grins. "How does it feel?"

Tobias smiles back. "Fucking terrifying—" he pulls me tighter to him and entwines our fingers—"but I'll . . . *adjust*."

Sean looks over to me, his eyes shining with pride. "You did good, Pup."

I nearly wince at the slip of his pet name for me and glance over at Tobias, who squeezes my fingers tightly between his.

During all of this, Sean and I have been in close contact because it was necessary, but during that time, we managed to strike up a different kind of relationship, a friendship close to the one we had years ago. The ease in which it happened surprised us both. It was *how* the friendship came about that I was uncomfortable with. Not because of any lingering feelings I have for Sean, but because of how it might affect Tobias. Tobias remains mute, his expression imperceptible as I look back at Sean. "Couldn't have done it without you."

"Yeah, well, it wasn't easy—" he smirks and nods toward Tobias—"I had to keep him distracted with heart-to-hearts a few times a week. He's a whiner, by the way; you might want to see about that."

Tobias scowls, a low growl sounding from his throat as we all share a laugh. I palm his chest. "I'll see what I can do."

Sean looks over to Tobias and I can feel the shift in the air between them as if they're really seeing each other for the first time in years. Sean's eyes rake over us together, and he nods, his eyes shining with acceptance. "But it looks like things are good now."

Without waiting for a response, he shifts his attention to Tyler. "Good to see you, man." He pulls him in for a half hug. They clap each other's backs and pull away.

"We need to catch up," Tyler agrees, and Sean nods.

"No time like the present. I could use a fucking beer."

I clear my throat as they all start talking at once, completely ignoring the fact that there's a French gangster in my living room. "Guys," I say as they rattle on. "Guys," I repeat, stepping between the three of them before nodding toward the door.

The three of us walk out as Sean approaches Antoine, looking down at him from the bridge of his nose. "What's next is—" he gives Antoine a maniacal grin—"I take out the *trash*."

Tyler moves to step in front of the window, and with the flick of his wrist the lasers disappear from Antoine's face and chest.

Sean bends so he's almost nose to nose with Antoine, clear violence in his posture. "Hope you ate well tonight, mother-fucker, because that was your *last supper*."

Antoine turns from Sean and addresses Tobias. "I have several associates who won't at all be pleased with you if I disappear."

"I wouldn't be so confident," Sean says, drawing his attention back, "they sold you out, and you came fucking *cheap*."

Antoine visibly pales as Sean reveals the ace up his sleeve. "Money talks, dickhead, and we used *yours* to pay them. Wrestle with that shit a minute and we'll be right back with you." Sean smacks Antoine's temple with his Glock for emphasis.

Antoine shifts black eyes to Tobias, who stares back at him, hellfire brimming in his eyes, but he remains mute. Sean nods to the kitchen as Tyler gets briefed by one of the men in charge, and Sean addresses the two of us.

"We've already eliminated his plan B, and if there's a C, we'll figure it out and handle it, but Palo hasn't left his side in weeks, and I doubt there is one." Sean looks to Tobias. "We're giving Palo a set of keys, but he's agreed to get wings and wing his men, so it's ours to *share*."

Tobias only nods, seeming introspective as Sean speaks up again. "We'll have a lot to work out down the line, and we will, but since we're now covered by the government, why don't you both take a little trip while I clean this mess up?"

Tobias turns to me with zero objection, and I can still see he's trying to work it all out. "Any ideas?" He narrows his eyes when I upturn my lips. "I've got just the place in mind."

Chapter Forty-Two

TOBIAS

Tossing the last of our suitcases in the idling Audi, I eye Cecelia, who's talking to Ryan on a burner phone while taking Beau for a walk before we head out on the road.

Fucking Ryan. Her source on all things Greg. She caught onto him before I even landed in Virginia.

I'm still so fucking blown away by what just transpired—shocked mostly, along with a thousand other emotions I'm having to constantly battle to keep my shit together. What she's done, what she managed to do while under my careful watch, is incomprehensible to me. And even though I'm filled with pride, I'm still fucking battling the urge to spank her or fuck her, or both. *Definitely* at the same time. Problem is, she likes the punishment too much.

But mostly, I'm just in awe of her, of her strength, her ability, and the woman she's become—fierce, brave, brilliant, powerful, and fearless.

I can't help the dopey smile on my face as I watch her scold her dog briefly like it's an everyday walk as she chats on the phone like she didn't just save both our fucking lives, and ensure our future while lifting a thousand-pound burden from my shoulders and preventing a war.

I've just been schooled by my queen.

Un-fucking-believable.

And she played me on an expert level.

Sean joins me where I stand at the trunk, my eyes fixed on the woman who retrieved my heart, healed my soul, and saved my life a thousand times over.

I can feel Sean's watchful gaze on me before he speaks up. "All set."

I nod. "Let me get her in the car."

An uncomfortable silence passes between us as I try to work my brain around the fact that Sean's here and the why of it. That he, himself, went through great lengths to prove a similar point to me.

"It's going to take you weeks to piece it together," he says, reading my thoughts.

I cross my arms. "I think she'll gloat way too much to give me a chance to work it all out for myself."

"I say she's earned the right." He turns in her direction, and she glances back at the two of us, her eyes darting nervously between us as Sean speaks up again.

"Think there will ever come a time when things aren't so fucking weird between the three of us?"

"I don't know," I say honestly.

"Or that you don't feel ill at ease when I look at her?"

I stare at his profile as he crosses his arms and leans against the trunk, his gaze still on Cecelia.

"I'm in love with my wife, Tobias." He turns to me, his expression genuine. "I'm convinced by my own experience that it's possible to love more than once in a lifetime. And honestly, I never thought I would see her again after she left Triple."

"Neither did I."

"What made you go after her, finally?"

"Because maybe you are capable, but I'm not. There's no one else for me but her. Never before, never after."

"I get that." Another bout of silence. "She's more than ready."

"She is, but I'm leaving the *when* up to her. I don't know how long it's going to be until then, and I really don't give a fuck. It's her call, *indefinitely*."

He nods, and I glance over at her, still on edge from how close things got mere minutes ago. No matter how well it worked out, I'll never truly be comfortable with her in harm's way.

"Dom told you about Antoine," I say, turning to face him.

"A long, long fucking time ago. Still looking out for you, even from the grave." He shakes his head. "Only Dom."

The truth of that sets in.

"It's the one good thing that came from our time in France."

I don't bother to hide my surprise.

"Yeah, man, of course we looked into him while we were there. We've had your back the whole time. Always. And would have had it well before that, had you not been so fucking tight-lipped about him. When you sent us away, we tracked him down from the information Dom had gathered over the years. Together, we learned the entirety of his operation, in and fucking out, and it wasn't hard to figure out you taught them everything you knew."

"*Almost* everything."

He nods. "Keep them confused, right? We worked out early on, through a faint text trail, that you already had Palo in your pocket, but we wanted backup, so we sent a few of our unmarked guys into his ranks over time. We have a lot more birds in his army than you can imagine. Question is, why didn't you do it?"

"I didn't want men capable of doing Antoine's dirty work working for me. They're a different breed. But I see now it was a mistake and a necessary evil. And I've made mistakes, Sean. Lots of them."

"I wish you would have asked for help."

"I didn't want you to know. He's—"

"He was only a worthy adversary because you made him one."

"I regret it every day."

"You don't have to anymore. We own him," he says, fishing a cigarette out of his jeans before striking his Zippo. He clicks it closed with the flick of his wrist before exhaling a steady stream of smoke. Another long silence ensues, and I turn his way to see him staring at me intently. "The worst day of our lives was the day we broke your heart."

The words strike deep and take away my ability to speak as we face off, eye to eye, for the first time since the night that tore us apart.

"If you thought we left willingly, that we would leave *her* willingly for the cause, you were fucking wrong. Of course, we cared, and we didn't want to lose it, but we left—" he exhales another drag as my chest tightens unbearably—"we left willingly and gave her up temporarily because of the sacrifices *you made for us*, Tobias. For the years you spent doing everything for us, risking your life, *for us*, because that's the type of man you taught us to be." His voice shakes as he speaks, his eyes darting down at the gravel between us. "And we started missing your love and loyalty the minute we lost it." He exhales a plume of smoke and lifts watery eyes back to mine. "The second worst day of our lives was the day you broke *our hearts*—" he clears his throat and cups the back of his neck as the burn in my own throat intensifies. "Motherfucker." He shakes his head as my heart cracks dead center, and I feel the years of separation between us, the longing I felt to get us back with no idea of how.

"But that very same day you broke our hearts, you showed us what true love looks like, and you gained it by sacrificing everything, *including us*, and our cause, for *her*." He glances toward Cecelia and then back to me. "Something we both failed to do. And in turn, you *earned* her, and you do deserve her for it." He swallows audibly. "When you tried to defend yourself, we knew you were right, but we were cut so deep we didn't want to fucking hear it. Because losing her completely was a good enough reason to resent you, and our hands weren't as dirty if you were equally as guilty."

He blows out a harsh breath. "But we knew you were right, and I think, deep down, we both knew we were on borrowed time with her. And fuck, how I hated you for it." He exhales again, his shoulders rolling forward. "Dom realized it that night because he caught on a lot faster like he always did. He understood. I didn't fucking want to. But he always saw things clearly for what they were, even if it hurt. It took me a lot longer to sort it out. And Tessa, that woman, she went through hell showing me where I went wrong, but you deserve to know you've had my forgiveness for a lot longer than you think."

I stand on the verge of eruption, the burn in my throat far too much as my eyes begin to sting.

"But the truth is now . . ." Sean admits hoarsely, his teary eyes lifting to mine, "I just want my fucking brother back."

In a flash, I cup the back of his neck and press our foreheads together.

A pained gasp leaves us both as he grips my shoulders, the pressure unbearable until I release it, my emotions taking over as I swallow continually and try to speak. Sean grips my shoulders as we stand there for endless seconds.

"Always brothers," I whisper through a shaky breath as we clutch each other tightly, mending the bridge that's separated us for years. Several seconds pass as we collectively choke on our emotions.

"We all got too fucking good at keeping secrets, even from each other," I admit tightly. "I'm sorry, brother."

He shakes his head, and we separate, wiping years of pain away.

"We all made horrible mistakes, Tobias, but just look at where we are *now*, and it's largely because of *you*. Take some fucking credit and let those mistakes fall to the wayside. It's time to forgive yourself." He sighs, running a hand over his face, his eyes shimmering again, his voice a plea, "But you've got to let him go. He wouldn't want you condemning yourself like this. We all deserve to see how the rest of this plays out, especially you. You've got to let him go, man."

I can barely manage my reply. "I'm trying."

"Try *harder*." He grips my shoulder and squeezes as I nod several times. "We need you."

When he releases me, I glance over to see Cecelia frozen in the middle of the yard, staring at the two of us. I lift my chin to her to let her know we're good, and she starts to make her way toward us.

A minute passes, maybe more, and Sean lights up another cigarette and passes it to me. I take a deep inhale, feeling lighter than I have in almost a decade.

"He never gave me a reason to suspect him, but it all makes sense now. It was so fucking obvious, Sean. So fucking obvious. I got a confession from Jerry that he sent Miami before I put a bullet in him but never asked for his *source*. I was so anxious to get back to Cecelia I didn't press any further. I never thought Antoine was equipped enough. He played me well, distracting me with his own drama, but the truth is, who the fuck else would've known about a loyalty dispute in our club? Who would dig so far to find out?" Fury buds in my veins at the idea that the man who tossed the grenade—who set the events of years of hell I've been through into motion—almost got away with it.

"There are no coincidences, not in this game, we all know that, but that's why you have us."

"Thank fuck for that."

"And what you did for *me*, for my *family*—"

"Don't, Sean, it's the least I could do. You joined a crusade to help avenge my family without anything—"

"I gained everything, brother, *everything*. And I would do it all over again in a heartbeat. The hellacious road less traveled has been worth it, man. I only wish he was still with us."

I give him a slow nod as Cecelia ambles toward us with Beau in tow, the serene expression on her face lit up by the single street lamp at the end of her long driveway.

"She's really upped her game," Sean says in contemplative

observance. "I was fucking blown away when she put this all together."

"I trust her with everything, Sean. *Everything.* I hope you're good with her making decisions for the club in the future."

"I'm gold with it. I think we all saw it in her." He turns to me. "And when you two are ready, it's time to get back to work." He drops his cigarette and crushes it with his boot before nodding toward the house. "See you inside."

Sean steps away, intercepting Cecelia a few feet from where I stand. I force myself to watch their interaction as they exchange whispers. She wraps her arms around him briefly, and he returns her hug before releasing her. The shared intimacy doesn't gnaw at me the way I thought it would, nor does her smile or their glance back at each other when they part. It's when her eyes flick to mine, and she gives me a pensive look before she ushers Beau into the back seat that the strain of our own exchange sets in.

I grip her hips and spin her just as she shuts the door.

"Don't feel guilty."

"I can't help it."

"Entertain Mr. Handsome? You like making me jealous."

She grins because she knows I'm still piecing it together.

"You left that *to-do list* in a rather convenient place, Trésor. But it was last on the list."

She twists her lips. "It was to throw you off his scent. He was mine to take down. I just didn't know he was going to bait you tonight. Antoine allowed it last minute, but I knew you could take him."

"Jesus, I've created a monster."

"Yes, you have, my king."

I shake my head. "Still not a king."

"Agree to disagree."

"I'm okay with you . . ." I look toward the direction Sean went, "having whatever friendship you end up having with him."

"Considering I've been talking to him daily behind your back, that means a lot, but I'm more concerned about *your* relationship with him. For a second, I thought you were wrestling until I figured out that hug was a way to keep your man chests from rubbing together."

I roll my eyes as her lips turn up before concern takes over.

"Are you . . . two . . . okay?"

"Yeah—" I nod—"we are."

"Is that the truth?"

"Would I lie to you?"

She narrows her eyes, and I can't help my chuckle as I grip her face before separating her pursed lips with my tongue. My cock stirs, and I break the kiss in an attempt to keep focus on my task. "We're not going to make it far on the road tonight," I say gruffly. "I'm going to have to fuck you, and *soon*."

"You'll hear no complaints from me."

"Dividends?"

"I'm cashing in, King," she assures, "get ready to empty your pockets."

"Everything I have is yours," I assure her. "Sure this is where you want to go?"

"Positive."

I search her face for shadows, in light of what just took place, and find none.

"I'm okay," she assures me, reading my thoughts. She just killed two men. One to keep her gun, the other to take out the only real threat in the room, but I see no trace of regret, no remorse. But I know her heart, and the act she committed is something that could very well begin to eat away at her. But right now, all I see is a woman who did what she had to do to protect *me*.

"I forgot something inside." I nod toward the house.

"No, you didn't," she says evenly. Searching for any sign of condemnation in her face, I find none. "Finish this," she whispers softly before pressing a kiss to my lips.

"I'll be right back."

She nods and buckles into the passenger seat as I palm the door closed on the frame, and Beau barks at me from the back seat.

The thought occurs to me then that my entire life exists inside her Audi, a small but budding family. And if this is all I ever have, it's more than enough.

Reining in my emotions, I straighten my spine for the task at hand and nod toward the men standing guard just feet away before I make my way back inside.

Chapter Forty-Three

TOBIAS

THE SHIFT IS instant when Sean meets me at the front door, a loaded offering in his hand. I gather what I need from the living room before stepping into the kitchen and onto the plastic.

"Tobias—"

"It's pathetic, really, Antoine," I cut him off, "seeing you this way after all I've taught you over the years. Clearly, you weren't paying attention."

"You forget so easily that it was me who you sought for help."

"I never needed help. I told you that. I needed resources, man-power, money, things I wasn't able to acquire in a time that suited me. My impatience has always been a flaw. And seeking you out was my biggest fucking mistake. I told you I was a thief. And you were too ignorant to it, way too eager to play some fucking mentor to me. There was a better way than through you, but it paid off because I started stealing from you week one. Thanks for the tuition money."

Antoine's eyes flare.

"First, I want you to admit your best play against me."

He doesn't hesitate, too eager to gloat. "I might have called Jerry and made him aware of Miami to take care of *your* problem. I was doing you a favor, Ezekiel. You were taking too long to move in on Roman."

He never knew I'd fallen for Roman's daughter and discovered the truth about the nature of my parent's death, which forfeited my vendetta against him. He assumed my fixation with Roman was the only thing keeping me from being at his side in France.

"So, if you got Roman out of the picture, you thought I would come running back to France and remain your errand boy?"

He shrugs. "I did not pull the trigger on your brother."

Sean lunges for him, and I turn and hold him back as he fights me to get to him, nearly knocking me back, and I grip his arms. "Look at me, brother," I urge as he grips my wrists to fight my hold. "Sean, look at me."

His nuclear gaze flits to mine. "Let's finish this, for us, for *Dom*."

Sean gives me a solemn nod, his trust, and steps back, his lethal gaze flitting back to Antoine.

Fury rolls through me as sweat gathers at my temple with my restraint. It takes every bit of strength I have to slip my mask back into place and keep my voice even as I stare down at the man responsible for the worst years of my life.

Instead of taking Roman out to get me back to France, he manipulated my own fucking club to try and teach me a lesson, all the while keeping his hands clean so he could continue to use me. Satisfied that's the totality of the truth of it, I make peace with it. It ends here. Tonight.

"Are you familiar with the game of chess?"

"Save me the theatrics, Tobias. I'm open for negotiations."

"I'll keep that in mind, but I think you'll find this interesting."

Sean smirks as Antoine glares between us both.

I produce the first chess piece out of my pocket and run it along his line of sight. "My grandfather's first lesson to me was about the pawn." When he drops his eyes to follow it, I backhand him. Head jerking back, he gawks at me as blood starts trickling from his lips. Satisfaction hums through my veins as I again wave the pawn in his face and let the monster out to play.

"You see the pawn . . ." The second his eyes focus, I slam my fist into his nose again and am rewarded with the crunch of cartilage as his eyes water and a curse leaves him before he spits out a mouthful of blood on the plastic.

"Are you paying attention, Antoine? I don't want you to miss this." The second he's focused, I slam my fist into his face again, and he lets out a yelp of pain as blood gushes in a free fall and he mutters something unintelligible under his breath.

"What's that?" I taunt.

"I'm listening," he wheezes out.

I look to Sean. "Where was I?"

"The pawn."

"That's right. Like I said, the pawn can be one of the most powerful players once in motion. If played just right, it even has the ability to check the king." I pinch the piece between my fingers. "The pawn is whatever it presents itself to be. I revealed my own weakness early by telling you exactly who I was in our first meeting. That was a rookie error on my part, not to be confused with the *rook*." I bury my fist in his face and this time he screams, before choking on the blood clogging his throat.

Giving him a few seconds to regroup, I grip his hair and jerk him to face me.

"Still listening?"

"Yesss," he hisses, his eyes filling with a rare fear.

"But you did the same thing the night we met. You showed me your weakness because you didn't see me as a threat, then or in the future, and you gave me everything I needed within a few words. And it was clear to me then—we weren't playing the same game."

He furrows his brows.

"Illusion is a powerful thing, Antoine. It can hide a lot. But you never really checked to see what was in my hand, not *once*, because if you had, you'd have spared yourself this humiliation."

I shake my head and sigh. "I guess I should give you some credit for reminding me of who I am, of my purpose, but my *weakness* is not something you should have ever tried to fuck with. You were always an afterthought for me and never part of the picture. If anything, you were my first *mark*, not a worthy fucking mentor. You never once had my respect, my ear, or my full attention. You want to fucking *be* me, but I've learned true leaders have to humble themselves to evolve. They have to recognize their weaknesses and use them to strengthen themselves." I avert my eyes to Sean as the after-taste of my medicine coats my tongue. "And they have to know when to ask for *help*."

Gaze lingering on Sean, I come to terms with that truth. Maybe at one time we were all phoenixes, baptized by our individual fires before rising from the ashes of our mistakes.

But after the transformation, we declared ourselves a different sort of bird and managed to find our way back to each other. The truth of that is more comforting than anything I've ever felt. I was never alone, not once, and it's so evident now. When one of us falters, when our wings fail us and we lose direction, there's always another to coast us in.

Although I've spent years adrift, attempting to coast alone to save those around me from the destruction of my hidden path, they've refused to let me fly solo.

The synergy is back, and it's powerful. I can feel it between us now as we crest on the same breeze, wings wide open, scars from our separation the same depth, shape, and color. Sean dips his chin, confirming my line of thought as we feel the absence of one, never to be forgotten. And it's then I let the rage totally consume me.

"This is the illusion, Antoine. Ready? Watch closely." I cup the king in my palm, making sure he sees it before effortlessly shifting the pieces with a sleight of hand. "But *this* is who I am." I pinch the pawn between my fingers and lift it an inch from his gaping nose. "It's who I've *always been*, and I accepted that early on."

Cupping the back of his head, I press the chess piece against his gaping nose as he shrieks in pain, his body shaking violently in his chair as I lean in and whisper every word.

"But as I told you in the beginning, I never make the same mistake, *twice*. And because of that, you'll die a coward because you showed me your weakness in our first meeting—*ego*."

I glance at Sean, handing him the king. "Shall we feed his greed?"

Sean nods, taking the king from my hand as Antoine jerks

violently in his hold while he shoves the chess piece in, breaking some of his teeth while forcing it to the back of his throat. Antoine begins to choke, his face beet red as he gags.

Sean allows him some air as he tries his best to spit the piece out, blood pouring from his mouth between gasps.

"So, let's move down the checklist, shall we, Sean?"

"Let's," he says, as he holds a struggling Antoine in his iron grip.

"We stole his money?"

"Yep."

"Palo took his wife?"

A nod.

"We've trashed his reputation?"

"He's a fucking laughing stock, but in truth, he did that himself."

"We stole his kingdom and gave a set of keys to the lieutenant fucking his wife, and positioned him to our advantage?"

Sean's menacing smile appears, and he nods. "Palo is going to have a damn good year."

"Did I leave anything out?"

"His mistress just fled France." He shrugs. "Something must have spooked her."

Antoine snaps his gaze between the two of us, his features twisted in utter defeat as I step toward him and press the barrel of my Glock to the center of his forehead.

"And I didn't have to lift a finger because I'm just a *pawn*, who managed to find a *queen* and make her fall in love with me. But what good is a pawn, who can *check*, without a *mate*?"

I press the gun into his skull, tilting his head up, forcing his eyes to mine and pull the fucking trigger.

Chapter Forty-Four

CECELIA

"NO, NO, NO. Come on, man, no!" Eddie all but shrieks as we enter his bar. I can't help the laughter that bursts out of me as Tobias scowls at him. The last time we were here, Tobias all but destroyed this place due to our stand-off. From the looks of it, Eddie put the consolation money I left him to use. Glancing around, I give him a low whistle. "Looks great in here. New lighting."

Eddie towels off a glass. "Wonder how long I'll keep it."

A voice sounds up from behind us. "Chill, Eddie, we might only swing from the chandeliers once tonight." I turn to see Jeremy at the door, a grin splitting his face as I rush to him and he catches me mid-flight.

"Damn, girl, you only get more beautiful," he whispers as he lifts me from my feet in a bear hug before gripping my arms. "How you been?"

I gesture over my shoulder and raise my brows.

"Yeah, I get it. He's a jagged little pill, isn't he?"

"Watch it," Tobias snaps, and we both look over at him. He's completely relaxed, a gin in hand, dressed from

487

head-to-toe in a newly cut Armani. For a second, I get lost in my attraction, and Jeremy slings an arm across my shoulders.

"Up for a game of pool?"

"I'm going to wipe the floor with your ass," I promise.

"Either that or she'll tap your nuts with her stick. It's a dirty trick." The sound of Russell's voice has me turning out of Jeremy's grip, a second before Russell sweeps me into a hug.

"You ass, I only did that once."

"*Twice*, my nuts were counting."

"Not that you need them. You'll never settle down," I say as he glances over at Tobias.

"Well, if he's not willing to secure you long-ter—"

"Finish that sentence," Tobias says evenly. "*Please*, finish that sentence."

Russell rolls his eyes. "Wouldn't want you to wrinkle that suit, Hugo."

Tobias sets his gin on the bar and discards his jacket, rolling up his sleeves, giving me a shot of arm porn. Memories surface of my time here, of days gone by, as the burn starts in my throat and Eddie brings out a pitcher of beer while Jeremy racks the pool balls. Stick in hand, Tobias glances over at me and lifts his chin in question as I nod in reply while my emotions threaten to take over just as "Wish You Were Here" begins to chime from the jukebox.

It's not perfect and not altogether the reunion I hoped for. Some of us aren't here. But this isn't then. It's in my love's eyes I see the same hint of sadness, and we hold our gaze until we're both strong enough to break it. For the next hour, I watch the three of them drink and bullshit, chiming in here and there. For the most part, my enjoyment comes from watching the camaraderie from nearly a lifetime of knowing each other, growing up together, a foundation built long ago before me. And while some things change, love remains the same. So we drink to that. We celebrate now, the new normal even as we tiptoe around the absence of a few irreplaceable Ravens—those who have passed and those who moved onto a different present as we all will when our time comes. And our time is coming sooner than later.

But we have tonight, and it's enough.

Buzzed from a few hours of beers with the boys, I light my red sparkler as the band marches by playing Christmas carols and catch Tobias scanning the crowd for the umpteenth time from where I stand at the edge of the street. When the sparks run out, I walk over to where he sits.

"If this makes you nervous, we can go."

"We're covered," he assures me, his posture rigid as he sits back, bundled in a snowman blanket in a lawn chair we picked up on the ride over.

"Is that why you look constipated?"

"Yeah," he says absently, and I burst into laughter and join him in the chair, kissing him in hopes of erasing the confusion from his expression. Instead, he tilts his head, returning my kiss, so he's got one eye on the crowd. Laughing into his mouth, he pulls away and gives a sheepish upturn of his lips.

"We can't live like this, Tobias."

"Just give me some time to adjust," he assures.

"How long?"

"Around seventy years," he says matter-of-fact, and I shake

my head and smile. He taps the plastic arm of the chair and I lift his fingers and kiss them in an attempt to quiet some of his anxiety.

"We've got eyes everywhere, so what is it that's bothering you so much?"

"Cecelia, I do want to marry you."

I turn in his lap and look him over to see his expression is grave.

"Color me confused, Frenchman, but you don't seem too excited about it."

"That ends now. I'm not going to push important shit to the back burner anymore, and I've kept this confession to myself long enough. This is a conversation we *need* to have."

"It can all wait, Tobias. I'm no . . . I mean . . . put it this way, my biological clock is completely silent for the moment."

"I'm kind of hoping you'll wait on a different clock." He swallows. "Before we do *anything* permanent."

I frown. "What?"

"I'm . . ." he shakes his head, emotion flitting over his features. "I would marry you right now, Cecelia. Right fucking now, I would give you a ring, a wedding, big or small, pledge my love, but I can't give you those promises because I might not be able to see them through, to keep them."

"If we're talking about fidelity, I may just fucking shoot you."

"I may be sick."

My body jars as volts of shock slice through my veins. I can barely manage to get the words out. "What do you mean sick?"

"You know. You've always known."

Two seconds is all it takes as he conveys to me the truth in his eyes.

"For everything I do, there's a reason behind it."

His reasoning for a lot of his actions all those months ago is the shame shadowing his features—his true weakness, the fear that plagues him the most.

My love.

My fucking love.

How blind I've been. How wrong I was in assuming I knew the totality of his fears, especially that day in his office when he let me walk out of his life. I always believed it was the danger that kept him pushing me away, nothing *but* the danger he could be to me. Over the years, I have been forced to assume a lot of his reasonings because of his evasion, and that's on him—but I'm done playing the blame game of where we both went wrong.

From this moment on, I'm done with assumptions because with this man, nothing has ever been what it seems. And in doing that, I can see the reasons for some of his past actions.

"You're afraid of schizophrenia? You're afraid you'll get sick like your father?" My eyes pour over.

"The woman I've been speaking to, Sonia—" he pushes out as if he's terrified of the words themselves—"was my father's psychotherapist at the mental institution. While he was being treated there, she started conversations with me. She could tell I was struggling with the fear, with my own issues. She's been helping me find my focus when my mind sometimes betrays me. There's no genetic testing for it . . . but some of my behavior is indicative that there's a possibility I could get sick."

"It's anxiety and OCD. There's a huge difference. He was

twenty-eight when he was diagnosed, Tobias. You've lived almost ten years past that, already."

"It could still happen." He swallows. "I've got seven years until the 'what if' clock ticks out, and even after there's a chance. There's a *real* possibility it could happen, Cecelia. And I do lose myself sometimes. Especially in the paranoia."

"It's to be expected with the line of work you're in."

"That's what she says." His eyes are cast down, and it devastates me—he's so deeply ashamed. "But she's more realistic than you are. There's a chance, Cecelia. I need you to acknowledge it."

"Okay." I close my eyes and hate the fact that I called him a coward just months before because the battle he faces daily makes him more heroic to me than anything ever could.

He shifts me on his lap, his knuckles running along my jaw.

"You know my . . . habits. You saw me get lost in my head in Virginia. I've been in several *questionable* states like that . . ." His eyes shine with fear as he looks to me, completely lost. "I have no control over if this happens to me. I'm not going to put you in the position my mother was put in, a young child to raise while her husband went fucking mad."

"Is this the reason you refused me when I showed up?"

"One of them. You're young, Cecelia. I've already robbed you blind. How much more could I take? I'm not that greedy." With that statement, my heart shatters into a million pieces.

"You take everything, Tobias, because I'm no good for anyone else. I won't ever be. It's only you. And I know what you're thinking, and you're right, I won't. I'll never leave your goddamn side. Never for that reason. Not *ever*. So don't ask me." He remains silent, his eyes dropping as I again force him to face me.

"Damnit, Frenchman, you don't get to hide from me anymore. Do you understand? Tell me you believe me, Tobias. I will never purposefully leave you for that. What hurts you, hurts me. What scares you, scares me," I murmur to him as he runs his nose along my jaw. "If we fail," I assure him, "we'll fail together. You'll never be alone again. Not ever."

Red-rimmed eyes lift to mine. "If there ever comes a time where I can't . . ."

"Stop. We aren't going to do that."

"This is where you let me be realistic."

I concede due to the sheer determination in his eyes. "We do it together unless I become incapable, which brings me to my next point. You decide."

"Decide what?"

"When to go back in, if we go at all."

"And what about what you want? What about my king?"

He nuzzles me. "Still in the making. For now, the queen is the one in control of the board."

Chapter Forty-Five

TOBIAS

OPENING THE HOTEL door, I pause when I hear the familiar melody of "K." by Cigarettes After Sex. My woman is in a mood. Grinning, I shut the door and stalk into the living room of the suite in search of her. A freshly made drink waits on the antique bar cart, and I retrieve it, taking a healthy sip.

"Trésor?"

As expected, I get no reply. Walking into the bedroom, I see it's also empty aside from the garment bag laying on the bed with a note attached.

Tailored for a king.
Merry Christmas.
   X

Setting my drink down on the dresser, I walk over to it and unzip it, revealing a classic Armani with a skinny tie and freshly starched white pocket square.

"Trésor," I sigh, running my fingers over the material in appreciation; I can't help my grin.

It's fucking perfect.

This woman knows me, my story, my beginning and my middle, my flaws, the history of my scars—my strengths and weaknesses. She sees so clearly past my armor and is the only one capable of going further, penetrating flesh and blood to get to the beating heart beneath. I gave that power to her, to hold it in her hand and do what she will with it. And even with it—knowing what she's capable of doing to me—she continues to love, accepting the burden fully while remaining loyal and faithful.

The liberation that comes with her acceptance is one I unknowingly searched for and found in her. In these precious seconds, I bask in the understanding that I have someone to share myself with; a partner, a lover, confidante, and friend. Her love is all the validity I'll ever need.

Just beneath the collar lays a small leather box. I pick it up and open it to see two custom-crafted cufflinks, painstakingly molded in great detail. A raven, wings fully stretched. Any doubts I had about her message vanish as I begin to shed my clothes.

CECELIA

Anticipation thrums through me as I run my keycard across the screen and open the door. The melody still plays as it did when I left it hours before. I abused my powers today—as Tobias has so many times in the past—to execute my personal plans. Over the past few hours, I used my birds to track his movements, knowing when he would arrive.

Sure in my stride, I walk into the living room to find it empty, but it's the lingering scent of spice that has me changing direction—the hairs on my arms spiking to life as heat gathers at my core. Entering the bedroom, I come up empty but see the patio door open. It's when I step in, I spot him on the far side of the balcony, and it's enough to make me pause. The sight of him with his back turned, one hand resting on the balcony, the other cradling his drink, robs me of breath—knocking me into an immediate state of arousal. His hair is slicked back just enough, longer now with the ends curling slightly around his ears. It's when he turns to face me fully that I'm rewarded in whole.

Jesus Christ.

Timeless, intimidating, formidable, and a brilliant menace. The most incredible picture of unrest. The flames waltzing in his eyes slam into me. He's the most alluring of men and the most lethal. The heat radiating between us is already too much. The fact that he is more than capable of burning when he touches has me gravitating toward him, all too ready to thrust myself into his inferno. I've spent an entire day being waxed, polished, dyed, and cut, specifically for the reward of the look in his eyes. With a subtle lift of his chin, he orders me forward, and I obey, taking the strides toward him and discarding my jacket along the way without breaking my gait. His eyes drift up my frame pausing at the spiked leather boots and trailing up the sheath dress that hugs my every curve. Simmering in the possibilities, I'm granted the payoff for my efforts when he thrusts his hand through my hair, gripping it just enough so I feel the sting.

He's back, my broken king. Though forever scarred, he's whole again, and he's completely mine.

"This is what you want?"

"Yes. It's time."

"You're sure?"

He loosens his grip on my hair, his warm breath hitting my lips as he bends. Molten eyes penetrate mine, the only sign of emotion in his otherwise stoic expression. Only this man could make the possibility of dying together seem romantic. But he's searching now for any trace of fear. Fear that no longer exists and won't as long as we're in it together.

"Positive."

His reply is a slow nod before his eyes dip, and his free hand wanders to the slit of my dress, his finger gliding up my thigh. His nostrils flare when he finds me bare, gathering evidence of my need for him on the pads of his fingers.

"I hope you weren't planning on leaving this room tonight, Trésor."

He separates me before pressing his fingers in, his hold on me tightening as he feels my desire. My mouth parts as he leans in and runs his tongue along my lower lip. Body humming, I slide my hand down the silky material of his tie and down to cover his cock, which jerks in reaction to my needy touch. Fingers entangled in my hair, he tilts my head, taking advantage of the access before pressing his full lips to my throat. My moan fuels the movement of his finger, and in seconds I'm moaning his name.

Taking his time, he thoroughly covers every inch of exposed flesh at my nape before staring down at me with satisfaction—a man on fire, as whole as a man can be after all he's endured, as I whisper the words he's been waiting for.

"Let's get back to work."

Chapter Forty-Six

TOBIAS

THE TICK OF a grandfather clock and the intense stare of the woman sitting across from me has me on edge. It's been a solid minute of uncomfortable silence since we sat down. She lifts her teacup, never taking her narrowed gaze off me as I clear my throat. It was a short trip from Triple Falls back into the pits of hell, and this is part of my penance and one of Cecelia's few conditions for re-entry. I was told in great detail of how it was "on me" to right the wrongs of my past and explain my behavior to the people who mean most to her outside of our exclusive world. One of whom is now looking at me as though plotting my slow and painful death.

Cecelia bristles at my side before bursting into laughter. "Christy, ease up on him. I don't think I've ever seen the man sweat this much."

I keep my stare on Christy, another oversight and the very "best friend" of my future. A friend who's had to pick up her pieces over the years due to the nature of our relationship. It's clear now, even with ample warning from Cecelia, I wasn't prepared enough when she opened the front door of her colonial-style home in suburbia Atlanta. When we arrived, Christy rushed her husband away, along with their two children to Home Depot—which was, I'm guessing—a safe enough distance from where the inevitable mushroom cloud couldn't be seen.

For me, this is both penance and Cecelia's price—for Christy, this is a day of reckoning.

She seems ready to burst now as she slurps from her cup again and darts her eyes from Cecelia to me in accusation.

"I'm listening."

Cecelia looks over to me. "The floor is yours."

I open my mouth to speak and close it, unsure of why I agreed to explain my motives to the Atlanta Housewife from hell. Well, I do, but I'm not happy about it.

"We are together now—" I slice a hand through the air—"*end of.*"

"Tobias," Cecelia hisses in clear warning.

I can practically see the steam coming out of Christy's ears and I relent and take a patient breath. "Why don't you ask me what you want to know?"

She comes in, guns blazing. "Have you stopped punishing her for sleeping with your brother?"

Cecelia sucks in a breath, and I glance her way before turning to address Christy.

"Nothing to forgive."

"Bullshit, you tortured her for years."

"Christy, there's a lot you don't know," Cecelia interjects. "A lot."

"Yeah, like what? This asshole didn't claim to love you and then toss you to the side? He didn't rip your heart out a second time a year ago and stomp on it for good measure?"

She stands abruptly, discarding her tea and saucer on the table, before putting both hands on her hips. "I understand you were grieving your brother, and I'm truly sorry for that, but that's no excuse to treat a woman the way you treated her. It's unforgivable, and you're here now, for what, my blessing? *Fat chance*. It will be a cold day in hell. She faithfully loved you for years, but did you? Did you ever once ask about *her* life or the people in it? Have you even bothered to meet her *mother*?" Christy's scold shifts to Cecelia. "And you brought him here thinking I would be okay with it? I'm not okay with this!"

She's lied to her, repeatedly, to keep me safe, damaging her own relationships with the people closest to her for my protection while alienating herself in the process. And through it all, she's been alone—alone with her knowledge, alone with the truth, and isolated because of it, her pattern mimicking my own.

"Christy," I address her, and her attention slowly shifts to me. "Please, for her, not for me, for *her*, listen to what I have to say."

"Now you have something to say?"

"Plenty. And you're right, I am the bad guy, and I treated her horribly. I don't deserve her."

"No shit! And maybe I don't want to hear your excuses." She stands and begins snatching toys from her carpet, and with the death glare she grants me between her hostile cleanup, I'm sure it takes great effort not to hurl them at me. After a few restless seconds of watching her, I stand and join her, picking up a teething ring. She snatches it from my hands, and I can see the fear in her eyes as I try and level with her.

"I love her."

"You're terrible at it."

"I will do better."

"Not good enough. Can you really blame her for moving on after you—"

"His brother didn't die in a car wreck," Cecelia says softly, and Christy flinches with the revelation. "He died from several gunshot wounds at a gunfight at my father's mansion, saving us both." Mouth agape, plastic keys in her hand, I guide Christy back to her seat on shaky legs.

She gapes at Cecelia before looking up at me, and I attempt to crack a joke to take some of the tension away.

"And we know who shot JFK."

Chapter Forty-Seven

Cecelia

"Holy fucking shit," Christy utters for the umpteenth time as Tobias chases her two-year-old around his playground while Josh mans the grill.

Midway through our confession, she switched her tea for wine. Not long after she finished her first bottle, Josh came home and decided to barbecue in the dead of winter, which led us to huddling on her back porch as the two men juggled both the grill and one of her toddlers.

"It's insane, I know. And I really don't think you should tell Josh. At least not *all of it*."

She looks at me with the stress of a thousand spilled secrets etched into her face and practically screams. "How can I not?!"

"I mean, you can, but I doubt he'll let us back in the house if you do. I don't want that."

"You wouldn't put me in danger," she says confidently. "Never."

"We have the Secret Service protecting us now, and you're right, I wouldn't."

"This is absolutely crazy. I don't know whether to be

pissed, or amazed, or excited or—good God, that man has me wanting to make another baby."

Tobias stands with the toddler in his arms as the baby points to the slide. "Don't get me wrong, I love Josh—" she glances at her husband, who's wearing an "eat my meat" apron over his hoodie—"but door number two sure is appealing."

"Door number two is a reformed egomaniac and gigantic ass, who I'll have to fight every day for the rest of my life."

"Hot," she says, eyeing Tobias and completely unfazed by my words as she looks back to me. "You know, even if I told Josh, he wouldn't believe it."

"Do you believe it?"

An emphatic nod. "Every word. There were too many holes in your other stories and too many inconsistencies. Now it all makes sense. I thought you were losing your mind for a while, then you seemed to get straight with Collin, so I figured it was just a spell."

I haven't heard Collin's name since we parted, easing some of the guilt associated with it. A sudden sting of remorse eats at me now at the mere mention of him. In my grief-stricken state, and my will to start a new life, I'd shifted from grieving one to another, but the full weight of my destructive path rears its ugly head now.

Christy reads my expression. "He's okay, you know. He's met someone."

"How do you know?"

"I saw them together at a swanky restaurant in town on our last date night."

"Really? Did he look happy?"

"Yeah, he did."

"Why didn't you text me?"

"Because ever since you moved to Nowhere, Virginia, you haven't been texting much either."

"I got in my head again, and I was tired of burdening you with it."

"That's not what this is about," she snaps. "There's no limit in being a friend, in being *there* for a friend. There's no limit."

"I'm sorry if my distance hurt you."

"Well, it did."

"I'm sorry. And it won't happen again. I swear to you. I'll never lie to you again. I don't want us growing apart."

"I don't either, and I know why you did it. I understand it now. And I've got your back. But my God, Cecelia . . . I'm still crazy numb. Like, this shit is real?"

"One hundred percent, and mostly because of him." Tobias glances over at the two of us after uncapping a fresh beer Josh offers him. Tucker runs up to us, bundled in his winter coat.

"Mommy slide, pease, pease, Mommy!"

In a flash, he's pulled from the ground and hoisted over Josh's shoulders. His sweetheart eyes shining down on us with apology. He's a considerate husband and knows our time together is limited.

"Daddy's got this." Josh bends and kisses Christy, and I can see her inwardly swoon. She's happy, truly happy, and I briefly wonder if my life will ever resemble hers in any form. But the truth is, I don't care, as long as I have them both in it. As long as I have the man who looks at me now with flaming eyes of observance, no doubt wondering the same thing as he looks to Josh wrangling his son and then to me.

I try to picture us in her scenario, in the suburbs and it doesn't at all compute. And I know for certain it won't be us, not anytime soon.

"So, what will you do now?"

"We're going back in." I sip my wine.

"Seriously?"

"With the protection and aid from the government, we're going after them—*all* of them. Any we can get to while Monroe is still in office. We're not going to poke the bear. We're going to fucking bitch slap him."

"This is . . . so crazy."

"I know, I came in somewhere in the middle of this, and it took me years to fully wrap my head around it all."

"I really should have ignored you and come up to see you anyway."

"Christy, I had to protect you."

"I know. I'll try not to hold a grudge, but it will take some time. But we'll be fine. You and me, we'll always be fine. And I'm behind you a hundred percent. But—" she shifts her gaze to me, her tone growing serious—"shouldn't there be some perks to this arrangement?"

"Like?"

"Think you can get us out of paying taxes?"

We both burst into laughter, and two curious male heads turn our way. Tobias reads my expression and gives me a whisper of a smile before going back to his conversation with Josh.

"What in the world could those two be talking about?" Christy contemplates watching them interact. "What could they possibly have in common?"

I study Tobias, who's at this point completely at ease in

suburbia with a practical stranger. He's here for me because this family, these people, matter to me—because he loves me. And hopefully, our future consists of more gatherings like this even though our future doesn't look a thing like the Baldwins.

"You see a refined, nearly impenetrable man in an expensive suit. And he is that, but I don't see that anymore. I see a boy who started as just an orphan determined to protect his brother. Just a poor kid living on a bad street, intimidated by a world he didn't understand and determined to change it for himself, for his brother, and for us. I see the man he's grown into, who's never forgotten where he came from and how it shaped him, no matter how much he's evolved."

"It's admirable . . . he's truly . . . he's some kind of man."

Tobias's gaze drifts over to me as electricity spikes in the air between us.

"He is," I agree.

A true king.

I turn to Christy. "I know I've asked a lot of you today, but I need a favor."

I run my fingers along Beau's ears, fighting tears. Tobias bends, repeating my movement, his suit jacket brushing the frozen grass.

"We don't have to leave him here. We can—"

"There's no safer place than here. It's okay. I'm okay."

He tilts my chin up and knuckles away the evidence of my lie. "What hurts you, hurts me."

I manage a laugh. "You won't miss him."

I can tell by his expression that may no longer be the truth.

My pooch has grown on him. And maybe one day we'll be able to give him a home, but he doesn't belong in our world for the moment. He runs a hand along Beau's back.

"Are you sure?"

"We don't know where we're going to end up. He needs a good home until we figure it out."

Christy stands feet away, her eyes drifting between us before I walk him on his leash over to her.

"He's a good boy. He shouldn't give you much trouble." The shake in my voice gives me away, and Tobias curses behind me, no doubt out of guilt. But it was my call, and I made it. Mustering my strength, I make it only seconds before Christy pulls me into her arms.

"When will I see you again?" she asks as I hold her tightly to me.

"I'm not sure, but I'll call you as soon as we get somewhere."

"I love you."

"Love you too."

We hug until the blacked-out Mercedes pulls up to the curb, cueing the end of life as I know it. Christy releases me, her pleading gaze on Tobias. "Don't give me a reason to come after you."

He gives her a nod before ushering me inside the idling SUV.

And with the slam of the door, we pull away from the curb. I can feel Tobias's gaze on me a second before he shouts to the driver.

"Arrêtez!" *Stop.*

The driver frowns as Tobias shakes his head, giving the order in English. "Stop!"

Confused by his outburst, I turn to him a second before he leaps from the SUV. The driver glances back at me, equally as confused as I scan the streets for any threat I might've missed while grabbing my Glock from my purse. A minute later, Tobias opens the door with my other Frenchman in hand, both of them panting as he climbs back into the car, the dog clutched tightly in his embrace as Beau licks his jaw. Tobias flicks his gaze to me, daring me to argue with him before his lips tilt up and he speaks. "I can teach him to shoot."

Relieved laughter bursts from me as Beau settles across our laps, resting his head on Tobias's thigh as he lovingly strokes his ears.

"You're getting soft, King."

"I don't give a fuck."

"I knew you loved him," I insist as I kiss his upturned lips.

We lace our fingers together in anticipation as we're swept away from the curb and hurtle into the unknown, hearts pounding, excitement building between us as we speed toward our future.

"We loved with a love that was more than love."
—Edgar Allan Poe

Epilogue

TOBIAS

Age Forty-Four
Saint-Jean-de-Luz, France

Meet me at the finish line.

WE COLLIDE IN the middle of the balcony and I lift her from her feet.

"Goddamn you, you bastard!" she cries into my neck. "Please tell me being here means what I think it means."

Eyes glazing, I inhale her scent as she shakes in my arms. It was close, too close, and we both know it. For the last seven years, we set out on a thousand-dream adventure—mostly mine—and not once has she complained. We fought as often as we fucked. We moved twelve times, dodged bullets, lost friends, fought the good fight, together, and mostly side by side—which was the biggest fight of all. We struggled, felt defeated, rallied, and came back swinging. We utilized our position in every imaginable way, going head-to-head with the biggest threats—mostly corrupt corporations and media conglomerates controlled by deep state. With Cecelia's help, Molly implemented several programs and passed numerous bills to give aid to those less fortunate.

We fought hard, and it's been fucking bloody, but we've managed to accomplish a lot—and mostly come out unscathed. Preston reigned both his terms with an iron fist, and with the government's backing and the support of the people, we managed to take out a good amount of trash. My sole focus over the last seven years was to flush out the terrorists who became notorious during Preston's second year in office. Adversaries who made themselves known to me as I sat on the couch in Virginia years ago during our snow day. When the hairs on my neck rose, and that familiar zing struck me like a bolt of lightning, I knew, I fucking knew that I would make it my mission to rid the world of them even if I had to hunt them down and eradicate them myself.

And two days ago, with the help of the US military, we assassinated the five heads responsible for the movement before we immobilized and imprisoned the rest of the key players. And with that war officially over and the bullets coming too close for comfort, and a long exchanged look with my brothers as we all let out a sigh of relief when we made it into the air, we concluded that the war we waged years ago was over for us as well.

We'd done our part, risked our lives, and the lives of those we loved long enough, taking back control of a corrupted government. We won far too many battles to consider our efforts a failure. And what we fought for were the people we once were and will become again, world citizens—Cecelia, the daughter of a single, struggling mother, and me, an orphan left in the wake of a greedy white-collar emperor who turned out to be a man with a heart a lot like mine. Our worlds collided as those people, and since, we've manifested a different reality. One that we worked a lifetime toward.

We have enough birds up to continue our legacy or let it die out—the choice is theirs.

The sad truth is, there's already a new and unseen threat coming because there will always be more. No one can rule the world. In good versus evil, there will always be two sides, an opposition.

"Tobias, does this mean what I think it means?" Her blue eyes search mine for answers as to why we're here, and she knows, but I know she needs the words.

"It means we're in negotiations," I whisper hoarsely. "I'm sorry, Trésor. I'm sorry I scared you."

She pulls away, and I can clearly see the worry I've caused—small black rings under her eyes.

"Sean?" she asks, her voice shaking, too afraid of the answer as she runs her hands up and down my chest.

"He's fine. He'll be landing in Charlotte in a few hours. He's going to make a full recovery. Everyone's okay."

She nods, her posture relaxing substantially as her hands continue to roam. "Okay." She bobs her head. "Okay."

"I told you this was going to be—"

"Doesn't make it easier! After seven fucking years of this, I'm losing my mind! Tobias, our luck is going to run out one day soon—you narrowly made it out of this one. How many times do you have to risk your own neck to see your crazy plans through?" She shrieks all of this out, examining me like I just fell off the jungle gym in a schoolyard. She brushes over the cut beneath my eye, and I grip her hand before kissing the back of it.

"We got them, Cecelia. We got them. We did it, baby."

She gazes on at me, her lips parting at my revelation.

"It's really over?"

"Yes, it's over."

She lets out a long, relieved breath.

"We lost signal on our way to the airstrip. We were fucking running to the plane when I sent you the message. We got detained at the border for a full goddamn day before Tyler got it sorted. And by the time I could reach you, you were already in the air."

"If you want to reach me, *Frenchman*, then maybe you don't put yourself in these positions like some stupid Rambo commando. You're *too old* to be taking these risks!"

Unable to help it, I toss my head back and laugh, hard, which earns me two angry fists against the chest. I grip her arms to stop her assault, and she smiles up at me begrudgingly. "God, I hate you."

"I love you, too. And how many times do I have to demonstrate that I'm. Not. Fucking. Old?"

She clasps her hands around my neck, pushing up on her toes and pressing her perfect tits to my chest. "Maybe one more time."

"Only one?"

"Or two." Her face falls of all pretense as she lays her head on my chest and grips me tighter. "God, I was so worried."

I tilt her head up. "I know, I'm sorry. I'm sorry. Never again, Trésor. I swear to you."

"Yeah, I've heard that be—"

I kiss her soundly to cut off her snarky reply and she draws me in further, a moan escaping her throat. Briefly, I indulge my desire and sweep her sweet mouth with my tongue before I still her, intent on my purpose. "We'll get to that."

"*Okay.*" She glances over my shoulder. "Tobias, this house is a dream."

"Is it?"

"You haven't seen it?"

"No. I came straight from the beach to you. I was waiting for you."

Her eyes soften. "Come see. You've waited for this day for so long." She grips my hand and I manage to pull it away just in time.

"That can wait, too. As I said, we're in negotiations."

She glances up at me, brows drawn. "For?"

My insides rattle as I grip her to me. In her eyes, I see it all, including my redemption.

"Life."

"We're negotiating life?" She cups my face as emotions swell inside me, past the point of holding it. I choke several times before I'm able to speak.

"Tobias, what is it?"

"I love you."

"I know. Please tell me what's going on. You're scaring me."

"Don't be scared. I have a favor to ask."

She sobers considerably when she sees the visible change in me. "Okay, I'm listening."

"I'm done scaring you. Completely fucking done. I'm done making you worry. I'm done plotting. I'm done with the board altogether."

"You're serious?"

"We'll never be *fully* done. You know that. But I'm done with every part of the heavy lifting."

She swallows. "Okay."

I lift her hand and kiss the back of it. Her eyes fixed on where my lips caress her skin before I open her palm and place the sand dollar inside it. "I've been saving this for you. For *today*."

"It's beautiful." She runs her finger over the shell.

"My father reminded me of a memory the last time I saw him. It was the day on the beach, the only memory I have with him. Break it in half. Right down the middle." I cup my hands beneath it to catch the spoils.

She snaps the dollar in half, and the contents fall in my palm. I give a nod to luck when five perfect bone-shaped doves appear in my palm. She studies the evidence in my hand and lifts one to inspect it. "They look like little birds."

"Kind of ironic, isn't it? Even before I knew what my destiny was, it was handed to me by a man I never really knew. What's even more ironic is that these birds represent the five of us." I lift the birds one by one. "Me, Sean, Tyler, Dom, and *you*. The beginning and the end—even though technically they're doves—in the religious sense, they represent sacrifice and peace."

"I didn't know that," she says softly, studying the pieces, "that's . . . really beautiful." She lifts her deep ocean eyes to mine.

"It's time to change our wings, Cecelia."

Her lips start to tremble, and I know she's feeding off my emotions. We've reached a point in our union where there isn't an ounce of separation. We've been one for a long time.

I take the birds from the dollar and set them on the balcony.

"You," I manage to strangle out through the ball in my

throat, "you did this for me. I demanded the sacrifice, but you, Cecelia, you brought the peace."

Her eyes glisten as a suggestive smile plays on her lips. "Have you been drinking?"

"Not a drop."

"Sorry, it's just that you rarely get this sentimental unless—"

"Not this time." I close my eyes and hang my head as more emotions seep from me. All I feel for her is raging in my head and chest and refusing to be held back a second longer. "I don't need alcohol, and I don't need to hide anything from you."

"Tobias, what are you saying?"

"Where I go, you'll go?"

"I'll follow you anywhere," she assures without hesitation. "You know that."

"As I will follow you. And from this day on, I never want to take a single fucking step without you beside me. I love you, Cecelia, so much." She cups my jaw, the evidence of my undoing dampening her hand.

"I love you, too. Tobias, but you're still scaring me."

"Don't be. I'm not afraid of *anything* anymore. And you gave that to me. There's no opponent strong enough for us, Cecelia. You have to believe that by now."

"I do."

"God, I'm—" I dip my chin to my chest. "I have so much to say, but I don't think I can get through it all . . . will you forgive me that?"

I take a knee, and she recognizes my intent. It's the most beautiful sight. I burn her expression and the love in her eyes into memory.

"I . . ." I hang my head. "Fuck . . ." I run my face along the sleeve of my shirt and see her visibly starting to come as undone as I am.

"No man on earth has ever loved a woman more than I love you. I'll prove this every day for the rest of our lives. I love you more than any cause, any ambition. The sight of your face over any other on earth." I choke on every other word, frustrated by my inability to carry out my plan but too emotional to give a fuck. I'd humiliate myself a million times over because she's shown me, repeatedly, the beauty in a bare, stripped heart. "You own me. You make me so fucking happy. You are my purpose now, and *forever.*"

Her eyes shimmer and spill over as I pull the ring from my pinky, lifting the diamond into her line of sight. Her breath catches briefly, her eyes drifting from the ring and back to me as I gaze up at her and blink, clearing my vision.

I'm so fucking gone.

"I didn't steal this," I manage to say, with a slight lift of my lips.

Her lip quivers with her reply. "Non?"

"Non. I earned it."

She slowly dips her chin.

"And I've earned your trust?"

"Yes."

"Your loyalty?"

"Yes."

"I've earned your faith?"

"Yes."

"I've earned your heart?"

"Wholly."

"Your body is mine?'
"Yours. Only yours," she swears.
I push the ring onto her finger.
"Make me king?"

One month later

CECELIA

I HANG MY favorite photo of our wedding day and polish the white solid matte frame with my dust rag. It hangs just next to a floor-to-ceiling window, giving ample view of the sea. It's a black and white candid of Tobias kissing my ring finger as I gazed on at him, a woman utterly in love.

We were standing just outside the arched doorway of the little church where we recited our vows. It was just the two of us, the priest and his designated witnesses, and it was perfect. We honeymooned at home and then informed our family and friends after, most of whom are due here tomorrow for a delayed reception. Tackling the last of the boxes that finally arrived from overseas, I set out to finish my task. For the last month or so I've been nesting in a dream-like state, pinching myself mentally, not only because of the palace we now reside in permanently but also because of the shimmer of the three-carat teardrop diamond on my finger and what it means—a cure for the sickness I've harbored for so long, a lasting end.

In the last few weeks, we've settled into a routine, taking long walks on the beach, visiting our new town, eating seaside, introducing ourselves to our new life. What I thought would be the hardest part of all of the adjustment was truly unplugging from the life we've lived since we left Virginia. A life where we'd been fully immersed in the brotherhood, making calculated moves and setting into motion dozens of Tobias's schemes. I'll never fully understand the way he'd constructed it all, but that's some of the mystery of his genius.

And after doing years of grunt work and stepping back, I can clearly see the bigger picture; each note he chose to compose the most mind-boggling symphony. I married a king and a legend and all he sees in his reflection is a flawed man.

He slept for days when he got home. It was as if he finally felt relief enough to grant his body and mind the reprieve. There's a peace inside him now, in his fiery eyes, and honestly, I never thought it would come, not so soon anyway. I feel the same contentment, knowing that for the most part, he's winning his battle with the guilt that's plagued him for years. This morning was another turning point. I woke to the sight of him naked, tangled in white cotton, his eyes roaming my face, my body with urgent need as I roused, facing him on my pillow.

"Puis-je demander une faveur de plus?" *Can I ask for one more favor?*

"What is it you want now, my needy Frenchman?"

"Un autre trésor." *Another treasure.*

Taken completely aback, I burst out an incredulous laugh. "We got married five minutes ago, and you already want a baby? Want to try a little marriage first?"

"Non," he says softly, pinning my wrists and settling between my legs, his eyes dropping down to my breasts and beyond, before bringing them back up to mine.

"I'm still on birth control."

He dips and kisses me. "Stop taking it."

"You're serious?"

He gives me the dip of his chin, his eyes filled with hope. "Tu apprendras à notre bébé à aimer comme toi." *You will teach our baby to love like you do.*

"You love just as fiercely, Tobias."

When I lifted and kissed the crease of worry between his brow, our discussion ended with a little baby-making practice. Minutes after he spilled himself inside me, I joined him in the bathroom while he showered, his eyes searching mine when I opened my vanity drawer, took out my birth control, and tossed it into the trash. The light in his eyes, the joyful upturn of his lips, and the look we shared in those seconds is one I will never, *ever* forget. No part of me thinks we're rushing into anything. We've put our life together on hold long enough, but a ticking clock is no threat to us, not anymore. We've accomplished so much, come so far—now is a time of celebration, and that's exactly what we'll do.

And now, as I unpack our things in a palace I never imagined I would reside in, a place so far removed from the one-bedroom apartment I shared with my mother in Georgia, I can't help but be grateful for the road that took us here, to this point. A point of appreciation that's only been made sweeter because of the nature of the road we traveled. When Delphine died, Tobias had packed up her house alone, carefully preserving the belongings of three lives, two of which had ended far too soon. I can't at all imagine that, and the fact that he's gone through so many hardships by himself, trying to be strong for those around him while never really having any one constant of his own. From the looks and weight of the boxes, it seems he couldn't bring himself to throw a single thing out.

Opening a cigar box, I sort through pictures and fixate on the image of a young Delphine and a man who I assume was her husband. They're in the backseat of a car, Delphine sitting across his lap as they gaze at each other with smiles, undeniably in love.

It's a visual of the love that broke her, and I can only be grateful I didn't suffer the same fate.

I came so close.

I know most of her story, but not the details, and it saddens me she cut her life, and herself, off from possibilities when he left her. I'll always have mixed feelings about her, about the role she played in my life and the threat she was to me. But I also identify with her in a way because of the loyalty of her heart. If I hadn't pulled myself together, I might have turned out just like her, letting lost love ruin me to the point of no return. She'd lived as a casualty of love, and her path is proof that even the strongest of women can fall victim to its destruction. Thankful for the time she had with Tyler, for the healing it brought both of them, I place the photos back into the box to keep them away from prying eyes. Lifting the lid on a Nike shoebox, I falter when I see the matchbox car sitting on top of a stack of folded drawings. Lifting the car to my line of sight, my heart begins to bleed.

"I know what I'm holding. I know her worth."

It's an echo, this part of my heartbeat that thrums in my chest, an echo of a life I lived long ago and a man I loved whom I spent my rainy days with. My love for him is still so distinguishable, and for that I'm grateful. Tobias told me years ago in Virginia, that he was happy I was the woman to love him, and I can't help but to feel privileged because of it, as selfish as it may be. Running a finger over the hood, I reminisce about the star-filled nights we spent exchanging whispers and refusing to acknowledge the guilt those memories evoked. I can't forget my second love, and I never want to. I still carry him with me—through time.

"His favorite," Tobias says softly, speaking up from behind me. Turning, I see him standing in the frame of the doorway, his eyes fixed on the car in my hand. "Even when he was little, he knew what he wanted. It was like he saw his future. Looking back now, as far as I can remember, as crazy as it may seem, I believe he did."

"I believe it, too," I say, staring down at the car. "There was something about him that was so . . . it's indescribable."

He joins me, glancing down at the shoebox, and I can feel the sight of it is painful for him, but he doesn't back away.

"I was trying to sort things out before everyone gets here. I'll put this in a different room." I move to close the box, and he stops me. "Don't, Trésor. I've spent a lot of time remembering . . . the wrong things." He gently plucks the car from my hand before he kisses my ring finger. The hurt I can feel rolling off him stings, the longing, the piece of himself he'll never get back. He'll never stop grieving his brother, and I'll never ask him to because, in truth, I don't think any of us ever will.

"You can tell me," I say softly. "Whatever you're thinking."

He clutches the car in his hand and nods. "I know," he says softly. "I'm thinking of him in his pajamas as a little boy with a smart mouth." He gives me a sad smile. "I'm going to go take a walk."

"There's a storm coming." I nod toward the window.

"I'll make it quick, wife."

I beam at the title as he presses a kiss to my lips before he leaves the room, lingering sadness in his wake. Heart heavy, I watch him descend the stairs before looking back at the box, my curiosity winning over my need to recapture the peace I felt just moments ago.

I open the closest piece of folded construction paper to see it's a drawing. At the bottom of the page is a label in a teacher's handwriting, title—My Family—Dominic King—Age six. A lemon-yellow sun sits at the top right of the page finishing off a dark-blue sky. Inside of one of the puffy clouds dead center are two stick figures labeled Maman, Papa. Below stands Tobias and Dominic in the middle of light-brown colored mountains. Tobias is much, much larger in size. He might as well be a giant compared to the way Dominic drew himself.

They're holding stick hands, and I can clearly see the dynamic in the relationship—so much trust, love, and adoration. Dominic spent more time on Tobias's details than he did on any other aspect of the drawing. And it's because he loved him, idolized him, because Tobias was his world, his brother, his teacher, his mentor, and in essence, his father. Eyes stinging, I gaze on at the clear picture of devotion of one brother for another.

As much as I thought I knew about these men, as deeply as I've loved them and understood them as they were when I entered their lives, Tobias was right—there was an evolution that took place *long* before me, that didn't include me, and had absolutely *nothing* to do with me. And these are the times for which Tobias grieves most, for a relationship I only got a rare glimpse of before tragedy struck. The end to a history I was never privy to. Though Tobias has told me stories, I didn't quite understand it fully until this moment, the meaning behind every action, every detail, because I'm holding the original blueprint in my hand.

This isn't just my love story. It never was.

Carefully folding the drawing, I place it back into the box and walk over to the window, catching sight of Tobias just as he reaches the beach.

Beneath his purposefully constructed armor is the bleeding heart of an orphaned little boy who was forced to grow up way too soon. A heart that suffered years of neglect, of rejection—including his own. He kept it that way to protect himself and those around him until I retrieved it. And he let me discover him, knowing he would become his most vulnerable.

He told me once his admiration for me stems from the fact that I've always been vocal about my heart—while he's carefully hidden his to protect those he loves. And it's here, with me, where he's finally unshackled himself from the obligation of being so selfless. It's here with me that he's freed himself to love the way he was meant to. I raise my palm to the window.

"You'll never be alone again. You'll never be alone. I promise you. It was never *my heart*, Tobias. It was *yours*."

TOBIAS

Age Eleven

"COME ON, DOMINIC, grab your backpack. We have to go." Dominic doesn't move. Instead, he kneels on his carpet pushing his car along a track he made from electrical tape on his threadbare rug.

"Did you hear me? Come on, or we'll be late."

"So what."

"So what your red butt if you keep talking back to me, that's what."

"Why do we have to go to school for *five* days?"

"Because those are the rules," I snap, reaching for the car in his hand.

"Who makes the rules?"

"People."

"What people?"

"Dom," I sigh as he pulls it out of reach. "We don't have time for this shit."

"Then tell me who makes the rules."

"I told you, people."

"Why do we have to listen to people?"

"Because they made the rules."

"We can make our own rules. Papa said so."

I pause. He hasn't talked much about our parents lately, nor recalled his memories of them, but I always try to engage when he does to keep them fresh.

"Papa said we have to make our own rules, or the bad guys will win."

"He said that?"

"Yes. School for *two* days."

"It doesn't work like that, Dominic."

"Why?"

"Dom," I grit out and snatch the car from his hand.

His lip quivers with anger as he looks up at me. "*We* are people. We can make rules, so the bad guys don't win."

He looks up to me with such conviction that, for those few seconds, I believe him. I'll believe anything he tells me.

"Then maybe one day we'll change them."

"Promise?"

"Promise."

The hairs on my neck rise as storm clouds cover the sun on the horizon. The sea rages below as the rogue waves roll over the silky sand in front of me, a strong and fitting parallel to the way things happened. For a majority of that night, I stood out in my clearing as Dominic's words circled my head, the simplicity and brilliance of them—a heavy implication to the solution of every problem.

Change the rules.

His words triggered a butterfly effect and supplied me

with some of my first notes, the first images for the composition of my blueprint, the ignition that sparked the cogs into motion.

I haven't spoken a word to him since the day he passed — even when I visited his grave, because words always failed me — because I felt I failed him.

But it's different words that have kept me mute over the years. Words Dominic spoke the night he died that haunt me most. Indicative to the way he thought, of what I know he believed about himself, about his fate. Even those who didn't understand him personally — which was only a select few — could recognize there was something more to him.

I still don't know what I believe about the afterlife. I hope, and mostly for those I love, that there is a place where nothing is ever left unsaid. That all we suffer to say to those we lose, there's a place to confess — because I have so much to say.

I run my hands through my hair as I work around the burn in my chest. "Sorry to report school is still five days long." I shake my head and grin, clearing my throat. "You forced me to take all the credit for being the man behind the curtain, but that's not how it started, is it, Dom? And I don't think anyone would believe that it was the suggestion of a five-year-old boy who saw the world for what it is, that set it all into motion."

Choking on the never-ending snapshots of him flitting through my mind, I close my eyes and cradle the car in my palm. "I made you a promise, Dom, but I lost you to keep it. And looking back, I don't feel it was worth it. As selfish as it is, I would trade everything we've done, just to get you back."

Always brothers.

I hear him speak the words so clearly that my knees hit the sand. It's as if he's whispered them in my ear. Closing my eyes, I pray it keeps him with me just a little longer as every hair on my body stands on end.

"You were so fucking intuitive, but did you . . . did you really know?" Swallowing, I let hot grief stream down my face. "I fucking miss you. Every single day. Every goddamn day. And if I'm destined to live a long life without you, I guess the least I can do is thank you. Thank you, Dominic. Thank you. Fuck—" opening my eyes, I gaze out to the rapidly darkening sky. "I g-guess . . . I guess if you can hear me, save me a place in the passenger seat." I think of my parents and how it seems like a lifetime ago that they existed—a different life. "I hope you're with them. I hope you're . . ." I let the grief take over as the wind kicks up. I open my hand to see the car roll back and forth on the flesh of my palm as the white foamed waves crest in and snatch away the shoreline. A stronger breeze follows as if urging me to my feet, and I dust my pants off and walk over to the sea wall and set his dove atop it.

"I'm tired, Dom, so help me watch over us, okay?"

Starting my walk up the cliffside, rain begins to pelt my face just as thunder sounds at my back. Another gust of wind has me hastening my steps toward my future, but I can still feel him, and so I speak once more.

"We did it, brother."

"I don't want to live in a country with a brittle spirit, I want to live amongst soldiers."
                                                    —Dave Chappelle

Two years later

SEAN

M Y PHONE BUZZES again on the nightstand, and I silence it and lift to sit stretching my neck.

"Jesus," Tessa groans, burrowing deeper into her pillow. "Is that French son of a bitch not aware there's a time difference?"

"He doesn't care."

"I'll be calling his wife to air my issues."

"Might not want to if you still want to vacation there again this summer."

I run my hands along the fading wings on her back and turn her over, and she groans as I push her champagne-blonde hair away from her face. Her blue eyes narrow with a clear grudge.

"They'll be back soon. And things will calm down."

"Like that means anything with your work schedule."

I lean down and kiss her, and she draws me to her as I slide my hand down her body, appreciating the difference between now and when we met. She's given me three children and fifteen of the best years of my life. She still puts up with my shit and welcomes me home with open arms, asking me for zero explanation. She deepens our kiss, and my cock springs to life in my boxers.

"Woman, don't start anything I can't finish."

"Then finish," she taunts, drawing me deep into her. I lose myself briefly before reluctantly closing our kiss.

"Hold that thought," I whisper before drawing on her lips once more. When I pull away, I see the familiar worry that I've drawn out of her too many times to count.

"Good night or bad night?"

"Not sure."

"Come back to me."

"I will," I try to assure her, but make no promises. She's aware of the trade, so she doesn't ask for any.

"You're going to be an old man one day, and then what?"

I grab a smoke from my pack and strike my Zippo. "We'll do old people shit."

"I said you, not *me*. And if you light that in this house, I'll put a bullet in you before anyone else can."

Closing my lighter, I ditch my cigarette and stand, pulling my jeans with me. She stretches out, tossing off the comforter, fully naked, knowing what it does to me. "You're cruel, baby."

She shrugs, a sleepy smile on her face. "I love you."

"I know."

I pull on a T-shirt and slide into my boots before I hit the safe in our closet. I grab my Glock and creep into the kitchen, using the porch light to check the magazine. When the kitchen light flips on, I turn to see my son watching me carefully.

I drop my head. "Fuck."

"I'm fourteen, Dad. I've known for a while you aren't just a mechanic." He walks toward me and nods toward the gun.

"And Jesus was just a carpenter and a messenger who washed feet. Look at what they did to him. Everyone needs protection. Go back to bed, Dominic."

He jerks his chin, a gesture so familiar it gives me pause, and I swear I hear his predecessor laughing at me from wherever he is. But this version of Dom looks a hell of a lot like me with dirty blond hair, my eyes, and on bad days, my attitude.

"You know better than to question me."

"Dad, please, I'm old enough."

"Go to bed."

With that order, I step out onto the porch and light my cigarette, and sigh when I hear the creak of the screen door behind me.

"I'm fucking scared, okay? I don't know what you do when you leave at night or if you'll come back."

"Language."

"Mom's not here. And you're fluent in fucks to give."

"Monkey needs to neither see *nor do*." I inhale the smoke deeply, swearing this pack is my last.

"She gets up the minute you leave, you know, and she paces until she sees you pull back up. Then she plays possum."

I do know, and guilt eats me raw as I exhale.

He sits down beside me on the steps, nearly dwarfing my height as I crack my neck. I knew this day would come. I just didn't think it would come so early.

I look over to him as my own eyes plead with me, unbelieving of just how much of myself I see.

I run my knuckles over his head, and he shakes me off. "You're too smart for your own good. This isn't something I want for you."

"If it's good enough for you, it is for me. Dad, *please*, just tell me what this is."

I pull my cell from my pocket and begin to type out a text.

"Whatever," he grumbles and stands before turning toward the door.

"Grab your shoes," I order as I read the reply.

Family first.

"Sir?"

"And the next time you whatever me will be your last."

He flashes me a smile. "Where are we going?"

"For a drive."

He's back in less than a minute and flies out the door with his shoes untied. Once we're in the car, Tessa steps on the porch with her arms crossed. From the driver's door, I stare at her for a long minute with the question in my eyes, and she hesitates before she slowly nods in reply.

Trust and permission.

My love for her only grows, and I swear then and there that I'll do whatever it takes to show her how much I need her, to continue to never make her pay for choosing me, or the life we have. But it all comes down to decisions.

But for now, I still have a part to play.

Dom bristles at my side as I pull out onto the abandoned road and turn on the radio. I drive for endless miles before he begins to stare at the side of my head.

"Dad, we can go for a drive anytime," he reminds me as I try to hold my smile.

"It's a decision."

"What is?"

"To drive right now. Wouldn't you agree?"

I can sense his deepening frown in my peripheral vision. "I guess."

"There you go."

"That doesn't make any sense."

"It makes perfect sense."

"Shit," he sighs, slumping in his seat. "You go driving with a loaded pistol at night? *This* is the big secret? Pretty anticlimactic."

"I was your age when it started."

"That's some epic tale, Dad."

"That mouth of yours—" I glance his way, giving him a look reserved for few—"can you keep it shut?"

When he remains quiet for several minutes, I pull over and put the car in park. We idle on the side of the road, gazing on at the black outline of the mountains in the night sky. I turn toward him in the seat. "I guess what I'm really asking is, can you keep a secret?"

LA FIN (*THE END*)

Acknowledgments

Thank you to my readers. Without you, there's no story worth telling. You bring me so much joy, and I'm so grateful for you.

Maïwenn—for whom the book is dedicated to. I'm so thankful to you for taking the time out of your busy life to painstakingly go through every word for French translation to make it the best it could possibly be. Our friendship is by far the bigger blessing, but your devotion to this project was mind-boggling, and I'm so grateful. You, Cherie, are a rare treasure.

Donna—you've been there, from day one, for so many of these, and continue to remain there *through* the first day of the next one. I thank God for you. You are a magnificent human, and I'm so blessed to have you in my life. Thank you for the insane and countless hours you've spent on these books. Your sacrifices and sleep deprivation will never be forgotten. We did it again, Mon bébé.

Grey—thank you for all your help with inspiration, for replenishing my well when it gets too close to empty. You were blessed with both a love and way with words, and I'm so thankful for your dedication to help me with my own. I adore you.

Autumn—our talks, our exchanges—especially the humor—are absolutely everything. Our friendship continues to be one of my greatest blessings. Another thing to tick off daily on what I have to be thankful for. Your phone calls and 'I'm really proud of you' mean so much. There's no level of functioning without you.

I want to thank my dear betas—Christy, Maïwenn, Maria, Marissa, Kathy, Malene and Rhonda— for once again, coming through, for both your critiques and encouragement. I love you ladies.

Thank you to my dear PA, Bex-a-million-Kettner for putting up with me once again, with my demands, with my crazy banter, all the while manning the camp. You are one in a *billion*, my friend.

Thank you to my darling PA Christy, for being so much of an unforgettable presence you co-starred in this series. Thank you for being a *real-life* ride or die. My love, there is *no one* like you, and I'm so blessed to know you. Book twenty-four baby!

Marissa—I'm so thankful for the phone calls we shared before and after, and for your help in easing the headache and smoothing out my worry lines in helping to sort this plot. I love you, babe. No character I write could ever truly do you justice.

For my proofers—Bethany and Joy—thank you so much for sorting through my Kateisms, polishing my words, and reeling me in. I adore you so much. My books wouldn't be what they are without you. XO

A HUGE thank you and shout out to my sister, Angela, for the phone call that saved EVERY-THING, and the endless ones before. My rock, my best friend and sister, I love you.

Another HUGE thank you to my other rock, my Krissy Bear for keeping me laughing, organized, and on occasion slapping my hand. You are such a joy, such a bright light. I'm so blessed to call you sister, and I love you madly.

Thank you to my amazing ASSKICKERS, you continue to amaze me daily with your encouragement and support. A huge thank you to those in the Recovery Room, who post your love for these characters daily, and made all of the work a thousand percent worth the effort. You've brought me so much joy between the madness.

Thank you to my ever-supportive family for grounding me, having my back, and making me laugh. I love you.

Thank you to my faithful husband, Nick, who put up with way too much crap this round and loved me through it. You're an incredible man and husband.

Discover the TikTok sensation:
The Ravenhood Trilogy

Kate Stewart's Ravenhood Trilogy is a sexy,
unconventional modern love story, a fresh take on
Robin Hood, full of breathtaking twists.

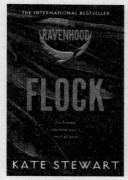 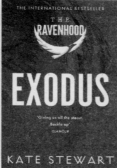 

Flock

The deal is simple: all nineteen-year-old student Cecilia
Horner has to do is survive a year in the small town of
Triple Falls, living with her estranged father. But everything
changes when she meets sexy bad boys Sean and Dominic,
both of whom have the same raven tattoo . . .

Exodus

Cecilia is reeling from the discovery that Sean
and Dominic are members of The Ravenhood,
a secret group of vigilantes. But at the head of the society
is The Frenchman, a man she has every reason to hate . . .

The Finish Line

The Frenchman has lived most of his life in the shadows.
His life's ambition has always led in one direction –
revenge. But he's determined to have it all: to settle old
scores, and win back the woman he loves . . .